THE CHRONICLES

OF KALE

A DRAGON'S AWAKENING

BY AYA KNIGHT

AN OLD LINE PUBLISHING BOOK

Printed in the United States of America

ISBN-13: 978-1-937004-29-3
ISBN-10: 1-937004-29-5

This book is a work of fiction. Any references to real people, events, establishments, organizations, or locales are intended solely to provide a sense of authenticity and are used fictitiously. All other characters, incidents, and dialogue are drawn from the author's imagination and are not to be construed as real.

Cover art created by Diego Jose
Map art created by Ariana Fauzi
Author photo by Aimee Carey

Old Line Publishing, LLC
P.O. Box 624
Hampstead, MD 21074
Toll-Free Phone: 1-877-866-8820
Toll-Free Fax: 1-877-778-3756
Email: oldlinepublishing@comcast.net
Website: www.oldlinepublishingllc.com

DEDICATION

To Manon for being my hero, my dad for being an inspiration, and my mom for being the best friend I could ask for.

Hiro and Ryu, you are my world; thank you for always being the motivation to achieve my goals.

TABLE OF CONTENTS

PROLOGUE: SYLICIA - THE ICE MATRIARCH   II

CHAPTER 1: THE BLACK DRAGON, FIREHART   20

CHAPTER 2: TRANSFORMATION   33

CHAPTER 3: THEY STALK AT NIGHT   41

CHAPTER 4: THE MONSLOTHS   61

CHAPTER 5: THE MYSTERIOUS ENCOUNTER   77

CHAPTER 6: INTO THE PAST   90

CHAPTER 7: BITTERSWEET   100

CHAPTER 8: A NEW LIFE   105

CHAPTER 9: A MYSTERIOUS MESSAGE   114

CHAPTER 10: YOU CANNOT RUN   126

CHAPTER 11: A DARK REUNION   136

CHAPTER 12: UNCERTAINTIES   150

CHAPTER 13: BROKEN TRUST   160

CHAPTER 14: IT'S TIME   171

CHAPTER 15: TO BECOME A WARRIOR   193

CHAPTER 16: SHE LIVES   209

CHAPTER 17: REES'LOK   224

CHAPTER 18: THE ELDERS   234

CHAPTER 19: NEELAN'S SECRET   249

CHAPTER 20: WHO IS BRIG?   258

CHAPTER 21: MALAKHAR'S TRUTH   270

CHAPTER 22: A WARNING ARRIVES   279

CHAPTER 23: THEY COME FOR BLOOD   293

CHAPTER 24: THE DARK ELF'S RETURN   309

CHAPTER 25: TO FREEDOM   332

CHAPTER 26: INTO THE KINGDOM   345

CHAPTER 27: THE KING'S PLAN   370

CHAPTER 28: KALE'S ULTIMATE DECISION   381

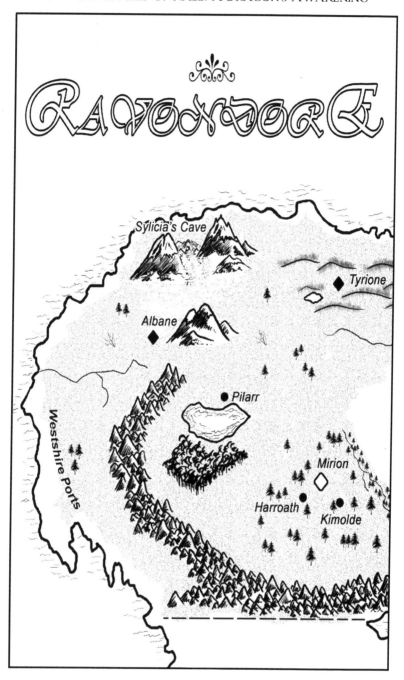

Necron

Forest of Forgotten Whispers

Perun

Eldawin

Braxle

Firehart's Cave

The Great Desert

Sulbrooke

REVAXIS

PROLOGUE

SYLICIA — THE ICE MATRIARCH

The sun descended over the horizon, tucking itself behind tall, lush pine trees looming high above from the top of a deathly steep ledge. The sky filled with a surreal orange glow as the white, snow-covered ground became eclipsed with a swelling horde; their footsteps pounded the earth, multiplying as they echoed against the icy cliffs. Heavily equipped warriors gripped forged steel blades and polearms within their sweaty palms, which trembled with anticipation. They wore full mail chausses, laced finely up to a belt that held the weight of the heavy garment. An outer cuisse topped the mail, packed with layers of thick linen and horse hair to aid in additional protection for any heavy blows they might receive in combat. Their torsos were heavily guarded by many ringlets of steel linked around one another in a perfect formation, resting beneath a coat of plates.

The army was a walking fortress, prepared for battle. Warriors of a broad age group marched on through the unpleasant, frigid weather. Some were fathers, while others were merely children who had begun to enjoy their adolescent life when General Jedah—the leader of this destructive army—sent notice of the war against dragons.

The frozen valley was enclosed by steep, jagged cliffs which warded off all outside sounds, adding to the anxiety of the already nervous knights. There were no owls hooting or wolves howling, nor were crickets chirping to welcome the nightfall—there was a ghostly silence. It was deathly quiet, aside from the steel soles of their feet crunching atop the bed of snow. As the large battalion of warriors rounded another bend in what felt like a never ending maze of ice, the overwhelming cave entrance greeted them, towering before their eyes. Its appearance resembled a colossal open mouth, anxious to engulf each of their warm, fleshy bodies as they entered. The frozen water, which cascaded over the top of the cave, created sharp pointed icicles seeming as though they were jagged teeth—the wide, dark entrance appeared to be the throat that would swallow them all.

"It's times like these I wish me and my wife had left Mirion and started a simple life farmin' in the country, gettin' safely away from any kings or lords to mold us into doin' their biddings." The tall, muscular knight exhaled, closing his dark eyelids. "I've heard that old Sylicia is a fierce ice dragon, and few have ever lived to lay eyes upon what we see now before us." He took another upward glance at the dark, uninviting entrance, wiping an ebony hand across his unshaven, stubbly mustache while shaking his head. His dark skin dampened with perspiration, despite the chilling temperature.

A young knight at his side was trembling; the ringlets on his mail softly chimed, clinking together in an unsteady rhythm. The boy panted, causing thick white fog to escape through the open slits on his steel great helm. Horrified, reddened hazel eyes could be seen peering out from within.

"I...I...," the youth's voice trembled. "I want to go back home. I don't want to be here."

"Silence, you foolish cowards!" a voice bellowed as a sizeable figure weaved his way through the battalion— approaching the two. They instantly knew it was the general from his distinct armor. He wore wide, steel pauldrons upon his broad shoulders, marked with the personal crest of a cobra snake and a red surcoat—which some rumored was stained of blood. The general eyed the older of the two knights. "Tell me your name."

"My name, Sir, is Illadar Ranclef," the man replied, holding his posture in a stiff, upright position. His dark brown eyes stared directly into the general's as he tightened his well-defined jaw line in apprehension of what was to come.

"Let me remind you that we are walking in a valley, bordered by stone cliffs." The general removed his helmet, handing it to his lieutenant. They could now see his slick, bald head, piercing, dark eyes, and the long, deep scar tissue which ran from the top of his left brow to just above his jawbone. "Your voice is amplified, and I must say...I did not fancy what was heard. We have no room for weaklings who cannot stand and fight to protect their kingdom from danger."

"General Jedah, with all due respect, we have yet to be attacked by any dragons." Illadar spoke in his and the boy's defense. "It seems as though we are the only ones doing the attacking on these creatures. I'm uncertain of our cause."

"That is enough!" With a swift thrust of his forearm, the general jabbed the hilt of his sword into the warrior's gut. Although shielded by layered armor, General Jedah's strength was superior and the unexpected blow caused Illadar to instantly fold over in immense pain. "Do not judge my course of action again. If not for me, you would still be a poor, worthless peasant, struggling to feed your loved ones." He spoke not only to Illadar, but the surrounding knights as well.

Illadar gripped his gut, cringing in pain as his stomach turned in knots.

"The dragons are our enemies." Jedah paused a moment to graze his palm over the hideous scar; this motion appeared to send his mind back in time to reminisce a bitter event. The side of his upper lip lifted as he silently snarled at the thought. "Let this be a lesson to all!" the general exclaimed as he stared down at Illadar, who remained folded over in pain. "If anyone of you is not willing to fight like a true man, then come stand before me now and meet your fate."

No one moved–no one flinched. Each knight stood frozen in place, intimidated, and fearful of Jedah. They knew attempting to leave would surely result in a blade to the throat. The general was merciless and would gladly kill anyone who dared disobey him.

"Well then, I believe the time has come to slay yet another foul beast." A sinister laugh escaped his lips. "She lies unaware of what is to come; slumbering within her den–a den that will soon become her frozen tomb." Jedah's eyes looked crazed as his lieutenant returned his steel great helm to him. The general slammed it down upon his head, fueled by an adrenaline rush of hatred. He then unsheathed his sword, aiming it toward the sky.

"We march!" he called out, pointing the tip of the blade forward.

The knights slowly crept forward at a steady pace. Sylicia's cave was dark and held the strong odor of rotting flesh. Many men attempted to stomach the stench, holding back the reflexive urge to vomit.

"Shhh...," whispers could be heard throughout the mass of knights, hugged together in a tight, yet sloppy formation. As they ventured deeper into the cave, a small sliver of light led the way as though their guiding North Star. The golden ray expanded in size until they piled into a large circular room. Crystals protruded from the floor and walls which emitted a mysterious glow. It was absolutely stunning. The knights felt a wave of momentary ease wash over them as they gazed upon the majestic scenery.

Then—they heard it. The loud grunt sent tremors through the frosty floor; so strong the men could feel it vibrating at the steel soles of their footwear. That's when they first glimpsed upon the mighty dragon, Sylicia. Her pearlescent back repeatedly rose and descended behind a significant glacial mound as she heavily breathed—completely oblivious of the threat that entered her chamber.

"You will swim in a pool of your own blood, you sickening creature," Jedah whispered. "Tonight you die."

The general stood before the army, a look of hostility upon his face. A man by his side, clad in black robes, held a red banner attached to a tall pole. He extended the pole into the air for all to see; the banner bore the crest of Mirion; an eagle's claw with sharp black talons and two crossing navy ribbons in the background. The knights knew that upon the general's word, the banner would drop. If they cared to live another day they would need to fight with all their strength.

Illadar looked to his side. The same young boy from his earlier encounter with the general trembled far worse than before; the veins in his eyes were irritated and red, as if he were about to break into a panic, or cry. Illadar reached over and placed a hand upon the boy's shoulder, attempting to add comfort in the intimidating situation. Deep within his heart, Illadar knew the chances of survival for the youth were slim. The boy was lacking in both stature and weight; Illadar could only assume he came from a poor family who could not afford the luxury of hearty meals. The boy's armor looked two sizes too large as it hung off his scrawny arms, dangling noisily with every step he took. He looked as though he might collapse at any moment from the struggle of supporting the armor's weight. The whole scenario seemed quite pitiful; it was obvious the boy could hardly lift the sword without using both his hands.

Illadar swallowed. Although he did not know the boy, he felt the need to say something to ease his worries. "It will be fine, son. Soon this will all be over and you can return home to your family."

The boy said nothing, but nodded his head. He was clearly trying to convince himself he would make it out alive.

Before Illadar could say more, the general, his right hand man, and the figure clad in robes carrying the banner began to slowly advance toward the area where the dragon lay sleeping. The knights followed, taking great caution with each step. Through the sound of heavy breathing and clinking of their steel soles, the men could hear a faint noise which sounded as if something was cracking. The general immediately raised his sword into the air diagonally. This was the signal to halt. It started with the knights directly behind him and had a trailing effect all the way to the rear of the battalion.

General Jedah turned to his lieutenant. "Saldin, it would appear this den has a few tricks we did not anticipate. Below our feet is a layer of ice that rests above water. We are treading upon a frozen lake."

Saldin barred his rotted yellow and brown teeth in what

appeared to be a smile; his wrinkled, worn skin revealed more bags and creases.

"I do believe we may be able to use this to our advantage. Sylicia must be using magical abilities in order to bear her weight over the ice." He brought a hand to his upper lip, wiping a clear string of snot across his face as he sniffled.

The general cringed.

Saldin then gripped the helmet which had been resting within the nook of his elbow, pushing it down over his slick, oily, brown hair. "You see, Sir, if we can weaken the beast, then her magic will in turn weaken as well." Despite his unmaintained appearance and crude behavior, Saldin was quite intelligent and often aided the general with tactical strategies or advice.

"You make a fine point, Saldin. I'm impressed with your keen eye to such details," The general replied.

He lowered his sword and began to slowly advance once again. By now, many of the knights, including Illadar, were aware of the circumstances involving the glaciated layer beneath them. They took each step with caution, warning those who were not perceptive of the situation to take heed.

"We're going to die... We're going to die..." the dismayed boy mumbled to himself as if in a delusional state of mind.

Finally, they made their way to the opposite side of the mound and stood a mere fifty feet from the enormous creature. With each breath, she exhaled an icy gust that would weave around the knights' bodies, chilling their flesh, even through the layers of armor.

Her head was ivory with many round, hardened, leather-like pieces of skin all bound together across her aged face. Upon the top of her skull were three horns tipped with a sky blue that protruded down to her snout like sharp, jagged, white teeth.

Sylicia's body was corpulent and covered in beautiful scales which held the same appearance of oil being spilled into a pool of water. As the light of the mysterious crystals cast a luminous glow upon her, the coloration swirled and glistened– she was a glorious dragon. To her side lay a pile of rotting animals she kept close in case the urge to feed overcame her. They had been there for quite some time as the flesh had taken on the texture of jerky. The chilling atmosphere in the room was apparently not enough to preserve the meat and the putrid stench engulfed their nostrils.

"We need to make our move soon, General. The ice is going to give out beneath our feet if we do not make haste." The figure in the black robe said in a low tone; his voice raspy and mysterious, almost sounding inhuman. His face could not be seen through the heavy hood draped over his head. Only his bony fingers, abnormally pale and long, remained visible.

"All right..." General Jedah tightened his fingers around the hilt of his sword. "On my word–drop the banner." His eyes narrowed as he glared in bitter hatred toward the dragon.

Once again he raised his sword into the air; this time directing the tip forward to alert the knights it was time to prepare for the fight to begin. Within mere moments, fate would determine who was to live–and who was to die.

Jedah took a deep breath as he mentally prepared himself for the blood thirsty battle. "Now, charge!" he cried out. Obvious veins pulsed on his forehead, throbbing against the inner walls of the steel helm as though purple worms lived snugly beneath his flesh.

The man in black lowered his arms as the banner dropped to the floor; it hit the sheet of ice with a clang. He immediately turned to run, scurrying to a nearby ice mound where he ducked snugly against the protection of the outfacing side–a routine he had done many times before. Footsteps rang out as the knights rushed forward; the general taking the lead as they closed in on Sylicia.

As Jedah lifted his sword to strike the dragon, a cry rang out from behind him, echoing off the cave walls.

"I can't do this! Mother... Mother where are you?!"

General Jedah immediately noted it was the same young boy from earlier. The boy's knees hit the floor in a moment of utter despair—his fear had completely consumed any rational thoughts as he tossed his helmet to the icy floor. He tugged at his blonde hair in a frenzy of frustration.

Fury ran through the general. "You stupid, little coward!"

Suddenly, the ground began to tremble as an ear piercing roar consumed the room. The force was so powerful it caused Jedah to stumble backward. His feet slid on the ice as he struggled to maintain his balance, nearly dropping the weapon gripped within his palm.

Sylicia had awoken.

CHAPTER I

THE BLACK DRAGON, FIREHART

The general staggered into the castle's royal hall, straining as he lowered himself to a knee before the King. His journey home had been enduring, and despite the minor care he had been provided, many of his wounds were still healing. He glanced up toward the King who was seated upon a grand golden throne, clad in a floor-length, blue velvet robe.

"We have risen victorious over the beast! Sylicia is dead."

King Valamar rested his chin on the palm of his left hand. His gentle, green eyes were directed toward the general. "Are you sure all this violence is necessary, Jedah?" Doubt swarmed within his mind.

The King was a respected and kind ruler of Mirion. Over the previous years, Jedah had proven himself time and time again until the King felt confident to place full trust within the general's hands. Yet, there were still uncertainties about his actions that caused the King to feel apprehensive about his judgment. There had always been a working balance until the war upon dragons. Although conflicts arose in the past, it never came to the point in which eliminating an entire species was necessary.

"Of course, Your Highness, do not forget it was those vicious creatures who took your only daughter from you."

The King looked to the floor; it felt like an emotional stone hit him in the chest.

"Yes... I suppose you are right," King Valamar replied.

The general stood, grunting in discomfort. "Do I have your authority to train more citizens for our final mission to eliminate the youngest and last living dragon, Firehart?"

The King sighed, "Yes. Go." He motioned General Jedah to leave the room. Jedah bowed and exited the hall. "I do hope this is the right decision." King Valamar muttered to himself in uncertainty.

~~~~~~~~~~~~~~~~

As the months passed, the forest where Firehart dwelled grew lush and thick as the spring season blended into summer. The small bonfire flickered vibrantly, casting a soothing glow against the stone cave wall. Its warmth circulated throughout the room, creating the perfect atmosphere for relaxing. The old sorcerer stroked his grey beard as he pondered in deep thought. It had been three months since the news of Sylicia's death spread across Ravondore. She had been one of the final two remaining dragons and a respected elder.

"It won't be much longer, you know, Kale," The sorcerer spoke as he adjusted a steel pot which held a delicious smelling stew he was preparing for dinner. "The general will come for you too."

"Then let him come! I'll rip his repulsive, bald head off between my teeth." The black dragon shuffled around before finding a comfortable spot to lie down on the cool, stone floor. His dark scales reflected a bluish tint as the flames fed off the crackling wood. "I'm not afraid of them, Thomas. Humans disgust me; all they care about is what they can take and who they can kill." He snuffed. "And they're ugly too."

The old sorcerer laughed. "Now, now, Kale, let's not forget that although I do have magical abilities, when it comes down to the facts—I too am human." He chuckled again before spooning a hearty portion of stew into his mouth. "Mmm, delicious—very hot—but delicious." He smiled. "See now, Kale, if you were a human, you too could enjoy this magnificent meal."

The dragon huffed. "I prefer something more fresh." Kale slid his foot out, digging his claws into an animal he had caught earlier in the day. He then tossed it up into the air and caught it within his mouth full of sharp white teeth.

The sorcerer wrinkled his nose as Kale crunched down on his dinner; the bones loudly snapping as he chewed. "How barbaric," Thomas said, rolling his eyes.

The two friends laughed. Kale—known to most as *the black dragon, Firehart*, had been friends with the wise sorcerer, Thomas, for many decades.

Thomas had spent many weeks debating Kale's predicament. He knew General Jedah was a cold-hearted man with bitter hatred in his heart and the lust for power. Jedah would stop at nothing to ensure Kale's death. As Thomas finished slurping the last of his stew, he intertwined his fingers, resting his bearded chin upon his knuckles.

"So then, what do you intend to do?" his bushy eyebrows narrowed as the mood shifted to a more serious tone.

"If you want the truth—then I don't know. Stay and fight, I suppose. Sylicia was old; she couldn't defend herself the same as when she was youthful. If they are ignorant enough to trespass within my home, I'll fry them alive." Kale opened his mouth and flames shot out, licking at his snout.

"Jumping balt toads! You nearly hit me, Kale!" Thomas leapt up, nearly stumbling on his crimson robe as strands of his grey beard smoked. "Do you know how long it took me to grow this?!"

"I'm sorry..." Kale lowered his silvery eyes.

Although Kale's age surpassed any normal human's, among his kind he was still very young and had trouble controlling his emotions.

Thomas patted at the ends of his beard to ensure nothing still sizzled.

"You'll need a plan you know," He moaned, lowering his achy body to the floor, situating himself into a cross-legged position. "If you intend to sit around waiting for them to come, then I presume you're as good as dead."

"Great. Thanks for the support." Kale rolled his massive body over, turning his back to the sorcerer.

Thomas grew quiet as he pondered yet again. He knew his dear friend was very strong; but not enough to defeat the incredible army that would soon come for him. The sorcerer was friend to both human and dragon kind. Because of that, he was able to obtain information from both sides in order to implement the perfect plan to help save Kale. Yet, every time he tried to think of an idea, his mind remained clouded and uncertain. He had overheard gossip at the tavern in the town of Kimolde. General Jedah had devised an army much stronger than before; ensuring each warrior underwent rigorous training. Jedah was determined to rise victorious as the *Man Who Rid the World of Dragons*.

"Maybe you could leave this area. There's more out there in this world than just the continent of Ravondore–I've seen it, you know." Thomas felt disappointed with himself for falling short on ideas. The old sorcerer was renowned for being exceptionally wise, and he knew that although Kale would never admit it—the dragon relied on him for help with the situation.

"What about Sundra? I doubt you would be bothered there," The sorcerer suggested.

"Thomas, this is my home. I'm not leaving—let them come." He rested his head heavily on his clawed front feet as a puff of smoke emitted from his nostrils. "Besides... Sundra is a big block of ice—hardly compatible. Not to mention, humans are bitter beings. It doesn't matter where I go; being the last of my kind, there will always be someone who will seek to slay the only remaining dragon."

At that moment Thomas knew there would be no way to take Kale willingly to safety. However, he wasn't ready to lose hope. Kale had always been a loyal friend—quite moody, but loyal none the less, and he wasn't about to abandon him in a time of need.

"I need some fresh air. Let's go for a walk to the cliffs." Thomas needed an excuse to get out and gather his tangled thoughts.

"I suppose we can. I presume there won't be nights like this once they find me." He turned to Thomas. "Want a lift?"

Once Thomas was securely positioned on his back, taking caution to seat himself away from the dragon's massive folded wings, Kale lifted to his feet. Small pebbles and dirt tumbled to the floor from Kale's torso as his massive feet tromped against the ground. The two made their way to the cave opening as the crisp night air filled their lungs; it smelt like a blissful combination of pine and jasmine. A soothing ocean breeze sifted through Thomas' long grey hair, causing him to grip his pointed, crimson hat, pulling it down firmly upon his head to ensure it wouldn't fly away. Kale made his way through the wide forest path he had formed from many of his previous outings to the cliffs. It was a favorite seclusion he and Thomas shared. They could hear animals scurry away as Kale's feet tromped the ground.

As they approached the cliffs, the forest scenery slowly merged with tropical foliage. Palm trees and wildflowers bordered the trail. Finally, the beautiful panoramic view of a vibrant starlit sky came into view.

"Ahh, here we are, my dear friend," Thomas said as he slid off of Kale's back.

The two sat beside one another, admiring their surroundings. The steep ledge declined down to a rocky bay where waves crashed in a repetitive pattern, creating a soothing ambiance. They enjoyed the moment, watching silently as a far off transport ship sailed along the horizon; the large white sail faintly noticeable through the darkness.

Finally, Kale broke the silence. "Why does General Jedah hate dragons so much? I don't understand the purpose of this war against us." He exhaled heavily.

"Well, I do know a thing or two about the general's history." Thomas replied. "I was in collaboration with the King when Jedah had his first encounter with a dragon. Would you care to see?"

"You know, for a wise old man you sure do ask pointless questions. Of course I want to see! I am the one who questioned the situation after all."

Thomas chuckled as he waved a hand slowly in an upward direction. *"Mortana nul kardenea,"* he chanted.

Instantly, a puddle-like mass appeared in front of them, floating in a stationary position. An image of the general appeared within it. He stood inside a stone room, occupied with a row of many narrow beds. Thomas quickly explained it was the sleeping quarters near the barracks for lower ranked knights in training. Kale could immediately see that the vision was from many years ago, as Jedah looked much younger. He was clad in dingy cloth with a lightweight chest plate commonly worn by squires while sparring. Kale found Jedah's short curled, frizzy, red hair to be amusing.

"Are you sure you're ready for a delivery mission?" a voice chimed in.

It was Saldin; his face was dirty with very uneven patches of hair growth around his chin and upper lip. Although this was from many years ago, his smile was already repulsive with yellowish stains across all his teeth.

"What good are you to have around as a friend if you don't have more faith in me?" Jedah continued to prepare his things for the trip "Besides, it's only a sack of eggs I'm ordered to deliver—hardly an epic task." He rolled his eyes.

"Do you know why the King wants these sent to Eldawin? They must be the eggs of a bollusk, or another large animal. Look at the size of those things." Saldin held his hands up to visually measure them. "Maybe they aren't even real; I've never seen an egg so colorful and shiny." He scratched his scalp between long, greasy strands of brown hair.

Jedah ignored his friend as he carefully placed the eggs into a sack, harnessing the straps over his shoulders so it hung comfortably against his back. He had no concern about the reasoning behind the delivery mission. All he cared about was the promotion in rank he would receive upon completing the task. He would finally become an official knight; someone respected and held in high regard—he longed for the moment. There would be no more catering to the veteran knights, no more polishing armor, or carrying shields—he would finally be the one with power. The thought alone put a smile upon his face.

"Are you ready to begin your journey, Jedah? You'll want to make it to the twin stones by nightfall."

Kale immediately recognized the voice—it was Thomas. The vision they watched had been seen through his eyes.

"I've always been ready, old man," Jedah replied.

Thomas held out a pendant that dangled on a golden chain. He informed Jedah that King Valamar sent instruction for the talisman to be worn at all times. Disgruntled, and slightly confused, Jedah snatched the pendant and placed it around his neck. He sheathed a small broad sword and gripped a sack filled with generous food rations over his left shoulder. Without saying a word, he turned and left to begin his mission.

"What was the pendant for?" Kale questioned.

"King Valamar requested I place an enchantment upon the pendant so he could view Jedah's progress and actions throughout his journey. Because I was the sorcerer to conjure the spell, I too was able to view Jedah as he moved toward his destination." Thomas smiled, "And now, it is time to accelerate this story, or else I'll be decrepit and staring at my grave by the time this is over." He chuckled to himself.

With another wave of his hand, they watched as Jedah sped in movement, traveling from village to village, covering many miles of ground. They viewed as he ventured across forest, river, and desert. If Kale didn't already know of Jedah's cold and hateful heart, he would've thought he was watching one of the bravest and devoted warriors in Mirion. As Jedah traveled, not once did he detour from his mission. He handled the sack full of eggs with care, always taking caution to ensure they were safe and unharmed.

"And here, my friend, is the answer to your question," Thomas said as he slowed the vision to a normal pace.

They continued to watch as Jedah approached a range of sand dunes. It looked dreadfully hot as the sun blazed down, blistering his face. He mumbled to himself about being thankful he had taken the inn keeper's advice involving the intense heat and left his chest plate and heavier clothing at the last village he visited. One of the King's couriers would be able to retrieve it on his next arrival. Jedah knew there would have been no way he could endure the sweltering heat with it on. The mission was far more enduring than he had anticipated from the start; however, he trekked on—determined to succeed. He staggered as he crawled up a tall dune before pulling out a canteen of water, stopping briefly to take a conservative gulp—and that's when he heard it.

His heart raced as he listened closely to the flapping sound high above. Something was flying toward him, and fast. He saw the significant, green mass from the corner of his eye just in time to dive down against the hot sand. Jedah spat as the dry sand stuck against his moist tongue.

"You dare take that which is not yours?!" a booming voice called out.

Jedah could now see that the green creature was a dragon. The mighty beast landed on the dune near Jedah, glaring down with intimidating, black eyes. His skin looked as though it was composed of smoothed rock slates. As Kale watched he could see the terror in Jedah's eyes–something he never knew the general was capable of feeling. Trembling, Jedah unsheathed his inadequate broad sword, aiming it toward the dragon.

"Leave me be, beast! I am on a mission for King Adrian Valamar of Mirion to deliver an important package. Do not interfere, creature!" The blade wobbled as Jedah's hand trembled. Though he knew of the dragons' existence on Ravondore, he had never until that day crossed paths with one. His chest felt tight as he struggled to take in each breath. For the first time, Jedah was feeling genuine fear. Yet, despite his emotions, he knew he had to remain strong in order to complete his mission.

"Give me the bag if you wish to survive," The green dragon demanded.

Without hesitation, Jedah tossed his satchel filled with food rations at the dragon in an attempt to mislead the creature and entice him with the freshly baked bread inside.

The dragon roared, "Do not toy with me human! The pack you carry on your back is what I desire–this is your final warning."

Jedah sheathed the sword; appearing as though he intended to obey the dragon's command. He removed the pack from his shoulders, gripping the bulk of the bag by a handle. Jedah took a step forward, insinuating he was willingly about to hand over the eggs, when a smirk crossed his face.

"I don't think so you grotesque abomination!" He quickly pulled out the sword, hurling it into the air toward the dragon as a method of distraction. He turned and briskly ran.

The dragon grew furious as the weak attempt of an attack rebounded off his stone-like skin. As Jedah ran he could hear the loud flapping of wings once again. Sand spiraled and flew in all directions from the violent gusts of wind. Within seconds, the enormous shadow was nearly on top of him. He quickened his pace, panting heavily as he struggled to take each breath. Suddenly, as his right leg shot forward in a sprint, it penetrated through the sand, sinking rapidly below the surface. The soft area was fairly large and caused the rest of his body to follow, dropping into the sandy pit. The more he struggled, the faster he sank into the earth. He was now waist deep, fighting to hold the sack of eggs safely above his head.

Laughter rang out, and the dragon spoke, "You're quite an amusing human—but now it is time for you to die." The green creature swooped down, swinging a massive foot toward Jedah in an attempt to lift him and the eggs to solid ground before devouring his meat and bones. As the dragon struck, the impact was so heavy his smallest claw caught Jedah in the face, snagging his flesh.

Jedah cried out in pain as the force of the blow plucked him from the sinking sand, tossing his body hard against the solid ground and knocking him unconscious. The dragon immediately noticed Jedah was no longer holding the egg sack and quickly landed. The weight of his feet created small, crater-like indents in the sand's surface as he hit the ground. Frantically scraping his claws around the sand pit, the beast searched anxiously for the eggs. His attempts however were futile; the pack had already sunk too deep below the surface to be retrieved.

As Kale continued to watch with undivided attention, Thomas once again moved the time sequence along at a rapid pace. Jedah had been rescued by a small group of knights the King dispatched. Thanks to the magic Thomas had placed onto the pendant, they were able to locate the general area where he had fallen. As they journeyed back to Mirion, Jedah's wounds were treated, leaving his head bound with heavy gauze. Finally, they returned to the kingdom; Jedah feared the results of his failed mission meant the promotion into knighthood would not occur. The King, however, was a caring and compassionate man; he had observed the struggles and hardships Jedah underwent to succeed. In the end, a ceremony was held and Jedah achieved his goal, becoming a knight. The image faded until the last remnants of the puddle-like mass disappeared.

"So, he became a knight in the end. I'm even more confused now than I was before." Kale crossed his front legs.

"Patience, Kale, patience. There is more to this story than what you've seen." He patted the dragon on the snout. "For many years after his promotion in rank, Jedah was mocked and ridiculed by the others as the man who couldn't deliver a simple pack of eggs. The other warriors harassed him and treated him as an inferior knight. They would throw chicken eggs at his back as he walked by and would jump out from behind corners, pretending to be a ferocious dragon. This mockery went on daily, driving Jedah into a bitter and hateful state, determined to rise up above them all. He longed for the day he could use the men who looked down upon him as pawns to seek revenge on dragons. In his mind, his torment was the dragon's fault. Eventually, his lust for destruction and fearless sense of battle caused the other knights to fear him. Jedah fought hard and gave his devoted efforts to King Valamar. In time, he earned the trust of the King, ranking his way up to general of the royal army. Throughout this time, Jedah's mind remained hell-bent on ridding the world of every last living dragon—beginning with the Emerald Prince— the green dragon Jedah encountered on his delivery mission years before."

"What a sick individual. That's hardly a reason to loath *all* dragons. Jedah deserves a tortured death; one that leaves him suffering until his last gasp for air," Kale muttered in disgust. "Humans..." He shuddered at the thought.

Thomas yawned. It was time for him to return to his own home. He stood, gently brushing the sandy debris from his robe. He smiled at his friend, who was obviously upset with what he had just observed. Thomas rubbed his hand over Kale's neck. The dragon closed his eyes momentarily, humming softly as he enjoyed the soothing sensation—similar to a cat purring upon its owner's touch.

"Get some rest, my dear friend," Thomas whispered as he rubbed his green eyes wearily. "I'm not going to give up, you know. I'll find a way to ensure your safety."

Kale huffed. "You worry too much; I'm going to be just fine. No human will ever take me down," Kale lied. His stubborn personality would not allow him to reveal his uncertainty.

Thomas knew his friend well enough to see the truth behind his wide, silver eyes. "Goodnight, Kale." He did not wish to argue. Thomas held his palm out, caressing the air with his fingertips as he softly recited words of ancient magic–Thomas vanished, returning to his home.

Kale remained at the cliffs, enjoying the cool breeze as it brushed his scaly cheeks. As he drifted to sleep, listening to the waves crashing below, he had no idea of the life changing event that was soon to come.

CHAPTER 2

TRANSFORMATION

Two more months passed and Thomas continued to assess the different outcomes for spells he could use to protect Kale. Everything he devised thus far concluded with often disastrous results. In one scenario both he and Kale would die from the wrath of the general's army. In the other, they managed to escape, but were then left with the constant need of finding large secluded areas in which to hide the dragon from the world—something Kale would surely be against. He was a hard-headed creature who always placed his pride before logic.

Thomas began to dedicate a great amount of his time to researching books and old scrolls with the hope of acquiring new spells. As each day passed, his determination shifted toward frustration. He knew time was of the essence, and yet the old sorcerer felt as if he was getting nowhere. Thomas began to sense the villagers had grown suspicious of his sudden irregularity in behavior. He had always been collected, calm, and polite—now he was an anxious mess, remaining bottled up within his home, only leaving to purchase food and other necessities. His long grey hair appeared untamed and oily, as if he hadn't bathed in days. He knew he had to find an alternate method of obtaining information before time ran out. His determined state of mind kept him willfully trying to find the answers on his own, but now the time had come to seek the aid of another.

Thomas knew exactly where he needed to go—the home of a great philosopher and friend. If anyone was going to be able to assist him, it was Rogerick. His home was a sanctuary to many old tomes; there had to be something hidden inside to point Thomas in the right direction. Thomas slid circular, frameless spectacles into the pocket of his robe as he exited his home for Rogerick's. Thankfully, his friend's house was located within the same village.

As Thomas briskly walked through the village square, many individuals stopped briefly to stare. Some whispered among one another as he passed and young children pointed as if he was some sort of peculiar attraction. The village Thomas lived in was small enough to where most people had known one another for many years. Because of this, if anything was out of the norm, gossip would flood the streets.

I knew I should have taken the back route, Thomas thought to himself. *But that would have taken me twice as long, and time is not on my side.* He exhaled in relief as he approached the white stone home. The yellow flowers that landscaped Rogerick's yard were an inviting welcome. As he reached out to knock on the wooden door, it swung open before his knuckles touched the surface. There stood a very weary-eyed Rogerick. He looked as though he had not slept for many nights and his usually well-maintained blonde hair hung, sloppy and askew.

"I was wondering when you'd arrive. Get in—get in. The last thing I need is everyone thinking I'm crazy too!" He motioned for Thomas to step inside, quickly closing the door as the sorcerer entered. "Just what is going on, Thomas? I've always been a good friend to you. Now, it seems as though you've gotten yourself in a pickle and yet you won't even discuss the situation with me? Everyone in the village is talking about you, you know." Rogerick walked over to his bookshelf, placing his hands upon his hips as he hung his head down, sighing.

After a moment, Thomas sat down, wrinkling his forehead in thought. "Wait a moment... How exactly did you know I would be arriving at your doorstep today? It's as though you were awaiting my visit."

Rogerick gripped a thick book within his hands, disgruntled Thomas had not shared his hardships. He carried it over to an oak table next to where Thomas sat; ensuring careful attention to not disrupt the cover as he gently sat it down. Rogerick wiped his brow, taking a step back from the tattered, black book.

Thomas glanced toward the end table as he pulled his spectacles from his pocket, resting them upon his long nose. The book was mysteriously magnificent. Hand-carved symbols were engraved onto the leathery cover and in the center was an image of an oversized black eye which looked reptilian.

"A woman named Zasha delivered this to me yesterday; she said you would be coming today and I was not to give it to you until you arrived." Rogerick crossed his arms. "She said if I dared to open it, she would turn everything I tried to drink into sand until I died of dehydration... What a foul woman she was. I don't know why she chose to give something of apparent importance to me and not come directly to your home—I didn't bother to ask." Rogerick felt that questioning Zasha would have resulted in another threatened curse upon him, so he obediently accepted the delivery in silence.

Thomas quietly chuckled to himself. *That sounds like Zasha all right*, he thought. Although he did not know much about Zasha's personal life or past, he had encountered her twice over the years. She seemed to follow trouble. He could vividly remember her short, wild, red hair which hung to her shoulders in tight curls, her middle-aged complexion, and the thick, wooly, black scarf she always kept wrapped around her neck.

"So, the old witch wants to help...or meddle." His fingertips grazed the book's cover, gently lifting the edge. Without warning the pages began to flutter, rapidly turning themselves. The speed in which the pages moved created a light breeze that sifted through Thomas' beard. After what seemed like hundreds of pages, the book finally stopped moving. It landed conveniently and 'oh so cleverly' on a chapter about dragons—Thomas rolled his eyes.

"I can see this *wasn't* planned," Thomas emphasized the sarcasm.

Rogerick threw his hands up in the air. Thomas had never seen his friend this upset. Rogerick was usually a very collected individual.

"You're unbelievable Thomas-dragons?!" He brought a hand to his face, rubbing his temples. "Just what have you gotten yourself into this time? I know you've always been friend to their kind, but if General Jedah were to find out you're interfering, he'd have your head on a stake." Rogerick sighed in concern for his friend.

"*My* head?" Thomas laughed. "I may not be as fast on my toes, but this old sorcerer still has a few tricks up his sleeve. I'm not planning to be an easy target. Besides, this is why I'm not involving you."

As Rogerick opened his mouth to speak, Thomas held out his palm to insist he needed a moment of silence. Thomas' face crinkled as he thoroughly read through the page in heavy concentration. Suddenly, his green eyes lit up—he had found exactly what he needed. Joy swept through his heart as he felt a strong sense of hope.

"Zasha, I don't know what you're up to, or how you are even aware of our predicament, but I'm thankful for this," Thomas muttered toward the book. He recited a section of the page repetitively in his mind, until he felt fully confident it was burned into his memory. He then stood, slamming the cover of the book down in excitement. "I have to go now, Rogerick. I'm sorry I can't tell you more, but please understand that it's for your own benefit and well-being."

He bid his dear friend goodbye as he left through the oak door, heading back out into the bustling village. Thomas briskly walked toward his home to begin the necessary preparations. As he rounded the bend which led to the village square, a small group of women were gossiping loudly enough for him to hear. They were so engrossed in their conversation they did not hear as Thomas approach from behind.

A robust woman with a round red face gripped a woven basket full of clean linen in her hands; her laughter rang out down the narrow street. "General Jedah should be at Firehart's cave by now with his men. The filthy nuisance won't be able to destroy a single town after today. Give any dragon a chance and they'll demolish everything in their path... Horrid things they are—good riddance."

Thomas had never hurt a woman before; but if they had been alone, there would have been no containing the fireball which would have shot toward her frumpy bottom.

"Beatrice, you always speak such nonsense." another woman in the group replied. "I personally think this whole war is foolish. I've never even heard of a dragon attacking a village in Ravondore. Besides, *your* husband wasn't recruited as a pawn in his army, risking his life out there."

Thomas had heard enough. He knew he needed to reach Kale—and fast. He frantically slipped down a secluded alley to the side of the tailor's house so no one would see him conjure a teleportation spell. Thomas would only have the ability to teleport outside of Kale's cave. His spell was limited to places not enclosed by walls and a covering. Long ago, another sorcerer attempted to see if he could test the laws of magic and defy the rules. In the end, townsfolk found his mangled body twisted in unnatural directions with miscellaneous objects imbedded in his flesh. He had met a terrible death.

Horrible thoughts ran through Thomas' mind; his friend might already be in grave danger, or worse—dead. He waved his hand, softly speaking an incantation. Thomas closed his eyes, and within seconds, he vanished from the village. In mere moments, an apparition of his body began to solidify in the forest outside Kale's cave.

As Thomas opened his eyes, he was overwhelmingly relieved to see the entrance to Kale's home was clear of armored warriors. The general's army had not yet arrived. Still panting for air after teleporting a great distance across Ravondore, Thomas ran as fast as his old bones would move toward the cave entrance. His bright green eyes widened in surprise as he could now make out the faint sound of marching footsteps moving along the main trail within the forest. There wasn't much time left before they would arrive—prepared to slay the final dragon.

"Kale!" Thomas' eyes needed to adjust as he entered the cave. "Kale?!" He could finally make out the black lump at the far end of the room. Kale was peacefully sleeping, ignorant to the oncoming threat. "Wake up! You foolish dragon, you're about to sleep through your own execution! We've got to move—now!" Thomas shoved his hands against Kale's rib cage. "Come on, you lazy dragon, it's time to leave."

Kale opened his silver eyes, shuffling his body to get a better view of the sorcerer. "Hmm? What's happening, Thomas? Are you all right?"

"No...no, Kale, as a matter of fact I'm not all right. And neither are you. Now lift up onto your feet and let's get moving." Beads of sweat trickled into his beard as he continued to push against Kale's side.

As Kale rose, they both heard a steady rumbling sound which grew louder with every passing second.

"They're here?!" Kale exclaimed as flames spat from his mouth, impacting against the stone floor. "I'll obliterate their flesh!" He snarled; barring his pointed teeth which dripped with saliva.

The footsteps suddenly ceased, insinuating to Kale and Thomas that the army was most likely standing outside the cave's entrance. General Jedah was preparing his men for the attack. It would not be long before they entered Kale's home.

Thomas looked up at the dragon and could see the rage in his eyes. The old sorcerer knew there were no other ways for them to escape with General Jedah's army positioned outside. He originally planned to take Kale into the forest, which would have allowed more time to devise appropriate actions. But under the current circumstances, he knew he needed to use the information obtained through Zasha's book—and fast.

"There will come a time to be a hero, Kale—but now is not that time. Please forgive me..." Thomas pointed his fingers toward the dragon, lowering his head as he concentrated on the incantation he had earlier memorized. "*Zaraba michelea itone motinar.*"

His sweaty palm began to illuminate with a blue hazy glow. Thomas grunted as his hand began to shake, releasing a stream of light which shot from the sorcerer's fingertips, striking Kale in the chest.

Kale arched in pain as his limbs contorted. His flesh was burning. "Ow!! What in Pan's name are you—" he stopped short. His voice sounded different than before; it wasn't as loud or raspy as it had been moments ago. Kale's silver eyes grew wide as confusion, disgust, and anxiety overwhelmed his thoughts. He exhaled, extending his arms as he viewed his new appendages. Kale wiggled his fingers.

"No! No, you've got to be joking."

Kale had become a human.

CHAPTER 3

THEY STALK AT NIGHT

Kale pinched and pulled at the skin on his arms. "What have you done to me, Thomas?! Turn me back!" Without his shielding scales, Kale's bare body felt cool and uncomfortable.

Thomas ignored Kale's ranting as he turned to the cave entrance, listening closely for any sign the army was approaching. He could hear nothing, which told him that the general had already given orders and the men were slowly advancing into the entrance.

Thomas quickly looked back toward Kale; his eyes wide with fear as tension struck. "They're here—we must hide, now!" Thomas whispered while panning the cave for a good place to conceal themselves. By this point their options were limited. Had they made it to the forest, the task would not be nearly as difficult.

Kale, having a stubborn personality, attempted to protest against Thomas. "I'm not going to..."

Before he could finish, Thomas brought a hand to Kale's lips, gently applying pressure. "*Silant devorda,*" Thomas whispered. Kale's vocal abilities immediately went mute. The sorcerer had cast a temporary silencing spell upon Kale so he would not be heard by the army.

Thomas discovered an area within the cave where they would have a remote chance to not be seen. The sorcerer gripped a hand around Kale's arm, tugging him as he staggered on wobbly legs in the direction of a dark crevice in the massive wall. He pushed Kale firmly into the dark nook so there would be little risk of him running out to confront General Jedah. Thomas followed directly behind, positioning himself uncomfortably within the narrow space in order to tuck his body from sight. Luckily for the two, despite its outward appearance and tight squeeze, the crevice was deep and allowed them to tuck far back into the darkness. Thomas hoped they would remain camouflaged and unnoticed among the many other nooks, crannies, and cracks within the cave.

Kale moved his lips in an attempt to speak, wrinkling his forehead in frustration as no sound emerged from his mouth. Before Kale could create anymore commotion, Thomas pressed a hand firmly against his chest to keep him still. At that moment, the echo of many footsteps rang out against the stone walls. The army poured into Kale's home, led by General Jedah. They watched as the army invaded the one place Kale had always considered his sanctuary from the bitter world.

Thomas was an amazing sorcerer, but even he knew there would be no way to stand and live against such a vast army. He had already exhausted most of his energy on Kale's human transformation spell. Even the simple silencing spell had been a great task for him to complete in his current state.

As the two watched from the narrow, dark crack, Kale felt a wave of fury run through him. He fought within himself to maintain a hold on his common sense and not run out to confront the intruders. He was well aware that the consequences of doing so in his current state would certainly ensure a swift death to both he and Thomas.

They watched from the darkness as a wave of confusion swept over the warriors. The men visually inspected the room in all directions. They had expected to be confronted by a vicious dragon at any moment, yet there was nothing in sight.

"Something is amiss. This whole situation is not right," General Jedah muttered.

"Maybe it is a trap, Sir."

Kale and Thomas could recognize the rotted teeth, even through the darkness from where they hid—it was the General's lieutenant, Saldin.

"Hmm, quite possibly...but doubtful." Jedah rubbed his chin, "Firehart would have already made his move. Dragons are full of pride and would never allow a horde of humans to stroll into their dwelling without a sudden confrontation or consequence." He began to explore the cave, taking note of every pebble and imperfection he saw. "Saldin—come!" Jedah motioned a hand in his direction.

Obediently, Saldin approached the General, following him toward the far end of the cave wall.

"Look at this, it's fresh. The beast has been here since this sunrise; I'm sure of it." Jedah tapped the toe of his steel boot against the lifeless, hair covered creature. The limp body rolled over and they could see a puncture wound on its neck that formed a matted cake of blood. "The carcass is still soft and tender; it would also appear rigor mortis has not yet set in. This tells me

Firehart was here even more recently than I first presumed." He turned to face Saldin. "If I were Firehart, and the last of my kind standing on the edge of extinction, would I stay and fight?" he paused a moment, "Or would I run? But how could he have known of our plan...?"

The general walked back to the army of men. "It appears we must have a traitor living within Mirion. Firehart knew we were in route to slay him. It appears the beast has run away like a coward," He yelled loud enough for his voice to echo against the cave walls, amplifying so that every knight could hear. "We shall find the filthy waste—no matter where he runs. This war is not over until his body falls lifeless to the floor." He gritted his teeth in anger, "Firehart will die!"

Kale leaned forward; his chest pounding in fury. "Did that ugly, bald monster just call me filthy?"

Thomas jumped in surprise, reaching out with impressive speed to cup his hand over Kale's mouth. The silencing spell had worn off sooner than anticipated. He knew his magic had been weakened after transforming Kale into a human.

"What in bloody hell was that?" General Jedah spun around, turning in the direction where the two hid.

Both Thomas and Kale pressed as far back as they could squeeze into the dark crevice, holding a pocket of air within their chests so their breathing would not draw attention.

Jedah paced toward them, his head slightly tilted and eyebrows lowered as if he was carefully listening for something.

Thomas' chest burned horribly. His old body didn't have the same stamina it once did.

"What is it, General?" Saldin inquired, baffled by Jedah's actions.

"I am positive I heard someone speak over here." He

narrowed his eyes as he examined the wall, stepping even closer to where the two concealed themselves. It looked as though his piercing eyes were staring directly toward them.

Thomas exhaled slowly and silently, unable to hold his breath any longer—his heart raced.

"Sir," Saldin placed his hand upon the general's shoulder, "I believe the sound you heard was one of our own men. This cave is formed purely out of stone; everything we say—every move we make echoes off these walls."

General Jedah now stood mere feet away; so close they could hear his heavy breathing.

It's over—we've been spotted, Kale thought. He was fearful that because of him Thomas would be slain in the most vicious way by the general's army for betrayal to the kingdom.

The general snickered. "What am I thinking, Saldin? There is no logical way a dragon, so massive in size, could possibly hide within these walls—right before our very eyes." He paused. "Then again, not everything is logical in this world." Jedah gave a final glance toward where they hid, as if to satisfy his suspicions that there was indeed no one there. He turned, walking toward the assembly of knights. "We march men!" the general called out, gripping his sword by the copper-toned hilt carved in the shape of a serpent. He raised it above his head, "Make way for the kingdom of Mirion!"

To the far right of their narrow span of sight, Thomas and Kale could see someone approach the general wearing flowing, black robes. His long, pale fingers clutched a rod topped with a red banner. They could only assume that he had been cowering in safety for what he thought was going to be a grand battle against a fierce beast.

"Do not worry, General—we will find the dragon," he spoke

in a low, dark tone. "Although gone, the smell remains." Hidden beneath the darkness of his hooded robe, they could hear someone—or some*thing* take in a long whiff of air. "I will not forget the beast's scent."

Thomas quickly realized the man in black was a figure who he had heard about from the philosopher, Rogerick. As he could recall, General Jedah found him, starving, weak, and alone. As Rogerick had explained, the origin of the being was unknown, but it was rumored he was an outstanding hunter and had an exceptional sense of smell that could not be matched. It was said that Jedah only rescued the being in order to bind him to an oath—taking on the role as a servant, answering to every demand, and executing his abilities to carry out both the righteous and immoral requests of the general until all dragons were slain.

Thomas closed his eyes, hoping the man—or being, in black would not capture the scent of his perspiration. He watched silently in relief as they made way for the forest. The plan had worked. Thomas was proud he managed to conjure the spell with enough time for them to seek refuge within the cave walls. As the final knight's footsteps echoed upon his exit, Kale and Thomas breathed heavily—the air felt exhilarating as it filled their lungs.

The two remained cautious, holding their bodies up uncomfortably for what felt like hours, expecting General Jedah to surprise them with a sudden ambush. Finally, the cave grew dark, filling them with the confidence that nightfall had washed over the blue skies, and it would be safe to emerge from the crevice. They each stretched their achy limbs which throbbed from being held in awkward positions for such a prolonged duration.

Kale had been so focused on the recent events with General Jedah's army his mind wandered in distraction nearly forgetting the life altering changes which occurred earlier. As he shook his tingling arm that had been pressed between his body and stone for the past hours, reality struck him.

"Oh no...no, no, no." He glared angrily at Thomas. "All right, we're safe—now turn me back!"

Thomas shook his head. "If I were to do that, Kale, you would be dead within the week—at most. The general's army will not rest until they find the black dragon, Firehart, and slay him. Besides..." he looked down. "The book that had this spell did not say how to reverse the process. I only know how to transform a dragon into a human—not the other way around."

"Ugh!" Kale tugged at his black hair in frustration. "Hair...Great—just great, I'm hairy now too!" His eyes fixated downward, as he investigated his new body in better detail. "What in Pan's name is wrong with this body?!" He pointed downward.

Thomas placed a hand upon his stomach as it pulsed with laughter. "I see we're going to have quite a bit of work ahead of us with getting you used to your new body."

"New body? *This* body? I don't think so, Thomas! I'd rather have died earlier than to be stuck within this flesh for the rest of my life. To live among humans..." Kale's face cringed in disgust. "No way. I'm not staying like this, so I suggest you start looking for ways to change me back. I'll go to the frozen island of Sundra—I'll go anywhere you want me to as long as you return me to my former self."

Thomas held a hand up, motioning Kale to stop carrying on about circumstances that could not be altered at the current time. "All right, Kale, all right. But, for now, let's make the best of this situation; it's not going to get any easier if we stand here all night." He glanced toward Kale's lean torso. "We can start by finding you some clothing. It won't make for a very good first impression if you are nude when encountering other humans. And," he extended his arm, spreading all five of his fingers apart, "we will need to rectify your features at once–we can't have a silver-eyed young man roaming around without drawing too much suspicion." With a wave of his hand, Kale's eyes transfigured to a crystal-like blue.

After Kale grew weary of arguing, he finally agreed to leave behind his home—the one place he had grown to love—his sanctuary of solitude for most of his life. He staggered and stumbled his way toward the cave entrance, struggling to walk upon his new legs. As they emerged into the open fresh air, relief swelled within their chests. They were safe for the time being; no one from the general's army was waiting to ambush them from the surrounding darkness—an assumption that had weighed on their minds since the knights left the cave.

A cool, ocean breeze sifted through the nearby leaves, making its way to Kale as it grazed against his human flesh, causing the hairs on his arm to prickle outward. He made a discomforted face, creating a warm friction by rubbing his hand quickly in both directions on his forearm. Kale repeated the process on the other arm until the tiny bumps faded.

What is wrong with humans' bodies? he thought to himself, *this is ridiculous.* The wind never bothered his hardened dragon skin which had been protected by flaky scales. This new exterior was so soft and delicate.

"Can't you just chant some fancy words and teleport us to your village? I just want to go somewhere safe where I can close my eyes and pretend today never happened." Kale glanced down. "Not to mention getting something to put over this hideous body." He sighed.

Thomas turned to face Kale, who was slightly taken back by the sight. The old sorcerer had dark bags beneath his reddened eyes. His eyelids weighed heavily over his pupils as they struggled to remain open. Within the short walk to the forest, Thomas had grown horribly fatigued after exhausting all of his energy on the transformation spell.

"We won't be going back to my home." He breathed heavily as though out of breath from speaking. "It's too close to the kingdom of Mirion and will no longer be safe for us to take refuge. The general's men will surely search for information in all surrounding locations to the castle. I'm sure it will not be long before they realize I have been missing, soon after invading my home to find books and scrolls pertaining to dragons. I anticipated having more time with preparing for this moment and was planning to destroy all the evidence. It surely won't take much for General Jedah to realize it was I who warned you of their arrival." He paused. "I do know of another location that will be safe. It's a place where we would both be welcomed without question. It is just to the north and out of the rule of King Valamar." He held out a bent elbow. "Hold onto my arm, Kale. I'll take us just outside the town walls. I can gather clothing for you from within the inn; the innkeeper and I are acquaintances and I'm sure he would be glad to oblige. This way we do not draw attention from you strolling in—like this."

Kale did as instructed, grasping his fingers tightly around Thomas' arm, unsure of what to expect from the spell. Just as Thomas began to mutter a few foreign words, his legs gave out, causing his body to crumple wearily to the ground.

"Thomas!" Kale quickly knelt by his side, gently shaking his friend. As he helplessly tried to aid Thomas, a faint popping sound was heard off in the distance. Although Kale knew that most likely this had come from an animal on the prowl for his supper, no chances could be taken. His blue eyes panned the area, ensuring they were alone. He knew that he needed to keep a clear head and get both he and Thomas to a safe location for the night.

~~~~~~~~~~~~~~~~

Thomas' eyelashes fluttered against one another as his eyes slowly opened. The bright orange and yellow light caused him to wrinkle his forehead, squinting as his pupils dilated. He licked his tongue against his dry lips, adjusting his crimson pointed hat as he sat upright.

Where am I? Thomas thought to himself, peering around the area as he investigated his surroundings. He noticed a wooden caravan which was immobile and missing a wheel. It looked as though it had been ransacked. There was a large red splatter on the side he was able to view from where he sat. The rear door had been ripped from its hinges and remnants of what was left behind remained scattered within the bed of the caravan, trailing out and onto the ground outside. He could not see any horses in front to pull the vehicle, nor could he make out any other people around.

The fire snapped and popped as a log settled deeper into the hot coals which caused Thomas to focus his attention in that direction. He immediately noticed the silhouette of a figure moving on the opposite side, causing Thomas to hunch down instinctively.

"Who's there?" Thomas called out to the mysterious figure.

Whatever it was, mumbled and spoke in an indistinguishable voice. As the figure stood, Thomas raised his arm, facing a palm toward the person. *We must have gotten caught by the General's men,* Thomas thought in panic. He knew that in his current state, if he didn't act now, there might not be a second chance to escape. As Thomas opened his mouth to begin chanting a magical attack, a voice shouted out.

"Stop!" It was Kale.

Thomas had nearly turned his friend into a pile of ash. "Jumping balt toads, Kale, I could've killed you! Why didn't you say something when I asked who you were?"

"Well, for one, I was eating when you asked. Secondly, in your current state, I would be impressed if I saw even a spark flicker from your fingertips. You've only been asleep for a couple of hours—hardly enough to rejuvenate your energy for spell casting. I assume that in your condition it will be a few more days before you're able to conjure anything. You've expended everything on turning me into this ugly heap of human flesh." Kale flicked a twig into the fire. "Just be thankful I don't know any magic or I'd change you into a cockroach—the only thing filthier than a human." He laughed at his own sinister joke.

Thomas disregarded Kale's threat. He knew how childish Kale could be when upset and had grown accustomed to it over the years.

Kale reached his arms above his head to stretch and Thomas could now clearly see that he had somehow acquired clothing.

"How did you get those?" He pointed toward the shirt and pants Kale now wore. "While you're at it, you can also explain where we are and how we arrived." Thomas scanned the area; his mind filled with questions to be answered.

Kale explained that after Thomas collapsed, Kale carried him through the woods, still staggering as he slowly mastered how to properly walk on human legs. They detoured from the main trail, venturing through the thick forest vegetation to avoid any possible encounters. Kale assumed there would be lingering knights stationed nearby in case Firehart returned to his den. Kale continued, informing Thomas how he journeyed through the darkness until discovering a dirt trail deep within the woods, bordered by thick pine trees.

In all his time living nearby, he had never known of the trail. Because of the small trail being placed in such seclusion, he could only assume it was used by thieves and tradesmen to transport goods between villages. After a brief debate, he decided it would be less risky to follow the trail versus carrying Thomas aimlessly through the forest. He hoped luck was in his favor and there were no humans traveling in the darkness aside from them. Even if there had been a thief making his way to raid another nearby town, Kale assumed that he being naked, and Thomas having only a tacky robe, a silly pointed hat, and slippers would hardly be something of desire to steal.

As Kale's story progressed he told Thomas about discovering the ravaged wooden caravan. He revealed that upon approaching the rundown transport he could see that someone—or something—had gotten away with many provisions. To make matters even grimmer, whoever had attacked, completely slaughtered the three travelers who occupied the caravan. One of the men was hardly distinguishable and his limbs appeared ripped from his torso. The petrified look upon his face could only suggest this had been done while the man was still alive. The other male traveler was much larger and must have proven to be more difficult to kill. His arms had chunks of meat missing which oozed darkened blood. Bone fragments protruded from his forearm, revealing he had gone down fighting for his life. The third human had been a woman whose body remained halfway inside of the caravan where she must have been riding. She was completely lifeless, though her body appeared to be unharmed.

Kale, unaffected by the death of humans, began to explain how, after visually inspecting the area, he laid Thomas on a nearby section of tall grass while searching for any leftover food rations or clothing. After rummaging through the leftover materials, most of which were useless to them, he came across three ripe apples and half a loaf of bread. Both were without mold and the bread felt soft, which told Kale that what happened to the caravan was most likely within the past day.

"Pardon my interruption, but you still haven't enlightened me on how you've obtained clothing. Was it found inside of the caravan as well?" Thomas raised his right eyebrow, glancing at Kale's oversized ivory shirt and brown pants held up with twine and splattered in various areas with blood.

Kale smiled proudly as if he had accomplished something grand of which Thomas would be pleased. He pointed toward a section behind the caravan where the grass grew tall.

As Thomas squinted through the darkness, he could faintly make out the light peach skin of a hand. It stuck out from the tall green blades, lying limp and motionless. He instantly knew it was the dead body of the larger man Kale described. It didn't take a genius to figure out that Kale had stripped the deceased man's clothing from his bloody body.

Thomas scrunched his face as though he had swallowed something incredibly sour. "Kale, that's disgusting! Have you no morals?" He looked away, revolted by Kale's actions.

"Well," Kale replied without remorse, "it's not like he is going to miss them. At least the clothes are getting some usage."

Thomas shook his head in disapproval. As Kale returned to a sitting position near the fire, Thomas' mind began to wonder. Although he was very grateful for the enduring walk Kale had gone through to carry him to where they now sat, he couldn't help feeling apprehensive about where they intended to camp for the night. He pondered the dangers they might soon face. Something had attacked the three dead travelers—something emotionless to human life—something that would tear them apart given the opportunity. No humane person, or average thief, would have gone through such lengths to kill the travelers. Whatever had done this most likely did not venture too far. Thomas could tell from the many empty baskets inside, there had been far too much to carry for a single person planning to travel away from the area. Unless it was a large group who ransacked the caravan, they would have no way to cover much ground while carrying such an abundance of rations.

Although tempted to relocate, Thomas realized he was still too exhausted to travel at such a late hour. They would have to wish for the best and start their journey toward the new town first thing in the morning. Spending another night in the area was too great a risk.

"Here—catch. I almost forgot to give you your share." Kale tossed Thomas his portion of the bread. "I can't breathe fire, you know," Kale randomly stated as he glanced toward the flickering flames in disappointment. "I had to use human materials from the caravan to start this thing—what an inconvenience. It's really quite pathetic, you know." He felt hopeless and weak inside. For the first time it was as though he had fallen lower on the food chain—vulnerable and unable to protect himself.

Thomas allowed himself to relax for the time being, leaning his back against an old tree stump. He was quite impressed with Kale and commended him for a job well done on the fire. For someone who had become human mere hours ago, Kale caught on amazingly quick to the basic ways of life and motor functions of his hands and fingers. Prior to this moment, Kale had merely glanced upon Thomas during his visits as he would slap flint and steel together until a small pile of dry pine needles or leaves would kindle. Not to mention the fact, Kale had always been able to huff a stream of fire at will if he ever desired to sit next to the comforts of a warm fire. To build a fire without help was quite an impressive feat.

Thomas smiled. "You'll soon learn, Kale." He bit down on one end of the bread, swallowing hard as the semi-moistened piece slid slowly down his throat. "You don't need to be a large, frightening dragon who breathes fire in order to take care of yourself and get through life. Though humans may be small in comparison, some possess a heart that could eclipse even the largest of obstacles. Within yourself," he gently placed his palm onto his chest, "is a heart that will guide you to overcome anything that stands in your way."

"All right," Kale rolled his eyes, "so, you're telling me that my heart will help turn me back into a dragon? Because, quite honestly, Thomas, this is a massive obstacle to me."

"You never know my friend... You never know. In the end, I'm sure everything will fall into place as it should. Things tend to have a way of working out, one way or another." Thomas shoveled another chunk of bread into his mouth. Although slightly uncertain of the food's quality, after such a mind-numbing day, the tiny meal tasted like the best thing he had eaten in ages.

Kale rested his head on the sandy, pine needle covered ground, as he swallowed the final portion of his meal. He placed the apples, flint, and steel into a small pouch he found in the caravan. He rolled onto his back, staring up at stars that glowed vibrantly and contrasted against the night sky. The heat from the flames radiated against Kale's skin, which felt surprisingly nice.

There were so many new sensations he had already experienced as a human. Although his mind clouded with uncertainties and doubt, at that moment everything temporarily drifted away—he was able to truly allow himself to relax for the first time that day. The bread satisfied his aching stomach and Thomas was doing well; he could now focus on the simple pleasures such as the comforting night they shared. He continued to stare upward, enjoying the majestic scenery as his eyes rolled upward beneath his lids until he simply could not hold them open any longer. Kale drifted away into a peaceful slumber on his first night as a human.

~~~~~~~~~~~~~~

The first sound to stand out against the repetitive crackling of the fire was the rustling of nearby bushes on the perimeter closest to where Kale slept. The leaves shook against one another as something moved—hidden within the darkness. Neither Kale nor Thomas woke to the noise. To Kale, the sound of creatures scurrying about in the forest was normal, and although it was quite close, his mind did not register it as a threat which allowed him to continue dreaming without interruption.

As the flames licked against the center of one of the larger logs, it eventually weakened, snapping in half and causing the two halves to land onto the bed of coals. The fire hissed upward, brightly illuminating the surrounding area as if hungrily pouncing upon the wood. The momentary increase in luminosity cast an orange glow upon the bordering vegetation, reflecting off a pair of large yellow eyes. Whatever was camouflaged within the bushes let out a soft grunt as it shunned away from the sudden burst of light. As the fire settled into place, the yellow-eyed stalker resumed its position. The being spread the branches of the bush apart as it watched Kale and Thomas soundly sleeping—ignorant to the threatening gaze cast upon them.

The creature waited a brief while longer, until it felt assurance that the two had not awoke to the noise. It then stood, towering above the bush. The yellow-eyed creature had smooth skin resembling the color of a severe bruise; purple, blue, and slightly red with discolored spots throughout. Its limbs were slender and long, with an abnormal pliancy to them. The creature's arms were lengthy and attached to raised shoulder joints which protruded upward. It had a very flat face with the distinct feature of having no lips. The creature's mouth revealed an open set of sharp teeth and considerable gums which were shown at all times. Because there was no tissue to hold its saliva in, drool constantly ran down its chin. The creature's nose was quite small, yet it picked up the scent of the sleeping humans with ease. Its frame was so thin that as the creature stood, the flesh hugged its rib cage tightly, revealing each bone's formation. The creature cautiously maneuvered around the twigs and dried leaves scattered around the sandy ground. Any wrong move posed the risk of waking the two sleeping men.

The being focused intensely forward making its way toward Kale, stopping only momentarily to wipe a glob of drool from its slightly pointed chin. The creature approached Kale, widening its yellow eyes with thin pupils that shifted along the length of Kale's body in overwhelming curiosity. It lowered its monstrous head near Kale's messy black hair, inhaling quietly to capture the scent. The creature briefly closed its eyes as if to savor the moment. Soon after, it brought its face mere inches above Kale's light-toned arm, extending a grotesquely long and narrow tongue just above the hairs. It seemed to be utilizing another method of smell, much like that of a snake. The creature then grew bold, gently caressing Kale's cheek with its crooked fingers. It seemed to be rather intrigued by his body. As the being lowered its gruesome face closer to Kale's, a long string of drool slipped through its vicious looking teeth—dropping directly onto Kale's forehead.

Kale flinched, rolling onto his side while muttering unclear babble. His body turned, causing the glob of saliva to slide at an angle and pool in the corner of his eye. His natural instinct and reflexes took over as he lifted his arm, balling his hand into a fist and rubbing his eye socket. As the wet slobber sloshed around beneath his fingers, he shook his head. His mind quickly grew alert to the situation—he was not dreaming. He pinched his eyes tightly shut, attempting to remove all of the liquid, before slowly squinting, allowing his eyes to adjust to the bright glow of the fire.

*It's not raining...*he thought, *then what in Pan's name was that?* He used his index finger to wipe away the remaining wetness from beneath his eye, bringing it close to his nose. He then sniffed and analyzed the clear fluid-like substance. *Useless human sense of smell.* He rubbed it between his two fingertips and, although he didn't dare admit, his newly acquired ability to touch was quite amazing and he was able to feel textures like never before. He continued to ponder, *It's not rain...not dew drops from the leaves...is this —saliva?*

Kale immediately went into a defensive state of mind. His former instincts as a mighty beast that longed for a good hunt returned. He wasn't about to allow an animal to get the best of him. He crouched to the ground, examining the sand for footprints—there were none. He glanced over toward Thomas who was softly snoring, deep asleep. Kale knew Thomas was overly exhausted and it would pose a greater risk to attempt waking him in order to join in on the investigation. Thomas would not be able to cast any magic without a severe strain on his already weakened body. Kale stood, tightening the twine that held his oversized pants up around his waist. He was incredibly thankful to have remembered the way Thomas would often knot up a small pouch around his robes.

He stared into the darkness surrounding them, taking caution to stray from looking toward the fire in order to allow his pupils time to adjust. His hopes were running high that whatever had come so close to him was no more than a coyote or gnarlcat, which spooked away at his earlier movement or the crackling of the fire. He licked his lips, thinking how delicious it would taste after being roasted. If he could somehow catch the creature, they would be able to fill their stomachs, giving them energy to continue their journey tomorrow. He realized that as a human, he was not naturally able to kill unless he was quick enough to grasp the animal within his bare hands. He needed to find something—a weapon—and fast. Whatever ventured into their camp could already be scurrying away to safety.

He rummaged through the caravan, but to his disappointment, there were no swords or other larger weaponry. Kale did manage to dig out a small dagger, which seemed to be freshly sharpened. To his side, there was also an iron pole that looked as though it had been used to hold the caravan window open. He grabbed both, just in case, placing the dagger's blade through his twine belt to hold it snugly in place. Kale then crept slowly toward the darkness, unknowing which direction the creature had gone—a blind hunt.

He grew discouraged after many minutes of searching, and the temptation to return to the camp was becoming more appealing. Suddenly, he heard a twig pop—something moved, and in the direction he was headed.

Here, little gnarlcat. He thought, hungrily anticipating an attack on what he still assumed to be a small animal. He smiled as he felt close to enjoying a scrumptious meal.

As he continued to follow the direction where he had heard the noise, the ground beneath his bare feet grew damp and sponge -like. Kale glanced around, soon realizing he had approached a pond which appeared quite unwelcoming and murky. He could scarcely see his surroundings, given the few twinkling stars which shone their faint light through the leaves of surrounding trees. His enthusiasm faded. What stood before Kale in the center of the pond was the very last thing he could have ever fathomed. It was certainly no coyote, definitely not a gnarlcat—but a dragon—it was him.

CHAPTER 4

THE MONSLOTHS

Kale pinched his eyes tightly shut and shook his head in disbelief. *Was this a dream?* He slowly lifted his eyelids—the dragon was still there. Mesmerized by the sight of his former self, he took a step forward into the cloudy brown water. He sloshed his way toward a relatively small sandy island in the center where the dragon stood. The massive beast filled nearly the entire piece of land. Cypress trees bordered the lake; their roots protruding from the ground, creating an eerie, haunting appearance to the area. The body of water was surprisingly shallow, only rising to his hips at the deepest points—which, for Kale, was quite lucky considering he never swam a day in his life. As he made his way to the center section of land, Kale came face to face with the replica of his mighty former body.

"Just who are you!?" Kale tightened his grip on the iron rod, furious someone would attempt to play such a sinister trick on him after all he'd gone through. "I know you aren't another dragon—and you're definitely not me. So tell me, what sick game are you trying to play? Are you truly so cowardly that you fear to show me your true face?"

Kale couldn't imagine who, other than Thomas, could possibly know the truth about him. "Have it your way then—I'll force you to answer me, you gutless fool!" He swung the rod violently toward the black dragon. Kale was taken aback as his feet slid, nearly throwing him off balance, and causing him to fall. The weapon had gone completely through the dragon's face—it was an illusion.

"So, you are a dragon!" An incredibly gruff female voice mysteriously echoed around him.

It sounded as though whoever it was spoke to him from all directions. The effect caused Kale to lose any chance of tracking the location.

"I knew I could sense something...different about you." It paused. "You did not smell like a normal human."

Kale realized this must be the same creature that woke him from his sleep. He began to piece the whole scenario together, coming to the conclusion it was also this creature which must have attacked the travelers in the caravan—killing them all. Kale stood, like an animal lured into a trap, helpless, isolated, and alone, surrounded by water. He slowly spun around on the small island, investigating his surroundings in an attempt to determine where the stalker camouflaged itself.

Although his eyes had adjusted to the blackness of night, he still found it incredibly challenging to see through the cypress trees. Their trunks were rooted so closely together it created a wall of bark, nearly impossible to see through. The only noticeable clearing was the path where Kale originally approached the lake.

The voice broke through the silence, speaking to Kale once again. "So curious you are. My ability to conjure illusions is intended to show foolish and greedy humans what they desire above all else. To most—gold, riches, and power...But you—you are quite different. For a human to desire a beast is laughable. It was then that I felt confident with my earlier assumptions about you. You are not a human...but a dragon. I sense a deep, bitter hatred within you. Could it be, much like myself, you too despise humans?" The creature cackled.

Kale realized the illusion he saw was a method the creature devised in order to lure humans—to trap them.

The creature spoke again, its voice slurred, much like someone who was attempting to speak without having the ability to pucker their lips. "It's a shame that you are now one of them; because we've grown hungry and your flesh smells so delicious."

We? Kale thought as his heart began to quicken in pace.

Suddenly, the water began to bubble as four arms darted out toward Kale's ankles. His animalistic reflexes allowed him to quickly dodge the attack, leaping toward the island's center. Being in a human body did have its advantages; he was lighter and much more agile than he had been as a large dragon. He was stranded and his soaked clothes weighed down heavily upon his body; he had no idea what type of monster he was up against. The blue and purple tinted appendages were long and outstretched onto the sandy shore. They moved around frantically in search of Kale's legs. Almost as if they could sense where he stood, they lashed out in his direction, causing him to dance around in order to avoid being caught.

The water began to ripple as two oblong hairless heads emerged; their bright yellow eyes rest deep inside of their sockets, staring directly toward Kale. With every movement the creatures made, a sickening pop could be heard. Their many joints were so disfigured that every time the monsters took a step forward, their bones shifted constantly within the joint sockets. The creatures moved their bodies in an abnormal fashion and kept their necks constantly bent to the right as if permanently looking sideways.

Kale cringed as the pointed teeth within a lipless mouth parted as the two creatures snarled at him, inching their way closer to where he stood. It was fight—or be eaten alive. Kale lifted the iron rod above his head; he prepared to thrust the weapon down toward one of the approaching creatures.

Without warning, another monster leapt down from the only cypress tree on the border of the small island and slammed into Kale's shoulder. It landed with ease on the wet ground in front of him.

Kale lost his footing, slipping backwards into the thick, sticky mud. In the midst of surprise, Kale kicked out his left leg and knocked the creature backwards into the water.

"Do not resist, boy. The pain will not last long." The creature stood, approaching the island rapidly.

The other two positioned themselves on opposite sides and closed in on Kale's body—attempting to trap him for an attack.

Kale had already lifted himself onto his feet, shifting his eyes around to view all three of the creatures. He knew he was outnumbered, yet, after having fled from General Jedah, his pride would not allow him to run away a second time. One of the creatures managed to creep close enough to Kale to extend its long, slender arms outward, wrenching its hand forcefully around Kale's bicep. He grimaced as his arm burned horribly. It felt as though it would be ripped out of the socket at any moment. He struggled to keep his footing.

Kale knew he needed to make his move before it was too late. He angled his free arm back, preparing to swing a powerful blow. As the rod swooshed through the air, it made contact with the creature, slamming hard against its rib cage. The monster cried out, buckling over and gripping its side. Before Kale could feel any enthusiasm about his accomplishment, he felt an agonizing sensation on his leg. He glanced back just in time to see the third monster gnawing viciously as his calf. While focusing on striking the other creature, Kale had not noticed another of the monstrosities returning from the water. Vulgar words spat out from Kale's mouth as his body filled with a combination of pain and anger. His thought process quickly focused as he reached down to his belt, grasping the handle of the small dagger.

Kale maneuvered his fingers around the weapon until they pinched the tip of the blade. He bit his lower lip, preparing for the intense pain he was about to endure as he jerked his leg from the monster's mouth snugly clamped onto his flesh. The skin tore and blood splattered to the ground as it oozed from his wound. As Kale's anger rose, so did his determination to live. His palms began to feel hot. The temperature increased with every passing moment. He flung the dagger as hard as his wrist would allow toward the creature that had bitten him. As the weapon spun through the air, Kale developed a perspective on his situation. He became fully aware of his surroundings and managed to duck downward to avoid another incoming attack as one of the other creatures reached out to grab his neck.

Kale watched in awe as the dagger's tip pierced through the creature's forehead, sliding smoothly through its skull. The dagger exited out the backside of the creature's head, taking small pink pieces of brain along for the ride. As the dagger hit the lake's surface it sizzled loudly before sinking out of sight. The monster's yellow eyes rolled back into its skull as it plummeted face down into the mud.

Kale felt a refreshing sense of confidence after his successful kill. There were only two opponents left—he had a chance. Kale gripped the rod with both hands, prepared to finish the fight. His palms were now emitting even more heat than before as he swung the rod fiercely toward the next closest creature which had its disgusting mouth hung open, preparing to rip a chunk of flesh from Kale's bicep. The rod struck the monster's jaw with amazing force. Kale's eyes grew wide as the upper half of the creature's head spun through the air. Blood and chunks of innards that resembled maggots flung in every direction. The creature's body fell lifeless and limp to the ground.

The remaining monster took a step back, now intimidated by Kale.

From his peripheral vision, Kale could see a faint orange glow which transmitted from the iron rod. It had the same appearance as metals heated to extreme temperatures.

What is happening? Kale thought. He blinked, quickly shaking the thought from his mind. There was still one creature left to fight—he had not yet won the battle and this was no time to become reckless, or allow his mind to wander. He dug his toes into the mud as he prepared his footing for another swing. His calf muscle flexed and pain seared through his body from the open wound. Kale could feel blood trickling from the gaping hole where the monster had torn a chunk of flesh. He gritted his teeth and forced his eyes to focus on the monstrosity before him.

The creature lowered its lids as if pondering where to lash out for an attack. The skin above the creature's top set of teeth raised as it snarled, wrinkling its nose. Then, unexpectedly, it parted its pointed teeth, releasing an ear piercing scream.

Kale was momentarily stunned. He had not yet struck the monster, and thus, there was no reason for it to cry out in what sounded like bone-chilling agony. The creature soon ceased screaming and began to chatter its teeth together. Kale was baffled by the gesture, unsure of how to react.

Is this abomination attempting to surrender to me? Kale wondered.

The creature continued to hammer its top and bottom rows of teeth together in a repetitive, steady rhythm. Within seconds, Kale heard multiple splashing sounds as a dozen pairs of yellow eyes blinked along shore of the lake, positioned in a perfect circle—surrounding him. Kale realized the scream had been a battle cry, used to summon more of its kind to aid in the fight. He swallowed hard, knowing that swarmed by such a large number, and already injured—things were not going to be in his favor.

Kale looked toward the sky. *Pan, I hope you're watching over me...* he thought while wishfully praying to the mighty dragon god who was said to live among the stars. He took in a deep breath, holding it as he ducked down before springing back to avoid another swing of the creature's long arms. The surrounding monsters began to rhythmically chatter their teeth in unison as if it were their drums of war.

"What did I do to deserve all of this?!" Kale yelled out in anger. The veins on his neck pulsed as he tightened his jaw. "At least when I was to die as a dragon I could have kept *some* dignity!" He began to recklessly swing the orange glowing iron rod in a mad frenzy. "I'll kill you all!"

The rod struck the creature standing closest to him. As it made contact, the weapon sliced through the monster's torso with ease. Its smooth skin singed and the smell of burnt flesh filled Kale's nostrils. The creature staggered toward him, still determined to attack as if hunger was the dominant thought on its mind. It stepped forward, a long string of intestines discharged out of its gut and it fell to the ground in a heap of bloody mess.

The monster glanced down at its torn torso as its yellow eyes widened before collapsing into the murky water.

Kale barely found the time to inhale, before many of the surrounding creatures thrashed angrily through the water toward him. The chattering of teeth ceased and they were now threateningly hissing as they closed in on him.

"It looks as though my time has come, my brethren." Kale whispered into the air, speaking to the fallen dragons. Although Kale intended to fight until his last breath, the thought of death weighed on his mind, causing the joyful times he had spent in life to flash before his eyes. He pulled back the rod, readying himself for his final battle. The creatures were only feet away from arms reach when Kale noticed a spark of light, followed by a loud snapping noise—something approached in his direction.

"Kale, do as I say and do not move!" a voice bellowed out above the sound of hissing. Kale could immediately distinguish that it was Thomas.

"I sure hope you know what you're doing!" Kale yelled. He knew that with one false move he would become a feast for the creatures. They were so close now, that should Thomas delay, Kale would meet an inevitable demise.

Kale froze in place—his mind swarming with doubt as half a dozen creatures advanced toward him. He pinched his eyes tightly shut, placing his life within Thomas' hands.

Thomas' open palm rose to the sky. "*Mischenda lok vixairea.*" He then tightly balled his fingers into a fist and struck the ground. A large, red nova of light flashed brightly outward around Thomas' body. It hovered inches above the ground as it made way for the island at an outstanding speed. Brief cries rang out as the red blast struck the creatures and seared through their flesh as if it were a sword made by the finest blacksmith and sharpened to perfection.

Kale slightly lifted his eyelids. He viewed in amazement as the red blast split directly in front of where he stood and created a V-like shape around him. The magical barrier deterred the spell from striking him. He watched as the creatures' skin turned to ash, beginning in the area where the attack first struck and expanding in both directions until their ugly faces disintegrated. The pieces fluttered down in grey flakes to coat the surface of the murky water. It looked as though snow had fallen before the ashes melted away, sinking below the surface. Kale widened his eyes; the nova was gone—so were the creatures. He glanced around to view the damage done by the blast. To his surprise, none of the surrounding foliage was harmed. Everything stood as it had when he first arrived— completely untouched by Thomas' spell. The attack was able only to affect breathing organisms with flesh and bones.

Thomas pointed at Kale, shaking his finger, "You should count your blessings that my bladder isn't what it used to be! I'm sure you can imagine my surprise when I awoke, only to see you were nowhere to be found!" he called out from the bank of the pond as his grey brows descended over his eyes in anger. "Just what were you trying to prove by running off alone? You've only just become a human; it's amazing you survived as long as you did before I arrived. These creatures are called monsloths. You're incredibly lucky they didn't rip the flesh from your body and feast upon your innards."

"*Those* things were monsloths?!" Kale remembered a story Thomas once told him about the creatures.

They had ambushed a very small village to the west of Mirion many years ago, slaughtering men, women, and children—there had been no survivors. The King dispatched a small, but elite group of knights to hunt the attackers. At the time, a description was unknown other than the assumption it had been a sizeable animal. After three days on the hunt, they had finally managed to devise a plan to lure the beast out by roping a sheep to a tree. The knights' plan proved to be a success as hours later, two monsloths emerged from the brush. They appeared hungry and prepared to indulge upon the helpless animal. The knights were utterly repulsed. They had never seen nor heard of such a monstrosity prior to this encounter. The knights watched in silence as the two creatures walked toward the sheep. The men had no doubts the monsters were responsible for the horrible murders, judging by the savage look they bore. The warriors jumped out from their hidden location and ambushed the two creatures. The end result was a victory and both monsters had been slain—however, it came at a price. They lost one of their own men, along with the sheep. It was a bittersweet ending.

Kale's memories were interrupted by the sharp affliction in his calf that felt as though his lower leg was on fire.

"We'd better head back to camp, Kale. You're soaked and need to dry by the fire. I'm afraid the only spell I know that allows an individual to walk across liquid is limited to only myself." He sighed regrettably, feeling sorry that his friend would now have to wade through the remnants of monsloth particles. Until this point, Thomas had not foreseen becoming part of a war in which he would have needed to know such a spell. He now wished he had dedicated more time to the study of spell books in his youth.

Kale nodded as he began to trudge through the water. Once

THE CHRONICLES OF KALE: A DRAGON'S AWAKENING

he arrived at the deepest section of the lake, his leg felt cool and relieved from pain. This lasted briefly as the agony soon returned. With every step he took, he could feel a chunk of loosely attached meat from his wound swaying in the water. The sensation felt as though the flesh was being tugged from his body, slowly ripping away. Kale had never been so glad to stand upon dry land as he made his way up onto the shore. At this point, he wanted nothing more than to return to their camp to enjoy the comforts of a warm fire and rest. It had been the worst day in all one hundred and twenty six years of his life. Between General Jedah and the monsloths, he couldn't tell which was worse; both were equally ugly and vicious—then there was the whole being transformed into a human issue. He sighed, grunting and groaning, as he limped his way back to the camp.

~~~~~~~~~~~~~~~~

When they arrived back at the ransacked caravan, Kale had a much better understanding of what really happened to the travelers. He tried to shake the thoughts, knowing he needed to rest his mind and body. The once cozy fire had dwindled to nothing more than hot coals and embers. Thomas began to gather nearby twigs and sticks in order to salvage the dying fire, instructing Kale to rest and warm himself. After the fire began to feed off the small pieces of dry wood, Thomas carried a small log to the flames, gently laying it on top of the coals; as he did, his eyes widened. Thomas jerked his hand back, pulling it under the sleeve of his robe. He was thankful Kale was so exhausted that he did not notice the blackened veins which ran through his hand.

Thomas knew he had exceeded his magical limits. Even supreme spell-casters such as sorcerers had boundaries on how much power they could expend within a certain amount of time. Each caster was different and had their own extent of what would push them over—Thomas had met his. When a caster went beyond what their physical and mental strength could handle, the magic would react against them, absorbing into their body as a poison.

"Can't you just conjure us a fire? It's a bit ridiculous to watch a sorcerer tending to a fire as if he were an average human." After seeing him in action, Kale felt confident Thomas had his strength back.

Thomas glanced up toward Kale, who still sat in his sopping clothing. "Magic is not to be used recklessly, Kale. It's not wise for a skilled spell-caster to ease their way through life using only their magical abilities. Any decent sorcerer should be self-sufficient without the need to use spells on basic daily tasks." He tossed another small bundle of twigs on top of the flames, gently blowing downward onto the sparkling embers until the fires intensity increased. The larger flames now hugged the logs placed into the pit. "I think it would be best for us to sleep inside the caravan tonight. It will provide cover against any unexpected weather and it is much less of a risk in case there are further night creatures roaming about." Even with the door missing from its hinges, the caravan would still provide better shelter than sleeping vulnerably out in the open.

Kale nodded in agreement, so tired at this point that he truly did not care where they slept. They spent a very brief amount of time engaging in conversation before neither of them could hold their eyelids up any longer. They slowly made their way toward the wooden caravan. Thomas gave a final glance over his shoulder to ensure there was no debris surrounding the pit which could catch fire while they slept. The last thing they needed after such a horrible night would be to wake and find themselves surrounded by flames.

Suddenly, Thomas paused, stopping in his tracks as he pointed toward the inside of the caravan.

"I'll leave that to you, Kale."

Kale could immediately see that Thomas referred to the corpse of the woman traveler within the wooden vehicle. He had forgotten all about her until now. Her body hung halfway through the side window, as though she had been trying to escape when the monsloths attacked. Her attempt to flee had failed horribly. Kale sighed at the inconvenience as he made his way around to the side of the caravan. All he wanted to do was sleep. He wrapped his arms around her torso, tugging forcefully in an attempt to dislodge her from the small square opening she had tried to squeeze through. His muscles ached as he struggled to battle his fatigue. The deceased body inched forward, until the woman's feet slipped down from the window frame. Kale released his grip around the torso as her body crumpled to the ground in an abnormally grotesque position. Her neck bent to the side, and Kale could now see that beneath her auburn locks was a hole where her face had been eaten away from the skull. He cringed. Even for a dragon who had devoured animals whole, this was disgusting. A single eyeball remained, sagging loosely in globs of thick oozy blood.

Thomas peeked around the corner of the caravan, "How long must an old man wait?" As he saw the woman, he choked back the vomit that slid up his throat like a scorching volcano about to erupt.

In a poor attempt to cover the bloody remnants of what once was a face, Kale picked up as many pine needles as he could fit within his grasp and tossed them onto the woman's head.

Thomas smacked his palm to his forehead in disbelief at his friend's shameful method of hiding the corpse. He wrinkled his nose as he eyed Kale's blood-smudged arms.

"You are sleeping on the opposite side of the caravan, young man." He waved a finger as he spoke. "Tomorrow we will need to find a clean source of water to hydrate and wash." Although friends, Thomas often behaved as the adult and father figure of their relationship. Kale had lived longer than most humans; however he was still a juvenile among his kind and revealed a great amount of immaturity and reckless behavior.

Kale paid no attention to his sticky hands as he walked back toward Thomas. "Why do you think the monsloths ate only portions of these people? From the story you once told me, and from what I've seen tonight, I would think that there would be nothing left of them."

"Well, I've never encountered their kind prior to tonight— I've only heard stories as well. I would assume they rummaged through the caravan and found that between the chunks of meat they indulged upon already and the stocked food within the vehicle, it was enough to satisfy their temporary needs."

Kale then explained to Thomas about the one who stalked him as he slept.

"I'm sure they were returning to recover the bodies and bring them back. Then to their surprise, fresh meat had arrived." Thomas shook his head, attempting to remain awake.

Kale limped his way over to the caravan, planting his bottom onto the wood as he scooted toward the far end. He was completely exhausted.

"Jumping balt toads, Kale, why didn't you tell me you were wounded?! How did this happen?" Thomas earlier assumed Kale's stagger to be a normal strain on his leg due to the adjustment into a human body. "Let me have a closer look," He demanded.

Kale rolled his weary eyes, explaining to Thomas it was just a small wound and he would be fine after a little rest.

Thomas dismissed Kale's sorry attempt at pretending to put on a tough exterior. He firmly gripped Kale's ankle and pulled the leg toward him to better analyze the injury. He pulled out his spectacles, placing them upon his face as he maneuvered himself to allow the light of the camp fire to illuminate his view.

"My goodness...you hardheaded dragon." He exhaled, "You were bitten by a monsloth—and don't you dare try to deny it, boy. I once read a book which spoke of various venoms across Ravondore, and this is most definitely from a monsloth. I can't tell whether your brain is filled with pride—or stupidity." He continued to investigate the open wound, gently pressing against the sides as he watched a green pussy substance squirt down Kale's calf. The wound advanced with infection at an accelerated rate; it had already begun to fester and smelt putrid. Thomas increased the pressure on the red swollen tissue of the wound and Kale moaned in pain. "My, my." He removed his spectacles, returning them to his pocket. "You're in for a rough night, dear friend." Thomas' green eyes narrowed sympathetically. "From what I've read, those who are bitten by one of these creatures will suffer with symptoms for a day at the least. You can expect severe vomiting and temporary hallucinations. I can however, offer you a bit of relief." He held his hand up above Kale's wound, ensuring the sleeve of his robe shielded the blackened veins from sight. He knew that using even more magic in his current state would not be wise, but he could not allow his friend to suffer throughout the night in agony. Healing spells of this magnitude were fairly easy. The wound was not extremely large and he was only going to use a little of his strength to ensure comfort, not cure the entire opening in the leg.

"*Xaranthium mendona.*" With a painless *zap* the red inflamed tissue returned to normal and the puss seemed to evaporate away. Though the chunk of flesh was missing, the opening was much smaller in size and the pain relatively gone. Thomas informed Kale it would still need more time before fully healed and his body would naturally run its course to do so. The old sorcerer could feel the veins on his hand pulsing as the black magical poisons ran up into his arm. He would need to refrain from using any spells over the next couple of days if he wanted to survive.

"Thank you...I mean it." Kale yawned heavily. "You're the best friend I've ever had Well, the only friend—but still the best." He smiled as his tired eyes finally closed.

CHAPTER 5:

A MYSTERIOUS ENCOUNTER

Kale drifted into what would normally have been a peaceful rest, but tossed and turned as he passed from one disturbing dream into another. In the final and most troubling dream, he stood before Pan, the mighty dragon god. Pan held his enormous grey head up, gazing forward with wide, hazel-toned eyes. Every step he took pounded against the ground, sending tremors across the area. His body was covered with bone-like spikes aligned down his spine. Above each eye were two rows of small horns which were embedded into his skin, nearly hiding his webbed ears. Alongside Pan stood many other dragons; they walked in a significant herd toward a pink horizon. Kale immediately recognized a few of the dragons within the group. He saw the beautiful pearlescent torso of Sylicia, the Ice Matriarch, shimmering with each stride; the large blue fins of Xelanthos, the Ocean Dweller, slapping against the ground; and Zandol, the Emerald Prince, who tucked his large wings upon his back. They looked proud, magnificent, and very much alive. Kale's heart leapt with glee as he took off in a sprint toward them.

"Pan! Sylicia! Everyone, it's me, Kale—the Black Dragon, Firehart!" He called out as loud as he could.

They didn't respond. They didn't even glance his way or acknowledge his presence; it was as though he were invisible. He waved his arms high above his head, continuing to shout as loud as his puny human lungs could handle. "Everyone, please! It really is me, I swear!"

He continued to watch them roaming past him in silence as his eyes grew wide with horror. Each dragon plummeted head first toward the ground; their bodies exploding into thousands of bloody chunks upon impact. Kale fell to his knees in despair as his eyes began to glass over with tears. The vision of dragons was suddenly eclipsed by the image of General Jedah who now stood before him and laughed profusely as his dark eyes pierced Kale's. His armored foot lunged forward, slamming forcefully into Kale's gut.

Kale awoke from the dream, vomiting brown and yellow chunky fluid from his mouth onto the bed of the caravan. His stomach ached terribly. He crawled his way out of the vehicle and inhaled the overwhelming scent of urine which caused him to choke back even more fluid from rising in his throat. The sun beat down on his head as he emerged out into the open air. Although still shaking from the ill feeling churning in his stomach, to be awake and outside in the sunny cloudless day was pleasantly refreshing. His leg felt amazingly better, with only a minor wound remaining. As he glanced around the camp, squinting to adjust to the bright light, he noted Thomas was missing. Before panic could take effect, he heard someone walking toward his direction.

Thomas emerged from the foliage carrying a bucket filled with water. He wobbled, holding the handle within both hands as he brought it near the caravan, setting it down near Kale.

"Good afternoon! Glad you're finally able to join me in the realm of reality!" Thomas chuckled, patting Kale on the shoulder. "I mean no disrespect when I say you look—and smell—horrible. Wash up boy, you've been asleep for the past two days. I've tried to keep things tidy, but between your constant vomiting and *relieving* yourself, it's been quite a task and hard to keep up with."

Kale glanced down at the bucket, peering toward the waters' glassy surface. He tilted his head to the side in a combination of confusion and curiosity. It was his first glimpse of himself as a human. He squatted lower in order to better examine his facial features, lifting a hand to his smooth cheek. Kale's black hair and eyebrows contrasted in a most appealing manner against his blue eyes which caused them to appear as though they were two gems of sparkling ice in the reflection. He quickly shook his head, feeling slightly disappointed for having had any interest with his human body—after all, humans were disgusting. Kale quickly dunked his hand into the bucket, distorting the reflection into a rippled blur. He quickly withdrew his hand, shaking it to remove the water droplets as he peered down at the ashy flakes floating around within the water.

"Thomas, I can't clean myself with this filth; there are monsloth remnants. I'd rather stay damp with my own stench before I rub those monstrosities all over my body."

"You're too much, boy." Thomas laughed. "The water is clean; I retrieved it from a tiny stream just to the east. Those ashes you see are from the fire. Stir the water and they'll dissolve."

"Oh, sorry. Thanks for bringing this to me," Kale muttered, feeling slightly guilty for having had to rely on an old man to help care for him. "Thomas... Why do I look so young? I saw myself—my reflection. I look like a boy."

"Because you *are* a boy, Kale. I'd go as far to say a young man—but you do still behave as though you were a boy at times." Thomas chuckled. "As I've told you before, a dragon's lifespan is scaled much differently than that of a human. You have lived for one hundred and twenty six years. If you were to convert that into a human equivalent, you would be a maturing man of eighteen years—which is exactly what you see in the reflection."

"I am no ignorant human child." He raised an upper lip in distaste as he removed his soiled clothing. Once again he dunked his hand into the bucket, scrubbing away at the sweat and vomit that had seeped through his shirt and covered his torso. It felt amazing to have the cool water trickle down his body, countering the blazing sunlight that drenched over him. He ran a hand through his wet hair causing black spikes to stick out in all directions. Having the filth removed from his body felt invigorating. Using the remaining water within the bucket, he soaked his putrid smelling clothing, dunking each piece repeatedly until the orange chunks were no longer present on the cloth.

Kale, carrying his dripping wet garments, walked over to where Thomas sat with his back turned. "What can I do with these until they dry?"

The old sorcerer glanced over his shoulder, "Jumping balt toads, Kale! You can't go around walking up behind people unclothed!" He quickly snatched the clothing, turning away. "I'll help you—this time."

"You have no right to get upset, Thomas. Let's not forget it was *you* who did this to m—" Before Kale could finish, he heard a loud gasp that caused him to spin around on his heels. For the first time in Kale's life, he leapt in fear, wrapping his arms around his body.

Before Kale's blue eyes stood a very petite, young woman with a tattered, oversized brown hat. She wore a black tunic, obviously not made to fit her thin frame, and red tights that hung from her skinny legs. A grand wooden bow hung over her back with a leather quiver stocked full of arrows.

"Hello?" Kale questioned.

The woman peeked between the cracks in her fingers as her porcelain-looking cheeks flushed red with embarrassment.

Kale reached out to move her hand from covering her face. He was unaccustomed to proper greetings.

"Do not touch me!" She pulled away quickly, cringing at the sight of Kale. "What is wrong with you? Are you some sort of dim-wit who runs around the forest without clothing?"

By this point, Kale appreciated her previous silence much more. Before she once again buried her face within her palms, Kale caught a glimpse of her unusual violet eyes from behind shaggy brown bangs that covered her forehead.

"Now dear, please do not be frightened." Thomas approached her. The gesture seemed to cause even further uneasiness as she had not noticed the old man's presence until that moment. "My friend was simply bathing here at our camp before we make way to the next destination. He was unaware that there were any other travelers nearby or he surely would not have been so careless." The sorcerer threw Kale his clothing which was surprisingly dry.

Kale could only assume magic had been used.

"*Your* camp?" She snickered, tossing a lock of brunette hair over her shoulder. "This happens to be a road, you know. Traders have used it in secrecy for years. No one camps here unless they care to sleep with one eye open for risk of getting their throat slit as they sleep. Thieves are wise to the goods transported through this forest and have been known to attack unsuspecting travelers." She cautiously glanced toward the ransacked caravan. "You wouldn't happen to be thieves, now would you?" Her eyes narrowed. "I'd advise you to answer if you wish to live. Thieves are scum." She bravely tilted her body to give the two men a better view of her longbow.

Kale took notice of its magnificent craftsmanship. It appeared as though the bow was infused with both wood and gold, intertwining around one another to create an impeccable weapon of range.

"We're definitely not thieves. And despite your attempts to frighten me, I don't fear you." Kale smirked, pulling his pants up and tightening them around his waist. "Do such threats actually work on humans? You don't even reach my shoulders." He held a hand out, measuring her height in a mocking gesture.

Thomas immediately cut into the conversation, fearful Kale might reveal too much information to the stranger. "I assure you—we mean you no harm. Allow me to introduce ourselves— my name is Thomas, and this is my good friend, Kale."

He went on to explain that they were travelers, new to the region, and were en route toward the town of Braxle to rest and recover after a long journey. Once Kale was fully clothed, the young woman appeared more at ease, no longer hiding behind her hands or shunning their presence. Without an invitation, she took it upon herself to sit upon an old tree stump as she continued to listen to Thomas speak of their fictitious travels. He had a habit of elaborating even the smallest of tales. Although he enjoyed telling grand stories, even more so he loved having others to share them with.

"Now then," Thomas sat, resting his bearded chin onto his knuckles, "you know a bit about our lives, please enlighten us about yourself." He smiled welcomingly.

She immediately grew defensive, crossing her arms over her chest. "Who said I was planning to stay? And, I don't recall telling either of you I wanted to share my life story and become friends." She paused, glancing toward the ground and sighing. "But, I guess if we're all heading in the same direction anyway, it wouldn't hurt to travel together." The young woman stood, brushing stray hairs from her face. "My name is Neelan. I suppose it's not such a bad thing that I ran into you." She shot a glance toward Kale as if to say, *I still don't want you to get close to me.*

"Neelan, you say?" Thomas lightly stroked the hair beneath his bottom lip. He eyed her curiously, inspecting her structure and movements while taking note of her unique violet eyes.

Neelan shifted uncomfortably as her eyes quickly dodged Thomas'.

Kale could sense that Neelan was uncomfortable with the conversation. He groaned loudly, rubbing his stomach in hunger, suggesting they find something to eat before traveling to a new location.

Neelan agreed, explaining she had not eaten in over a day. She continued on to tell the two men she had spotted a grand army traveling from Eldawin, which caused her to flee into the forest. Neelan expressed her assumption that it was the nefarious General Jedah whom she heard had performed so many abhorrent deeds across Ravondore.

Kale swallowed hard, trying to conceal his bitter hatred for Jedah. He knew from stories Thomas had told that Eladwin was a town to the northwest of his cave. He shifted his thoughts toward the young woman, trying to determine why she had decided to conveniently invite herself to join them. Kale noticed the deep look of loneliness within her eyes that she shielded through a very assertive attitude and reinforced with sarcasm. Whatever her reasons, Kale's aching stomach stole his focus. He did not care to concern himself any further on the subject of Neelan's reasoning.

"We should try to hunt something for lunch. After the past few days, I need something more than an apple before I exert this puny body any further. I'm quite familiar with the variety of animals within this forest—many are quite tender, juicy, and delicious. I would love to sink my teeth into something fresh," Kale licked his lips at the thought.

Neelan lifted the bow from upon her back. "You have an odd way of speaking, you know. If I didn't see you standing before me now, I'd be tempted to assume *you* were an animal yourself." She paused a moment in thought. "Wait a moment; I thought you both were new to this region?"

Kale chewed on his bottom lip at a loss for words.

Thomas stepped in to salvage the situation. "My dear, we are indeed new to this area, however, Kale is quite familiar with its wildlife through numerous books and documentations he has read."

Kale smiled uncomfortably. He would have to choose his words carefully from this point on. Neelan was much more observant than he assumed.

"All right then, Kale," she smacked him on the back, "Let's get something to eat."

"If you don't mind," Thomas spoke as he lowered himself to the ground, sliding off a slipper-like, black shoe, "I'm going to rest my feet awhile. You two go on ahead." He gave Kale a look of warning as if to tell him to watch his tongue.

Neelan and Kale nodded, beginning their hunt as they silently made their way through the forest. They took great caution not to step on any dried leaves or other debris that would reveal their location. Neelan scouted many steps in front of Kale and he couldn't help but chuckle to himself as he watched her movement. Her outfit was as pitiful as his, drooping ridiculously off her small frame. The whole scenario seemed comical to him.

Before Kale could further amuse himself, Neelan turned to face him, holding a finger to her lips, and using her free hand to point through a growth of green ferns. He gently moved a cluster of leaves to the side so he could view the creature on the other side. It was a large bald animal with a long wet snout and stiff thick whiskers protruding from its wrinkled cheeks. It curiously moved around the tiny clearing, baring bucked front teeth and hissing viciously. Kale immediately recognized the creature; he had eaten many of its kind in the past. They were carnivorous beings called sugalrats that savagely digest smaller animals, preferably rodents, much like a snake.

"Give me the bow," Kale softly whispered. He had no idea how to properly hold a bow, let alone shoot one, but his mind could not fathom such a small female having the ability or skill to hit the target.

"Never!" Neelan quietly snapped back. She withdrew a steel-tipped arrow from her quiver, steadying it upon her fingers as she tugged back firmly on the string. The arrow shot rapidly through the air toward the creature, striking it in the side. The sugalrat released a shrill cry before collapsing onto the ground. "Right on target." She smirked, winking at Kale.

"Lucky shot." He rolled his eyes, too proud to admit she had skills he did not possess.

The two gripped the animal's legs and carried it back to the camp where Thomas hungrily awaited their return.

"Magnificent work, you two!" He clapped his palms together, eagerly eyeing their catch.

It wasn't much longer before the animal had been prepared and speared to roast over the open fire. It smelled delectable as the aroma filled their nostrils. Once the sugalrat's outer layers had turned a leathery golden-brown, they removed it from the heat and began to slice the tender meat onto a smoothed rock using Neelan's pocket-sized knife. Kale shoveled a hearty helping of meat into his mouth, rolling his eyes upward in pure bliss. It was remarkably delicious.

After they could eat no more, it was time to depart. Thomas knew they would only have a few hours before darkness consumed the sky. It was imperative for them to make haste and find a new place to camp.

Kale groaned in discomfort as he lazily struggled to stand. He watched as Thomas dumped the bucket of dirty water over the dwindling fire. It sizzled as a cloud of smoke rose into the sky. Before leaving, Kale retrieved the iron rod he had previously used as a weapon.

"Just in case," He said while tapping it against the palm of his hand. Kale still had not told Thomas about the mysterious orange glow of the weapon, or the exceptional strength he possessed during the fight against the monsloths.

~~~~~~~~~~~~~~~~~

The three began their journey along the traders' path as the sun peeked through the foliage above, beating down upon their heads.

"I must admit, I'm looking forward to taking a relaxing soak in a cool tub of water once we arrive at the inn tomorrow." Thomas wiped many beads of sweat from his forehead.

Kale could only imagine how hot the old sorcerer must be in his long robes. Yet he knew there would be no convincing his friend to remove them, despite the horrid heat. As they continued on, Kale's mind drifted in thought. He couldn't help but wonder about Neelan, the mysterious woman who unexpectedly showed up at their camp, revealing only miniscule details about herself. A smile crossed Kale's face. Neelan had already gotten under his skin numerous times, yet he saw a bit of his own personality within her. Although he wasn't about to tell her, he did enjoy having conversation with someone other than Thomas for a change.

They walked for many miles through the humid forest before Kale finally decided to press Neelan for more information.

"Where are you heading?" he asked while running his fingers through his matted, sweaty hair which caused it to stick out in an untamed appearance.

Neelan glanced up, giggling childishly at the sight. "I'm heading to the—" she paused a moment, "to the north." Her light eyes once again were dodgy, avoiding contact. "That's all you need to know."

Kale sighed. Neelan's *secretive demeanor* was getting old. He pondered why Neelan was behaving so reserved. Scenarios involving her as a criminal on the run rushed through his mind. Thoughts continued to press on Kale's mind, as curiosity had certainly gotten the best of him.

Finally, the faint sound of running water could be heard bringing a wave of excitement to the group. All frustrations from the hot walk seemed to drain away as the thought of cooling off became a reality.

"I think it's this way." Kale pointed to his left, where the sound intensified.

They veered off the main trail, heading through a thick growth of bushes, hearty vines, and cypress trees. Kale thrashed the iron rod against the foliage, clearing an opening for them to pass. The walk was brief before they came upon an inviting river. The three were thankful to see the water moved slowly enough for them to enter without fear of being swept away. Kale was the first to approach the riverbed, dipping his toe into the water.

"It feels great!" he called out with enthusiasm.

"With a lady in our presence, I will simply soak my legs. These robes would take an eternity to dry and I don't think anyone would care to see this old, withered body without them." Thomas chuckled.

Kale nodded, knowing that as long as Neelan was around, Thomas would not be able to utilize his magic. Despite the fact that Kale's clothes had been dried only hours ago, he was determined to get into the water; this would be his first time swimming. He tossed the iron rod to the ground and glanced playfully at Neelan. Before her mind could register what was happening, Kale had cleverly lifted her quiver and bow, removing them from over her head.

"Hey! What are you trying to pull? No one — and I mean no one, touches m—"

Neelan's words were caught in her throat as Kale dropped the weaponry at Thomas' feet, sliding an arm around Neelan's waist. He smirked, lifting her petite body from the ground with ease, then ran them both into the cool water. Without warning, he threw his body backwards so they both sank beneath the flowing surface.

Neelan sprang up, spitting water from her puckered lips. "Are you an idiot?" she yelled, throwing her hands up above her head. "What were you thinking?!"

Kale stood, waist deep in water—speechless. His blue eyes bulged and his mouth hung wide open as he stared intently toward Neelan.

"What are you looking at?" Her cheeks were overcome with pink hues. "D-don't stare at me!" She was under the impression Kale might have been admiring her beauty which made her bashful and embarrassed. *For a crude and annoying man, he does have a certain appeal, I suppose.* She bit her lower lip, reaching up to playfully curl a lock of wet hair around her index finger. As her hand rose, she too froze in place. Her breathing intensified, realizing her hat was missing. When hitting the water, it had been pulled from her head by the current. She closed her eyes and began to move her fingertips upward as she traced her long pointed ears, pinching down on the tips and tugging them downward in a poor attempt to hide what she knew had already been seen.

Thomas lifted his robe above his knees as he sat upon a large rock which hung over the riverbank. He dipped his bare feet into the soothing water, as his lips curled into a proud smile. "Dear Neelan, I believe my presumptions were indeed correct after all. You *are* an elf."

CHAPTER 6

INTO THE PAST

Neelan sank down beneath the river's surface in utter embarrassment. At that moment she would rather drown than have to surface and face the two men who now knew her secret. As bubbles of air slipped through her lips, she drifted lower to the sandy bottom—moving slowly at the mercy of the current. Suddenly, she felt a strong hand grip under the pit of her arms, lifting her head up and out of the water. She coughed as water spat from her mouth. Her irritated eyes squinted until the blurred vision began to clear. Glancing forward, she saw it was Kale who stood before her, still holding her body in place.

The seconds passed and Neelan quickly snapped back to reality. She defensively shrugged Kale's arms from her. "Why did you do that?" She turned her back to him. "Everything is ruined now. Once people find out I'm not a human, they'll treat me differently. They'll stare and disregard me—see me as an outcast—just like I'm sure you do now..." Neelan sighed sadly. "I just wanted to fit in with your kind."

"Wait a moment. You actually *want* to be accepted as a human?" Kale exclaimed with a look of disgust. He could not fathom why anyone would want to become human.

"Of course I do! Being a human would mean I could live a free life. I could roam where I desire and no one would second guess my actions. No one would stare at me or shun my appearance." She turned to face Kale. "You must understand—you've lived as a human your entire life. I'm sure you've always been able to go where you wish without any strings attached. Elves don't have the best reputation, you know."

"Pardon my interruption, but I suggest you two begin making your way back in this direction. I've found a place where we can camp for the night." Thomas called downstream to them.

Although there was so much more Kale wanted to know about Neelan, he was grateful for Thomas' distraction. He knew himself enough to *not* trust another slip of the tongue while on the topic of humans.

"I don't want to go back with you," Neelan softly spoke. "I want to travel alone." She turned, pressing through the current toward the riverbank.

"Stop being so temperamental." Kale wrapped his fingers around her forearm. "Just because you're different, doesn't mean you have to run away from us. I'm not going to lie and tell you that finding out you were an elf wasn't a surprise, but it's definitely not a bad thing and certainly no reason to act like such a child." Kale did not know why he cared if she left. For the majority of the time he'd known her, he found the elf's presence to be a nuisance. The only explanation he could rationalize was they both shared similarities on how they felt—both living as something they truly were not—*humans*. Though her reasons were a personal choice and his were circumstantial, he felt there must be more to her story.

Kale pulled on her arm, turning her body to face his. "I suppose if you're not going to come willingly, I'll take you back myself." Kale smirked, lifting Neelan up into his arms as he sloshed his way back to where Thomas had called. He couldn't understand why, but deep inside he knew she didn't want to go— she didn't want to be alone.

~~~~~~~~~~~~~~~~~

Kale and Neelan sat close to the fire, allowing its warm flames to slowly dry their drenched clothing.

Thomas sat directly across from them, hacking at the tip of a long stick with Neelan's knife. He then withdrew a small beige sack Kale recognized from the caravan. He retrieved chunks of leftover meat from their earlier lunch. Thomas was not the type to waste good food, especially in circumstances such as theirs where a delicious meal was few and far between while traveling.

"It tastes better warm," Thomas said with a smile as he speared a chunk of the tender flesh, rotating it slowly over the open flames. "My dear," he looked toward Neelan who had not spoken since her conversation with Kale in the river. "You do not need to fear your true self while in our company. We are not here to judge you." He withdrew the stick, blowing on the meat until it was cool enough to pluck from the stick. "It's still good." He reached around the pit to hand the portion to Neelan. She immediately shoveled it hungrily into her mouth, barely chewing before it slid dryly down her throat. "I have a peace offering you may be interested in. It should at the very least, make you feel more comfortable." The old sorcerer winked pulling her brown tattered hat from behind his back.

"My hat! But how did you—"

Thomas' green eyes sparkled in the light of the illuminating flames. "I'm a sorcerer, dear, we have our ways. Now you know a secret about me as well." He smiled.

Both Neelan and Kale looked dumbstruck as she gripped the hat, quickly placing it once again upon her head. Kale could not believe that after all of the warnings he had been given, the truth about Thomas' magical abilities slipped out so easily. The anger fueled him to fulfill his curiosity about Neelan. He could no longer bite his tongue and needed to know more—especially considering the information she knew about Thomas.

"I want to know, Neelan," Kale shifted to face her as he shoved a handful of meat into his mouth, "Rhy roo oo khoo oo rhyd urr oo relf?"

She raised a brown eyebrow in annoyance. "Disgusting. Chew your food—I swear, you really *are* just like a wild animal."

After swallowing, he once again questioned Neelan. "Why do you choose to hide your true self?"

She heavily sighed, as if in self-debate on whether or not to reveal her story to them. "I suppose I could tell you. But I swear, if you tell another soul—" She hugged her bow warningly.

"Yeah, we get it already." Kale rolled his eyes.

"My father is a very proud man who holds our racial traits as elves above all others. He is incredibly narrow-minded to view and accept the world outside of our own. They only see *our* culture and beliefs as being right." She stared solemnly into the fire as if her mind was drifting back in time. "I can still remember my first true friend. I was playing just outside of our kingdom—something not fully accepted at the time, but not forbidden. I clearly remember skipping stones across a beautiful pond I had come across. The day was perfect and the weather felt amazing. Then, I saw her. She was a young, human girl who seemed in appearance to be the same age as myself. Although, of course, I was much older. Elves age much slower than a human and I still looked as though I was a ten-year-old child." Neelan tugged down upon her brown hat.

"Well, aside from my ears, and eyes. But the girl, her name was Gloria, never once seemed to care. She behaved as though she hadn't even noticed our differences. To her, we were both young girls who simply wanted to enjoy each other's company and play. Each day after my parents left, I would sneak away from Tyrione to meet Gloria. Then," Neelan looked to the ground, "one day while we were weaving crowns out of bright pink flowers we had found, my father appeared. He had somehow found me and his eyes were filled with anger. I...I just didn't understand. He looked to Gloria and told her she was born of filthy blood and to never come near me again. After that day, I was forbidden to leave the kingdom ever again." She buried her face into her hands, forcing back tears as she continued with her story. "I never saw Gloria again."

Neelan went on to explain that after the incident, her father did all in his power to shelter her from the outside world and to keep her from the only true friend she ever had. On her ninety-sixth birthday—equivalent to her sixteenth—her father announced she was to fulfill her life as a priestess, devoting her remaining years to the temple. The thought alone made her sick to her stomach.

The kingdom where she had lived was breathtaking, with masterfully constructed buildings and sparkling streams. It was protected by a barrier of combined magic and defense that ensured a safe environment for them to grow without fear of any outside conflicts. Yet, despite everything Tyrione had to offer, she longed to have the freedom to choose where she wanted to go and who she would befriend. The world was too vast to limit herself to remain within the walls of only one kingdom.

When she fought to compromise or reason with her father, he would punish her in an attempt to cleanse her mind of such desires. He locked her within a tiny, dark room beneath the temple, for days at a time. Neelan's mother, who remained fearful of her husband's rage, would stand back, doing nothing to defend her daughter against his cruelty. In time, Neelan grew to detest her father and lost all respect for the mother she still dearly loved. After two years of being a slave to her father and the temple, she knew it was time to make a stand if she ever intended to truly live her own life.

On the day of her one hundred and second birthday— seventeen in human comparison—she retrieved the bow which her great-grandfather wielded many centuries ago and devised a plan to escape. Once Neelan's parents left for the temple, she made her escape at nightfall to the kingdom sewers. She stealthily crept through the alleyways, remaining cautious and hidden within the shadows cast by the full moon. With ease, she slipped past the guards who kept their focus on the surrounding landscape outside the kingdom. Neelan swiftly dropped down into the dark tunnel of the sewer. She silently took each step upon a narrow brick walkway that kept her feet dry and away from the horridly putrid water. Finally, a stream of moonlight shone down above her head and she knew she had made it out—she was free. Her father's control had caused her to flee from her former life, to desire an alternate life among humans. She longed to be treated as an equal among human-kind, and so, for the past months she had lived as one.

Kale's blue eyes met hers. He hadn't expected such an elaborate story, nor did he anticipate the hardships she had endured.

"What about you?" She sniffled, still tucking back the urge to sob. "I've told you about my past, now it's your turn to share something with me about yours." Neelan regained her composure as she sat upright. "I hope you don't assume I'm *that* naïve. I find it very odd that a young and ordinary man is traveling alongside a sorcerer, secretly, through the forest."

Kale was taken aback by the sudden reverse interrogation. "I'm really tired right now, Neelan." It was the only response he could muster. He lifted his arms above his head, wiggling his fingers toward the sky as he faked a loud yawn. "Maybe tomorrow." He leaned back, staring upward. "Besides, my story isn't nearly as interesting as yours." He felt slightly guilty about hiding the truth from her, but he knew the risks were still too great.

Kale tried to convince himself that he owed Neelan no explanations, having only met her earlier in the day. It wasn't his fault she had spilled her entire life story to them. Still, he couldn't shake the sympathetic feeling he got when looking into her glassy violet eyes. She looked so sad—so alone.

Kale bit his lower lip, chewing gently as he thought about the situation. He had finally met a new acquaintance; as irritating as she was, he found himself enjoying her quick-witted personality. Kale wanted to share his secrets—he wanted to release the weight he bore and find if she too would accept him for what he truly was. For now, he knew it would have to wait.

"All right," she finally replied, glancing toward Thomas who had fallen asleep and was softly snoring. "I suppose I'll sleep as well, then."

"Smart decision," Kale softly laughed. "Thomas is obnoxiously cranky when woken."

Neelan caught Kale by surprise as she removed the brown hat, allowing her long brunette hair to flow freely around her long elven ears. She set it next to her bow as she positioned herself onto the ground which was uncomfortably covered with scattered twigs, pebbles, and leaves.

"Goodnight, Kale," she whispered. "And don't even think about touching me while I sle—" Before she could finish, a white shirt flew down upon her head, muffling out the remainder of her warning.

"Before you scold me, I'll save us both the aggravation by saying that the clothing is for you to use beneath your head. I know the ground isn't pleasant to lie upon." He turned, facing his back to her. "I'm used to sleeping on hard surfaces; it doesn't bother me as it does most. Just be sure to return it when you wake. I wouldn't want you to go into hiding again because I am indecent." He laughed.

Neelan remained silent as she tucked the shirt beneath her head. She closed her eyes, allowing her body to finally relax. "Thank you, Kale," she whispered.

~~~~~~~~~~~~~~~~

Kale laid on his back as tiny beads of perspiration scattered across his forehead. His body shifted as the peaceful dream he was having, slipped into darkness, replaced by the image of a middle-aged woman with short, spiraling red hair. Her golden eyes met his as she smiled warmly. The mysterious woman stepped forward in her plain and unflattering lavender dress that hung to just below her knees. She oddly wore a different shoe upon each foot, one black and the other red. Both looked old and worn. The woman then lifted her arm, gently tracing her fingers along a black scarf wrapped snugly around her neck. He could make out a small, golden bracelet which hung loosely around her wrist. Dangling from the chain was a jade pendant in the shape of a pointed tooth.

"Kale," her voice sounded distant, although she stood mere feet in front of him. "There is still hope, young one. I am aware you are traveling to the town of Braxle. Please know I will do what I can to help guide you along your journey."

"Guide me to what? Who are you?" Kale took a step boldly toward the woman. As he did, the floor beneath his bare feet felt soft, much like freshly kneaded dough, causing him to sink downward. He staggered to stand in an attempt to regain balance as he fought the wobbly sensation of each movement.

The woman glanced at him, watching as he struggled. Her eyes seemed to be filled with pain as if she wanted to reach out and touch him. Despite this reaction, she turned to leave, slowly walking away into the nothingness that surrounded them.

"Wait!" Kale called out, extending his arm toward the woman. He could not understand why, but he felt an unexplainable desire to continue their conversation. It was as though he could sense she had more to tell him. He continued to sink deeper into the ground until suddenly; an unknown force lifted him upward, pulling him free. Everything went black.

The next sight he saw was the warm rays of sunlight that broke through the leaves above. Kale soon realized he had awoken from a dream. He blinked numerous times before looking around to find Neelan and Thomas sitting nearby.

"'Morning, lazy, it's time to go." Neelan purposely tossed Kale's shirt upon his head.

He moaned, wrinkling his forehead as he forced himself to sit upright. *That must have been another hallucination from the monsloth bite. But, it felt so real...* Kale thought. As he reached up to pull his shirt on, something fell from a fold in the fabric. He tossed the shirt to the side, examining what had fallen into his lap.

"What have you got there, Kale?" Thomas inquired; his eyes curiously intrigued.

As Kale lifted the small, golden chain onto his fingertips, his bright eyes widened in astonishment—it was the same bracelet the woman had been wearing. Kale knew now that what he had seen was certainly no dream.

CHAPTER 7

BITTERSWEET

"What in Pan's name...?" Kale held the bracelet before his face to better examine the piece.

Thomas approached Kale, kneeling to inspect the object. A look of surprise crossed his face as he pulled back in astonishment. "Jumping balt toads, Kale—unless my eyes deceive me, I do believe that belongs to a witch who goes by the name of Zasha. Though she has always kept her distance from me, I have no doubt the bracelet you hold belongs to her. I recall on a previous sighting of her, that very object hung from her wrist. There was an oddly intriguing glow which emitted off of the pendant." Thomas narrowed his eyes. "What business do you have with her? I'll warn you now to be cautious—she is quite the meddlesome one."

Kale yawned, shaking in an animalistic manner to remove the debris from his body before dressing. "You're going to think this sounds insane, but I met her—at least I think I met her, while I slept."

"I don't doubt you, Kale." Thomas rubbed his beard. "What a clever woman. I'd like to know just what it is she's up to."

Neelan finger-combed her hair before tossing the brown hat up into the air and catching it, with ease, behind her back. She placed it snugly upon her head, ensuring her ears were concealed inside. "We'd better get moving if you two intend to reach Braxle by nightfall. It's unsafe to spend too many nights within this forest."

Kale and Thomas knew this all too well. It was surprising how different and intimidating the woods were as a human.

She began to make her way toward the traders' path, through the thick vegetation. "I'll be going my separate way once you've reached the town." Her pace quickened. "I just don't want you to get comfortable with the thought that I'll be sticking around."

"All right. Do whatever you desire, we will be just fine." Kale followed close behind, unwilling to budge with his hard exterior. There was no way he would reveal that he would actually miss her company.

Although Kale could not see, Neelan looked ahead with sorrow-filled eyes. Somewhere within her stubborn heart, she hoped for them to ask her to stay. Instead of allowing herself to feel sorry, she shook the emotion, putting up her inner shell which helped shield her from pain. "If we follow this trail, we should arrive by twilight."

The sky was nearly cloudless and they could hear the sounds of birds chirping cheerfully in the distance. Kale inhaled, enjoying the warm atmosphere from an all new perspective.

"Thomas," Kale broke the silence, "can you tell me more about this, Zasha? She seemed to know a great deal about us, although she only revealed a small amount of information. The woman knows we are heading to Braxle."

"To be quite honest, I know very little about her, aside from a couple of previous encounters in which I've seen her. Even then, she stayed back, almost as if she were trying to hide from sight. For this reason, I assume she is meddlesome and cannot be trusted." He leaned in toward Kale, whispering into his ear as they continued to walk, "I do, however, have a confession to make." He sighed, knowing Kale was not going to fancy his next words. "It was Zasha who provided me with the spell to transform you. This is why I did not doubt your dream. She is planning something—what it is I am unsure of, but I do know we must take caution. We do not know who we can trust and who will be against us. However—I do owe her great thanks for saving your life; even if there is an ulterior motive that lies beyond the obvious."

Kale abruptly stopped. "You're telling me that you placed my life within the hands of some loony witch?!" he snapped quietly at Thomas, waving his hands angrily as he spoke. "You didn't even know if the spell would truly work! You took a gamble at the cost of my well-being!" Kale grunted in frustration. He had always thought Thomas to be wise and rational. The entire situation was quite surprising. Luckily for the two, Neelan continued to pace herself in front, oblivious to their conversation.

"I had no other choice, you know. Had I waited even another minute, you'd be de—" Thomas glanced up, noticing Neelan had stopped and was impatiently tapping her foot for them to quicken their pace. He knew he needed to come up with a believable cover, otherwise she would surely grow suspicious once again. "Had I waited another minute, you'd be *de*hydrated. That is why I conjured such a water spell." Thomas sighed at his poor attempt to conceal the truth for what he so recklessly blurted out.

The old man is worse than me with his loose lips, Kale

THE CHRONICLES OF KALE: A DRAGON'S AWAKENING

laughed to himself. Luckily, Neelan appeared to have bought the story as she continued on without saying a word.

~~~~~~~~~~~~~~

The forest grew scarce and the trees were scattered about, leaving most of the area bare and sandy. The day's final rays of sunlight poured over the horizon, creating a natural display of colors.

"We're almost there!" Neelan called out to them as she pointed forward toward a large silhouette. Her stamina was exceptional and had allowed her to maintain a brisk pace throughout their entire journey.

Kale and Thomas finally reached her, panting loudly as they caught their breath. Kale's human feet were still tender and hurt badly after walking for miles upon stones and debris.

They finally arrived at the tall wall, built of many vertical logs sharpened into a point at the top. Beyond the wall, Kale could see grey smoke drifting toward the sky from many of the homes.

"Here we are—Braxle." Neelan tapped the tip of her green boot against the ground, pushing the powdery sand into a small mound. Her eyes wondered aimlessly, dodging Kale and Thomas.

"Well, I hope you have a safe journey to wherever it is you're heading." Kale gave a quick wave to Neelan, a human gesture he had seen Thomas do many times upon departure.

Neelan peered toward her boots, now hiding behind the curtain of hair that hung straight and sleek, despite the heavy humidity. "Sure...goodbye."

Without hesitation, Kale turned and began anxiously walking toward the wooden wall. Both Neelan and Kale's pride wouldn't allow them to be the first to give in and confront the other. It was easier to shield themselves from being hurt, rather than to face it head on—it was easier to say goodbye before either grew attached to each other's companionship.

Through their body language, Thomas easily picked up on the situation. "Are you certain you don't want to join us?" He gave Neelan a final offer, despite already knowing what her answer would be. A soft spot within his heart felt sorry for her.

"I'm very sure of my decision. I have something very important I need to do...alone." Though her time with Thomas and Kale had been short, she knew that there was no forgetting either man. They had welcomed her as a friend, and for that she was grateful.

"Well, my dear," Thomas bowed, "it has been a pleasure to have met you."

Neelan forced a smile, taking a final glance toward Kale, although unsure why. He remained with his back toward her, admiring the wooden wall—the simplest things were fascinating to him. It was his first time interacting where humans dwell. Neelan frowned, gripping the strap of her quiver as she turned to leave. She then walked away from the two men as something cool trickled down her left cheek, causing her to reach up and touch it with her index finger. As she felt the liquid, it was clear that tears were streaming down her face. For the first time in decades— Neelan cried.

CHAPTER 8

A NEW LIFE

Kale and Thomas were alone once again and eager to enter the town. Although Kale still despised humans, he was very intrigued with the town and wanted to see more.

"Hey Neelan, why don't you at least join us for din—" Kale turned to face an empty trail. He had forced his focus from her so intently he hadn't noticed she was already gone. He didn't know whether to feel guilty or angry at himself. His eyes pinched shut as he shook his head. *What am I doing? I can't allow this to bother me. It's not as though we were friends — she was another liability to get us caught. She's irritating too. It'll be nice to have some peace once again.* Kale couldn't differentiate if this was truly how he felt, or if it was a stubborn desire to be alone. With the reliable old sorcerer as his only friend, Kale knew that as long as it was only the two of them, he would pose no risk of growing attached and being hurt. After all he had been through, he did not want to feel pain within his heart again. For a dragon of fire—he now had a heart of ice. Four fingertips slid over his shoulder, breaking his chain of thought.

"Maybe we shall see her again, someday." Thomas spoke in comfort, as if he could read Kale's thoughts.

"I could care less," Kale abruptly replied as he crossed his arms.

Thomas shook his head, "Ah, to be young again." He gave Kale a firm pat before turning to face the town of Braxle. "I think it is in our best interests to make way for the inn. If we don't arrive soon, there won't be much left for dinner." He removed his pointed hat, tucking it securely into his robes to reduce attention being drawn toward them.

Although it was common within the town to see tradesmen come and go, a sorcerer clad in long robes and a tall pointed hat would be a sight to behold. Most individuals skilled with magic served a royal kingdom, or lived nearby to assist their higher authority in the times of need. The other handful which remained in smaller villages were natives and chose to remain to aid their loved ones. While it wasn't unheard of to see a traveling sorcerer, it was a rare sight, and some might take alarm, afraid the magic wielder might have foul intentions. Kale did not help the situation, and appeared quite shady with his ill-fitting clothing that hung sloppily from his body.

"Tighten your waist so your pants do not drape so loosely. We need to do all we can to appear as though we are simple travelers coming through." Thomas shook his head, knowing they would soon have to take the main street toward the inn as there were no back alleys leading to the building.

Once situated, they followed the wall until coming to an opening just wide enough to accommodate a small wheeled cart. As they took their first steps into the town, Kale was surprisingly enthusiastic by what he saw. From the outside, Braxle had appeared to be quite small, but once inside he could see many rows of homes and a variety of shops. Many of the buildings were constructed of wood with a thick straw roof, woven tightly together. Others were made with much higher quality materials such as stone walls and lumber roofing. They began their journey down a road which was made of firmly packed clay that stained the bottom of Kale's soles a bright orange.

Townsfolk, who were tending to their end-of-day routines, paused to watch the two as they strolled by.

Thomas had visited Braxle in the past, however he had done so without notice, arriving at night and quickly slipping into the inn. As he sensed more stares upon them, he raised a wrinkled hand, motioning a friendly wave. "Greetings!" he cheerfully called out. Since they had already been noticed, Thomas wanted to ensure there were no suspicious or worrisome feelings toward their entrance.

Once they approached the inn, the mouthwatering scent of food drifted to their nostrils. Kale had never smelled such a variety of spices and soon, the corners of his mouth were wet with saliva. The big grey building was quite plain in appearance. Its dimly lit interior and stone walls Kale saw through a pair of tall, rectangular windows reminded him of the comforts of his cozy lair. As they entered through a wooden door, Kale viewed a room full of square tables, each accompanied by two chairs.

"I hope you're hungry, Kale. Prepare yourself for a delectable and most satisfying dish. The innkeeper, Mortimer, makes the best seasoned hen and roasted potatoes I've ever tasted."

Within moments they were greeted by a short thin man whose white hair formed a horseshoe shape around his balding head. He wore thick glasses which caused his brown eyes to look amazingly large. Kale felt more at ease by the fact that the man's clothes were not fancy, but quite the opposite—a plain, light brown shirt, simple black pants, and worn brown boots laced up to his shin.

"Well, if it isn't my old friend, Thomas! It's been ages, how have you been?" Before Thomas could reply, the little old man pressed his palms against their backs, shoving them in the direction of a nearby table. "Come—sit. You look exhausted. Who is your friend?" He eyed Kale, adjusting his round glasses upon his wide nose.

Thomas parted his lips to speak, "Th—"

"Oh my, you must be starving, let me make you both some supper."

Kale caught on rather quickly that the old man's attention span was rather—lacking.

"You two just wait right here. I'll be back in a moment, then we can catch up on things."

As the innkeeper hurried off to the kitchen, Kale glanced around the room. It was his first time inside a human building, which surprisingly was much more pleasant than he could have imagined. He slid his hand slowly across the table, grazing his fingertips against the smoothed grains of wood.

Thomas smiled, "If I didn't know any better, I'd say you're enjoying yourself."

"Excuse me? No. I'm just exploring is all. Don't look into things so much."

Mortimer soon returned, carrying two plates piled high with meat, potatoes, and sliced radishes. "I do hope you've come hungry. I've made far too much and there is only one other occupant. It's roasted hen and potatoes."

Thomas chuckled. *Some things never change.* It was *always* hen and potatoes—with the occasional exception of vegetable stew or pulled pork.

"It sure is a nice night outside." Mortimer leaned back against an adjacent table, shifting the direction of the conversation yet again. "Eat—eat!" He nudged the plate closer to Kale, who unaware of human customs had no idea how he was supposed to begin consuming the food.

"Thank you." Kale's hand mashed down into the pile of meat, curling his fingers much like a hawks talons gripping its prey. He then shoveled his mouth so full he could barely close it to chew. Kale finally managed to clamp down upon the succulent hen as he packed another handful filled with potatoes between his lips. The excessive amount dribbled down his chin and shirt.

"My, your friend here sure is hungry." Mortimer sat wide-eyed as he watched Kale's unusual behavior.

Thomas inhaled loudly, embarrassed by his friend's actions. He now regretted not teaching mannerisms along their short journey. The old sorcerer quietly ate, hopeful Kale would soon finish, and thankful there were no others present to view them.

Once they finished their delicious meal, Kale leaned back in his chair. His belly had never felt so satisfied. He sipped down a small goblet of water, burping loudly.

Thomas closed his eyes and sighed.

"I presume you both will be staying the night?" By this time Mortimer seemed un-phased by Kale's crude behavior.

"Yes, my friend, I was hoping we could stay here—for awhile. Weeks...possibly months, if this is all right with you."

Mortimer leaned forward. "Over my many years running this place, I've learned not to ask too many questions, so I don't need to know why you're here. I do however ask that you don't bring any trouble my way. If you can promise me this, then you're welcome to stay as long as you desire."

"Thank you Morty." Thomas cleared his throat, as he reached into a pocket of his robe. "There is a minor complication..." His green eyes met with Mortimer's. "I was hoping my young companion and I could work for you in order to pay for our food and board. We would be glad to take on any tasks needed. I humbly apologize for not realizing much sooner we did not carry coins with us—I believe I let my hunger get the best of me."

Mortimer scratched his scruffy cheek, "Business has been slow as of late, so at this time I haven't any available work. I did, however, overhear Phyllis saying she was in need of an apprentice to work with her at the tailors'. I'm fairly certain Galin needs help, as well, over at the blacksmiths'." Mortimer's eyes suddenly seemed to lose focus on Thomas as if to queue his mind that it was time again to randomly change topics. "Need more to drink? I've brewed a lovely concoction of juices that I must say is quite delicious!"

"I appreciate the offer." He glanced up toward Kale, who shook his head, "but I think we're both fine. Thank you kindly for the delicious meal." Thomas paused, pondering their situation. He was unsure about their sleeping arrangements considering they had no funds to pay for a night at the inn.

As if Mortimer could read Thomas' expression, he offered them a room. He assured the two it was all right and to not worry about reimbursement. He knew when Thomas and Kale woke they would seek work and begin paying for their stay.

"I do not wish to further burden you, but would it be possible to borrow some clothing as well? I believe in our current attire, we will draw much unnecessary attention to ourselves." Thomas was aware of the storage area where Mortimer kept an abundance of clothing mistakenly left behind by travelers who never returned to claim their belongings. He was certain there would be something for he and Kale.

"But, of course. I have no need for them. I'm glad they've finally found a use."

Kale could see that while Mortimer was slightly disoriented at times, inside he was a good and honest man.

"I am in your debt, my friend." Thomas stood, reaching out to pick up his empty plate.

Mortimer's hand shot out at a surprisingly quick speed for his age. "I'll have none of that. No guest at my inn is going to clean up after themselves. Now, shoo—go relax in a warm bath, then get some rest. Your room is the one with the red door. It looks as though you both could use it! I'll have the clothing delivered shortly after I fetch more hot water for the tub."

Thomas insisted they help, but Mortimer would not hear of it. After Mortimer's wife passed away four winters ago, he made it a point to remain occupied. It was his way of coping with a broken heart.

Once they finished bathing and had chosen appropriate clothing from a large basket Mortimer left in their room, Thomas ensured that Kale learn basic manners before heading to bed. He couldn't bear to send him out in search of work while behaving as he did at dinner. He informed Kale that each night they would take the time to educate him on proper human customs and etiquette.

Kale rolled his eyes as Thomas spoke. "This is all so ridiculous—every last bit of it. *You* are the one who brought this fate upon me, and now you act as though you're upset my personality didn't transform along with it. I don't want to behave as a human does. I'm happy being myself."

"My dear boy, I've known you long enough to understand the

way your mind works. You won't ever truly be happy until you seek vengeance upon General Jedah. To do this, however, does mean you will need to mislead those you meet into believing you truly are one of them."

Kale thought for a moment. He knew Thomas spoke the truth. "Fine."

Thomas smiled, satisfied with the progress he had made.

As the two men lay in bed, Kale rolled to face Thomas. "I hope that was all part of our cover—when you said we would be finding jobs tomorrow."

"Quite the contrary, we are indeed going to find work tomorrow—and yes, Kale, by *we*, I do mean you and I. We will be staying here until we're able to figure out our next course of action. There is much that needs to be done in order to prevail over Jedah. In fact, at the current time, I wouldn't even know where to begin. I assure you though, Kale—we will figure it all out, just give it time." He smiled, closing his eyes.

~~~~~~~~~~~~~~~~

That night, Kale's comfortable rest was interrupted by a steady humming sound within their room. He squinted through the darkness to see Thomas had also awoken. The old sorcerer leapt out of bed in surprise as he swung his arm out defensively. Thomas mumbled softly and Kale watched as a radiant swirl weaved around the sorcerer's fingers.

"Kale, get off of the bed—now! It's coming from beneath you!"

Kale immediately scurried near where Thomas stood, knowing that without a weapon or knowledge of magic, he was relatively helpless.

"*Raynok tondelda.*"

A green sphere of light blasted from Thomas' palm, projecting forward with astounding speed toward the bed. Upon impact, they heard a loud *zap*. Both men watched in disbelief as the sphere appeared as though it had been sucked into an invisible black hole.

"Jumping balt toads, it's as if someone knew I was going to do that and countered it before the event even occurred. Stay behind me Kale—things might get turbulent very quickly."

Before Thomas could launch another attack, the humming ceased and all was quiet. Nothing moved. The only sound was their rapid breathing as they heavily panted in the darkness.

"Do not move, Kale." Thomas slowly made his way toward the bed. "*Viscolan illumin.*" A small, vibrant orb appeared by his side, floating along with his every step. He cautiously knelt down, prepared to attack should any intruders be hiding below. He peered under the bed, motioning his fingers forward. On command, the small orb zipped below, illuminating the entire floor.

"Interesting... Very interesting." Thomas grew silent in thought before reaching his hand beneath the bed, withdrawing a thick sheet of ivory parchment. "As I thought," he placed his spectacles upon the bump of his nose, "nothing—no words, which means...this was intended for your eyes only, Kale." He hovered his hand above the parchment, as if to ensure there were no harmful spells placed upon it, before handing it over to Kale.

Just as Thomas had assumed, the moment Kale's fingers gripped the item, many words began to appear. Someone intended this delivery to be just for Kale—someone knew who and where they were.

CHAPTER 9

A MYSTERIOUS MESSAGE

As the final sentence emerged into view, Kale began to read the message aloud. Unlike most dragons, Kale had learned to read thanks to exceptional lessons from Thomas. Kale could clearly remember that it was through such teachings he and Thomas had become good friends.

Dearest Firehart,

As you continue to grow within your new environment, you must never lose sight of your ultimate goal - revenge upon the one called General Jedah. Ridding him from Ravondore will open a new door which I cannot explain at this time. One year from this day, you must seek the tree which rains gold. Do not forget this, for a victorious fate depends upon it.

Within the Forest of Forgotten Whispers, you will find someone who will forever change your life. Your path to glory will become a reality. Do not give up, young one.

As he finished reading the mysterious letter it began to crumble away between his fingers, turning to ash as pieces fluttered to the wooden floor. Before Kale or Thomas could respond to the situation, Kale felt a warm sensation against his right thigh. He glanced down to view the dim glow shining through his pants pocket.

"It's the bracelet!" Kale reached a hand in to retrieve it. The two men looked directly at one another as the small golden chain dangled upon Kale's fingertip.

"Zasha!" Both men exclaimed simultaneously.

"Kale, it may be in your best interest to ignore the directions of this letter. You don't know this woman—quite honestly she seems a bit deranged. We don't know what sort of plans she has upon your arrival to this *tree*. It could very well be a trap. The Forest of Forgotten Whispers is rumored to be incredibly dangerous and filled with unimaginable beings."

"She already knows who I truly am, Thomas. If it were a trap, I think that by now I'd be dead, or captured at the least."

Though Kale's response proved to be a solid defense, Thomas was still apprehensive about the situation. "Well then, when the time comes, take heed and think before you take action."

Kale nodded in agreement, though he knew his mind was set. It was Thomas after all who taught him there are times in life when one must think with their heart. He needed to know what waited for him within the forest.

"It is time to sleep now, Kale. I can sense there is no longer a magical presence within the room. It's safe for us to get some much needed rest." Thomas caught the glowing orb within his index finger and thumb, pinching down firmly as it exploded into hundreds of tiny sparkling pieces that faded into darkness.

~~~~~~~~~~~~~~~~

The next morning came quickly and both men awoke to the sun beaming upon their faces through the tall rectangular window. They were unsatisfied with the amount of sleep they had gotten due to the mysterious occurrence in the middle of the night.

Kale stood, thankful to be in clothes that fit him snuggly, although he truly did not realize what a difference it would make. The only thing he could not find in his size was a pair of shoes which he hoped would not hinder his chances of obtaining work.

Thomas sighed in discomfort as he pulled up a pair of red stockings beneath a long matching tunic. He longed for the day when he could once again wear his robe.

As the sun continued to rise, they could hear the townsfolk beginning their day; this urged them to make haste.

"So, how do you intend to find us human work?"

"For starters, Kale, do not refer to everything as *human* activities if you care to maintain your hidden identity. Second, we shall begin by finding the sources Mortimer spoke of. He mentioned last night—if you were paying any attention—there were two individuals in need of help."

They made their way down a narrow flight of squeaking stairs to the dining room where Mortimer pleasantly greeted them with breakfast. "G'morning! Did you sleep well?" Before they

could speak, Mortimer continued, "I think there may have been—
" he glanced around to ensure no one walked in unnoticed, "rats
in the building. I heard noises last night."

Thomas and Kale said nothing, knowing the truth behind the
mysterious night sounds. Thomas gulped, feeling slightly guilty
that he had assured Mortimer they would bring no trouble to the
inn. Luckily, Mortimer's lack of attention saved them from the
awkward moment. "I've got to go clean the cobwebs from the
attic today. Good luck finding work!"

As they quickly ate their delicious bowls of warm porridge,
Thomas informed Kale they would be taking separate paths. Kale
was to seek the blacksmith, Galin, on the east side of the town
square, while he would find Phyllis at the tailors' on the west.

Although Kale despised the thought of doing human tasks, he
knew it was necessary for them to live within the town. He
needed to do his best until a year passed and he would be able to
see what the destiny of the mysterious letter held for him. Kale
knew that in his current state, he would stand no chance against
the general in battle. He had never trained nor even held an actual
weapon within his grasp before. Kale placed a hand over the
pocket where he kept his bracelet, feeling the rush of being one
step closer to achieving revenge upon Jedah. He had to remain
positive that whatever waited for him at the mysterious tree
would aid him in victory. Until the time arrived, he wanted to
learn as much as he could about the new body in which he was
forced to remain.

As Kale approached the building Thomas directed him
toward, he could hear the steady sound of pounding. He walked
past a front booth where many weapons were on display. He then
headed back into a darkened room. He saw a large man hunched
over and working so intently he hadn't noticed Kale's arrival. The

man's beige tunic was dingy and covered in soot.

Kale cleared his throat, "That's a very nice sword you're working on."

The man immediately paused, pulling out a piece of cloth to wipe the sweat from his ebony forehead. His stubbly facial hair was filthy and smeared with remnants of black coal. "This must be important for you to interrupt my work. Who are you and what do ya' want?" He rubbed his muscular forearm across his wide nose, sniffing loudly. "Irritating ashes..." the man mumbled.

"My name is Kale and I'm new here in Braxle; I was hoping you are still in need of help."

The man seemed to ignore Kale and returned his focus to precisely striking the blade of a sword.

What is his problem? Kale already grew annoyed with the man who he had only met moments ago.

"Kale, you say?" The man finally spoke. "The name's Galin and I guess I could use an extra hand; but only under the condition that you do as I tell ya' and keep outta' my way when I'm workin'." He placed his hammer onto a nearby table, turning to face Kale. "You have any blacksmithin' experience?"

Kale dodged his dark eyes, "Well...a little."

"I'm warnin' you kid, don't lie to me." He swung his index finger toward Kale's face. "Let's get this straight right now, as long as you work for me, everything that spats outta' your mouth better be the truth."

Kale bit his tongue, struggling to obey Galin who had already gotten under his skin. It oddly reminded him of the irritating small pebbles that would sneak between the layers of his scales. None the less, Kale knew he needed the job, so arguing was not an option. "Yes, sir," he replied.

~~~~~~~~~~~~~~~~

His first day of work was spent scrubbing the floors, wiping tools, polishing, and bending to Galin's every demand. By evening, Kale was soaked in sweat and his palms bore multiple blisters. He was amazingly grateful when Galin informed him the day's work was complete and he was free to leave.

"Here's your pay, kid." Galin flipped a single copper coin toward Kale who shot his arm out, catching it with ease. "I expect you'll have shoes upon your feet by tomorrow. I've never seen such a fool who walks into a blacksmith forge with his bare feet out. A hot piece of fallen metal could melt right through your skin."

On Kale's stroll back to the inn he could hear the faint rapping of Galin's hammer pounding down upon steel. By this time, most townsfolk had gone home to eat supper with their families and the streets were relatively clear of activity. Kale began to wonder if Galin had a family within the town. He wondered why Galin continued to work, despite the approaching nightfall. As the sun set behind the thatched roofs, Kale opened the wooden door to the inn. He was pleasantly surprised to see Thomas seated at a nearby table awaiting his arrival.

"How was your day?" Thomas glowed with anticipation— eager to hear the details.

"Well, the blacksmith is really callous. I think he hates me." Kale placed the coin onto the table, "But I did get this." He smiled proudly.

Thomas looked down at the copper piece in confusion; he had anticipated Kale would have earned a greater amount for an entire day of work. A single copper coin was the lowest payment one could receive—next to nothing. "I'm proud of you Kale—I really am." Thomas didn't want to discourage Kale.

"How did you fare today?" Kale took note of Thomas' prior expression and grew curious to see if his pay had been worth pressing his body so hard to fulfill the menial tasks Galin required.

"It was pleasant; Phyllis is a very kind woman." Thomas knew where Kale was going with the conversation and chose to play ignorant, changing the direction of the subject. "She hired me without question and even taught me how to sew." He smiled.

"Good, then you can make me a pair of shoes. The ill-tempered curmudgeon I work for said I must have them if I care to continue with him."

Thomas nodded, assuring Kale he would ask Phyllis about the issue the following day.

At the end of their night, Kale laid in bed, sore and exhausted from the long day. His mind began to drift as he thought about the town of Braxle. Aside from his experience with Galin, the small town was full of humans who were quite pleasant. Living at the inn was turning out to be better than he had anticipated; the beds were comfortable, the baths were warm, and the food was amazing. Mortimer took great care to ensure they were satisfied and Kale enjoyed not having to hunt for his food each night. Everyone so far had been welcoming toward him, despite that he was a stranger. Even Galin, with his rough exterior had still given Kale a job. Until now he had thought of all humans, with the exception of Thomas, to be cruel and uncaring. This experience was already altering his opinion and he began to perceive that humans were not as horrible as he had once assumed.

~~~~~~~~~~~~~~~~

The next few days went smoothly and, aside from Galin's routine bickering, Kale began to enjoy working at the blacksmithing shop. He had even managed to get a high quality pair of shoes thanks to a friend Phyllis knew who was a leatherworker. As each day would pass, he grew accustomed to a routine in which he would rise at dawn to join Galin. Eventually, a mutual confidence was established and Kale was taught how to forge the perfect blade.

Weeks turned into months and soon Kale became a well-skilled blacksmith. He was able to handle orders and craft weaponry without supervision. With his newfound experience came higher pay, and soon Kale was able to afford his entire half of room and board while still having a few copper pieces to spare.

On a beautiful day when business was running slow, and they had nearly caught up with their restock, Kale took a bold chance and requested to be excused for an hour to visit Thomas and explore the town. Until this point, Kale had yet to explore any areas aside from the town square and was excited to view more of what Braxle had to offer.

"Sure, kid, but don't take too long if you wanna' have a job when you return."

Kale thanked Galin. He had grown accustomed to the blacksmith's moody behavior and even adjusted to being called a kid—despite the irony of being nearly three times Galin's age.

~~~~~~~~~~~~~~~~~

"Good afternoon, Thomas." Kale smiled at him from across a long table covered with rolls of cloth. He choked back a laugh as Thomas finished the final stitches on a pink ruffled dress. "That will look great on you." He couldn't help himself.

"Jumping balt toads—hello, Kale. I hadn't expected to see you here. Shouldn't you be working?"

As Kale finished explaining the reason for his visit, an older woman approached the sewing table, wearing a white apron and plain brown dress. Her graying brown hair was held back with a small silver pin that gave a clear view of her almond eyes.

"So you are the Kale I've heard so much about." She smiled warmly. "You would think that Thomas here was your father by the way he praises all you've accomplished since your arrival in Braxle. He's very proud of you."

Kale began to formally introduce himself, as Thomas had taught him, when a young woman approached wearing very scanty clothing that revealed a fair amount of cleavage.

"Mother, I'm going to need a new dress. I ripped my skirt while out last night." She flipped her dark ponytail over a shoulder. "Men can be such animals."

"Theresa, I'm going to mend your tear; you don't need an entirely new dress. I've already made you three this year." Phyllis sighed. "I did not raise you this way. It also would not hurt you to come here and help me from time to time. You can't always expect your natural beauty to get you by in life. Trust me, the day will come when you're old and withered like your mother."

Theresa huffed, appearing as though about to throw a childish tantrum. Then, as if she had been in her own secluded realm, she took notice to Kale's presence. Her mood immediately shifted as she straightened her posture and quickly approached him.

"And who might you be, handsome?" She winked flirtatiously.

Kale took a step back, overwhelmed and uncomfortable by her presence. In an attempt to help Kale, Thomas stepped into the conversation, explaining to Theresa that Kale was on a short break from his job and needed to leave in order to have the time to explore the town. Kale took the opportunity to politely bid farewell to Phyllis and her daughter. He wanted to quickly leave the awkward situation behind him.

Suddenly, as if a brilliant idea sparked within her mind, Theresa's eyes lit up. "I'll show him around! I've lived here my entire life and know every nook and cranny."

Kale shot a glance toward Thomas for assistance. The old sorcerer sighed, shrugging as if to tell Kale that he was now on his own. By the look on Theresa's face, there was going to be no discouraging her from what she wanted. She didn't bother to wait for a response as her arm slid around Kale's bicep.

"What are you doing?" Kale questioned, confused by her gestures.

"My name is Theresa Vascallar and I'll be your guide today, handsome. Let's get going." She tugged him toward a narrow street to the right.

Kale frowned at the thought of having Theresa along for what would have been a relaxing stroll. However, he knew better than to upset the daughter of the woman who was paying Thomas.

They eventually came to a halt in front of the tallest building in town. Up until now, Kale had only seen its peak towering above the rooftops. The building was solid, made of grey stone and accented with large windows trimmed in white. The double cherry wood doors were only approachable by climbing a set of six steep steps bordered with square trimmed bushes.

"This is where the town Lord lives. If you plan to remain here in Braxle, you'll need to know where it is. Only Lord Zalimond has the authority to answer requests from the townsfolk." She leaned in close to Kale's ear as she spoke softly, "I don't think his wife favors me very much."

I can't imagine why, Kale thought as he glanced toward her low-cut bodice.

"I've heard the lord has a secret room beneath his home where he keeps his valuables." She continued to speak in a low tone. "I would love to get a closer look one day..." Her voice trailed off and Kale could see the look of excitement in her eyes at the thought of sneaking away with his wealth. "Anyway," she shook her head, tightening her grip on his arm, "let's keep moving. I've already said more than I should to a man I barely know. It'd be wise to keep that information between us."

Kale nodded, not wanting to cause any problems. They continued to walk around different sections of the town as she explained each area in brief detail. Finally, they came to a building where Kale noticed a great deal of commotion.

"What is this place?" Kale questioned, pointing toward the structure.

"That? It's the tavern; haven't you ever been in one for a drink?" She paused a moment to think. "I believe I understand. You've probably assumed the inn also serves as our town tavern. I've heard from travelers that most inns serve the purpose of both. I guess we, here in Braxle, do things differently. I couldn't ever imagine Mortimer converting his inn to such a place." She gestured toward the Tavern.

Kale shook his head, still unsure of what she meant. He had perfectly fine juice and water from Mortimer at the inn each night. He could only assume whatever drinks the tavern offered must be spectacular to draw in such a crowd.

"Hello, Theresa." A man walked by and tipped his hat to greet her. "Care to join me?"

His words triggered Kale to remember that he was supposed to be back at the blacksmith's ages ago. "Oh, no—I'm late! I've got to go, Theresa." He knew Galin was going to give him an earful and, hopefully, would allow him to keep his job. "I'm sorry, I really do appreciate all you've done, but I need to get back to work or Galin will have my head."

Theresa smiled, "I understand." She pressed closer to his body, ignoring the man who stood impatiently in front of the tavern.

Kale looked away, embarrassed by the scene she was making.

"I'd like to see you again," She continued. "You know, I've noticed you in town before today. But, I know you haven't noticed me." Her lips pouted as she traced a finger against his chest.

Kale shifted his feet in discomfort. He gently gripped her hand, removing it from his body.

"Playing hard to get?" Her lips curled upward in a sly smile. Theresa was used to men flocking toward her and wasn't about to accept rejection so easily. "Meet me tonight at the tavern—I'm not accepting no for an answer. I'll be waiting."

Kale sighed, irritated by her persistence; yet despite his distaste for the woman, he was curious about this *tavern* she spoke of.

"Fine. I suppose I'll come—but only for one drink, then I'm returning to the inn."

"Great!" Her eyes twinkled with satisfaction. "Meet me here after you've eaten, and bathed."

Kale did smell foul and his clothing was damp with sweat. He hadn't washed in nearly three days; but that was the last of his worries. At that moment he needed to return to Galin—and fast.

CHAPTER 10

YOU CANNOT RUN

"What could've possibly taken you so long? This is a town, not a bloody kingdom. I'm deducting half of your day's pay."

"What? Why?" Kale threw his arms up in frustration. "I'm sorry I was late, but we don't even have any orders due."

"Come here, kid." Galin motioned Kale over to where he stood. "Look into these eyes. Does it look like I care? Work, or no work, if I'm payin' you I expect you to be here—end of discussion." He angrily held a blade against the grinder as he sharpened its point.

Kale spent the remainder of the day working extra hard to reconcile for his careless behavior. He knew losing his job at this point would be a terrible burden on Thomas—even with the miniscule amount of coins he had saved.

Eventually, after the sun set behind the horizon, Galin informed Kale they had completed all the necessary tasks for the day and he was free to leave.

"Here's your pay." Galin placed half of Kale's usual earnings into his palm. "Now, go—and be here early tomorrow morning. There's a wealthy traveler in town and he's in need of some custom weaponry and armor. We've got a lot of work ahead of us."

Kale nodded, disappointed with his pay, yet thankful he still had his job.

The walk home was peaceful as usual until the moment he approached the inn. Laughter rang out from the usually quiet dining area as he walked through the wooden door. Kale immediately took note of a tall man standing near a group of peers who appeared to be of wealth. The stranger wore quality, tailored clothing and a short, black velvet cape hung around his neck on a golden chain.

This must be the person Galin spoke of, Kale presumed.

"Didn't I teach you it is rude to stare at others?"

Kale nearly jumped as he finally noticed Thomas who sat at a nearby corner table. Within minutes of Kale sitting down to rest, Mortimer walked briskly by, waving cheerfully as always. It was obvious he was very busy due to the new crowd. Kale smiled at the thought of more revenue coming in for Mortimer; he had grown quite fond of the old man.

As they patiently waited for their meal, Thomas intertwined his fingers, resting his bearded chin atop wrinkled knuckles. "How did everything go with Theresa?"

Kale grunted and could tell Thomas held back his laughter. "Nothing too exciting—I'm sorry to disappoint." He rolled his eyes. "She did show me around, though, which actually turned out to be quite helpful. Well—aside from her odd behavior of constantly touching me. Is that also a human custom? I didn't like it—at least not coming from her."

Thomas could no longer contain his laughter. "No, dear boy, that usually occurs when a woman fancies you. It would seem in her eyes, you are quite the catch." He winked as if to mock Kale.

"Well, I have no interest in a human like her; although, she did invite me to meet her at the tavern tonight."

"Oh? Are you planning to attend?" Thomas asked curiously.

"I think so. I'm quite intrigued by such a place. From the words she spoke, the place sounds quite captivating."

Their conversation came to an end as Mortimer approached the table with two plates of food. "I'm sorry about the wait. As you can see, we have new visitors who will be staying here for about a week. From what I gather, they have heard of Galin's exceptional ability to forge a blade. These gentlemen will be purchasing a significant amount of weaponry—although I'm sure you've already heard, Kale."

"He looks full of himself, standing there with his fancy clothing as though he were a lord." Kale blurted out.

Thomas quickly reached out, placing a finger to Kale's mouth.

Mortimer leaned in, softly whispering, "He's actually a very nice gentleman, Kale; please treat him respectfully while he is here. I've heard he is the leader of a noble group of warriors who have traveled very far. Well—that's what I've gathered through eavesdropping." He glanced around cautiously. "I'd better not meddle. As I've said before, I usually prefer to stay out of other's business—it's safer that way." Mortimer then glanced toward the floor as if he completely lost his thought process. "My, my, look at this floor. It's filthy! I must tidy up this place if I care to keep business coming." He stood up, leaving the table without another word.

Once they were alone, Thomas focused his attention onto

Kale again. He felt safe enough to speak while the loud conversation flooded the room. "Be cautious tonight, Kale. You are still adapting to life as a hu—" Despite the noise, he still did not feel comfortable enough to continue on. "Well, you know what I am trying to say. Please don't draw attention to yourself." He took a sip of water. "You'll also want to remain alert when around Theresa. I have heard a great deal about her from Phyllis; she's quite the promiscuous one. Apparently, she also has a very quick sleight of hand."

"You worry too much, Thomas. I'm not about to be fooled by some woman. Besides, I need a change from the walls of this inn; it's all I've seen every night since we've come to this town."

After dinner, Kale made his way to the bathing tub, using the remaining water to scrub himself clean of any unpleasant scents with a washing cloth. It was surprisingly warm which suggested someone had recently used the tub. After ensuring his body was clear of black ash, Kale pulled a linen towel around his body to dry himself.

"Pardon me; I assumed the bathing area was vacant." The traveler in the black velvet cloak startled Kale as he spoke. "I'll return later," The man eyed the dirty bath water, "once the innkeeper has refilled the tub."

"Wait a moment." Kale spoke as the man turned to leave. "Why are you in need of such a large order of custom crafted weaponry? Is there a war going on nearby?" Though his methods of questioning were blunt, if something big was happening close to town—he wanted to know.

The man paused, turning to read Kale's eyes. After a moment of silence, it seemed he felt comfortable enough to confide information. "My men and I are on a personal mission to ensure that a very cruel person who has inflicted great wrongdoings across the land will meet the wrath of our steel. Please do not pry any further as this is all I shall tell you."

Kale rubbed his cheek, respecting the man's wishes. "Can you at least tell me your name then? I'm Kale—Kale Firehart."

"I suppose, but I shall not reveal my family name to someone I am unfamiliar with. My name is Alden. It is a pleasure to meet you, Kale Firehart." He tipped forward a black velvet Robin Hood cap which was accented with a slender white quill.

Alden hadn't been nearly as bad as Kale first assumed. In fact, he seemed admirable with his cause, though vague in detail. It seemed all too familiar to Kale's own journey.

Kale knew there was no time to dwell upon the new travelers. Time was passing and he knew that Theresa, as irritating as she was, had most likely been awaiting his arrival for quite some time. He shook off his clothing to remove all ash, before getting dressed. Kale hoped the darkness of night would conceal the sweat stains which he had yet to wash. He yawned sleepily. The sooner he fulfilled his curiosity of the tavern, the sooner he would be able to rest on his soft bed.

~~~~~~~~~~~~~~~~

The gentle night breeze felt great as it sifted through his dampened hair. He approached the wooden sign of the tavern, glancing up to read the engraved words: *The Rusty Sword*. Kale found the title to be odd considering Theresa had earlier spoke of it being a place to converse and drink.

Upon opening the thick door, he was immediately overwhelmed by the number of people and level of noise. It was his first time in such an environment; it caused him to feel incredibly uncomfortable. The large room was much warmer than outside, and the air proved stuffy with the strong scent of liquor—something Kale knew nothing of until this point.

Suddenly, he felt an arm slip around his shoulders. "Hello, there." A woman wearing a black bodice tied far too tightly for her waistline stood beside him. "You sure are a cute one. I believe I've seen you around town before. You interested in having a little fun tonight?" She winked; lifting her long black skirt as she flirtatiously wiggled her bare leg in front of him. As she continued to speak, Kale cringed—her breath smelt horribly rancid. "Come spend the night with me, it'll only cost you ten copper pieces. I promise to make it worth your while."

What in Pan's name is she talking about? Kale thought. He casually eased his way in the opposite direction.

"He's accounted for tonight," Theresa spoke.

Kale found himself surprisingly grateful to see her.

"Go find someone else to dig your claws into." She gestured the woman to leave.

Kale couldn't help but look toward the woman's hands, ensuring that the claw comment was indeed a human form of expression.

"I'm glad you came." Theresa smiled, taking him by the hand and guiding his body toward a nearby long table.

As they walked past many individuals, Kale could've sworn he saw Galin out of the corner of his eye. Before he could confirm his assumptions, Theresa firmly pressed down upon his shoulders, forcing him to sit.

"Buy me a drink?" Theresa asked as she batted her long eyelashes.

Kale sighed, reaching into his brown pouch for coins. "Fine."

Theresa whistled; raising her hand in the air until a young woman wearing a white bonnet arrived.

"Two ales, wench—on him." She pointed to Kale, who smiled uncomfortably.

The bar wench nodded, leaving quickly to get their drinks.

"You know, Kale, I still can't get over the fact you've never been in a tavern before. For such a handsome man," she pressed herself against him, "you sure do come off as odd, yet somewhat intriguing."

Kale could feel her hand caressing his thigh which caused him to flinch, scooting slightly away from where she sat.

"You're shy—how sweet." She laughed obliviously.

By this time, the wench arrived with two large mugs filled with a yellowed liquid that foamed at the top.

"What in Pan's name is this?" Kale wrinkled his nose as he lifted the mug to his upper lip, taking in a deep whiff.

"You really are—different, Kale. It's safe, I promise." Theresa took a gulp of her own ale. "You see?"

His lips cautiously met the rim as he allowed a small sip of the cold liquid to enter his mouth. The taste was bitter, yet he couldn't help himself from wanting to drink more. As he finished the first mug, a warm sensation moved throughout his body—it felt good. As if on cue, the bar wench returned with another pair of full mugs which Kale immediately began to drink. He soon felt as though he was floating atop a cloud; glancing around the room with a smile upon his face. As he panned the room, Kale caught a glimpse of the man who he assumed was Galin, and to his surprise—it definitely was. He could recognize Galin's large stature anywhere. Kale took notice as Galin hung his head low; his facial expression appeared distraught, as if his heart was in turmoil. Kale continued to stare—he couldn't help but wonder if he should approach the blacksmith to say hello. Maybe outside of work, Galin wouldn't be so crude.

"Drink up!" Theresa's voice broke through his thoughts. "Don't bother with him," she continued, noticing Kale's attention to Galin. "I am aware that you work with him, but he is a very strange man—even more so than you!" She laughed. "He hasn't lived in Braxle for much longer than you, yet in all of his time here, he has barely spoken to anyone. It's as if in his mind, none of us exist. He works all day, and then comes to the tavern every night to drown himself with ale. I've never even seen him take notice of a single woman in town, and I'm certain he has no wife—something is just not right with that one."

Kale nodded, knowing that Galin would likely desire to be left alone—especially after their earlier tension. Yet, for some reason he could not shake the feeling of sympathy for Galin. Kale's mind began to drift as he took another large gulp from his mug. He soon had to squint his eyes to see clearly.

Theresa leaned toward him, softly breathing in his ear, "You want to go someplace quieter?" She playfully bit at her bottom lip.

The room now felt as though it was constantly in motion as he released a loud obnoxious burp. "You're not my type," he bluntly spoke, unable to watch his slurred words. "You human women haf weird headsch—and thosch tings on your chescht schare me, it'sch like you're a part of the cow family." He burst into maniacal laughter, banging his fist upon the table.

Theresa stared angrily at Kale. "I'm going to let that one slide since it's your first time drinking. Be thankful—I've never allowed a man to speak to me in such a manner. I have a piece of mind to slap that silly smile from your face."

Kale's head dipped as he struggled to keep focus. Through his goggled vision, he could make out a faint glow coming from a pocket on Theresa's skirt. It took him a few minutes of hard concentration to fully comprehend what he was seeing. Suddenly, in a moment of panic, he reached into his own pocket—it was empty.

"Give it back, right now!" Kale demanded. "You've been playing me for a fool thisch entire time!"

"My, my, handsome, I believe you've had far too much to drink. It seems as though you've grown delusional."

"Therescha, do not play gamesch wif me; I want my braschelet back thisch moment. Pleasche do not make me take it from you. I do not wisch to harm a human female." Kale stood in anger, swaying as he tried to maintain his balance and frustrated that he allowed such a common woman to trick him in such a manner. "You're schuch a foul woman—it'sch no wonder why you haf to trick men! It'sch becausch no one would ever want to truly be wif you for more than one night and the thought burnsch you. It makesch you reschort to petty theft tacticsh so you schtill feel asch though you have won in the end—you're pathetic."

Theresa's eyes swelled. No one had ever stood up to her before, and although it hurt to hear, she knew it was the truth. "Here — take your stupid, little bracelet. It looks worthless anyway." She flung it at Kale's face, causing it to hit his cheek before falling to the floor where he swiftly swooped it up.

Before any further words could be exchanged, she stood— dodging Kale's glance as she ran out the tavern door.

Luckily for Kale, few people noticed their scene and those who did were far too drunk to care. The night was growing late and Kale knew he had consumed too much ale and barely had the ability to stand upon his own two feet. He hoped that with a night's rest, the effects would disappear in time for work.

Kale slowly made his way to the door, gripping onto whatever he could find along the way to support himself. He could already tell it was going to be a long walk to the inn. As he approached the exit, a tall slender figure clad in black robes stood. Kale took little note of the stranger's movements until the hooded figure made way directly for him. Although intoxicated, Kale was certain he had seen the mysterious person somewhere before. Suddenly, his glassy eyes grew wide as he noticed the long, pallid, white fingers hanging at the stranger's side—it was the same man from General Jedah's army—Kale had been found.

CHAPTER 11

A DARK REUNION

The man in black paused, inhaling heavily in the direction of Kale before taking a step back.

"It can't be—impossible!" The man sniffed again. "My senses do not deceive me, I'm certain of it. But how—how can this be?! Never could I have imagined that coming to this pathetic little town on a mere scouting mission for *him*," he gestured toward Galin, "I would also find you, the one creature Jedah wants to slaughter above any other—*Firehart*." Raspy laughter could be heard from within the heavy dark hood. "I cannot fathom how it is possible that you now stand before me as a human—unless you are in league with a powerful spell-caster... Simply fascinating." The hood shifted as the man in black glanced around the room.

Kale felt sick as he fought the dizzy sensation in his head. *How could this have happened?* He couldn't allow the townsfolk to know the truth—he had to do something, and fast. He cursed himself for drinking; he could barely hold himself upright, let alone fight.

The figure in black lifted his arm, causing the cloth of his robes to hang loosely and drape down heavily as he extended his long, bony fingers toward Kale. "You are the key to my freedom, Firehart."

Kale could barely think straight, he felt helplessly frozen in place. Suddenly, two hands pressed forcefully against his side, forcing him to stumble over his own two feet before collapsing onto the floor. Kale turned his head in time to see Galin standing where he had just been. Galin's char-covered fingers and cheeks told Kale that he had come to the tavern directly from the blacksmithing forge. Kale could immediately see by Galin's staggering movement, he was sloppily drunk as well.

"I suggest ya' leave my good friend here alone, stranger." Galin cracked histhick, dark knuckles.

Good friend? Kale wondered *And I assumed it was only me who had too much to drink.*

"To think that you both would fall into my lap so easily is amusing. I assumed it would be a challenge to find you both— yet, here you stand, drunken and foolishly ignorant."

"Close your mouth and leave here at once. You're not welcome in Braxle ya' babbling idiot."

"You shall pay for those words, you mindless barbarian." The man in black shot his hand toward Galin who miraculously ducked, despite his excessive consumption of ale.

Galin then hopped on top of a nearby wooden table, lifting two mugs and slinging them at the dark figure. One missed, shattering against the wall; the other struck the man in black directly on his chest, causing him to stagger backwards.

Kale knelt in awe at how swiftly Galin moved, considering

the circumstances. By this time many others within the tavern were aware of the commotion going on around them. Two men stood and approached the table where Galin stood. One was a heavy set fellow who wore a shirt far too small for his build which caused his massive gut to stick out, drooping over his waist line. The other man was clad in a sleeveless tunic, showcasing his massive mountain-like muscles.

"Is this man causin' you trouble?" The overweight man spoke to Galin, pointing toward the figure in black.

"Stranger, we don't need any troublemakers coming in here and stirring things up. If you've got a problem with anyone who lives here in Braxle—then you've got a problem with us all." The other, muscular man chimed in, crossing his bulging arms across his chest.

Many others gathered behind them in support of the situation, glaring angrily toward the man in black. A tall, slender man extended an arm to Kale, helping him onto his wobbly feet. Kale was astonished to see humans working together to assist one another—to help him and Galin, without question.

"You all right?" The man who helped him up questioned in genuine concern.

Kale nodded as he gripped onto a nearby chair to maintain balance. He was thankful beyond words for what Galin and the others were doing to help—no one aside from Thomas had ever been there for him. Kale watched as the group of men closed in on the dark figure, causing him to step backwards until his back hit the tavern door. The man in black shifted his direction, taking careful note of the steel weaponry some of the travelers pulled from their sheaths.

"You will regret this day, you disgusting vermin. And you," the gaping black hood directed toward Kale, "we have unfinished business. Be grateful your comrades have come to your aid. However, I can assure you our next encounter will not end the same. I have found you and will not allow you to slip through my fingers as before. We shall meet again once my strength has increased—you cannot win this war."

"Get outta' here!" Galin shouted.

"Do not worry—I have not forgotten you either—Illadar." The man in black opened the door just enough to slip out, disappearing into the night.

Galin stood, frozen in place with widened eyes as if something horrible had just happened. Then, after minutes passed, one of the men smacked him on the calf, telling him to get off the table where he still stood in silence.

Galin shook his head, "Thanks everyone, what you all did for us tonight means a lot." He tried to behave as normally as possible. "Kale, let's get you home; you're in no state to be out, let alone walk home by yourself."

Galin placed his arm around Kale to support his staggering walk. He paused a moment to glance back toward the townsfolk who bid them goodnight. As Galin left the tavern, his heart swelled with both anger and sorrow as he began to recall his horrid past. "You're comin' back to my place tonight." His words were firm and short.

Kale didn't argue; he knew he was in no shape to confront Thomas about what had just happened. He also needed to overcome the drunken sensation in order to focus upon his next course of action. There was no more hiding within the sanctuary of Braxle—his identity was known.

As they approached the blacksmith shop, Kale couldn't help but wonder what exactly Galin had in store for them. Before he could question Galin's motives, he was led through the workshop to the farthest wall. Galin lifted a long ivory sheet of cloth to reveal a hidden black door behind.

"Home sweet home." Galin pushed the door open. He led Kale to a small room, completely bare except for the narrow wood-framed bed, small wood stool, and cooking pit in the center.

The room gave Kale insight on how simple a life Galin lived. Kale sat upon the stool, burying his face within his palms as he heavily sighed.

"Here kid, eat this, it'll help you sober yourself." Galin handed Kale a chunk of bread. "Eat." He paced the room, rubbing his fingers across his black sweaty brows. Many minutes passed in silence as both men pondered the night's events.

Finally, Galin broke the silence, "I'm leavin' Braxle before dawn's light. I don't know what type of business you have with the man we encountered tonight, but he's incredibly dangerous. Now that he knows I'm here, I'm confident he'll return should I remain within the town. I'd advise the same to you, unless you care to place the townsfolk in harm's way."

"I understand, but we can't aimlessly journey around Ravondore without a plan. I need to tell Thomas about what happened, he'll want to come with us."

Galin nodded in agreement. Then suddenly, he lost focus in their conversation as his mind began to drift. He pondered who Kale really was, knowing the man in black would not seek an average traveler. Galin knew there had to be much more to Kale than he could fathom. Finally, Galin could no longer contain his curiosity. "Tell me who you really are, kid."

Kale was taken aback by the unexpected question. Though, he felt better after eating the bread, his head still pounded. Mustering up the perfect answer was the last thing he wanted to worry about. Kale sighed, knowing that Galin's persistent personality was not about to let the subject drop until answered.

"I've told you before, I have been travelling with my friend Thomas in order to start a working life and settle into a nice town. We came from a very poor village to the far south." Kale decided to stick with his original story.

"Stop all of these constant lies!" Galin threw a loaf of bread hard against the wall, causing flakes to scatter upon the floor. "Where do you really come from? Were you once a knight in General Jedah's army?" It was the only logical explanation that made sense to Galin.

Kale looked to the floor. *Thank goodness, Pan; it seems he has no idea who I truly am.* "I've told you the truth. There isn't any more to say." He felt guilty about lying, but knew the options were limited. Kale still wasn't ready to openly trust Galin.

"Tell me then, why is your last name Firehart? That was the same name of the black dragon Jedah meant to slay. You can't fool me, kid, that's not your real family name." Galin sighed, "Forget it. You're as stubborn as me—I'm sure the truth will reveal itself eventually." He sat upon the floor, leaning his back against the wall and sulking as the minutes passed. "You know, kid, I don't know why I'm tellin' you this, but Jedah—that abomination—is the reason I'm bein' sought. I was in his army durin' the majority of the war against dragons; a pawn in his malicious scheme. He had no idea who I was until the day when I abandoned his command durin' a battle against the Ice Matriarch, Sylicia. Disobeying the general is a swift death sentence, but luckily for me, he was preoccupied amidst the attack and unable to take action—until now. Apparently, someone leaked the information that I've been stayin' here in Braxle. I knew I'd never be able to remain here forever; but I didn't think they'd find me so quickly. So, now you know the truth. Jedah doesn't dispatch his most valuable men for just any reason, so I'm certain that because they seek you as well, you're hidin' a great amount of information from me."

Kale's jaw hung low—he felt stunned, shocked, and enraged all at once. The man he worked alongside for so many months was a knight; a pawn who played a role in slaughtering his brethren. *I cannot believe I've shared so much of my time with this piece of filth.* Kale thought as he clenched his fists tightly.

"You do not deserve to breathe this air!" Kale cried out as he stood. He uncontrollably lifted the wooden stool, thrusting it violently toward Galin. The aftereffects of ale still caused him to move slightly disoriented and clumsy. He had recovered enough, however, to focus intently until the seat of the stool slammed into the side of Galin's face.

Galin fell back, instantly placing a hand to his cheek as the pain seared through his face. "What in Hades are you doin', kid?!" He yelled out as blood trickled down his rough, dark chin.

Before Kale could answer, Galin dove toward him, driving his massive knuckles into Kale's jaw.

"How dare you attack *me*! After all you've already done!" Kale jumped back, too enraged to succumb to the throbbing pain. "You fought with him—with Jedah. I'll kill that monstrous scum; and I'll kill you too! You've lied to me all this time; you killed the dragons. Scum like you does not deserve to walk this earth!"

Although Kale too had his secrets, he felt betrayed. Without hesitation or rational thought, Kale extended his arms, gripped his fingers around Galin's neck, and squeezed tightly. He could feel a surge of strength pulsing through the muscles in his hands and Galin began to gasp for breath while struggling to remove Kale's arms. "Why did you become part of such a vile group of men?!"

Kale spat in anger as he spoke, "Do you have no heart, you lowly cur?" He could now smell the scent of burning flesh as Galin's eyes began to flutter.

"L...let me s...speak," Galin managed to choke out in disbelief at how strong Kale's thin arms were.

Galin's knees hit the floor as Kale released his grip. He began coughing frantically as oxygen flowed into his lungs, breathing heavily until the dizzy sensation ceased. Galin gently ran his fingertips across his neck which felt warm and irritated. He narrowed his dark eyes, then whispered, "*What* are you?"

"I'm done answering any more of your questions. You said you had something to say—so spit it out." Kale crossed his arms, impatiently awaiting the explanation.

Galin coughed again before clearing his throat. His neck stung badly. "My name is Illadar."

"More lies," Kale mumbled loud enough to be heard.

"Just listen, kid!" Illadar demanded as his eyes began to glaze. An overwhelming amount of frustration and sorrow rushed through him. "I would never willingly fight alongside that poor excuse of a man had there not been severe consequences for declining." He glanced down, pounding his fist to the floor. "It was just me and my wife, Kleana; we had a very simple, yet extremely blissful life just outside the kingdom walls. Once, I was able to earn enough as an apprentice blacksmith workin' within Mirion's marketplace. We were gonna' plan for our first child and move away. Life seemed so wonderful—she was so beautiful." His jaw tightened, "Then, Jedah weaseled his way up in the King's ranks through lies and deceit. He became well-known to the others as the general—and that's when all chaos broke loose. Our once peaceful kingdom became filled with turmoil. King Valamar was a good ruler, but all too easily manipulated by Jedah's words. Upon hearin' the news that a dragon had attacked his only daughter, war was declared upon their entire race. Jedah convinced the King that they were all equally vicious and capable of slaughtering a child without second thought. Since dragons lived on unruled land, General Jedah had free reign to slaughter them as he desired. Many surrounding kingdoms and towns disagreed with Mirion's course of action, but having no authority over the free territories they could do little without endangering their own well-being. Should they attack Jedah's army, it would result in a declaration of war."

"Illadar," Kale cut him off, "if that *is* your actual name; why are you telling me all this? You stand before me breathing because I wanted to hear *your* excuse for fighting against dragon-kind. You are wasting my time and my patience grows short."

"Didn't anyone teach you how to remain quiet when others speak, kid? Just listen. What I tell you is necessary for you to fully understand." He waited for Kale to settle against the wall before continuing. "It was durin' this time Jedah began to enlist for battle. He issued a mandatory law that was placed into effect so anyone he deemed able would take an accelerated trainin' course. Those chosen would advance from a page to an able knight—ready for battle. The trainin' was rigorous and I barely had any time to visit Kleana. Jedah had pulled males from within the kingdom and all immediate surroundings to fight. There were young boys and elderly men who were stripped from their families."

"Why didn't you just stand up to him and say no?" Kale questioned.

"Didn't I tell you a law was in place? Had I disobeyed, it would have jeopardized my life. My wife couldn't bear the thought and pleaded with me to join. She told me that when I returned we would try for a family and get away from the madness. Although I despised Jedah, I went along with the trainin' for the sake of having the chance to hold a beautiful baby in my arms one day. I kissed her forehead and promised I would return. She feared for me, but told me she knew we would be together again." Illadar shifted uncomfortably. "With each dragon that fell, I acquired a bitter hatred toward the general. It tore me up inside to slay beings that had done us no harm—all because of Jedah's manipulation. He instilled fear upon the men, ranting about how the dragons could attack without notice, and take their families if not killed."

Illadar rubbed his temples. "Between many of the battles, we would return to the kingdom for recuperation and to train more knights to replace those who had fallen. On the day of our departure to hunt the Ice Matriarch, Sylicia, Kleana received news from the midwife that we were expectin' the child we dreamt about. Although the news had come sooner than we anticipated, both she and I were overjoyed. I was going to become a father—no words could explain how I felt inside." Illadar brushed his arm against his cheeks, wiping away the tears which he could no longer contain within himself. "I left with the army that afternoon, confident I'd return to my family—my beautiful family. But, everything changed. Upon arrivin' at Sylicia's cave, I met a boy; he made me think about my own unborn child and my heart filled with sympathy for what his parents must be goin' through—what *he* must've been goin' through. The boy was so scared and I knew he wasn't properly trained to fight such a mighty beast. And old Sylicia—she was sleepin' so peacefully—she just wanted to be left alone. I couldn't take it anymore!" The veins on his neck throbbed as he clenched his jaw. "After the battle began, the young boy was wounded by one of Sylicia's strikes. I had to rescue the boy. When I saw him lyin' in his own blood, I could no longer bow down to Jedah's cruel desires." Illadar stared deep into Kale's eyes. "I stopped fightin' and ran to lift the unconscious child into my arms—he was barely hangin' onto life. Despite Jedah's commands for me to stay, I left and brought the boy to the nearest town for immediate medical attention. I traded all my weaponry and armor to ensure he would receive proper care. After I knew he was safe, I expended my strength to quickly journey back to my wife. I'd hoped to beat Jedah's army so I could find her and escape to safety far away from Mirion. When I returned," he swallowed hard as his suppressed emotions flooded his mind, "they had already made it back—the general's army beat me to Mirion. I was stunned. It was nightfall, and I managed to make it to my home without the notice of any royal guards patrolling. I will never forget what I saw."

Illadar's thick fingers cupped his face as he spoke. "They killed her—that murderous devil, Jedah, killed my wife! She was carrying our baby! Before my very eyes, my dear innocent wife who had never harmed a soul in her life lay face down in her own blood. The weapon used went straight through her heart and struck so forcefully that I could see the exit wound on her back. Jedah must have had her held in place when he thrust his sword into her body. He did it all because of me—to spite me for my betrayal to his meaningless battle." His anger returned as he repeatedly slammed his knuckles to the floor.

"What happened next?" Kale's face softened as he felt the sting of Illadar's painful past.

"I heard *his* voice—Jedah." Illadar's tear-filled eyes burned with hatred as he spoke. "He knew I was inside; they had been awaitin' my arrival all along. The general asked if I liked my homecoming surprise. At that moment, my life shattered—I wanted to die too, I wanted to see my loving wife again. I knew she would be disappointed with such thoughts. Even though she was gone, I felt as though she was still watchin' over me—tellin' me I had to keep on livin'. My purpose in life had not been fulfilled, and I was then certain I needed to somehow escape. The time would come when I could seek revenge upon Jedah and rid the world of his cruelty. That would be the ultimate vengeance for my family." His swelled eyes locked onto Kale's. "Sayin' goodbye to my wife on that night was the hardest thing I've ever done. I poured oil across the floor and onto the walls; I knew I had to be ready for their entrance. As they infiltrated my home, I smashed a lantern and lit the place up. The intense fire seemed to distract them enough for me to escape from the rear. I ran all night and into the next day, until my body could no longer carry on and needed to rest. So you see, kid, those are the events which have led me here. I suggest you learn to control your temper and listen to others before actin' out so irrationally."

Kale looked down, feeling slightly guilty for his previous actions. "You could have made things easier, you know, by being honest with me from the beginning."

"And risk being caught by Jedah? I think not. You can't be too easy to trust others, Kale. One false move and your life could turn upside down. As you've seen tonight—word travels fast across Ravondore." He paused. "Though, I'm sure you are well aware of this since you also have been hiding information from me—I can feel the proof on my neck." Illadar wiped his cheeks, feeling as though a heavy weight had lifted from his heart.

"I'm very sorry for your loss." Kale truly meant his words, even though Illadar had participated in slaying his kind. "But I have to go; I can't do this right now. Though, you have valid reasons for what you've done, I am not able to accept your actions at this time." Without another word Kale left, making his way slowly toward the inn, still recovering from the alcohol.

He could not understand why he hadn't stayed with Illadar in his current state; they had both shared losses. Yet, he couldn't force himself to offer forgiveness. Kale needed to clear his mind before confronting Illadar again. In his heart, he knew Illadar's intentions were good. Kale knew that, in all honesty, he would have done the same if presented with the situation. Because of those who fought alongside Jedah—Kale was now alone as the last of his kind.

As he made his way past a row of smaller houses, he couldn't help but notice the vibrant full moon peeking through the abundance of grey clouds. He was captivated by the pale glow that washed over the town. Suddenly, his instincts began to send signals to his mind—someone or something was watching him— eyeing his every step. The hair on the back of his neck stood stiff as he began to glance around in all directions. *I wonder if this is the remnants of ale running through my body*. Kale remained alert as he continued his walk toward the inn when suddenly he saw it—the silhouette of someone perched upon the wooden barrier wall. The obscure individual gracefully balanced upon the spiked tips. They remained deathly still as if stalking him from afar.

Kale needed to know who was watching him; he wanted to get a closer look in an attempt to confront the mysterious intruder. To Kale's disappointment, the stalker leapt off the wall, disappearing out of sight as if they could sense his motives. Kale scrunched his forehead, baffled by the occurrence. The wall was easily ten feet tall and had no surrounding trees to climb. He couldn't understand how the individual managed to, not only reach the top, but also leap off so effortlessly. Tension quickly set in as he pondered the thought of the man in black returning to finish his mission. As much as Kale desired to release his anger upon the man, for once again ruining his life, he knew doing so would jeopardize the townsfolk—and his identity. His revenge would, yet again, require patience, something of which he had little. Kale struggled to calm himself, quickly returning to the temporary sanctuary of the inn. He needed to think. Over the next hours, action would be taken—he had to leave Braxle behind. A new and uncertain destiny awaited.

CHAPTER 12

UNCERTAINTIES

As Kale entered the inn, he was immediately bombarded by Alden who lightly gripped his shoulders. A few of his men gathered behind, all glaring intently toward Kale. Despite the late hour, Alden's eyes were wide and alert.

"Is he still here, boy? The man you met tonight, is he still within these walls?"

Kale was exhausted and desired nothing more than to return to his room. "No." He wearily replied. "He's gone." Although Kale was mentally and physically exerted, he couldn't help but wonder why the new travelers were inquiring about the dark figure. "Are you an acquaintance of his?" Kale's eyes narrowed as he read Alden's expression.

"No, boy, I am quite offended you would assume so. I suppose it is best that you ask though—one can't be too sure. He is a foul being and could have easily infiltrated scouts into the town without notice, for all we are aware. I cannot provide you great detail; however, we are fighting against the man you've encountered tonight, along with the general of a fierce group of knights. I'm sure you are already aware of Mirion's army, if you hold enough importance to be confronted by the dark man."

Then, as if Alden could read Kale's confused expression, he continued, "Word travels quickly within this small town. One of my men returned shortly after the incident with information on the encounter." His eyes pierced Kale's as he spoke, "I will warn you—at all costs, do not allow the man in black to touch you with his hands."

"What happens if he does?" Kale was surprised at the amount of information Alden knew about their mutual adversaries. He wanted to know more.

"Kale, where have you been?! I've waited hours in hopes you were all right. I was about to go in search of your whereabouts." Thomas made his way down the wooden stairs with dark circles beneath his drooping lower eyelids. "When Alden alerted me to your situation, I'm sure you could imagine my distraught reaction when you did not return to the inn right away." He approached Kale, conflicted with both relief and anger.

Although Kale was happy to see his friend, he still wanted to learn more from Alden who was slinging a green sack over his shoulder.

"I apologize, but we must leave this town tonight. The man in black will be on the move and we must attempt to find the location of their camp. He will not be traveling alone and I'm sure there is a vast amount of knights accompanying him on the journey. It baffles me why he chose to enter this town, appearing to come alone—unless he was searching for someone of importance." Alden then tossed a small velvet sack filled with coins onto a wooden table to his side. "I do hope that will repay

Mortimer for his generosity while we were here." He once again reached into his cloak, withdrawing a gold coin which he held out toward Kale, "This is for you—for your trouble preparing our weaponry order. It should suffice so that you may purchase any provisions for your journey ahead."

Kale's eyes grew wide. He had never owned nor touched a gold coin before and knew they were of great value. He gratefully thanked Alden for his generosity.

Alden then continued, "We will now make way for the blacksmith's; I do hope that Galin does not mind our abrupt arrival in the middle of night. We must retrieve any weaponry he has available to fill our caravan."

Kale knew that in Illadar's current emotional state, he would not want to be bothered by Alden and his men. However, he didn't dare confide Illadar's personal business to the men. Kale knew well enough that the blacksmith could handle himself—regardless of the circumstances.

Suddenly, a brilliant idea dawned on Kale, "Why don't we join you? We desire nothing more than to see the general's demise. Working together will only strengthen the cause."

Alden cleared his throat. "My deepest apologies; we prefer to travel alone, taking on no additions to our party. As I've mentioned before, you can't be too sure when it comes to the general's methods and anyone we meet could pose a threat. Maybe the hands of fate shall bring us together again someday." He smiled. "Until then," he bowed, "it has been a pleasure, and I wish you well."

~~~~~~~~~~~~~~

Kale dropped onto the bed as his head spun with thoughts.

The inn was silent without Alden and his men stirring about.

"I regret to say that there is no time to rest. Kale, we must pack and prepare to depart as soon as possible. Now that things have stirred, I am certain it's only a matter of time before they return with full force. We don't know their location... Warriors could arrive at any moment."

"Do you think I haven't already planned to leave? I'm not an idiot—I know we can no longer remain here. The man in black—he knows who I am."

Thomas rested his chin atop his knuckles, "Jumping balt toads, this is worse than I thought." He sighed. "We will need to go into hiding once again. They will certainly be scouting the area for you. I had assumed that the man in black was not human. It is simply incredible that he had such skill as to identify you so easily."

"It's not only me they're after..." Kale rolled onto his side to face Thomas. "They're after the blacksmith too. His real name is Illadar and he has been in hiding as well since he abandoned General Jedah's army—it's quite a long story." Kale fumbled with his hands in silence as he looked to his heart for answers. Kale gritted his teeth with determination as he came to a conclusion. "I want Illadar to join us. I wasn't sure if I was going to meet with him, but now I'm certain; we're all in this together from here on out."

Kale rolled onto his back, still clouded with uncertainties involving their future. Despite their growing party, they were still far from confronting Jedah and his army. "I feel lost, Thomas." He closed his eyes, "What have I done with my life? Although, I will likely regret saying this, Braxle has become my home. By leaving here, I will feel as though I am losing everything all over again. I don't even know what we're going to do now—we have nowhere to go. Why did this all have to happen?" He exhaled as he sat upright, already missing the soft comfort of his bed. "I'm ready, Thomas."

"Do not worry yourself; there is always somewhere to go, dear friend. It will all work out." Thomas smiled, knowing that although Kale didn't realize it, he had already grown so much inside. As Thomas continued to ensure their belongings were packed, he could sense big things were about to happen.

~~~~~~~~~~~~~~~

The moonlight leaked through the front windows of the inn and Kale blinked, regaining full focus on his surroundings as he scrunched the skin between his brows. The loud squawking of a black crow which sat perched upon one of the windowsills caused him to groan loudly. Kale rubbed his temples as the pain permeated his throbbing head.

"Drinking will do that to you." Thomas spoke as he slung his red pack over a shoulder. "Maybe next time you'll caution yourself to watch your pace."

"Though I'm sure the drinking is at fault, this wretched bird is not helping the matter." He growled in the direction of the crow.

"Is everything all right you two?" Mortimer spoke from the darkness, causing Kale to jump in surprise. "I apologize for startling you. However, I heard a lot of movement and wanted to ensure no mid-night guests had arrived.

"We are fine, Morty. It is we who should apologize for waking you," Thomas replied.

Kale glanced over to the velvet pouch Alden had earlier left behind for Mortimer. "The travelers left earlier. They wanted you to take that as pay." He looked down, feeling guilty that they too would soon leave Mortimer.

"My goodness." Mortimer held the sack in his palm as if to weigh it. "This is far more than the cost of their stay. What kind gentlemen they were." He glanced toward the window, "I need to purchase more tomatoes today." The old man's mind had begun to wander again.

Neither Kale nor Thomas wanted to deliver the news to Mortimer. They both knew he had truly enjoyed their company and would be incredibly lonely once they left. Though Mortimer portrayed a cheerful and content man, it was clear he anxiously awaited the arrival of travelers to keep him company.

Finally, Thomas spoke, "I'm sorry, Morty, but we too shall be leaving Braxle tonight. Our time has come to move on, as we do not wish to bring our burden upon this town. It would seem our luck has run thin."

"Oh—this is sudden." Behind Mortimer's thick glasses, his enlarged eyes filled with sadness.

"There have been some unexpected occurrences and we both feel it is in the best interest of the people here for us to leave. We thank you for all you've done; your hospitality has been far too gracious."

"Yes, thank you. The meals I've had while staying here are the best I have ever eaten in my life," Kale added, grateful for Mortimer's kindness.

"I understand, and do appreciate you are good to your word and will not bring your troubles upon us. However, I cannot say this doesn't come as an unfortunate surprise." He sighed. "I—I need to go clean out the storage area now then rest..." Mortimer's voice trailed off as he turned, leaving the room.

Kale and Thomas stood in silence, knowing Mortimer was

upset about their departure. Though unpleasant, they knew there was no other way to handle the situation. Kale rubbed his stomach as he realized just how much he was going to miss the comforts of the inn. Although Kale still wasn't keen on the thought of humans, he had grown to care for and appreciate Mortimer.

Before leaving for Illadar's home, Kale reached into his pocket, withdrawing the gold coin Alden had given to him. He smiled, hoping one day he would see Mortimer again as he set the coin onto the wooden table. "Goodbye, Morty," he whispered. "I won't forget you."

As they exited the inn, Kale could see a mass of dark grey clouds rolling in from the west. They would need to move quickly in order to make camp before the storm.

"Please, wait a moment!" Mortimer hurriedly approached them, carrying a wrapped bundle within his arms. "Put this into your bag, Thomas. You're going to need something to eat when you arrive at your next destination." He glanced from Thomas to Kale. "Please take care, you two." He forced a smile before quickly returning to the inn.

Kale sighed as they watched Mortimer disappear. "Let's go, old man." He rested a hand on Thomas' shoulder as they walked toward the town square.

Upon arriving at the blacksmith's, Kale briskly made his way through the forge and toward Illadar's small room. He shoved the cloth to the side and pushed open the wooden door.

"Illadar, we—" Kale's words stopped short as he glanced around the empty room.

He left already—I can't believe it. Kale turned to leave, with his shoulders dropped as he began to sulk.

"It will be fine, Kale." Thomas put a firm hand on his back.

Before any further assurances could be given, they heard sudden movement from outside a small, squared window.

Kale was certain he heard the sound of Illadar grunting. His blue eyes immediately lit up. He feared Illadar had left without him after their confrontation. Kale turned to follow the noise, without hesitation or second thought of the circumstances.

"We should take caution." Thomas gripped Kale's arm. "You do not know if this is a trap."

"I know it is him, Thomas." Kale pulled his arm free.

As they rounded the corner to the side alley, Kale abruptly halted, causing Thomas to stumble into his back. Kale raised a finger to his lips as he pointed toward Illadar who held a large claymore up in the air—unaware of their presence. Even at a distance, they could hear his heavy panting and see the thick beads of sweat which rolled down his dark muscular arms. He maneuvered his body flawlessly within the limited space of the alley, thrusting and swiping the broad blade in clean, swift motions.

As Kale continued to watch in awe, Illadar paused, momentarily resting the blade upon his shoulder as he approached a barrel topped with a single apple. Without hesitation, he lifted the apple, tossing it into the air. He took a swift stride back before gripping the claymore with both hands, preparing his body to swing. As the apple descended to the level of Illadar's chest, he swung at full force, slicing the fruit into two halves.

Though his back was turned to them, Kale could see Illadar's cheek muscles flex and knew he smiled at his accomplishment. He then watched as Illadar knelt to retrieve one of the apple pieces. The loud crunching could be heard as he indulged in the reward from his victorious strike. Thunder roared loudly above as the night sky became covered in grey, distracting Illadar from his snack.

"You never told me you were so good," Kale finally broke the silence. He knew time was of the essence.

Illadar started in surprise. "What are you doin' here, kid? I figured you'd be long gone by now." He glanced toward the dark clouds which were nearly above them. "I'd better get goin' myself. I just needed to ensure that I've packed the proper weaponry—you've gotta' be prepared in a world filled with chaos. I pity the man in black, should I meet him again."

"I want you to come with us." Kale didn't waste any time getting to the point. "We both have the same goals—and, I'm sorry..." He glanced down. "I'm sorry for my behavior last night. I want to learn from you. Your skill is amazing."

Illadar stared forward suspiciously, unsure why Kale could possibly have such a strong hatred for Jedah. He knew there must be a reason behind Kale's passion to fight. Another rumble of thunder filled the sky and Illadar knew that now was not the time to delay the situation with his stubborn pride. His priority was to leave Braxle and find a place to safely camp before the downpour.

"I suppose we can go together—for now, anyway. But run off like you did last night and next time I won't be around when you come lookin'. Comrades stand together." He smiled, as though relieved by the situation.

It was the first time Kale had ever seen Illadar smile, which in turn made his lips curl upward with satisfaction.

"Let's go, kid." Illadar continued, lowering his voice, "I know a place just outside of town where we can go. I've been there before and can assure you, we won't be found tonight." He slung a grey bag over his shoulder as he approached the two. "Nice to finally meet you—Kale talks about you often."

Thomas bowed his head, "Likewise."

Although Thomas and Illadar had worked so close in the town square, up until this point they had only exchanged a courteous wave in the morning and even that was a rarity.

A bright flash illuminated the sky, followed by a mighty boom of thunder.

"We need to leave," Kale spoke as a strong gust of wind blew through his hair.

As they made their way to the opening entrance of the town wall, a light drizzle began to fall. A crow flew overhead, releasing abnormally irritating sounds. Kale couldn't help but wonder if it was the same bird from the windowsill.

Good riddance, Kale thought as the noisy bird soon became a black speck in the distance.

By the time they reached the exit their clothes were damp and cold from the wind chill. Despite the need to press on, Kale paused, glancing over his shoulder toward the quaint town. The people of Braxle were so kind and caring. They had opened his heart to a whole new way of life and taught him not all humans were cruel. He would even miss Theresa, despite her persistent annoyance and clever sleight of hand. Throughout his time in Braxle, he learned to not judge others so hastily. Although, he still longed to return to being a dragon, he now held no regrets for his time spent as a human.

"Farewell, Braxle." Kale whispered as he turned to join his friends, setting off toward their new destination.

CHAPTER 13

BROKEN TRUST

They arrived at the forest border, chilled from the intermittent rainfall steadily growing worse. Kale shook himself, which caused a copious amount of water to scatter in all directions. He was thankful for the momentary relief the sky offered.

"It's just ahead." Illadar pointed forward. "Hopefully everything is as it was when I first prepared the site in case of an emergency." He glanced toward the threatening sky. "Either way, we'd better get movin'; it looks like things are about to get much worse." Illadar took the first steps into the dreary forest, weaving through the sagging foliage weighted down by water droplets.

Kale had anticipated that they would travel along another trail; not shove their way through wet vegetation in the darkness of night. He grunted, miserably pressing forward as mud began to seep into his shoes. It was amazing how many puddles were hidden beneath the leaves, and soon his feet squished loudly with every step.

After what felt like hours of discomfort, they finally arrived at a clearing where Kale saw a small, wooden structure consisting of four short posts and a log rooftop coated in dead leaves. It obviously had been created for no more than sitting and sleeping purposes.

Illadar chuckled. "I can't believe the thing is still standin'. It's no castle, but at least we'll be dry when it rains."

Kale exhaled, knowing time was going to drag on slowly as they huddled under the low roof, awaiting dawn's first light. The rain, as expected, increased and the thought of a warm fire pressed upon their minds as the chilling wind slapped against their flesh. They were grateful for the barrier of trees which surrounded them, aiding to block some of the rain that poured in at an angle.

"We owe great thanks to Mortimer; had it not been for his kind parting gift, we would not have a delicious meal in such weather." Thomas reached into the red sack, retrieving the thoughtfully wrapped bundle.

The three enjoyed the feast of roasted pulled pork, cheese, and bread. The late-night meal was incredibly satisfying and left each fully content. They laid back, listening to the pitter-patter of raindrops against the rooftop.

Kale rolled onto his side, admiring the hilt of the claymore Illadar had secured snugly in a hilt which only covered the tip of the blade. "Will you teach me?" Kale questioned hopefully to Illadar. "I'm never going to stand a chance in battle, let alone against Jedah, if I don't learn the proper techniques."

"Are you hardheaded, or just plain stupid?" Illadar replied as he lowered his eyebrows. "Do you honestly assume you'll be able to master swordsmanship, and then stroll up to General Jedah for a one-on-one confrontation?" He laughed in amusement at Kale's ignorance. "It's apparent you don't know that sly cur after all. You won't find him without his pawns around, so if you think you're gonna' have safe passage past a hundred knights—you've got another thing comin'."

"I'm no fool, I've already thought of such things." Kale replied hastily. In all reality, he had not given much attention to the details of the situation. He hadn't a clue of how he would handle fighting against such a powerful adversary. "I'd still like to learn." He finally continued, "Things are not going to fall into place all at once; I cannot begin to plan my next steps if I can't even swing a weapon properly. Besides, *you* can't expect to fight against him alone either—you need me." Kale smirked, knowing by the expression upon Illadar's face, he had won the argument.

"Fine, kid." Illadar grunted, annoyed by Kale's persistence, yet equally flattered that someone would desire his guidance. "We begin first thing in the morning after we eat. I suggest you get some rest now. You won't be sleepin' for long."

~~~~~~~~~~~~~~~

The morning air was warm and humid. Each gentle breeze sent water droplets trickling down from the night's rain. A few scattered clouds lingered across the sky, but the day appeared to be pleasant and filled with sunshine.

Kale awoke after an uncomfortable and brief amount of broken sleep. He stretched his limbs as he opened his mouth to release a loud yawn. His eyes shot open, filled with sudden excitement—this was the day he was going to train. He shoveled down a filling portion of leftovers before emerging from the small covering.

"You have got to be joking." Kale ran a hand through his

hair, frustrated by the sight before him.

The black crow caught sight of Kale as it began squawking loudly before swiftly flying away.

"Stupid bird," Kale muttered.

Illadar, already awake, was gathering wood to lay out for drying so they could later enjoy a fire. "Mornin', kid."

"Good morning." Kale rubbed his eyes. "I'm ready to learn."

Illadar laughed, smiling at Kale's eager attitude. "All right, kid, come stand here." He motioned his hand toward the location.

Kale hustled obediently. *This is it*, he thought, *I'm finally going to be a warrior. I'm going to avenge those who have fallen to Jedah's wrath.*

"Here you go." Illadar extended his arms, allowing a bundle of short logs to roll into Kale's bent elbows.

Kale's eyes met Illadar's with confusion. "I don't understand, do you need me to put these somewhere?"

"No." Illadar walked back to the wood covering, taking a seat as he picked up an apple and began eating. "I want you to stand there and hold 'em until I say otherwise. If you drop the logs or move, your trainin' ends." Pieces of fruit spat out onto his chin as he spoke.

"What is this? I thought you said we would begin training today." Kale felt furious.

"This is your trainin', kid. How can you expect to withstand a battle of endurance if you can't even hold a few logs for a little while? When swords clash there are no breaks. You can't expect your opponent to politely stand back and wait while you regain composure. Sword fighting will test your endurance to the limits. If you get tired and can no longer hold your blade—you can count yourself dead. All it takes is one second with your guard down to lose your head; don't ever forget that."

Kale sighed unhappily, grunting as he better positioned his body. The hours passed and he finally saw Thomas emerge from the wooden shelter.

Illadar immediately began to explain the situation and soon he and Thomas were engaged in conversation while Kale miserably looked on. The logs were surprisingly light and easy to hold; it was the continuity of standing in the same position for a prolonged period of time eating away at his nerves.

"Can I stop now? This is ridiculous. I find it highly doubtful a battle of swords would go on this long."

"The answer is no. You have to prepare for the unexpected— physically and mentally. Now don't ask again, kid."

Kale understood Illadar meant well, and when it came down to things, Illadar's strong personality was just what he needed. He smirked as he began to hum loudly as if to spite Illadar with annoyance for such a horrible task. Kale knew Illadar expected him to fail and quit the menial task, begging for the daunting challenge to stop.

There is no way I'm going to show Illadar any weakness, Kale thought as he grew even more determined to move forward with his training. He was anxious to put this petty task behind him.

Then, as if to mock Illadar even further, he began to lift the logs as though they were weights. He flashed a childish smile toward both Thomas and Illadar, who pretended as though they were unimpressed by his boasting.

As the day wore on and the sun began to set, beads of sweat continued to roll down Kale's body and absorb into his clothing. The feeling grew uncomfortable. The mental strain was now taking its toll on his mind and, although the weight of the logs were still easily tolerated, the flow of blood within his arms had slowed and his fingers felt numb—he didn't know how much more he could endure.

Illadar, who had enjoyed a day of recuperation and relaxation, glanced toward Kale. He could not believe such a thin, young man had held the heavy logs for an entire day. Even he would have collapsed by this time. "You know, kid—I don't think you're human."

Kale's eyes grew wide. *Did Thomas say something? How could he possibly know?*

His thoughts were broken by Illadar's laughter. "Your face is too much, kid." He smacked his knee as more laughter followed. "Learn to take a joke. After months of workin' with you I know better than most there's no way you have any amazin' abilities— Well, aside from bein' surprisingly strong— But I'd hardly call it inhuman." He lightly touched his neck. "Plus, you're clumsy and complain a lot—let's not forget the fact you don't even know how to fight. Even the dull-witted giants from the northern mountains aren't *that* bad." His infectious laughter soon had Thomas gripping his stomach as they both enjoyed the comic relief.

Kale scrunched his face; he wasn't sure whether to feel relieved or insulted.

"Go ahead and set the wood over here." Illadar motioned past Kale. "Those puny arms of yours are pretty strong, I'll give ya' that."

Kale hadn't realized the strain his body endured until taking his first step. His knee joints locked which nearly caused him to fall.

Thomas quickly rushed to his aid, helping him walk toward a pit Illadar had dug for the fire. As the logs rolled from his arms, Kale could see deep indentations on his skin where the logs had pressed. He balled a firm fist, flexing his forearm which immediately began to throb as the blood rushed through, circulating to his fingertips. Kale moaned as he lowered his aching body to a seated position.

Thomas followed, patting Kale gently on the back. "I'm very proud of you." He smiled warmly. "Now, eat this to regain your energy." Thomas handed Kale a bread roll stuffed with pulled pork strips. "Enjoy, for this will be our last meal on Mortimer."

"That's right, kid, tomorrow you'll be providing us with food so I suggest you sleep soon." Illadar began to pile twigs and leaves into the bottom of the pit as he spoke. He then withdrew a piece of flint from his pocket, striking it many times until he finally grew too frustrated with himself to continue. "Curses, it's still too damp to catch fire. I'll be back." He sighed, leaving in search of dry foliage to use.

After a few minutes passed, Thomas glanced around to ensure they were truly alone before turning toward Kale. "Your strength is remarkable! Though I must say, it is not a normal human characteristic to endure such a tedious task without years of training. I presume you've inherited some of your former traits. Have you noticed anything else aside from your exceptional strength? It's important you tell me if so; this is all new to both of us and we cannot risk something going wrong."

"Well," Kale thought of his unexplained ability to heat things with the touch of his palms, "there is one thing." He lowered his voice, looking around cautiously. "I'd really rather speak about this later though—when it's safe."

Thomas nodded. "Well," he winked "since he isn't back just yet, I suppose I could assist the situation." Thomas pointed a finger toward the pit and whispered, "*Eraton avoria.*" The twigs immediately ignited, creating a crackling fire that quickly fed off the pile of logs. "I think a little magic will be all right this time. It's getting late and we've all had a stressful past couple of days." Thomas pulled the flint close to him and Kale so it would not draw suspicion as to how the fire had started.

Upon Illadar's return to camp, he appeared to be full of enthusiasm—this, however, lasted only moments as he quickly took note of the crackling fire. He let the small bundle of dried sticks fall to the floor. "I see you were able to start the fire," He mumbled as he sat near the pit, enjoying the comforting warmth.

Not much later, Kale grew too tired to hold his eyes open. His strength was nearly depleted and he was ready to sleep. He crawled his way under the covering and instantly drifted into a deep slumber.

~~~~~~~~~~~~~~~~

The next morning, Kale awoke to a firm hand nudging against his shoulder. He opened his eyes to see Illadar kneeling outside the structure with a long pointed stick in his grasp. "Rise n' shine, kid. I'm hungry, which means it's time for you to go hunt for us."

Kale slowly sat in an upright position, dusting off his tunic as he emerged from the sleeping area. Hunting was something he was fond of, though he had never attempted to try since his excursion with Neelan—even then, he hadn't actually made the kill. As a dragon it seemed so simple to hunt for food—he towered over all animals with no threats. Kale took a deep breath and reached toward the sky to limber his body before taking the spear from Illadar's grasp.

"Shouldn't I be hunting while it's dark out?" Kale glanced toward the clear, sunny sky.

"A true hunter can catch their prey at any given time, regardless of it being day or night. You will find many animals are sippin' a mornin' drink or eatin' berries—it's pretty active and you shouldn't have a problem if you've got half a brain." Illadar extended his arm, pointing toward a thick patch of tall grass and bushes. "I'll be comin' with you to ensure you do things right. You take the lead—I will assist when needed, but you must make the kill. We won't be returnin' until you get us a meal." He nudged Kale to begin moving and bid farewell to Thomas who would be watching over their camp while they were out within the forest.

A couple of hours passed and Illadar watched as Kale frightened away one animal after another.

Although he had been a great hunter as the *Black Dragon, Firehart*, as a human Kale lacked coordination and the skill to move stealthily.

Over the course of another hour, Illadar explained various techniques to help Kale improve his skill at hunting. He watched Kale quickly improve and proudly smiled at the accomplishment. "Things take time, kid, but you're on the right track."

Kale couldn't believe Illadar was actually paying him a compliment. Maybe there *was* hope for their friendship to strengthen. Kale had to admit—for just beginning, he was getting quite good at creeping silently through the forest and steadily thrusting the spear. As his stomach rumbled, Kale couldn't help but think of Thomas who he knew by now must be craving food as well. It was an incredibly hot day which added to their increasing fatigue. The sun seemed to absorb more of their energy with each passing minute.

Suddenly, Kale stopped and looked toward Illadar. He brought a finger to his eye, and then pointed forward—a signal

Illadar taught him to alert others of nearby movement. Kale grasped the wood spear tightly within his right hand as he carefully stepped closer to the target so that the large trees would not obstruct his view. As his left foot came down, it softly crunched upon a twig he had not seen.

The grey animal's long slender ears shot up and its black oval eyes shifted to both sides. It dropped the grass from its mouth before taking off in a swift gallop.

"Curses! It saw me!" Kale whispered in anger to Illadar before sprinting after the briskly moving animal. "I'm not going to fail again!" He leapt and weaved around the thick vegetation, keeping within range of the creature. He still needed to get closer before his confidence would allow his hand to release the weapon.

As he continued to run, he could feel a familiar sensation returning once again—his palm was growing steadily warmer. Despite the distraction, he pushed onward while keeping focus on the animal. Kale could now smell the scent of burning wood as a light stream of smoke escaped from between his fingers.

Closer—closer—just a little closer, Kale narrowed his eyes, *now*! He thrust his arm forward as the weapon released from his grasp. Kale stood in astonishment as he saw the weapon ignite into a spear of flames which flew at amazing speed toward the animal.

The flaming tip pierced through the animal's skin with ease. They watched in silence as it took a few more staggering steps forward. The gaping hole in its round torso from the attack drained its remaining life. The grey-haired animal's long legs buckled, causing it to collapse onto its side with a thud.

Kale quickly ran to the animal which had small flames still feeding upon its stiff fur. He frantically began to pat at the hair to calm the fire. "Illadar, can't you help?!" Kale called out.

After managing to get everything under control, Kale turned to face Illadar. He was frustrated at the lack of help Illadar had offered, leaving him alone to preserve their meal from burning.

Illadar stood, frozen in place as his mouth hung open in a mix of confusion and anger. "I'm gonna' ask you one last time, kid— who, or *what,* are you?"

CHAPTER 14

IT'S TIME

Kale was so focused on recovering the burnt animal he hadn't taken notice of Illadar's expression of shock. As Kale realized the serious nature of the situation, he swallowed hard—unsure of what to do. He couldn't understand why his ability had come without warning.

"I," Kale fought to find the right words, wishing Thomas was around to assist as he always had before. "I'll tell you everything, I swear it—but not now. Please understand that I just can't."

"Curses, kid!" Illadar slammed his fist against the trunk of a large tree. "This is the same crud you told me last time, yet I was willin' to overlook it, and come with you anyway. I forced myself to believe I imagined the intensity when you gripped my neck that night. You've gone too far this time—it's just too much. I'm not going to continue travelin' with someone who can ignite wood into flames with a mere touch and won't explain why. Either you tell me who you really are, or you and Thomas are on your own." He locked eyes with Kale. "You're no normal human—that much I'm sure."

Kale had been backed into a mental corner. He weighed out the options of telling Illadar the truth or risk losing him forever. He knew in his heart that allowing Illadar to go was not a choice he was in favor of. Kale wanted Illadar to teach him more. Every ally he could gather to stand and fight against Jedah's army was a valuable asset.

Aside from the obvious reasons to keep Illadar with them, he had become a good friend, despite their disagreements.

"All right... I'll tell you the truth about my past." Kale took in a deep breath as he parted his lips to confess everything. Before the first words could escape from his mouth, an eerie howl sounded nearby.

"Shh..." Illadar urgently whispered, quietly moving toward where Kale stood. "They must know we're here."

"*They*?" Kale whispered back.

"The red beasts. They're from the *other side*. They can't harm us here, but they can send an alert of our presence."

"Red beasts? Other side?" Though Kale was relieved his confession had been interrupted, he was now struck with bewilderment.

"Come quietly, I'll show you." He led Kale to a nearby thicket of bushes. "Look through, but don't let 'em see you." Illadar whispered.

Kale brought his fingertips to the leaves, gently parting them to have a better look. *What in Pan's name are those*?! He watched as a pack of gruesome creatures paced alongside the tiny stream.

They appeared to be of the dog family and walked upon four thin legs. Their oversized paws had long, thick, black claws that dug into the dirt as they walked. The creatures' thin lips were curled back as they snarled viciously, revealing crooked teeth that pointed at the tips. Their bodies were hairless and coated in a thin layer of mucus-like liquid which secreted from their pores, causing them to have a slick appearance. Every so often a small glob of the fluid would slide down one of the creature's legs and onto the ground. This seemed to be a self-cleaning method to clear debris which would stick to their bodies. The creatures had no tails, but instead a sharp white spike which protruded from the base of their spines. Their slender heads had not one set of ears, but two, positioned just above their devilish red eyes.

Kale couldn't resist his curiosity and pushed the leaves farther apart. As he did, the soft rustling which had been barely detectable by human hearing seemed to stir the creatures. Their double set of ears perked into a stiff upward position as they began to huff. Kale and Illadar remained stationary, taking in slow and silent breaths.

The red beasts paced quickly on the opposite side of the small stream as if being bound by an invisible force. The stream was very narrow and could easily be crossed with a single step—it certainly was not an obstacle for the red beasts. Kale could not understand why they did not attack.

As Kale wondered if they would ever be able to leave their location, a prolonged piercing howl rang out in the distance. All the beasts turned their heads to listen before quickly sprinting off into the forest.

Kale and Illadar simultaneously released a sigh of relief.

"Why didn't they cross the stream to attack us?" Kale immediately asked, his heart still racing. "I don't understand... I'm sure they knew we were here."

"The red beasts are remarkable hunters who live within the

Forest of Forgotten Whispers. Centuries ago, an old sorcerer cast an enchantment upon the area as a method to protect nearby towns. He placed a barrier of runnin' water around the forest so that any creature born on the tainted land will turn to dust should they attempt to cross. They are prisoners to the land." Illadar cautiously peered through the bush to ensure they were still alone before continuing on. "As time passed it became common knowledge among natives surroundin' the area to remain safely on their own side of the stream."

"Is it really that bad over there?" Kale was intrigued to hear more.

"I'd bet so. I've heard stories you couldn't even muster in your worst nightmares. Though, I will say—rumor has it that not all creatures born on the other side of the forest are foul. They've just been struck with misfortune and are now bound." Illadar stood as he cracked his neck to the side in discomfort.

"Why did the sorcerer place a barrier in the first place if it's not *all* bad?"

"Because it wasn't worth the risk of allowin' the beasts to roam across Ravondore freely. They aren't even the worst threats that lurk in there."

A thought then crossed Kale's mind, prompting him to ask, "Why did we have to hide?" He tried to make sense of it all. "Couldn't we have picked them off one by one from where we stood?"

"I wish it were that easy, kid. Red beasts don't fend well on their own in life. They're mindless creatures who only live to kill. The beasts will often fight amongst themselves and kill their own kind. Because of this, most of them are led by a higher power— someone or somethin' more intelligent than they. A being that is stronger and has either conquered the creatures into submission, or raised 'em from birth. Red beasts are very loyal beings and will only obey a single master throughout their entire lives — unless of course, their master has been slain."

"So, you're saying there may be someone within the forest commanding them? Someone that *can* cross the stream?"

"Exactly," Illadar smirked. "Maybe you're not as dimwitted as I've thought." He then disappeared without a word, returning shortly after with the dead animal slung over his shoulder. "Go fetch some water in our canteens. We don't need to get dehydrated."

Kale quickly obeyed in hopes the tense encounter had caused Illadar to temporarily forget his previous concerns. Kale longed to learn combat techniques while trapped within his squishy human body and he knew having Illadar around would be the only means for it to happen. Having the ability to fight was a necessary step toward Kale's growth in defeating General Jedah.

"Hurry up, kid." Illadar demanded of Kale, who had drifted in thought about learning swordsmanship. "We need to move quickly toward camp before anyone catches sight of us. Leave no tracks or evidence of our presence along the way. We cannot afford our location to be revealed."

Kale hesitantly approached the stream, glancing in all directions to ensure he was alone. It seemed surreal that a stream, less than arm's length at its greatest width, could keep the red beasts away. He swiftly dunked the canteens beneath the water's surface as he shook them until all air bubbles had escaped, allowing the cool water to rush inside. He spun the cap onto each canteen when a *thud* on the opposite side of the stream caught his attention. Something had just fallen from the tree branches.

Maybe it was only a squirrel, Kale thought as he secured the canteens to his belt. *No, it couldn't be—it was far too loud to be a squirrel.* As Kale turned to leave, he caught sight of a shadowy silhouette from the corner of his eye which immediately caused him to refocus his attention. He could vaguely make out the figure standing there in what appeared to be a hooded cloak. Before he could investigate further, whomever it had been swiftly dashed behind the trees. Kale was certain this had been no animal.

A sense of *déjà vu* overwhelmed Kale—the encounter reminded him of the person who he'd seen perched upon the wooden wall of Braxle. Kale shot a glance toward Illadar who was looking in the opposite direction, picking at his teeth while he held the animal carcass in place.

Maybe there is no need to draw alarm. Maybe whoever it was didn't notice us. After a brief debate, he decided to keep what he had seen to himself unless another incident should arise.

"Let's get back quickly," Kale stated, anxious to get as far away from the stream as possible.

"Took ya' long enough. The last thing we need is to be around this area when darkness falls upon us." Illadar led the way as they moved through the cluster of leaves.

They maintained a steady pace throughout their hike and kept an awkward silence that made Kale uneasy.

The two men arrived at the camp and began to settle around the fire when Thomas' eyes grew wide with dismay. He ran a finger along the gaping hole of the grey animal's torso. Thomas' eyes peeked out from under grey brows as he saw Illadar lying with his back against the ground. With hope that whatever caused the damage to the animal had a logical explanation, he continued to prepare and cook their meal. The last thing Thomas wanted was to stir unnecessary alarm. He decided to wait until later into the night, once Illadar fell asleep to press Kale for answers.

Finally, after their stomachs were full, Illadar leaned his back against a tree as he crossed his arms. He stared toward Kale with a look of exasperation upon his face. "I hope you don't think you're off the hook. You've got some serious explaining to do, kid—or I leave at dawn's first light."

Kale glanced toward Thomas who shook his head with disappointment. The old sorcerer was well aware that something had definitely gone astray during their hunt.

"What is our friend referring to Kale?" Thomas questioned with purposeful ignorance while secretly hoping it was not the secret they struggled so hard to keep.

The look Kale returned revealed Thomas' worst assumptions were correct.

"How can it be?" Thomas glanced from Illadar to Kale.

"Well," Kale sighed, "remember when we spoke about my inhuman strength? You said it might be a trait I've inherited from my," he glanced toward Illadar, "former self—an innate ability." Kale cleared his throat. "There is still that *thing* I wanted to tell you the other night. My hands," he brought his palms up to his face, "they get extremely hot. I'm able to heat or burn the things I touch—though, I don't know why it happens and I'm unsure how to control its timing." Kale closed his palms. "Today, Illadar saw when it happened again."

"I see." Thomas folded his hands together, "So it couldn't be helped then." He glanced toward the fire as he pondered the situation.

"Enough with this crud!" Illadar sat upright. "It's pretty obvious you've both been hiding information from me." He paused a moment. "For awhile, I know I did as well—but now we're travelin' together and quite honestly, if I'm gonna' be sleeping next to someone who could torch me while I sleep—I'd like to know. So stop with all the secretive chatter and tell me what is *really* going on!"

After a brief moment of silence, Kale spoke. "I've made up my mind, Thomas; I'm going to tell him. I believe we can trust him." Kale's heart raced. This was the first person he had ever opened up to, aside from Thomas, whom he had known for decades.

Thomas nodded his head in approval, though, still keeping a cautious watch toward Illadar's expression.

"Illadar, I'm a—a," Kale sighed. *Just tell him*! He urged himself to continue, "I am the Black Dragon, Firehart–the final kill necessary for Jedah's ultimate victory over dragon-kind."

An uncomfortable silence followed before Illadar burst into laughter so hard tears swelled in his deep brown eyes. "Kid, you must really think I'm an idiot!" He smacked his knee, "A dragon? You?" More laughter erupted as he stopped only to catch his breath. "An apprentice spell-caster maybe—I'd even believe you were born from the blood of a sorcerer, but a dra— "

"Actually," Kale cut him off, "*he* is the sorcerer." He pointed toward Thomas.

"Oh com'on! You two are too much. First you expect me to believe that you—a puny kid—was once a dragon. But, then you take it beyond that to tell me the old man here is a sorcerer?" Illadar stood furiously. "I've had enough. Good luck on your own from here on out. I'm sure it won't be that difficult between a *dragon and a sorcerer* to take care of yourselves," He snickered.

Kale balled his fists angrily. "Just wait a moment! I'm telling you the truth!"

"Indeed, I assure you he is speaking truthfully," Thomas added calmly.

Illadar ignored their attempts to regain his trust. "I'm not even gonna' wait until morning. There's no way I could sleep next to the two of you. Who knows what you might do to me?" He shuddered in disgust as he slung his pack over a shoulder along with his blade.

Within seconds, Kale was at Illadar's heels. "I said to wait, you stubborn fool!" Kale demanded as he reached out and gripped Illadar's forearm.

Illadar yelled in pain as he ripped his arm from Kale's grasp. "Touch me again and I'll slice you down right where you stand!" He placed a hand over where Kale had touched.

The stench of burnt flesh filled Kale's nostrils. Kale could see the bright red enflamed skin which was already beginning to peel between Illadar's fingers. He knew Illadar had been badly burnt. Kale quickly closed his palm into a tightened fist, taking a step back in dismay. "Please believe me—I truly didn't intend to harm you." He looked toward the sky in frustration. "I hate this! It's not fair; I don't know how to control this pathetic human body. This must be a curse—or a nightmare I can't wake from. When I had the ability to use power as a dragon, I knew of Jedah and the war he engaged upon dragon-kind." His chest hurt as he spoke, "I knew—and yet I chose to remain secluded within my own cave and did nothing. I sat back while they all died alone. I assumed each dragon would have the power to handle themselves in battle. That stubborn thought remained within my mind although I knew better. Even after hearing the news of each dragon's demise, I still placed my own pride first." He bit his lip as he glanced toward the ground.

"The truth is—I was scared. If I had only gone to aid the others, maybe we would have won and ended this long ago. There's something I've learned during my time as a human—you can accomplish so much more if you work together. I don't want you to leave, Illadar. You're my friend and I know that, as a team, we can win this." Kale awaited a response as many minutes of silence passed. He gulped, wondering if something inappropriate had been said.

Illadar heavily sighed, rubbing a hand across his scrunched forehead. "Logs," He finally spoke.

"What?" Kale hadn't a clue what Illadar meant.

"I said—logs. Go—now!" He turned to face Kale, shaking his head. "I'm not gonna' stay if you intend to slack off. Get moving!"

Kale smiled, quickly moving toward the spot where he first endured holding the logs. A new pile waited, neatly stacked — compliments of Illadar. Kale was prepared to train harder than ever before. This time, he would stand by those he cared for until the very end.

"You know, kid, if you think I'm gonna' give you special treatment just because you're really a *big, mighty dragon*, then you've got another thing comin'." Illadar forced back a smile. "Get some rest after you've held the logs until the fire dies." He then turned toward Thomas. "And as for you—you sly, old man." His finger shook in Thomas' direction as he spoke. "I think it's safe to say we will need to catch up on the truth between ourselves tomorrow evening. It's apparent I know nothing of the real you." He chuckled to himself, mumbling as he crawled under the wood covering, "Who would've thought—traveling with a dragon and a sorcerer."

~~~~~~~~~~~~~~~

That morning, Kale awoke to the tip of Illadar's boot tapping against his feet. He rubbed his eyes wearily, still craving sleep, as he squinted at another radiant day.

"It's time, kid—now your trainin' will truly begin. Follow me," Illadar commanded.

Kale sprung up like a child who had just been presented with a grand gift. He knew it was the moment he had been longing for. It was the day he would learn to fight using a sword. Kale slid his boots on and followed Illadar to an area just outside of their camp, near a tree. Thick green moss swirled around the bark, making it distinct among the other surrounding trees.

"Here," Illadar tossed him a sturdy stick, "dig."

How delightful, another of his insidious tasks. Kale sighed, shaking his head in frustration. He did as instructed and began to scrape at the firm soil which appeared untouched until now; it had a solid coat of damp fungus on the surface.

He pushed deeper and deeper, which proved to be quite difficult while using a single crooked tree branch as a shovel. Kale devised a strategy to use his hands as a scoop in order to prevent the dirt from tumbling back in.

"I think I've hit something!" Kale exclaimed as his fingertips scraped against something hard.

"Dig it out," Illadar nodded as he spoke.

Kale continued to shovel handfuls of dirt, following the shape of whatever was buried below. He was certain at this point it wasn't a tree root—the smooth texture was sanded wood. Kale became confident the object he was digging at was a box. His curiosity rose and he wasn't sure whether to feel excited or worried of its contents. Finally, the rectangular box was uncovered. He wiped his brow as sweat trickled downwards toward his eye. The task had taken much longer than he originally assumed.

This would have been so much easier if I only had my claws.

Kale grunted as he began to lift the box from the hole. It was heavier than he expected and the weight seemed to be disproportioned.

"Watch it, kid!" Illadar scolded as he heard the contents shifting around. "You don't know what's inside, so how about bein' more careful."

Kale nodded. Illadar was right. He didn't want to cause any damage before revealing what the contents were.

"What shall I do now?" Kale questioned as he placed the box onto the ground.

"Open it."

A smile spread upon Kale's face. There was no challenge or tests attached—he could satisfy his eager curiosity without any delays. He dug his fingertips beneath the small lip on the box top. It was tight and snugly fit into the main shell. After a few good tugs, the lid creaked as it slowly slid upwards until finally popping off. The sudden release caught Kale off guard, causing him to catch his balance with a hand before falling onto his bottom.

As he peered into the box, his bright eyes marveled. The box contained three beautifully crafted weapons. There was a double-edged dagger with a steel grip which blended the entire piece together. The daggers' hard scabbard was created of polished steel, reflecting in the sunlight; its center was embossed with smooth bronze plates. A deathly looking combat flail was the next weapon Kale noticed. A blackened steel handle was attached to a black chain with a weighted ball on the end. Kale cringed as he gazed upon the large pointed spikes protruding off the sphere—he did not want to be caught on the victims' side of the flail's attack.

Last, resting beneath the other weaponry, was the most divine sword he ever laid eyes upon. The scabbard of finely polished steel contained ringlets of gold wrapped around in precisely proportioned sections. Along the scabbard's edge were golden studs which traced down from the opening to the point. The hilt of the sword was awe inspiring with a black grip, ribbed to allow the wielder ample traction when attacking. The guard and pommel were both gold and engraved with swishes and swirls that completed a stunning visual impact.

"How did you know these were here?" Kale questioned suspiciously.

"When I first arrived at Braxle and took over old man Galever's blacksmith forge, I had a grim feelin' the day would come where I would need to leave the town without warning—or an abundance of time to make preparations. When it comes to my life, good things don't tend to last very long, so I knew it was only a matter of waiting for something to happen. For many nights after the shop was closed, I would stay and work on these. I wanted them to be precise, strong, and deadly. Along with my claymore, these weapons are my pride and joy." He glanced toward Kale, "I've decided I want to share them with you—and the old sorcerer." Illadar called out loudly enough for Thomas to hear on the other side of a cluster of bushes. "You'll want additional protection on the battlefield—just in case."

"Amazing..." It was the only word that slipped from Kale's lips as he stared wide-eyed at the box.

"This is exceptionally kind of you." Thomas emerged from the foliage. His green eyes twinkled at the thought of having his own weapon. Until now, magic had always proven to be sufficient. "I think I shall choose the most simplistic to use—if you two don't mind of course. The dagger would be ideal as I can't imagine my old bones swinging anything heavier around. I don't foresee myself having the need to resort to weaponry unless an enemy was close and my magical strength was nearly depleted." The corners of his lips curled upward

.The two men could tell he was excited to have a dagger to call his own.

"Fair enough. You're up, kid, take your pick."

"You're all right with this? You did create them, after all; I wouldn't want to take something you desire." Kale wanted to be polite with the situation, yet he secretly hoped Illadar would allow him next choice.

"I've got my lady right here." He patted the giant sword over his shoulder.

He gave his weapon a gender? Humans... Kale laughed to himself.

"Go ahead and take your pick." Illadar gestured toward the remaining two weapons.

Kale could see that behind Illadar's toughened exterior, he was excited to share the objects he had worked so hard to create. There was a certain glimmer in his dark eyes that gave it away. Kale couldn't deny he was overjoyed; he had never been given such a magnificent gift in all of his life—then again, as a dragon he never needed anything aside from companionship, and Thomas had fulfilled that.

Kale's hand shot forward with his pointer finger extended— undoubtedly sure it was the sword he desired. From the moment he laid eyes upon the weapon, he wanted to touch it—to hold it. He desperately desired to master the art of wielding it in battle.

"It's all yours, kid. Go ahead and take it."

Kale inhaled, holding a breath within his chest as he wrapped his fingers around the hilt. Although he handled many swords throughout his time working at the blacksmith shop—this one felt right. It was as though the sword had been made for only his hands. He sat upon his legs, resting the scabbard in his lap as he drew the sword. The blade was perfectly balanced and razor sharp. It sparkled in the sunlight as he slowly spun the hilt within his grasp. *It's mine—it's really mine!* A wide smile crossed his glowing face.

"I'll hold onto this." Illadar lifted the flail. The chain chimed as the weighted spiked ball dangled. "You can never have too much protection."

"Thank you for this, Illadar," Kale beamed. "You won't regret it, I swear."

Illadar chuckled, "Don't thank me just yet, kid, it comes with a price." The left side of his dark lips snickered upward. "Now, the real training begins. Grab your canteen and sword, then follow me." He wrapped the spiked weight on the flail in heavy cloth before shoving it into his bag. Illadar then placed the bag in a concealed location near the wood covering.

Kale quickly looped the scabbard through his belt, tightening the strap to ensure it would hold the weight of the sheathed sword.

"Let's go." Illadar looked up at Thomas, "You're welcome to join us if you'd like, old man."

Thomas smiled. "I appreciate the invitation, but I think I shall wait here at camp. I'll leave the fancy battle stances to you two." He then locked eyes with Kale, "Don't get too hotheaded. Learning a new skill takes time and practice. Once you have completed your training for the day, bring your weaponry to me and I shall repair it for you. Also," his expression grew serious, "we don't need your powers to do any more unexpected harm. Tonight, you and I will begin working on controlling the ability. Be warned that while I can correct a dulled blade, my powers are not able to piece a sword back together that has been melted by your temper."

Kale nodded as he anxiously followed Illadar into the forest. Within minutes they arrived at a clearing that offered plenty of room for practicing.

"All right kid, draw your sword." Illadar stuck a long, slender fallen tree branch into the dirt. "Imagine this is your opponent." He watched as Kale lifted the sword, prepared to swing. "Now, wait a moment, kid. You don't wanna' go in swingin' around all reckless. There is an art to sword fighting. You must feel the weapon's movement within yourself." He patted his chest above his heart. "Every step—every swing, they must be in unison with the blade. When in battle, a true warrior's sword becomes a part of him. Now relax—clear your mind—and breathe. I want you to come at your opponent and swing—but do not strike. You must learn to control your strength."

Kale did as instructed and relaxed his mind before tightening his fingers around the hilt. He lunged forward and swung the sword at an angle from his side toward the stick. A roar of inner anger released from his lips as the sword struck the wooden target with amazing force. It easily sliced into two pieces as the steel impacted.

Illadar shook his head; he knew this was only the beginning of many necessary hours invested in Kale's training.

~~~~~~~~~~~~~~~~

They remained at the camp as the weeks passed. From the moment Kale woke, to the time he laid down to sleep, his day consisted of hunting, practicing with the sword, and training with Thomas to control his abilities. They had come to the conclusion there were multiple aspects rooting to Kale's powers. When he felt an overwhelming sensation of fear, frustration, or anger, his body would trigger its former element of flame. It had somehow conformed to fit with his human transformation. Thomas taught him how to cope with these feelings and soon, Kale was able to utilize his powers at will.

As sword fighting progressed, Illadar saw such exceptional progress in Kale he decided to advance his training. They would finally begin sparring together with their swords — a deadly practice if not prepared. Until this time they had only used sticks to replicate having an actual weapon in battle.

Thomas assured them he would continue to repair their weaponry with his magical abilities before each following practice. Both Kale and Illadar wanted to ensure their swords remained sharp and precisely balanced, hoping for the day they would cross paths with Jedah or his men.

"You sure you're ready for this, kid?" Illadar raised a black eyebrow.

"Most definitely." Kale gripped his right hand tightly around the hilt.

"Try to keep up." Kale half-jokingly mocked Illadar. He tried to steady his slightly shaking hand. Kale knew that Illadar was an amazing swordsman and although he had taken on the monsloths, it was by pure luck, and the aid of Thomas, that he survived. Kale breathed, recalling the intense training he had endured over the past few days. *I can do this—I know I can.*

Kale advanced toward Illadar, attempting to read his expression and body language. Kale leapt forward as he raised his sword above his head, parallel with the ground. The sword chimed as it crossed against the broad claymore; Illadar was incredibly responsive and swift. Kale pushed his weight forward which caused Illadar to stagger backwards, allowing space between them.

Unknown to Kale, Illadar had no intention to unleash the full potential of his skills. He knew that doing so at Kale's level of experience would surely result in a massive injury. Both men were aware of the purpose of sparring—to simulate a killing blow, but to not truly strike one another.

"Nice move—for an old man." Kale smirked.

"You just watch your pace, kid. Strike my flesh and you'll be sorry." The stern look on Illadar's face instantly told Kale he was not joking.

Before Kale could come up with a witty response, he saw the shining reflection of Illadar's blade swiftly flying toward his head. Kale quickly reacted and ducked below the claymore—listening as it whooshed by.

"Curses, Illadar! That could have hit me!"

"Stop foolin' around and pay attention. Losin' focus for any amount of time could easily result in death. Secondly, learn to better read your opponent—we've discussed this before. Some say you can read a person through their eyes." He wiped the sweat from above his upper lip. "I knew the blow would not land."

Without hesitation, Kale straightened his posture upright as he thrust his sword forward. Illadar effortlessly parried, riposting the attack as his claymore swung forward. Kale managed to block the attack as he deflected it with his own blade. His frustration increased with every following attack that was dodged, blocked, or countered.

Control yourself, Kale pressed the words firmly on his thoughts, *you know how to do this—don't let your emotions get away from you.* He lectured himself. Despite his attempts, he could feel his palms growing increasingly warmer. He breathed heavily as he fought the growing sensation. He had to make a move now — before it was too late. *Don't lose focus*. It was proving to be incredibly difficult to engage in combat while still attempting to tame his ability.

Kale lunged at Illadar with the point of his blade pressing forward toward Illadar's chest. Illadar's claymore swung up in a half circle which forcefully shoved Kale's weapon to his side.

Illadar's foot dug into the sand as he spun around, stepping outward so that his blade would land behind Kale's neck. As the mighty sword came to a halt, Kale could feel the cold steel edge pressing gently against his skin—he had lost.

"That's all for today."

"What? Why?" Kale questioned in confusion. He was so used to Illadar's demanding training routines it seemed odd to stop after such a short time.

Illadar glared at Kale's sword with a look of frustration upon his face.

As Kale glanced down his eyes grew wide. The blade emitted a dim orange glow—he had failed to control his power.

"You could've easily caused me severe harm should that blade have touched my skin; not to mention, if your sword had grown any hotter, it could've snapped in two. This is a problem we cannot allow to happen again. For today, your trainin' will be with Thomas. I suggest you go now and use your time wisely so you're prepared to resume again tomorrow."

Once back at the camp, Thomas knelt by the two swords. He shook his head while glancing upon the many small indentations in the hard steel blades.

"I see that using my magical abilities to repair your weaponry is going to be quite the tiresome task," Thomas chuckled.

"I'm sorry, old man, but the kid has to learn how to properly fight with an actual weapon. Sparrin' with only sticks will have him killed on the battlefield."

Thomas nodded in agreement as he closed his eyes. *"Cronex vilavaria,"* He whispered while running his index finger along the blade. Blood began to trickle onto the ground as the steel sliced through the layers of his skin.

Kale routinely grabbed a canteen of water and poured it over both the blade and Thomas' hand. His sword had been restored to its former glory with no imperfections along the razor sharp edge.

Thomas then moved to Illadar's sword before casting a minor healing spell upon himself.

"Ah, the things I go through for the two of you." He shook his head with a smile.

"I suppose this means I'll have to bring back a juicy hog for dinner." Kale grinned.

"I won't argue with that!" Thomas quickly replied as the three engaged in laughter.

The night continued on with a delicious supper and intense training between Kale and Thomas. Kale knew his journey to becoming an exceptional swordsman and mastering control of his abilities was not nearly over. He needed to remain focused upon his ultimate goal of defeating General Jedah.

More weeks passed and Kale continued to train. It was intense enough to drive a normal man to the brink of exhaustion—or insanity. Yet, Kale pressed on, more determined than ever to succeed. As time passed, he improved in both sword fighting and learning to control his power while in battle.

Eventually, he was able to fully master his ability and increase or suppress it at will, despite any ongoing distractions. In so doing, he found his emotions no longer controlled him.

Through his intense training to learn the art of sword play, he was nearly up to par with Illadar's level of skill. The results made Illadar proud, and every so often, Kale caught glimpse of Illadar smiling happily. Kale's achievements had taken Illadar many years of practice to master.

During their time together in the forest, Kale and Illadar's bond of friendship increased and soon they developed a strong trust for one another. To Kale, it felt as though he had known Illadar for years.

On a rather dreary day, filled with fluffy grey clouds, Kale and Illadar were routinely sparring in their usual location. Illadar had grown confident enough to unleash his full array of techniques upon Kale who had become a very worthy opponent.

Illadar lunged his blade forward causing Kale to deflect the attack before thrusting his own sword swiftly toward Illadar's face.

Kale mockingly spun the hilt within his palm as the blade tip twirled between Illadar's eyes. "I win," He smirked. Over the previous months, Kale had overcome many obstacles and felt confident with his exceptional skill.

Illadar felt Kale had earned the privilege and deserved to enjoy a night to himself. The remainder of the evening was spent at the camp partaking in a much needed rest around the fire. Even more surprising was that Illadar, for the first time in weeks, did the hunting and brought back a large, plump hog.

Kale licked his lips as his taste buds watered. This meal was going to taste even better knowing he didn't have to lift a finger for once. He smiled at the thought.

After the food was prepared and the fire had settled, Kale began to indulge in the juicy meat. Suddenly, he felt a warm sensation pressing against his leg. He immediately leapt to his feet under the assumption he somehow managed to sit upon a hot ember knocked from the fire. As he patted frantically at his thigh, he realized the source came from within his pocket. He reached in and gripped the golden bracelet. It had been so long since an incident, he had nearly forgotten about it—and the letter which he received before leaving Braxle. Kale held it up to his face, inspecting the pointed jade tooth which glowed luminously green.

A swarm of memories flooded his mind as he thought of the mysterious woman, Zasha. His blue eyes widened—how could he have been so foolish as to forget something of such importance. The Forest of Forgotten Whispers was so close all this time—it was the place where his destiny awaited. He needed to hunt for the *tree which rains gold*. One year had finally passed.

CHAPTER 15

TO BECOME A WARRIOR

"We must leave here tomorrow." Kale dangled the bracelet for Thomas to see.

"Are you certain you're prepared to trust the word of Zasha? The risk may be great."

"What other choice do I have, Thomas? We've been hiding here for months with no plans for progression. I'm definitely going; I don't want to always live in fear of what lies ahead."

Thomas nodded. "All right, we will depart first thing in the morning." He glanced toward Illadar, who stared at them with bewilderment. "Will you be joining us?"

"Of course, old man; there's no way I'm gonna' let you two venture into the Forest of Forgotten Whispers without me. You have no idea of the possible dangers. Besides, my options at the moment are fairly limited—stayin' here alone isn't very appealin'." He shot a look toward Kale, "I do expect you to fill me in on what is goin' on though."

Kale told Illadar all about the dreams and the letter he had gotten. They continued to discuss the situation until their eyes grew weary. As Kale laid beneath his covering in an attempt to sleep, he couldn't help but feel a mixture of anxiety and excitement for what was to come. Thoughts raced through his mind as he tossed and turned before fatigue finally overwhelmed his body. He tightly held onto the bracelet as he drifted to sleep.

His worrisome thoughts of the upcoming events triggered Kale to wake as the first rays of sunlight peeked over the horizon. His dark lashes parted and Kale could see the beautiful pink glow of the clear sky. He stood, rubbing a firm hand against his slightly sore neck as he inhaled the crisp morning air. Kale decided to take the time to enjoy himself before waking Illadar or Thomas, who were still sleeping soundly. He knelt by the fire pit, poking around at the underlying hot coals with a stick. The cheerful sound of birds chirping caught his attention and he turned to search the trees for their movement. He had grown quite fond of spotting the different breeds of birds as a pastime.

Kale gasped stumbling backward in surprise. A cloaked figure stood many feet in front of him, silently staring in his direction.

"It's you again," Kale whispered quietly, to not wake the others. "What do you want from me?" He was now certain this was whom he had seen before in the forest and atop the Braxle wall. The stranger was definitely following him.

The short figure did not respond verbally, but instead lifted an arm. The cloth from the beige cloak draped over its skin, concealing the person's entire appearance. To Kale it seemed as though the mysterious stalker wanted him to look behind where he stood.

Kale gulped as he wondered if he was about to face another

attack. He gripped the insignificant fire poker and turned to face whatever awaited behind him. He took caution to listen closely in case the mysterious stalker was attempting to fool him for its own opportunity to attack. Kale creased his forehead in confusion—there was nothing to be seen out of the ordinary. Kale grew frustrated and spun around to confront the stalker. He glanced frantically around, panning the entire area—the mysterious cloaked person was gone. Kale couldn't believe he had been so easily fooled. As he turned to ensure his friends were still safe, Illadar slowly sat up.

"Mornin' kid, you're up early." He licked his thick, dry lips.

Illadar's unintentional loud volume caused Thomas to groan as he too situated into a seated position.

"What does an old man have to do to get some rest around here?" Thomas asked, half jokingly.

"I think we're being followed." Kale bluntly stated.

Illadar immediately stood, scanning the area. "What makes you think this?"

"I saw someone this morning. They were standing just outside our camp—right over here." Kale pointed, "I saw them—or at least, I think I did—the day we came across the red beasts, and also back in Braxle," He confessed.

Thomas stroked his beard. "I must say, I'm quite disappointed in you for not telling us this when you first sighted the person. We don't know if they are friend or foe—it could have been very dangerous had they followed us with the intention to kill. It would be wise for us to move as soon as possible."

They gathered their belongings and smothered the last remains of the hot coals before saying farewell to the camp. Kale secured his sword and nodded to his friends; it was time to move forward.

The three began to make their way through the lush greenery toward the Forest of Forgotten Whispers.

"Can you tell me more about the forest?" Kale broke the silence. Illadar seemed to possess a great deal of information and Kale wanted to know what they would soon be up against.

"Honestly, I have never dared to step a foot in there. But I've heard many stories, and even met someone who has walked upon its soil. People say that the land itself is enchanted. Everything—even the trees are not always as they might seem. We won't know what is dangerous, so it's vital to proceed with caution." He looked forward, swallowing hard. "It's very important that you both remember not to eat or drink anything you should see. One bite of the wrong food and you can kiss yourself goodbye."

"That's all the information you have on where we are about to go?" Kale asked with disappointment.

"Be thankful you even know that much, kid. It's not like I've ever had the desire to visit the place." Illadar paused in thought. "There was a man, though—I met him long ago while still in Mirion. Many called him insane, sayin' that after he returned from the forest his mind went crazy. It was at the kingdom tavern where he spat nonsense about a massive green-skinned creature with long, horn-like teeth and walked upon two legs, as a human does. The man said he quickly fled to warn everyone back home. Everything after that was mumbled gibberish which couldn't be interpreted."

"Interesting, a creature with deep green skin and horns you say?" Thomas stroked his creased cheek with an index finger. "This *creature* could be many things—however, if it is what I am assuming, we must take heed to avoid crossing paths with such a monster."

"What do you think it is?" Kale curiously questioned.

"An orc—a very brute and savage humanoid. They are hell-bent on destruction and bloodshed."

The three walked on in silence, each lost in their own thoughts. Tension had overcome them at the thought of having a confrontation with an orc. After a long and enduring trek, the sound of flowing water could be heard. They weaved through a thicket of bushes as the narrow stream came into view.

The sparkling water glided over sand and stones which created a peaceful trickle. This was hardly the atmosphere anyone could have expected to be the entryway into a treacherous forest. They each took a brief moment to refill the canteens while paying careful attention to their surroundings.

"I hope we can find this tree you need and get outta' here before nightfall." Illadar's eyes revealed great apprehension. "Well—you ready, kid?"

Kale gulped. "Yeah, let's get moving." He knew this was *his* quest and therefore felt it would be appropriate for him to take the first step over the stream.

Kale effortlessly crossed the enchanted border as he entered the confined land. The air felt instantly colder which he thought to be incredibly bazaar. The eerie feeling sent shivers down his spine. He could see that both Thomas and Illadar also experienced the sudden shift in temperature.

"Fascinating," Thomas whispered as he rubbed his hand against his forearm.

The atmosphere of the Forest of Forgotten Whispers was astounding. Tall and slender trees loomed, their lush leaves overhead in a perfectly intertwining canopy, blocking out the sun's rays. It was dark and unwelcoming, as though the forest had been trapped within a permanent nightfall. With every soft breeze, Kale swore he could hear the forest whispering.

It's only the leaves stirring. He forced himself to believe.

They pressed on through the odd vegetation that grew in a rainbow of colors. Kale constantly had the sensation they were being watched, as though the forest itself knew they were there. The three covered ground quickly and Kale remained hopeful they would soon reach his destination.

"What in Pan's name is this place?" Kale whispered. He stopped dead in his tracks, eyeing the circular area before them.

"This does not look promising my friends," Thomas added.

They approached an array of twigs, dried wood, and small trees formed into standing figures with two arms and two legs. Instead of normal hands, they had long, claw-like fingers which looked as though they could rip a human's flesh with ease. Their height was intimidating, easily towering over Illadar.

Kale and his friends stood frozen in place as they stared toward the wooden statues. The figures did not move—they didn't shift nor make a sound. It was deathly silent as if no wind, animals, or other earthly inhabitants dared to come close.

"It's possible these have been created by someone, or some*thing,* living within the forest to ward off intruders. It would be wise to find another route." Thomas could sense a strong force, though he was too unsure if it came from the wooden statues to share this with his friends.

Kale and Illadar agreed without hesitation. There was something about the area that made them feel uneasy. Although the wood seemed to be lifeless, their appearance was taunting and caused the hair on Kale's arms to prickle up. As they turned to hike around the area, Kale could have sworn he heard his name being whispered. He quickly turned his head as he glanced over his shoulder toward the wood figures, yet nothing moved. They remained stationed in place—motionless and silent.

"Hmmm-hmmmm," Kale softly hummed to himself as he joined his friends. Something was definitely not right within the forest. He began to wonder if he truly had been tricked into a trap, but he also knew they couldn't give up yet.

As the morning passed, Kale began to notice that although quite dark and chilling, the forest was also very beautiful. He had never seen such a prismatic display of flora. The moss ranged from grey to a vibrant orange and plants he never knew existed grew in their surroundings. The terrain was unique in its own way, with new features around every turn.

Just as Kale began to grow an appreciation for the natural phenomena, the trees grew scarce. Soon, the men found themselves walking upon loose rocks in a near-barren area. Although there were no trees in the vicinity, the placement of large boulders seemed to conveniently shadow the area.

As before, everything was all too quiet. The only sound to be heard was the crunching of pebbles beneath their feet, amplified off the surrounding stone. By the time they approached a large, jagged stone that towered above their heads, Kale began to wonder if they should have gone in another direction. There was no plant life around—therefore, he knew his goal of finding *the tree which rained gold* was not going to be met in this area. Kale was about to return in the direction from where they had come when he caught sight of a bend ahead near the farthest wall of a massive stone valley.

"Maybe that path will lead us back into the woods," Kale stated as he led the way. He walked with a look of determination in his eyes as a black crow flew overhead. Kale couldn't help but wonder if it was the same bird he had seen at the camp and within Braxle. He shook the thought away, knowing there were much more important issues at hand. "Stay close." He motioned for

Illadar and Thomas to follow him down the intimidating valley of rock.

Although neither man complained, Kale could see his friends grew discouraged. They now seemed even farther from their destination than when they first arrived to the shadowy forest.

Please be here, Kale wishfully thought. He glanced up toward the tall bordering walls above their heads. In all reality, he had no idea what he was supposed to be looking for. His only notion was that it was going to be a unique tree—one that would stand out from the others. He debated whether it truly rained gold pieces, or if it had been used as a metaphor. Kale knew that either way, he had to keep his eyes focused and his will strong.

The stones on the ground increased in size as they continued down the path and soon they had to exert a great amount of stamina to press on.

Suddenly, Kale felt a strong tug on his tunic, causing him to stagger backwards.

"Wait!" Thomas sternly whispered.

Kale had been so focused on spotting the tree he hadn't noticed the large, dark cave entrance. His eyes lit up, "Do you think it belonged to one of the dragons?"

Before Thomas could respond, the low echo of howling could be heard ringing off the stone walls.

"Red beasts!" Kale and Illadar whispered in sync.

"I wonder if they know we are here..." Kale's voice was soft as he stood frozen in place.

"We must leave quickly, and with stealth. I assume they are not aware of our presence yet, but we must move as though they were. We cannot take any chances," Thomas insisted, silently turning to leave the area.

The three briskly returned down the path on which they had

come. They carefully stepped over each stone.

"Can't we fight them? Wouldn't it just be easier to get rid of them now? Then we can move forward without further worry." Kale whispered as they continued down their exit route. "They're only oversized dogs. With the three of us working together I'm sure we could handle them."

Illadar shook his head at Kale's ignorance, reconfirming his suspicions that Kale was still naive when it came to battle tactics. "It's not always standin' to fight that makes a man noble—but now is not the time for a lecture. Just know that we only saw a fraction of the red beasts. I've heard they come in massive numbers; and let's not forget their master still remains a mystery."

A loud thud, which sent tremors through the rocky ground, interrupted their conversation. They turned just in time to see a creature of considerable size leap down from atop a gigantic boulder. Its flesh was deep green with hints of grey. He stood much taller than Illadar and was incredibly muscular. The creature's jawbone was high-set and well defined, and his piercing orange eyes looked tauntingly vicious. Two ivory-colored teeth protruded from fat lips and looked as though they were short tusks. Straight black hair trailed down his back in a long, messy ponytail. To the creature's side was a huge morning star containing remnants of blood and meat on its massive spikes. He was no stranger to the weapon.

No sooner had Kale gripped his sword in preparation to fight the creature, than a chip of stone hit him on the top of his head. He glanced up to see dozens of snarling teeth angrily facing their direction. The red beasts had perched atop the bordering rocks— they were prepared to attack upon their master's command.

"Their master—is the orc!" Illadar whispered. "The old loon

from Mirion was telling the truth." He swallowed hard, knowing that orcs were not known to show mercy.

"Run." Thomas softly spoke.

"What?" Kale could not make out what he said.

"Run!" Thomas shouted, then pushed both Kale and Illadar in the opposite direction of the orc.

The large humanoid roared in fury as he slammed his weapon in the direction of Thomas.

"*Alaria!*" Thomas shouted while extending his arm toward the attack.

The spiked morning star slammed down upon an invisible force that protected Thomas from the blow. Thomas could see the intensity and speed of the orc's attack send a shock up the humanoid's arms—causing him to pause in confusion. Thomas took advantage of the moment. He ran to catch up with Kale and Illadar who had stopped to wait for him.

"Keep moving!" Thomas shouted as he approached where they stood.

The orc released a series of rhythmic grunts and Thomas could hear the pattering of paws behind him. The red beasts leapt down upon command and clustered around their master. Thomas glanced over his shoulder to ensure he had ample space between them. The ground surrounding the orc was now blanketed with red—there appeared to be over a hundred of them, trailing back as far as his eyes could see on the path. He knew it would only be a matter of seconds before they were at his heels. As Thomas continued to sprint away from the threat, the toe of his shoe caught beneath the edge of a stone. He collapsed onto his knees.

"Get him!" The orc bellowed.

Thomas felt a pair of hands grip him tightly in the pit of his arms, lifting him to his feet.

"Let's go!" Kale yelled as the red beasts advanced impetuously in their direction. The creatures dripped globs of mucus from their bodies as they ran, leaving a trail of secretion in their wake.

Thomas knew there was no way possible to outrun over a hundred red beasts; he needed to come up with a plan—quickly. Thomas suddenly stopped and turned to face the beasts.

Kale's eyes grew wide with horror as his friend halted. "Thomas!" He called out as he spun around.

"*Kruedia esonek!*" A ball of swirling flames shot from Thomas' palm, exploding upon impact against the wall of rock.

Chunks of stone immediately tumbled downward, piling upon one another and creating a barrier between them and the beasts.

"It won't keep them or the orc back for long. We must keep moving," Illadar spoke as he motioned for them to quickly follow.

They could hear the savage orc grunting as he and the red beasts began to climb over the rubble. As they fled, the whimpering squeals of red beasts could be heard from behind. It sounded as though something was attacking the canine monstrosities.

"Do you think we should see what's happening? Maybe someone has come to aid us," Kale panted.

"Keep runnin'! It could be a trap—don't be so naive, kid." Illadar shoved Kale forward, causing him to quicken his pace to avoid stumbling.

The colorful vegetation began to thicken as they made their way back into the jungle of trees. They could still hear the taunting howls from the beasts and knew it was imperative to keep pressing forward. The three aimlessly ran through the forest, losing all sense of direction. They had no hope at this point of remembering where they first entered the Forest of Forgotten Whispers.

Sweat poured down their faces as they continued to push their weary bodies.

"I hear water!" Kale stated hopefully. "It sounds louder than the stream barrier; I don't believe it is somewhere we have been before."

They hurried in the direction of the sound until coming upon a wide, shallow river.

"We can use the river to conceal our scent and hopefully lose those ugly red fiends," Illadar suggested.

Kale and Thomas thought the idea was brilliant and began to follow Illadar as they waded along with the river current. It felt cool and refreshing against their sore feet, despite the weighted sensation of water filling their shoes.

"Take a look at those." Kale pointed to a beautiful row of blue and pink flowers that stood out in contrast against the dark green surroundings. "I think we should continue through the forest here," Kale suggested.

Something about the delicate flower buds enticed him— almost as though the forest gave him a sign. "We've walked far enough and we are on the opposite side of the river. I doubt they will easily find us." He could see the glares of uncertainty from Thomas and Illadar as they silently followed. Kale swallowed hard, mumbling softly to Pan for strength to make it through the situation. Daylight was nearing its end and they would be at the mercy of the forest once dusk was upon them.

"Orcs are said to have exceptional vision in the dark," Thomas spoke as though he had read Kale's thoughts. "I do hope you are leading us in the correct direction. If not, I believe it's safe to say we are in for a rather rough night."

As they walked past rows of flowers, Kale's eyes lit up as he quickened his pace. "I see something!" He approached a thick mass of vines and immediately began to tug at a tangled clump to get a better view of what was beyond. A wide smile crossed his face, "I think this is it! I see a golden glow ahead!"

Relief swept over the three as they each peered through the thicket of vines. A massive tree—much taller than any they had ever seen—towered high above all else. Kale wondered how they had not noticed its leafy top when first heading toward the forest from Braxle. The bark wrapped around in an intertwined manner unlike any tree he had ever seen.

The trunk was so large that Kale, Thomas and Illadar could hold hands in an outstretched link and not even wrap around a third of its circumference. Kale could tell why it was given the name *the tree which rains gold*; tiny golden spheres which almost appeared dust-like gently floated around the tree. Each piece illuminated a yellow aura creating an illusion that the branches were raining down specks of gold. It was truly a mesmerizing sight.

"We have to get closer," Kale stated as he pulled firmly on the vines. They were tougher than he had assumed and did not budge. "Stand back, I'm going to cut through." He withdrew his sword from its sheath.

As the blade's edge tore through the tender intertwining green web, an ear piercing squeal rang out. It sounded as though it came directly from the vines. The green cluster began to twist and maneuver itself around until a thick vine shot out toward Kale. It smacked him hard against his cheek, causing him to stumble over his own feet and fall backward onto the ground as he gripped the side of his face angrily.

"What in Pan's name was that?!"

Before Kale had time to stand, the thick, and unusually strong, vines twisted and slid with amazing speed around the three men—trapping their limbs in an immobile position.

"Thomas, get us out of these!" Kale gritted his teeth as the vines constricted around his chest.

"I'm afraid my magic is no good here. I cannot decipher whether it is these vines blocking my magic, or the land itself. It appears as though we are at the mercy of the forest."

"Over my dead body!" Kale bit down, hard, into the vine, but to no avail. The vine retaliated by tightening firmly around his face so he could no longer move his jaw.

"There is no way I'm gonna' let a plant kill me!" Illadar thrashed in a useless attempt to break free.

Kale forced air into his lungs through his nose as he struggled to breathe. Suddenly, he saw the silhouette of many individuals who emerged from behind the incredibly large tree. As the figures moved closer he could see a group of women—very beautiful women. They each had long, silky hair which flowed to their waistline, gently swaying with each graceful step they took. Their skin appeared smooth and flawless—complimenting their alluring features. Their thick lashes, big round eyes, and pastel lips nearly distracted his attention from their short pointed ears which peeked out from between thick locks of hair—they were not human.

Each woman wore an outfit appearing as though it was growing on them. Their tops consisted of thin vines which traced their feminine curves, and greenery with flowers to cover their breasts. Their bottom skirts were in the same fashion and they wore no footwear. It was very apparent they lived within the forest. The females continued to approach the men in silence, a suppressed look of animosity within their eyes.

Kale wanted to speak, to find out who they were, but the

thick vine continued to tighten between his lips. Unsightly driblets of drool spilled down his chin.

"Ye dare to harm thy home?"

The group of women froze as they turned to the side, creating a clearing that revealed another, much taller woman. Kale was mesmerized by her lengthy, flowing white hair and skin so pale it almost appeared to glow. His focus had been so drawn by her unique features he almost didn't notice the hideous old lady who stood hunched over by her side. The aged woman had grotesquely large moles on her leathery, wrinkled skin. Her blue eyes glared into Kale's, and he could feel the hatred burning inside of her. A hissing sound escaped her toothless mouth through thin, cracked lips. If Kale had been able to move his facial muscles, he surely would have cringed at the sight. She had to be the ugliest woman he had ever seen.

"So, ye savages assume ye can come to thy land and take life without consequence?" The tall, silvery woman elegantly strode toward them. She wore lush, green shoulder garments which signified to them that she was held in higher ranking than the other women.

Neither man spoke as they struggled with the pain of the tightening vines.

"Release thy flesh, cocoons of evil souls," the tall woman spoke to the vines.

In an instant, the vines weaved and slithered their way loose, releasing the three men.

Kale immediately wiped the saliva from his chin, flexing his muscles to return the circulation to his tingling limbs. "I don't know who you all are, but you don't understand..."

Before Kale could continue, the old woman reached into a green pouch, pulling out a handful of brown powder.

"Sleep now." The tall, white-haired woman softly spoke.

As if on cue, the shabby old woman blew the powder from her palm into the unsuspecting faces of Kale, Thomas, and Illadar.

As the brown substance hit Kale's face, he heard the swooshing sound of something flying through the air. He was certain it was an arrow—someone had shot toward the group of women. Their amazing senses allowed them to move out of harm's way as the arrow struck the ground.

Who is attacking? Are they trying to save us? Why—can't I see properly? Kale's vision shifted in and out of focus and his mind spun. Through the mass of colors, he could vaguely see the cloaked figure that leapt down from a nearby branch. Though everything was foggy, he was certain it was the same individual who had been following him. As the figure gracefully landed upon the ground with bow drawn, the stalker's hood fell back upon their shoulders. Kale squinted, fighting against his impairment in an attempt to see what the person looked like.

The stalker turned to aim the bow directly toward the tall white-haired woman, and Kale—though his vision was blurred—knew exactly who had been following him. He instantly recognized the petite build, stringy brunette hair, and pointed ears.

Kale reached out longingly, trying to speak, yet his vocals would not work. He could no longer fight the overwhelming feeling of fatigue as his body crumpled to the floor. Kale's eyes slowly began to flutter until the effects of the powder consumed all his functions and everything went black. The one who had been travelling alongside him within the shadows—was Neelan.

CHAPTER 16

SHE LIVES

"Kale, wake up!" A female voice rang out.

Kale felt an uncomfortable finger repetitively pressing into the tender skin above his armpit. He groaned, running his hand along his forehead, which throbbed profusely. Kale parted his eyelids to see a bright-eyed Neelan staring down at him with a joyful look upon her face.

She smiled, placing a hand behind his back to help him into an upright position. "It took you long enough!" Neelan softly laughed.

Kale could already see she hadn't changed a bit and was still her usual spunky self—yet he was glad to see her.

Neelan bit her lower lip, shifting her eyes nervously, before finally lunging herself toward Kale, pulling him into a tight embrace. Kale kept his arms loosely hung at his sides, dumbstruck by her sudden behavior. It wasn't long before she picked up on his lack of response, pulling back to allow space between them.

"You," she fought for the right words to say, "looked like you needed a hug." Beneath her shaggy bangs, her violet eyes dodged his as she turned to hide her ruby cheeks.

Kale could hear Thomas and Illadar laughing, and relief swept over him as the memory of what had happened returned. "You're both all right?"

"Indeed we are." Thomas smiled. "And I must say, you should try some of this honeydew berry mixture—it's refreshingly tasty." He took a long sip out of a wooden mug.

Now that Kale was sure his friends were safe, his focus returned to Neelan, who remained silent by his side. He inspected her garments, confirming his earlier assumptions it was she who had been following him.

"Why?" Kale questioned.

She glanced up in confusion. "Why what?" Her dark eyebrow tilted upward.

"Why have you been following me for so long? And why have you been doing so in secrecy? Do you desire something I have?" Kale placed his hand securely over his pocket where the bracelet snugly rest. "If so, I am afraid it will only lead you to an inevitable demise."

"I hope you are aware that you're a real idiot, Kale." Neelan looked down, hurt by his accusation.

"Kale," Thomas cut in, "you should mind your manners. You've yet to allow the young lady to explain herself."

Kale could also hear Illadar mumbling something about being an insensitive jerk. *Him, of all people,* Kale thought to himself.

"I just," Neelan sighed, "wanted to make sure you were all right, that's all. You didn't need to be so cruel; I was only trying to care about your well-being. At this point, I honestly cannot understand why I was such a fool as to return to a person like you." She stood, storming out of the circular room where they sat.

Thomas shook his head. "If you only knew what that young elf has gone through to ensure your safety—you'd think twice before opening that mouth of yours."

"How would you know what she's been through? She's stalked me since Braxle without a word—I'm sure there is an ulterior motive behind her actions." Kale crossed his arms in frustration.

"Is it so difficult for you to believe someone truly values you, Kale? While you were still recovering from the poisons, Illadar and I had the opportunity to speak with her. We've also been introduced to some very interesting individuals whom I think you are going to want to meet." He smiled. "But first, I believe it would be most wise to apologize to Neelan. She cares a great deal about you—you are the first friend she's had since she was a child."

"You would also be long dead had it not been for her. Be grateful." A young woman appeared within an arched opening across from where Kale sat.

Kale's mouth hung open. He wasn't sure if he had gone insane, or if it was possible he had adapted to being a human—sharing their emotions. His body felt warm upon glancing at the unknown woman. Her beauty was unparalleled; there was a sense of overwhelming feminine allure as she entered the circular room. Her wavy golden locks rested upon white shoulder pads that swooped upward. Kale gazed along her body, taking note of her white top and matching leggings. Upon her feet were superior quality black leather boots laced up to her knees. *I wonder if she is a warrior of some sort.* Kale knew no peasant could afford such lavish garments.

"My word—it cannot be!" Thomas broke the momentary silence, walking briskly across the room with Illadar at his heels to where the woman stood. They both appeared astonished by her entrance.

"Is that you, Thomas?" She stared as her fingers rested upon her mouth, which gaped open in surprise.

"Indeed. I cannot believe it's really you, Judith. We all thought you to be dead."

"Princess." Illadar knelt before her. "General Jedah has told your fath—"

"Jedah..." She clenched a tight fist.

"Can someone please tell me what is going on here?" Kale couldn't contain his curiosity any longer.

"This is the Princess of Mirion, and her father is King Valamar." Thomas explained. "We all assumed her to be dead after the announcement given by General Jedah. He told the King she had been viciously attacked by a dragon and their entire race posed a threat on the world. Thus, King Valamar accepted Jedah's proposal to begin war upon all dragon kind."

"Please, Princess, you've gotta' tell us what's happened with Jedah. I'm sure after your father found you to be alive, many things have since changed." Illadar stood from his lowered position.

Judith looked to the toes of her boots. "That's the problem, you see—he doesn't know." She sighed, "I love my father dearly, but he is a fool. Jedah has manipulated him from the beginning. I continuously warned him not to trust that demon of a man, yet he only saw a brave and trustworthy knight. He always scolded me to behave myself and to not judge others with such negativity." Her blue eyes narrowed.

"Jedah knew I despised him and saw me as a threat to his

plans. There was always something within me that knew he was interested solely in self benefit. Through my ignorant father, Jedah would alter situations so he could control the outcome." Judith leaned her body against the wall as she stared blankly.

"It was a warm spring day when my father told me I was traveling to Albane to meet with their Lord and present a diplomatic treaty. Unlike other diplomacies in the past, this was to be done in person by a member of high royalty. My father wanted to go in my place, but knew he could not abandon the throne when so much needed to be done within Mirion. He soon informed me that Jedah, along with a small group of his best warriors, would be escorting me to ensure my safety. I'm sure you could imagine my overwhelming joy," Judith huffed angrily as she spoke in a sarcastic tone.

"I knew he disliked me, but never did I imagine he would go as far as he did. Instead of escorting me to Albane, he restrained me once we were out of our territory. They forced me here within the forest where a dark elf that obeys his every command placed a horrid curse upon me. The elf goes by the name of Malakhar— and though a peon to Jedah's army—he is a very dangerous individual when given the opportunity to come in contact with another being."

Judith began to choke up as she spoke, causing her voice to crack. "Jedah obviously could not risk me returning to my father—and for some reason he did not want me dead. I can only assume his intention was to use me as a bargaining pawn when he felt his power had grown strong enough to overtake the kingdom. He commanded Malakhar to ensure I could not leave the Forest of Forgotten Whispers without turning to ash. To make the situation even worse, the curse transformed me into a disgusting old woman. The women here were kind enough to grant me temporary relief from the transformation while within this tree. It was the best they could do against such a powerful curse."

"That *thing* was you?!" Kale blurted out in shock. He could not believe such a hideous old woman could truly be this beautiful Princess.

Her face reddened with embarrassment. "Yes, I would prefer you not bring it up again—it was certainly not my choice."

She's even radiant while upset. I wonder if she is the reason I was sent here, Kale pondered.

"Princess Judith, with all due respect, couldn't we help you send a message to King Valamar?" Illadar questioned. "If he knew of your situation, then he could send help and remove Jedah's authority. Though, I'll admit, I'd love to have his head fall by my blade—I'd support any means of riddin' the world of that abomination."

"Do you truly think I have not thought of such things? I've spent over three long years pondering every possible solution. Although Jedah is a brute, he is very intelligent. Whatever cure there may be for me lies with Malakhar." Judith crossed her arms, sighing heavily. "Should I even attempt to contact my father at this time, Jedah would ensure that Malakhar was sent far from Mirion, leaving me stuck in a withered body—unable to leave this forest until the day I die."

"Could your father not send those he is certain to trust here to confirm the message? Then they could report back that you truly have been placed under a curse," Thomas suggested.

"If only it were so simple. Any member of the royal army to disrupt Jedah's plan for power would surely be persuaded into telling lies to my father—or killed. Jedah has a way to ensure *accidents* happen to those who disobey him, or interfere with his goals."

"We must find a way to rectify this situation. It is vital we conjure a means of returning you to your father before Jedah obtains too much power." Thomas ran his fingers along his grey beard. "If only I could teleport myself close enough to the royal castle to make it to the King." He sighed. "However, I know this is not a feasible option. I am certain I would be spotted and captured instantly; there are far too many guards within the kingdom for me to risk such a feat. It would be a foolish attempt and we must choose our actions wisely, if we intend to succeed."

"Is Malakhar the man cloaked in black?" Illadar questioned.

"Yes, he is," Judith replied. "I have honestly never seen what he looks like—he cowers behind his attire."

"Maybe we could find him," Kale suggested. "He has crossed paths with us once before, so it's quite possible he is still seeking both myself and Illadar."

Judith glanced toward Kale in surprise. "You—"

"Jedah wanted to eliminate all dragons from this world because of his own hurt pride. He initiated a war over something which never happened. Here you stand before me, living and well." Kale unintentionally interrupted the Princess. His blood boiled at the thought of Jedah and the strife he had caused.

"Trust me, I know this. I could not believe my father would agree to such a war. Regardless of my wellbeing, it was a terrible thing to do. I do not feel that all dragons had to be slain over such an occurrence—fictitious or not. I just wish I could have lifted this curse in time to stop it all." She looked forward sadly.

Kale's insides felt fluttery. She was both beautiful and sensitive toward dragon-kind. "It's not your fault," Kale attempted to reassure her. Kale's mind was set, he was going to try and help Judith.

"I see thou hast awoken." The tall, pale woman appeared

behind Judith. Her long, white hair gently brushed against the back of her knees as she took a step forward.

Kale could now see how tall the woman was in comparison to Judith. Her height was too grand to be human, and her appearance was unlike Neelan's, which left Kale baffled. The woman's ears, though pointed, were not nearly as slender or long as Neelan's.

"Come, boy." The woman held out a long, pale arm.

"Where are we going?" Kale felt nervous and confused as to why she called solely upon him.

"I request thee to speak outside."

Kale's chest tightened. "Is that really such a good idea? What about the red beasts? We encountered them earlier, along with a savage orc, and they may still be on the hunt for our scent."

"Ye orc, Rees'Lok, nor his beasts may enter thy ground. Tis a treaty in place for centuries. Should he disobey what hath been written—we shalt kill him." Her tone was so casual it sent shivers down Kale's spine. She seemed to have no fear of the monstrosities within the forest.

"Have you no manners? This is Elanya's home, do as she requests. I assure you, it's safe to trust her." Judith scolded Kale, who was still seated.

"Fine, I'll come with you." The last thing Kale wanted in the already tense situation was to upset Judith—or Elanya, who seemed mysteriously powerful.

~~~~~~~~~~~~~~~

Although the sky was painted by darkness, Kale could easily see his surroundings as they emerged outside. The luminescent golden specks floated around the tree as though they were drawn to its life force.

"So," Kale wanted to end the awkward silence, "you live inside this tree?"

"Tis true in a sense. Ye tree is thy home, but also thy source of life itself. I call thy tree, Orea."

Kale stared toward her blankly, unsure as to what she meant. Nothing seemed to make sense in his whirlwind of a life.

Elanya took notice of Kale's expression. "I shalt explain." She extended her arm, which resembled the pallid tone of the moon. "Thy body thee sees is but a solid illusion of thy true self."

Kale watched in astonishment as the flesh on her arm cracked, quickly exploding into thousands of tiny specks that fluttered in a circular motion around the area where her limb once was.

Elanya closed her diamond-like eyes, concentrating as the small pieces bonded back together to recreate her arm. "Tis dryads we are—not human, nor elf as thou assumed." She watched as Kale glanced away in embarrassment. Elanya had read his thoughts. "We hast been brought into ye world as energy and hast chosen this form to live as guardians of ye forest. Every dryad arrives to ye world within a single seed. As ye seed sprouts life, we are born. We are one with ye tree which giveth us life. Should destruction befall ye tree, ye dryad bound to it shalt perish."

Another young woman approached them, silently handing Kale a mug filled with red liquid. Kale glanced up toward the auburn-haired woman who also had the same distinct pointed ears as Elanya.

"Is she also—what you are?"

Elanya smiled for the first time, revealing a perfect set of white teeth. "Thou art correct. She too is a dryad."

The young woman appeared bashful, hiding her face beneath

her spiraling curls before hurrying back to the tree.

Once she was gone, Elanya returned focus toward Kale as she swept her long white hair behind an ear.

Kale could clearly see her rather interesting features. Her thin, white eyebrows gave a frosty appearance to her nearly transparent, light grey eyes.

"Now ye time hath come to discuss thee. I can sense thou hast a life aura unlike other humans." Her eyes locked with his "Thou art not human."

Kale's eyes grew wide. He hadn't even been with them an entire day and yet his secret was already revealed. Elanya's power was amazing.

"I desire to know what thou true self is."

Kale sighed. He knew that he must confess the truth to Elanya; yet he hoped she would not tell Judith or the others. He still had extreme difficulties trusting others and didn't want to be judged by what he was—or was not. Kale hesitantly explained everything to her while she sat in silence as if absorbing his words into her mind.

"I hast a request for thee," She spoke, surprisingly calm after many uncomfortable moments had passed. "Kale Firehart, thou must help restore Judith to her former state. Ye foul Jedah mustn't succeed with his treachery. No human hath come to thine land since her arrival and I am certain none shalt again for many moons. Hope lies with thee."

Kale nodded. "What do you want me to do? I want to stop General Jedah at all costs."

"Thou must travel to ye elven kingdom, Tyrione, which lie to ye north. Thou will require assistance from ye little elven one, Neelan. Only thou—Kale, can persuade her to return. Thee, not of elven blood, cannot enter ye city without an escort. Once there, thou must seek an old elf by ye name of Brig. Tis a dark elf who devotes his life to good. He is wise beyond most and can assist with removing ye curse." She paused, placing a firm hand onto Kale's shoulder. "Thou mustn't let Judith know, for I cannot say whether the outcome shalt be a success. I dare not break her sorrow-filled heart with false hope. Since ye day we rescued her from ye dangers of this forest, she hath dreamt of returning home."

"I understand." Kale glanced up at Elanya. "I have a request for you, as well."

"Speak."

"I would prefer if you keep what you have learned about me between us. Only my comrades are aware—and now, you, as well. The consequences could be great for me if word ever traveled back to Jedah of my whereabouts."

Elanya held her hand up toward Kale's mouth to hush him. "Unfortunate." She walked toward the entrance hole of the tree. "It appears I was distracted by thy words to you and did not sense ye presence which hath joined us tonight." She glanced over her shoulder. "Thou should look to ye stars." She smiled mischievously before leaving him.

What? Kale wrinkled his forehead as he glanced up at the towering branches. "Neelan!" His jaw dropped, watching as the hooded, cloaked figure huddled against a cluster of leaves. He knew something needed to be said. "Neelan, I *can* see you. Why are you still stalking me? Come down here."

Neelan leapt down as her layered skirt fluttered outward. She silently landed on the ground beside Kale with ease. Her agility was amazing. Kale could immediately see the glare in her glassy, violet eyes. She had been crying.

"I'm sorry." Kale finally had the opportunity to apologize for his earlier behavior. "I didn't intend to hurt your feelings." He felt uncomfortable as she continued to silently stare intently into his eyes. "I said I was sorry." Suddenly, it hit him—she must have heard everything he said to Elanya.

Without warning, Neelan threw her weight against him, wrapping her arms tightly around his body. "It doesn't bother me. I don't care that you aren't human; I just wish you had told me before. I told you everything—as hard as it was." She shook her head. "It doesn't matter now. I just want you to know I'll always be here for you, should you need me." She withdrew her body from his, once again looking deep into his bright blue eyes. "I never thought I'd return to my homeland. I've fought for so long to escape; but I'll go—for you."

Kale's eyes grew wide. Neelan's words meant so much to him and all his previous concerns with her melted away. He now knew she truly did care for him; she accepted him for all he was. Relief swept over him and he did something he never tried before this moment. His arms reached out, forcing Neelan's body against his—returning her embrace. "Thank you," he whispered.

"Am I interrupting?" Judith stood in the entrance of the tree, keeping her feet on the interior floor.

Kale felt his chest tighten as he nudged Neelan from him. "N-no." He stammered in embarrassment. "I was just saying thank you to my friend." He forced an awkward smile.

"Friend..." Neelan softly mumbled under her breath as she glanced down.

"Would you care to join me, Kale? I would like to show you something."

"I'd love to." Kale boyishly smiled. He couldn't understand what it was about Judith that made him behave so differently while in her presence.

"Your friend Neelan may join us also. Please, follow me."

Neelan reluctantly followed as they walked behind Judith, who led them to a spiraling staircase within the tree. Though the tree was massive in outward appearance, it felt even larger from the inside. As they circled toward the top, Kale could hear the wheezing sounds of wind. The three walked through a small hole that caused both Kale and Judith to duck. Kale found it amusing that due to Neelan's petite build, she was able to walk beneath with ease. He couldn't help but wonder how Elanya could possibly fit through such a tight opening.

The refreshing breeze caressed Kale's cheeks, inviting him beneath the open sky which was heavily sprinkled with vibrant twinkling stars. They now stood at the top of the tree on a wide sturdy branch. The leaves were parted to allow a breathtaking view of the surrounding land. Kale could see the vast canopy of treetops and a faint speckle in the distance that he knew was Braxle. The sight reminded him of what it had been like to fly above the forest as a dragon—carefree and on top of the world.

"This is a magnificent spot, Judith," Kale stated. "Thank you for sharing it with us."

Judith chuckled. "You are too kind, but my intention was not to show you the sights of this land, but to speak privately—without interruption." She boldly sat upon the edge of the large branch, dangling her legs over the side. She inhaled deeply as she closed her eyes. "It feels so good to be up here. This is the only place where I can enjoy the fresh air as my true self."

Kale carefully walked across the branch to sit beside her while Neelan distantly positioned herself behind them.

"What was it you wanted to tell us?" Kale pressed the subject curiously.

"Yes, I apologize; sometimes when I am up here I get lost in thought. I have a request for you, Kale."

Not again. Why me? Kale blankly stared at her, waiting to hear what she could possibly want.

"Should things not go as I hope and I'm forced to remain this way, I need you to promise me you will seek Jedah, and stop him at all costs. Should he obtain power above my father, it will be tragic for Ravondore. Since I have been here, Jedah has wreaked havoc across the continent. Children have been used as meat pawns—brutally murdered if their parents do not obey the general's every request. Women have been unwillingly bedded by he, and his closest men. Those who dare to disobey—or threaten to tell my father of Jedah's deeds—have met an agonizing and torturous death. He must be stopped, Kale; the people are suffering."

"It's far too dangerous for Kale." Neelan jumped into the conversation. "And besides, how do you know all this information, *Princess,* if you've been stuck here within the Forest of Forgotten Whispers?" She couldn't help but feel jealous toward Judith.

"Nature is amazing. From birds to trees, we have many ways of acquiring information of the outside world."

Kale wasn't sure what Judith meant, but after such a long day he had no intention of asking.

"It's all right Neelan." Kale glanced outward. "I need to accept this request—not only for Ravondore, but for myself as well. It's the reason I have trained so hard. Jedah took so much from me, and those I care for."

"Thank you, Kale. I knew from the moment I saw you it was fate that brought you here, to us."

I don't know if I'd call it fate—but someone, for some reason led me here.

Judith smiled at Kale, gazing toward him with her blue eyes locked onto his as she leaned in and pressed her lips gently to his.

Kale's eyes widened with surprise—it was his first kiss. It was soft and warm, sending a tingling sensation down his body.

Suddenly, a soft whimper interrupted the moment, breaking through the silence. Kale quickly pulled from Judith, glancing over his shoulder. Neelan was gone.

CHAPTER 17

REES'LOK

"My apologies," Judith exhaled, "I did not intend for anyone to be hurt by my actions." She glanced off toward the distant land.

"It's all right." Kale's cheeks were noticeably red. "I do need to find Neelan though—please, excuse me." He hurried inside to the main room where he originally awoke. Thomas and Illadar were feasting happily, accompanied by four, beautiful, dryad women.

"There you are!" Thomas chimed as he caught sight of Kale.

Kale was pleased to see him looking so cheerful. It had been awhile since he'd seen Thomas so joyous, which made him smile at the sight.

"I'm glad you're back." Thomas continued. Come celebrate with us!" He had a slight slur as he spoke.

"What exactly are you celebrating?" Kale raised an eyebrow.

"The Princess, of course! Finding her alive and uninjured is wonderful news. You have no idea of the hope this brings." Thomas took another slurping sip from his wooden mug, releasing a loud burp—something Kale never heard him do before. "Jumping balt toads! Excuse me!"

They all laughed as Thomas flushed with embarrassment.

"I'm actually looking for Neelan at the moment, so I'll have to join you a bit later. Have you seen her?"

"I think she went that way." Illadar pointed. "She seemed in a hurry and didn't say much. Is everything all right?"

Kale nodded hesitantly, "Y-yeah, I just need to speak with her." He quickly left in the direction Illadar gestured before they could further question him. The last thing Kale wanted was to reveal he had just kissed the Princess of Mirion.

"Neelan?" Kale quietly spoke as he entered a dark room. It took a few moments before his eyes adjusted enough to make out the silhouettes of large baskets which hung down from the tall ceiling.

As he walked closer, he could see they were woven hammocks made from long palm leaves. *This must be the room where Judith and Elanya sleep.* Kale turned to leave, under the assumption he had found an empty room, but a faint noise at the opposite side caught his attention.

"Hello?" he whispered, slowly approaching where the sound originated. "I can hear you." Kale could definitely distinguish the sound of breathing, though he still could not see who was in the room. He inched closer toward one of the dangling hammocks which slightly shifted. "Please say something, I know you're there." His fingers slid over the edge of the basket-like bed as he rose up upon his toes to look inside.

Relief swept over him when he recognized the long stringy hair belonging to Neelan. She was nestled in a fetal position within her cloak. Kale smiled down at her. *She's cute when she isn't running her mouth,* he thought with a chuckle. Kale gently grazed a hand upon her face as he brushed a lock of her hair from her lips.

"Goodnight, Neelan," he whispered.

~~~~~~~~~~~~~~~

Kale woke in the common room the next morning to the sounds of his friends conversing. He could smell the sweet scent of fruit nearby as he eagerly rose, rubbing his stomach. *I'm starving,* he thought hungrily. Kale enjoyed a hearty buffet of the juiciest and most gratifying fruits he had ever tasted, when Thomas approached his side.

"Good morning, Kale." Thomas chimed in, "I must say, this is quite luxurious compared to our previous camp. Who could have imagined such a gem rested within the center of a dark and dangerous forest?" His tone suddenly dropped as his words grew serious. "I've spoken to Elanya about embarking to Tyrione. It would be wise for us to leave today—there is no time to waste. Each passing day, Jedah is destroying the lives of many while growing more powerful. Illadar and I are already prepared to depart. Lifting the curse on Judith will play a vital role in ending the general's reign."

"I need to find Neelan first," Kale stated after swallowing a mouthful of yellow berries.

"She's already waitin' outside for our departure." Illadar slung his pack over his shoulder.

"Do either of you have any idea how long it will take on foot to arrive at Tyrione?" Kale questioned from within the arched entryway.

Thomas pulled his shoes onto his feet. "It's been many decades since I've traveled near that region; however I would estimate it will take a few weeks—possibly a couple of months or so."

"More than a month?! That's far too long; we cannot spend months on our journey while Jedah sends his men to ravage towns in search of us. If Jedah truly is increasing his authority by the day and tormenting the lives of the innocent, we must find a way to travel with haste," Kale huffed heavily as he paced in a small circular motion.

Thomas laughed as he approached Kale. "Dear boy, you are traveling alongside a sorcerer." He smiled proudly, "I will get us there—we will arrive with time to spare before nightfall."

Kale felt a weight lift as relief swept over him. "Thank you, Thomas. Since Neelan is already outside, I'm going to bid farewell to Judith before we leave. I'll meet you shortly."

Kale had a hunch where he would find her. He made his way up what felt like an endless amount of spiraling steps. Finally, he arrived at the branch, winded, but glad to see both Elanya and Judith seated near the ledge. Even with the sun's bright rays of light shining down upon Elanya, her pallid appearance seemed frost-like, and devoid of color.

"Good morning, Kale." Judith greeted him with a smile that appeared oblivious to the previous night's occurrence between them.

"Hello, Princess," He said while attempting to casually look away in order to conceal his reddened cheeks.

"Please call me Judith. I do not care for such formalities among friends."

There's that breathtaking smile again. How does she do this to me? Kale's body once again felt warm and his fingers fumbled nervously. "I wanted to say goodbye." He quickly spoke in hope of suppressing the tension he felt. "We are leaving today." Kale caught Elanya's stern glance as if to caution him not to reveal their plan. "We have some business to handle."

Judith gazed outward.

Kale could sense her disheartened emotions by the look upon her face. "I will come back for you, Judith, I promise." He wanted to comfort her. "Myself, Thomas, Illadar—even Neelan, we're your friends now. We aren't going to leave you behind."

She forced a smile and Kale knew she doubted his words. Judith had unwillingly been forced to live with her curse and over time grew to accept the fact that no one would have the ability to rescue her.

"Thou must leave while ye sky remains bright," Elanya urged his departure.

"I understand." He paused before turning to leave. "Thank you for all your kindness, it won't be forgotten." Kale waved as he stepped through the hole.

"Kale..." Judith spoke so softly Kale nearly missed it.

"Yes?"

"Take care of her. She behaves as though she is strong, but I can tell she's really quite fragile—she needs you."

Kale's confusion by her statement was quickly resolved as he followed Judith's gaze far below. Through the thicket of branches he could distinguish the figure of Neelan, who stood alone with her shoulder resting against the tree.

Kale smiled. "I will, Judith, you can count on it." And with that, he left to join his friends.

"I must know if you are willing to take an extreme risk." Thomas nervously spoke which in turn made the others uneasy as well.

"What exactly do you mean by *risk*?" Kale was certainly not about to agree to something when he was uninformed of the circumstances.

"You see," Thomas said as he fingered at his beard as he often did while thinking, "teleporting us to the elven city, Tyrione, is the only way for us to save many weeks worth of traveling. Even by horseback, I would assume the journey to take a month at the least. I believe it is our only logical option to conserve time."

"All right, now explain to us why it poses such a risk."

"I have never actually attempted to teleport more than just myself. To be quite honest, I'm unsure if it will work properly or what the consequences may be. So again, I ask—are you willing to take the risk?"

"I'm always up for an adventure," Illadar replied with his usual fearless attitude.

Neelan rolled her eyes. "I would hardly call allowing unknown magic to be cast upon oneself an *adventure*. The chance of being split into millions of particles isn't my top choice." She gave Kale a quick glance, "But I'll do it. So count me in as well."

"You know my answer is yes, so, let's get going." Kale replied.

"All right, first we must leave the enchanted ground as I cannot cast my magic here. We need to make way for the river we crossed yesterday. Take heed and move quietly; we do not need to attract the orc or his red beasts."

Neelan sniffed the air. "I do not smell them nearby at the moment. However, he is correct. We must take caution not to draw unnecessary attention to ourselves. I have heard stories of the orc called Rees'lok. He is even shunned by his own tribe."

"His own tribe?" Kale scratched his head.

"Yes, Rees'lok once lived among a tribe of orcs to the far south. As the story has it, he was more barbaric than all the others and longed for nothing more than to kill. One night he went into a mad frenzy and began slaughtering those who lived within his own tribe. He held no remorse, and even seemed to enjoy each deadly swing he took. By the next morning, he was gone. No one knew of his whereabouts, until about a decade ago when wondering travelers would accidentally venture into the Forest of Forgotten Whispers."

"Wait a moment. If he was not born onto this land, isn't he able to leave? Why does he remain here?" Kale couldn't understand the reasoning behind it all. "I mean, if he is so hell-bent on destruction, you would think he'd desire to unleash his fury on the entire continent."

"I do not know. Maybe he has chosen to stay by the side of his beasts. But that is only my assumption." Neelan continued to look ahead as they walked.

They trekked through the forest, passing the thicket of vines which now conveniently slithered aside to allow them passage. *I wonder if they work as a barrier to keep out intruders.* Kale thought while continuing through the array of vibrant flowers.

Neelan took a quick whiff of air. "We are still safe from the beast, for now."

"Neelan, I have a question for you." Kale's mind was drifting through a series of thoughts.

"Yes? What do you want?"

"How did you expect to smell the red beasts when I can neither see nor hear a threat nearby? They would be much too far to pick up their scent."

"Have you forgotten I am an elf? I want to ensure they are not scouting the forest for prey nearby. Our senses are heightened from that of a human." She crossed her arms, "It's one of the only good things about our race."

"My senses are more sensitive than humans as well." Kale smiled proudly. "Though not nearly as good as yours, in *this* body."

Illadar coughed. "Hey, you two, there *are* normal humans here ya' know. How about not rubbin' in your extraordinary abilities while in the presence of us *common folk*."

They all laughed as they continued on their path.

"So, are you and Malakhar the same race? I mean, you are both elves, right?" Kale wanted to know more about the man in black—and Neelan.

"I do hope you are making a joke. I cannot fathom anyone truly being so ignorant." It was obvious Neelan was insulted. "He is a *dark* elf, the worst kind of filthy creatures, really. There is the exception of a few good ones, but most are horrid. Within Tyrione, the kingdom of high elves, there are a small group of *them* whom now reside with us. Most, however, are forbidden to enter our kingdom because of their use of the forbidden magic known as Drell."

"Did you know Malakhar?" Kale continued to press the subject.

"No, I haven't a clue who he is; but I'm certain the council will. We will need permission from them to visit Brig. Outsiders are not welcome to walk the streets within the kingdom unless granted approval. Tyrione remains locked away from the rest of the world—it's truly a shame..." Her voice trailed.

"I am afraid this enlightening conversation about elves will have to halt for the moment." Thomas motioned toward the river directly in front of where they stood. Kale had been so engrossed speaking to Neelan he hadn't noticed the sound of trickling water.

"We should use these stones to cross; it will keep our clothing dry." Neelan led the way as she gracefully leapt from one stone to the next.

Thomas and Illadar followed, making their way across with ease. Kale was the last to cross as he cautiously stepped onto the first couple of stones. His feet wobbled and he struggled to keep balance. *Come on—you can do this. There is only a couple more to go.* Kale extended his arms out as he lifted his foot, moving toward the next stone.

"It's amazing, Kale, I think an old man could have crossed faster than you." Neelan's laughter stopped short as she bit her tongue, glancing toward Thomas. "Oh, sorry—although, it does prove my point."

"Ugh!" Kale lost his balance, causing his foot to slip into the cool water. "Neelan!" He growled, "Why did you have to distract me? Couldn't you see that I was—"

"Hurry, kid!" Illadar extended his arm, pulling Kale to dry ground. Nearby, within the forest, they could hear the all-too-familiar sound of howling. "Those ruthless monsters have been waitin' alongside the riverbed for us! They must've been campin' in the place where we first entered the river downstream." Illadar shot a glance toward Thomas. "We've gotta' go!"

"All right, I do hope this works out." Thomas extended his arms. "Everyone, please grab hold, and absolutely do not let go."

"Hurry, Thomas—I smell something foul within the air," Neelan quickly spoke.

They heard the sound of persistent battering upon the ground. Something was closing in on them, quickly.

"Tear them apart!" A deep booming voice yelled.

"Rees'Lok!" Neelan cried out. "He is coming, please get us out of here." She tightened her grip on Thomas.

Within seconds, the large orc tore through the nearby brush, surrounded by oozing red beasts. His orange, fiery eyes burned with a savage desire to destroy them.

Thomas closed his eyes, parting his lips, "*Kalora Xenari.*"

Rees'Lok quickly closed the distance between them as he violently swung his morning star toward the four. The massive spikes swooshed forward with a thirst for their blood. The weapon closed in mere inches from where they stood.

Kale swallowed hard.

As Rees'lok staggered forward from the force of his blow, the orc growled out in anger—he hit nothing more than air. They had vanished.

CHAPTER 18

THE ELDERS

Everything went black and the heavy pressure that weighed upon Kale made his chest ache. The gravitational pull was completely astray and gave the sensation of being forcefully tugged from multiple directions. Then, without warning, sunlight hit Kale's face as he and the others were flung in separate directions onto a grassy hill. Kale gripped his stomach which churned terribly as he glanced over to see Illadar kneeled over, vomiting profusely. Kale groaned and rolled onto his back.

"My apologies, I should have mentioned the nauseating side effects of teleportation. I have utilized this method of transport for so many years the thought did not cross my mind." Thomas glanced down at his friends sympathetically, before noticing his own reaction to the spell. The veins near his knuckles were slightly tinged with a blackened color and he knew transporting so many individuals at once had used up more strength than he expected.

"At least, we all made it here in one piece." Neelan staggered to her feet as she withdrew her bow and inspected it for damage. She seemed to be the least affected by the sickening sensation out of the three. After confirming her bow was still in flawless condition, she released a deep sigh of relief. "Thomas," she glanced up in concern, "why did you bring us here? We are an hour away from the Kingdom of Tyrione."

Kale and Illadar gazed up bearing looks of disappointment.

"Sadly, my powers are limited to places I have been to or seen. I once travelled to this location as a young man while on a training mission for spell-casters. We were en route to the quaint city of Perun, which lies north of Braxle, along the coast."

They took a few more minutes to regain themselves before beginning their journey toward the elven kingdom. The terrain was unlevel with many hills, forcing them to strenuously work their legs with each climb and descent. As they drew closer, Kale sensed the tension growing within Neelan.

"It will be all right, Neelan." Kale wanted to ease her nerves. He understood this was a difficult time for her and returning to her homeland was the last thing she ever wanted to do again.

She said nothing, but continued walking in silence as she crossed her arms tightly around her body.

"Can you tell me more about the dark elves? I would like to know more about our opponent." Kale made another attempt to break the uncomfortable atmosphere between them.

More silence followed before Neelan finally sighed, giving in to his request. "I've told you before that only a small amount of dark elves have been accepted to live within Tyrione. They are rarities among their kind who have chosen to leave behind their roots of chaos and the forbidden magic—Drell. Though the council wanted to be diplomatic and granted them approval to live within the kingdom, the dark elves are still carefully monitored and not trusted—though this accusation will always be denied. I know the truth; I've seen it with my own two eyes. There has been an age-old rivalry between the dark and high elves, though, it was long before my time, and I know little about the reasoning. The dark elves I have encountered within the kingdom seem fairly normal to me, although they appear to be closed off from interaction with many of the high elves—it's as if they are still frightened that one day we will suddenly turn on them all. Nearly all the dark elves have settled into the Catalythe district of the kingdom. It's a dark, overshadowed section near the rear of Tyrione. My impression, from what I have seen, is they prefer to be where there is minimal sunlight."

"Where do the dark elves come from? And why do they behave so differently from high elves?" Kale's hunger to obtain more knowledge about the elves continued to increase.

"You sure ask a lot of questions." Neelan shook her head. "Honestly, I only know what I've heard in stories told by elders at the summer festival. They say the dark elves dwell upon the island called Necron."

Thomas' eyes widened. "I have heard many foul things of that island. It's a place of death and darkness. Though, I have never dared to step foot on its cursed soil, I have been close enough to hope I never return near again."

"How?" Both Kale and Neelan spoke simultaneously.

"It was another of our many training excursions. We set sail to the frozen continent Sundra in order to master the art of conjuring flame while amidst extreme incompatible conditions. A dear friend of mine, and fellow student, saw something from our boat which must have been of great interest on the shores of Necron. Although, we warned him to stay, he seemed crazed and commanded us to stay back or risk being obliterated by his magic." Thomas sighed. "Something had happened to my friend—it was as though he became an entirely different person. He certainly wasn't the soft spoken, kind-hearted individual who had left Ravondore." Thomas rubbed his hands together as he solemnly spoke.

"The training was intended for senior students who were already experienced and trustworthy with the usage of magic—thus, no master spell-caster had come to supervise us. We were being monitored by a direct apprentice in his final years of schooling; he was to score each of us on our performance." Thomas cleared his throat. "As I was saying, we were so stunned by my dear friend's behavior that not a single one of us thought to use our magical abilities to restrain him, not even the direct apprentice, who seemed to buckle under tension. My irrational thinking and lack of judgment on that day is something I will regret until the end of my life." He exhaled. "Before reality sunk in for any of us, my friend teleported off our vessel and onto the shore of Necron, which was completely veiled in shadows. We sat impatiently and waited for him to return; each of us too frightened to venture after him. When nightfall arrived, we made the decision to anchor in the distance offshore. Each of us agreed to rotate watch in case our friend could be seen. We would continue to yell out to him in hopes that he would come to his senses and return." Thomas looked forward and Kale could read the expression of sadness upon his face.

"So, what happened?" Neelan inquisitively asked.

"The sun rose the next morning—mysteriously seeming to pass right over the land of Necron, which remained dark and gloomy. We continued to call his name for hours, shooting our magic into the sky in desperation, hoping he would see it and make his way to the shore. Finally, we knew that we must redirect our ship and return home. I was the one voted to teleport back in order to return quickly with the report on what had happened. The direct apprentice was to remain onboard to ensure the others returned safely."

"Did ya' ever find him?" Illadar was now equally interested in the story.

"I'm afraid so..." Thomas' voice dropped. "That morning I bid farewell to my friends who were to remain on board and sail home. I was prepared to teleport to Ravondore as we had planned when I heard the first of many horrified screams. It came from a female student who had glanced overboard. I ran to see what happened, following her paralyzed stare. It felt as though a weight dropped within my gut as I gazed upon her findings. There, floating in the water alongside of our boat was the mangled and torn body pieces of my friend. He met an unimaginable fate. To this very day, I cannot fathom what sort of brutal beast could have done such a thing. It wasn't as though this was your average wild creature for he had not been eaten. His body was simply ripped apart and tossed without remorse into the sea for us to find. It seemed apparent that whoever it was— mocked us from afar. For that reason, I am quite biased toward the continent of Necron. I believe I shall always have a bitter place for it within my heart."

"I'm really sorry." Kale was at a loss for what else he could say after such a horrible story.

"I wonder if it could have been the use of Drell that drove your friend to insanity. It surely sounds as though it was that foul magic at play," Neelan huffed in disgust, glancing toward Kale. "I do hope this clarifies why I say we are absolutely nothing like the dark elves. Though, I am not fond of my own heritage, the high elves believe in balance within the world and would never seek to obtain great amounts of power or destruction as the dark elves do."

As they climbed to the top of another sizeable grassy mound, the massive white city came into view. Tyrione—the kingdom of high elves; it was astounding. The tall, white cylinder structures peaked toward the sky, towering above the massive ivory stone walls that bordered the entire city. It was a grand sight to behold. They could see a large tower within the center of the kingdom. Its nearly pearlescent walls and cone-like rooftop were detailed with gleaming gold decorative accents that added to its stunning impact. The high elves obviously took great pride in their homeland.

Upon descending the hill, Kale saw many elven men stationed upon the wall. As they approached the massive steel gates, Kale could tell by Neelan's movements that she desired to turn and run, escaping the situation entirely.

"Shenu!" A man called down to them from within the gatehouse.

"Ken en ei, Neelan." She pulled her hood back to reveal her long pointed ears. "Ei neishen quey eerend."

"Morila ke, eitte raylea te shaelya censal," the guard replied.

"Their native tongue is English; they do not understand Ceruya. Please refrain from speaking it while in their presence."

"I see—outsiders." The male elf glanced toward them scornfully. "Please move; the gates will be opening. The council will be notified of your arrival, as well."

Neelan bit her lip, nodding, as she led the three men away from the gates reach. The engraved steel groaned as it slowly began to open toward them—driven by a magical force that would not allow access into the city unless granted from an insider.

"Welcome home, Neelan." The elven man who had been inside the gatehouse now stood within the entrance. Clad in thin, silvery armor with gold-dipped edges, his features were flawless with skin appearing as though made of porcelain. The man's golden hair was pulled back into a neat ponytail which trailed down to his mid-back.

"Thank you," she replied standoffishly.

"Is your father expecting you?" The guard questioned.

"No, Lorin, and I ask that you do not tell him I am here. My business does not lie with my father."

"As you wish." Lorin paused, "Are you going to introduce me to your companions?" As he glanced up to better view the three men, his near perfect face wrinkled in disgust. "What is this?! Neelan, you bring humans into Tyrione? The council will not be pleased with this."

"They are my friends, Lorin."

"You must bring them to meet the council at once. You know very well that humans do not have the authority to walk our streets until formal permission is granted. I am worried for you Neelan, and I fear the council will be enraged. You have been gone all this time, after having fled from your duties at the Temple of Enya, and now you bring...*them* here."

"You know nothing of my past, Lorin," Neelan's voice grew grim.

Lorin sighed. "Please forgive me, Neelan, I only meant they are quite displeased toward your actions." He flashed a flawless smile. "I am just glad you are back."

"Do not grow accustomed to seeing me. I am not staying long." Neelan glanced in the opposite direction of him.

Kale was unsure why, but Neelan's lack of attraction toward the impeccably handsome elf made him happy.

"Where do you plan to go? Tyrione is your home. You know very well the human kingdoms will not ever fully accept you." Lorin side-stepped into her line of sight.

"Tyrione *was* my home—it is no more. And I do hope you open your eyes one day to see that not all humans are as vile as you have been led to believe. Besides, I am not leaving Kale." She glanced toward Kale with her wide violet eyes that twinkled under the sun's rays of light.

"I see." Lorin glanced bitterly toward Kale. "So you are the one Neelan fancies—how disgusting." He turned, heading toward a set of stairs to the gatehouse. "I must return to my post now, before the commander takes notice. It was good to see you, Neelan."

Once Lorin was no longer in sight, Kale exhaled a lengthy breath. "I dislike him." He snarled.

"I am very proud of you; the old Kale I once knew would have spouted out some insulting reply directly to his face. I'm thankful you have grown inside and are able to mind your tongue. Had you not, we surely would have been removed from Tyrione before ever making it within the walls." Thomas smiled warmly.

"You'll have to excuse Lorin's poor manners. This is one of the reasons I desire to fit in with human life. The high elves feel they are far superior to humans and look down upon the race. Though, there are some who remain unbiased within the kingdom, they are few. I feel that humans are prone to be open-minded and not afraid to explore a broader view of life."

Kale glanced down, feeling shameful and guilty inside. Viewing the way Lorin had behaved was a direct reflection upon how he once felt. He felt sickened by how he had seen the world. Kale had wasted so many years of his life secluded within the walls of a cave.

"We need to head toward the central tower to speak with the council." Neelan glanced around in confusion before noticing the tall elven guard approaching. She sighed. "I knew they would send someone."

"I am here to escort you—and your *friends* to the tower." His light turquoise eyes glanced toward the three men. He wore the same style of armor as Lorin and had equally handsome features, though, he appeared to be older.

They followed the elven guard without question, making their way through the city. Kale was amazed with every turn they took—the kingdom was beautiful with clear streams trickling down each main street. Vibrant fish swam within the floral bordered water. It was nothing like what he experienced in Braxle. The rows of houses within Tyrione were nearly all identical in construction, made of solid white stone and topped with bright red roofs. The windows were arched and many had vibrant blooming flower baskets hanging from the base. Surrounding the homes were more colorful plants which created a rainbow of beautiful contrasting hues. As they neared the rounded tower, the area grew more lively as cheerful elves could be seen bustling about their daily routines. There were guards patrolling the streets with bows upon their backs, men and women working, and children playfully laughing. The surrounding shops had beautifully hand-painted signs to distinguish their specialties. Had it not been for the occasional contemptuous glares and gossiping whispers as they passed, the city would have seemed a very charming place.

"We arrive at the central tower," The elven guard who escorted them announced.

Even more incredible up close, it caused Kale to crick his neck while attempting to view the entire structure. The tall pearl-like tower had golden accents which had been formed to look as though vines were climbing around the cylinder walls. Each golden vine shimmered in the sunlight, creating the visual of the tower itself sparkling. There were no windows or balconies; the building was completely solid aside from a single entryway.

"Come." The guard urged them to continue up a short flight of stone steps ending at two enormous green doors.

Kale could see a pair of guards, stationary, staring with a blank expression.

"Well, don't they look delightful?" Kale softly joked.

"Close your mouth, Kale!" Neelan scolded, nudging her elbow into his side.

Their escort spoke to the other two men in Ceruya, the language of high elves, and Kale could only assume it was about meeting with the council. He could instantly tell when the subject of humans was mentioned by the disgusted stares they gave Kale and his friends. After the conversation ended, the two guards moved from their position to push the grand doors open. They creaked inward, revealing a large open room lit by hundreds of candles.

"You may enter." The guard bowed toward Neelan, "Farewell and good luck." He turned and left down the stone steps.

The other two guards held their arms extended toward the room, signaling for them to move inside. Neelan led the way as the group entered the area. Their shoes pattered against the ivory marble floor. Aside from the many flickering candles and white stone pillars, there seemed to be nothing—and no one occupying the room.

"What are we supposed to do now?" Kale whispered.

"Patience, Kale," Thomas quietly replied. "I can sense a

magical presence nearby. We are not alone."

Neelan took a few steps in front of them. "I must call for the elders of the council. Please remain silent." She took a deep breath, nervously fidgeting her fingers before speaking. "Ei makeel ulo te laylune queysel o Tyrione."

A heavy silence weighed upon them as they awaited a response.

"We came all the way to the elven kingdom to stand alone within this room?"

"That is enough, Kale!" Neelan snapped.

Before Thomas could comment on Kale's behavior, the ceiling began to shift and they heard the sound of grinding stone. They glanced up to see circular carvings rotating in a clockwise direction high above their heads. Kale wanted to ask Neelan what was happening, but knew well enough by this point to bite his tongue. This was a mission for Judith—for Ravondore—for the dragons that had fallen to Jedah's blade; it was not worth risking their approval to move forward.

Four stone circles descended on heavy metal chains and soon revealed a golden throne upon each. Seated atop each red velvet lined seat was an elderly elven male. Each of the men appeared equally wrinkled with thin, white hair that traced around their long ears, falling in length to the legs of their thrones. Their silver robes draped against their bodies as though made of a liquid substance.

"Humans, eunae raylea neishen helst?" One of the elders spoke, bringing a hand to his chin. His circular oasis gently swayed above Kale and his companions. The elder narrowed his eyes, awaiting a response.

"Reynessa shi yoria elukatayne reuk oleay shimoy re English moewa," Neelan replied, obviously intimidated by the elven men.

The same elder who had spoken interlocked his fingers beneath his pointed chin. "I should have known. What a foolish gesture to assume they spoke our tongue." His cold eyes locked onto the three men. "Tell me, *humans,* why have you come to our kingdom?"

"We request permission to visit a resident of the city," Neelan spoke before the others could begin responding.

"Silence, young elf! Do not speak out of turn—traitor to the temple of Enya. You should be grateful to have entry here." The elder returned his focus to Kale, Thomas, and Illadar. The other three council members adjusted their focus onto them as well, which intensified the already uncomfortable situation. "With whom do you desire to speak and for what business?"

Kale and his friends anxiously looked toward Neelan; they did not want to reveal any inappropriate information that could possibly jeopardize their mission. Neelan returned the stare as she widened her eyes and gestured with body language to answer the question. She knew that any disobedience on her part would result in removal from the kingdom, and in turn, her human companions would be forced out as well.

"You there." Another member of the council extended a bony finger toward Kale who in return pointed to himself in question. "You will speak on behalf of your party," The elf commanded.

"I—well, we, must speak with a citizen of your city. It is of dire importance in order to return the Princess of Mirion to her throne."

"We do not dabble in petty human affairs boy." The second elder replied.

"Please, listen to me." Kale couldn't give up after coming so far in his journey. "The entire continent of Ravondore depends upon ending General Jedah's destructive path. Returning the

Princess will help ensure his demise is met."

The elders grew silent as they looked toward one another. It appeared as though they were speaking telepathically.

Finally, a third council member spoke, "Tell us the name of whom you seek."

"His name is Brig," Kale quickly responded.

All four elders began whispering to one another in Ceruya.

Kale watched as Neelan nervously listened, biting down upon her bottom lip. Finally the room grew silent once again as the four council members directed their attention to Kale

"Request denied," The first elder spoke.

"Why?" Kale blurted out in an overwhelming bout of frustration. He had come so far since being transformed and was not prepared to return to Judith and Elanya without finding answers.

"You dare to question our authority—*human* boy?!" The first elder, who appeared to be the head of the council, raised his voice. "Our decision has been made and is final. We do not know why you desire to seek a dark elf—even one within our own kingdom—nor do we desire to know. However the man you wish to find suffers from insanity and delusion. He treads a fine line within Tyrione and cannot be trusted; therefore, you cannot be trusted to collaborate with such an individual. We have only granted him permission to remain within these walls because of a plea from a respected high priestess—your mother, Neelan."

Her eyes shifted with surprise. She could not have fathomed her mother to be fond of dark elves. Neelan's father had always made it quite clear about his disgust for their race. She had always assumed her mother to share the same feelings.

"Neelan, though you are no longer welcome to live within Tyrione, I will grant you and your companions a brief stay under guarded supervision to visit your family." The elder's narrow face locked eyes with hers. "This decision is not for your benefit, but your mother's. You must leave here immediately after."

"T-thank you," Neelan replied.

Kale couldn't figure out if the sad look upon her face was due to the finalization that she was no longer welcome in Tyrione, or that she would now have to face her father—the one person who scarred her emotions for so many years.

"However," the elder continued, "should we find that you attempt to seek the dark elf named Brig, you shall be exiled from Tyrione, and banished from contact. Go now and make haste, your time here runs short."

They did not dwell or further question the ruling. The four companions quickly turned to leave, thankful for each step they placed between themselves and the council. The same two guards awaited their exit, still stationed beside the immense doors. As they made their way outside, Kale felt the sunlight wash over his face and was thrilled to smell the fresh air. Though, his time within the tower room was brief, it had felt like an eternity of awkward moments. Never before had he required permission or authority to do something he desired—it irked him to no end.

"That was truly horrible, Neelan. I can now see why you fled from this place. I would too, if I had to deal with those four skeletons."

"Kale, lower your voice! If any of the citizens hear you speak in such a manner, we're through here!" Neelan snapped.

"From the way things went back in there, we are already through here." Kale crossed his arms in frustration.

"Calm yourself, I have a plan." Neelan spoke softly.

"What sort of plans are you discussing?" The four turned in surprise to see Lorin standing next to Neelan. His suspicious glare locked upon Kale. "I do hope you aren't going to do anything that may jeopardize Neelan's wellbeing here within Tyrione."

"It's nothing like that. We were planning where our next destination would be after leaving Tyrione." Neelan quickly thought up a witty response to quench his curiosity. "Why are you here anyway?" She raised an eyebrow.

"I was sent to escort you to your home."

They sure don't waste any time maintaining control here, Kale thought bitterly.

"Perfect." Neelan began to walk, wrapping her arms tightly around herself. "Let's get this over with quickly."

CHAPTER 19

NEELAN'S SECRET

Throughout their walk, Kale found himself frequently dodging the cold glares from Lorin's grey eyes. Curiosity at what Neelan planned tugged at his thoughts. He knew that, whatever it may be, it was their final hope for finding the answers they desired.

"Pardon my prying, but how do you two know one another?" Thomas broke the heavy silence.

Nicely done, Thomas, Kale thought sarcastically with a sigh. He knew that Neelan already had enough on her mind with the upcoming family reunion, and now she would have to endure a stroll down memory lane with the unpleasant male elf.

"Considering most of us have lived within the walls of this city since birth, it's hardly an interesting story. Most of the citizens know one another," Neelan quickly replied.

"I'd bet that's why you've been gettin' so many foul stares since we left the tower. I'm sure a lot of them don't fancy your arrival after what happened in your past." Illadar glanced around at their surroundings.

First Thomas, now Illadar? And they say I am the one who cannot bite my tongue? Kale shook his head.

"Let them stare, I truly could not care less. I am sure it was the words of my father that established all this negativity toward me. His only priority in life is the temple—not the emotions of his family."

Kale glanced toward Lorin, who had remained silent with a glum look upon his face.

"Neelan," Lorin finally spoke, "you make our history seem as though it was meaningless. I cannot understand how you speak so carelessly about me. I have known you since you were a baby."

"That is true—but it's not as though we were very close to one another."

Lorin looked as though Neelan had shot an arrow through his heart. "I disagree." His voice lowered to a whisper, "I was always close—even if you never realized."

As Kale overheard, for the first time since he met Lorin, he felt sympathy for the elf. Unsure how to react to the situation, Kale attempted a friendly gesture to ease the tension; he gave Lorin a pat upon the back of his armor.

"Do not touch me, you foul and insignificant peon!" Lorin immediately pulled away from Kale's reach.

"Excuse *me* for trying to be friendly with the likes of you," He huffed bitterly. "I can see why she doesn't care to be close to you. I can't see how *anyone* would want to be."

"Would you two stop?" Neelan snapped, looking forward. "We are here..." Her voice trailed off into silence.

Kale glanced up, confronted by a wide, white building. The front was unique from all others within the city with three stained glass windows in a row. They seemed to be symbolic in some way, though Kale could not interpret how. In the first panel there was a sun and a moon; in another a variety of plants, and in the last a woman draped in gold with a yellow glow surrounding her body.

Interesting, Kale thought.

Near the top of the building hung a large golden bell which Neelan explained was used to summon the citizens for worshiping ceremonies to the Goddess Enya.

"Is this your home?" Thomas questioned, in awe at the structural details.

"This is the temple," Neelan's voice was grim and her breathing rapid. A flood of horrible memories invaded her mind. She closed her eyes, shaking her head as she regained composure. "My home is around back." Neelan looked nervously toward Kale, "Will you hold my hand? I cannot do this on my own."

Lorin grunted his disapproval. "Disgusting," He whispered loud enough for Kale to hear.

Thomas fought the sudden urge to freeze Lorin's lips shut. He knew better than to risk their mission for a petty quarrel.

It took Kale a few moments before Neelan's sudden request registered within his mind. "Sure," he finally responded.

Neelan slipped her surprisingly soft hand into his then interlocked their fingers together. As they began to walk in the direction of her home, Neelan tightened her grip on Kale's hand.

Soon he could feel a gentle tremble. He responded with a light squeeze in an attempt to assure her everything would be all right.

"Thank you," she spoke softly.

"You don't have all the time in the world. Let's get moving," Lorin insisted coldly.

They made their way to the rear where a small extension to the temple could be seen. The front entry path to the home was bordered with beautiful pink flowers that made the surrounding area smell sweet. A narrow brick chimney released a stream of grey smoke and Neelan's grip tightened to the point of discomfort, causing Kale's fingers to swell as blood rushed to the tips.

Lorin took a step forward, raising his fist to the green wooden door.

"Wait!" Neelan called to him. "I have to try and do this part myself—I need to face my fears and overcome these never-ending nightmares."

Lorin nodded. "As you wish." He stepped to the side.

She confronted the door with a clammy cold fist, finally rapping her knuckles against the wood. "Kale..." she whispered.

"Don't worry, it will be all right." Kale had not realized the true extent of fear her father had instilled for so many years.

A few silent moments passed before they heard stirring from within. The door swung in to reveal a woman who was undeniably Neelan's mother. They shared very similar facial features and the same thin, sheen of hair hung long and straight. The woman immediately gasped, pulling Neelan into her chest.

Neelan's eyes widened as her hand was pulled from Kale's grasp.

The situation made Kale smile as he watched Neelan hesitantly wrap her arms in return around her mother's waist.

"Bry oneya, Neelan!" The woman's voice was filled with excitement.

"Mother, I am so glad only you are here. I have missed you so much," Neelan confessed in an almost childlike manner as she pressed her head into her mother's chest.

"English?"

"Yes, mother, my friends whom I have travelled with use this language. I prefer it as well." Neelan glanced up at her mother's eyes, awaiting a response.

"I see." More silence followed before she spoke again, "Well then, I too shall use the language while in your presence." She smiled. Her mother was unlike the other elves they met within the city; she was kindhearted and accepting. "Please, come inside." She smiled toward Kale and his friends.

"Thank you for your hospitality." Thomas bowed as they entered the home.

The atmosphere inside was cozy with minimal furniture which reminded Kale of Illadar's home back in Braxle—yet much nicer.

"I shall stand guard outside, humble Priestess. I was sent here to escort Neelan and—the *humans*." He forced the last part through gritted teeth. "It is not my place to enter your home."

"Oh, mag weed. Lorin, I have known you since you were a plump little infant." Neelan's mother pinched his cheek which caused him to blush in embarrassment. "Get inside and have a cup of bossberry juice." She smiled maternally. "And call me, Lelain. We are in my home, not the temple."

Kale was completely baffled by Neelan's previous accusations about her family. Her mother seemed amazingly kind and humble.

"I have missed you dearly, my beautiful little girl."

"Mother, I am not a child." Neelan hid her face to conceal her pink cheeks.

"I know, dear, I know. But you will always be my little one." She glanced up toward Kale, Thomas, and Illadar. "Now tell me—who are your friends?"

Neelan introduced them, explaining how they met and about their travels. Lelain wisely picked up on her daughter's constant stares toward Kale. She softly chuckled to herself which made Kale uncomfortable.

"Now, explain, why have you returned?" Lelain smiled. "As much as I would love to believe it is to see your old mother, I know this is not the case." She forced a laugh that caused the corners of her eyes to wrinkle, revealing an aged appearance for the first time.

"I came to speak with a dark elf named Brig." Neelan sighed. "The elder council denied permission." She paused in thought. "They said he—Brig, that is—was granted the ability to remain within Tyrione because of *you,* mother." She locked eyes with Lelain, "So please tell me, how do you know him, and why won't they allow us to speak with him? You have no idea of the importance it would have on Ravondore."

"I see. Well, to be quite honest with you, I felt as though it was the will of Enya which brought me to my decision of fighting for him to remain here. Though, he is of dark elven blood, his intentions are pure. He is incredibly intelligent, despite his— oddities. When the council was prepared to banish Brig from the kingdom, there were many signs presented to me. I knew that there was some meaning—some purpose as to why he had fled here. I suppose you could say that I utilized my authority as head priestess to grant him the ability to remain within Tyrione." Lelain smiled. "Since that day, he swore an oath to repay me for my kindness. The gesture was kind enough for me; I expect nothing in return for fulfilling the will of Enya." She placed a hand upon Neelan's. "Aside from all else, I get to see my daughter again. What more could I possibly desire?" Lelain pulled Neelan close.

THE CHRONICLES OF KALE: A DRAGON'S AWAKENING

"I am not staying, mother. The elder council has forbidden me to live within Tyrione for my abandonment to the temple—though honestly, I would not wish to stay on my own will anyway. Not that it matters, but I am sure father had a great deal to do with the council's decision." Neelan curled her fingers into a tightened fist.

Lelain appeared hurt by the news. "I am sorry, my daughter." Her mood shifted. "Your father was very upset when you left."

"My *father*," Neelan bitterly spoke, "treated me as a prisoner. He locked me away from the world and took everything I cared for away."

Kale cleared his throat, growing more uncomfortable with each passing moment that the conversation continued. "Excuse my interruption, but I think it would be best if we allow you two to speak in private—especially considering that our time here is short." He shot a meaningful glance to Lelain as if to remind her once again that Neelan would soon be leaving.

"Kale—no!" Neelan's hand reached out, gripping onto Kale's arm like a lost child. He had never seen her behave so vulnerably before.

"It's all right, I'll be just outside. Trust me, with Lorin watching me like a hawk scoping its prey, I couldn't run off even if I wanted to—which I don't." He quickly added the last part to avoid any further insecurity.

She hesitantly nodded, allowing her fingers to slip from his arm.

~~~~~~~~~~~~~

The sunlight felt invigorating as it warmed Kale's cheeks. "This is much better." He lifted his arms above his head to stretch as he seated himself upon a log bench against the front wall of the home.

"Indeed." Thomas smiled, positioning himself next to Kale's side. "I do hope Neelan is able to find peace with her mother."

Lorin glanced to the vacant space to Kale's other side. He then glanced toward Illadar to see that he was occupied with inspecting the surroundings of the small front yard. Lorin exhaled before giving in to sit upon the empty section of the bench.

Kale looked up in surprise. "You *are* aware that you're seated next to a *human*, right?" Kale joked, secretly laughing at the irony behind his words.

"I can obviously see this." Lorin replied with resentment. It was apparent that he did not have the best sense of humor. "I wanted to speak with you about Neelan."

Kale could see by the look upon Lorin's face this was incredibly difficult for him.

Lorin swallowed hard. Then, as if regaining his pride, he adjusted his posture and sat upright, his head held high.

Kale in turn faced Lorin, squinting as the sun reflected off the elf's shoulder guards. He couldn't imagine having to wear something so heavy and suffocating over his flesh in such humid weather.

"So what did you want to tell me?" Kale pushed the subject. He grew impatient waiting for Lorin to find words for what he wanted to express. Kale assumed it would be an irritating speech on why he should stay away from Neelan because he was a *filthy human.*

"Neelan," Lorin finally spoke, "she is very special."

That is one way to put it, Kale thought, secretly amused. *Let's not forget her other attributes of annoyance, overly clingy, and horribly stubborn.*

"Growing up, we didn't get to see each other very often. Her father would always keep her occupied with temple duties. She was to become a devoted priestess, despite her own desires." His jaw tightened, the veins within his neck pulsed. "I hated what her father did, but could never find the courage within myself to help. I will always regret how cowardly I was." He shook his head. "When she was free to walk the city, I tried to be friendly and make attempts for her to notice me." He glanced up toward the sky, shorter strands of blonde hair which had come loose from his ponytail hung disheveled across his face. "I longed to be more than just an acquaintance—I wanted more than friendship. I did all I could think of to win her heart. I brought her flowers, wrote letters, and did my best to be there when she needed assistance with tasks. Despite all my attempts, not once did she ever return my feelings. I felt so dearly for her." His voice shook with pain as he struggled to hold himself together. "And now—you come along. Someone she barely knows—a *human*, yet she is drawn to you and comforted by your touch. I see the way she looks at you, Kale. I was in question at first, but even after the short time I have watched the two of you, I am now very certain—Neelan loves you."

CHAPTER 20

WHO IS BRIG?

Kale stared forward, stunned. "No, I think you are mistaken with your accusations. She cares about me only as a friend." He had never experienced love toward a female before, and the thought alone was frightening. "Please trust me, Lorin, there is no way she would love someone," he sighed, "like me." In his mind, he found it impossible for anyone to ever love a dragon.

"At first, I could not believe it either. Just look at you." Lorin gestured in Kale's direction. "You are an inferior, puny, unattractive being." There was no remorse in his voice as he spoke. "But, sadly I am certain she does..." His voice trailed off. After many minutes of awkward silence, he spoke again. "Take good care of her. Should you ever harm her in any way..." His cold stare locked onto Kale. "I shall kill you."

Kale knew that Lorin meant his threat by the look in those pale grey eyes.

Before the conversation could go further, Thomas quickly

stood, and Illadar forced a series of fraudulent coughs.

"What in Pan's name are you two doing?" As Kale turned to face Illadar he froze in place. A tall, slender man clad in white and golden robes scowled at them. His teeth were bared and clenched, contrasting against his black beard falling to his mid-chest, bound together by a white string.

"Greetings," Thomas attempted to break the silence, although it was very clear the man was not about to return the welcome.

Lorin immediately stood, holding a perfectly upright posture with his arms hung straight at his sides. "High Priest Zalura!"

"Mekton nen treyae?!" The man gestured toward Kale and his friends with a look of disdain in his eyes.

They continued to speak in the elven tongue and Kale was certain it was about them. Kale's memory traced back to Neelan's story about her father forbidding her from playing with the only friend she had—all because her friend was human. Kale then heard Lorin mention Neelan's name to Zalura, who Kale decided must indeed be her father.

The high priest growled furiously as he shoved Lorin to the side—forcefully pushing the green door inward. They could hear both Neelan and her mother gasp in surprise as he stormed into the home. Her father's voice filled with rage as he yelled loud enough to be heard outside.

Kale could now see a glimpse into the reality of Zalura's cruelty.

"What a cold waste of flesh," Illadar shook his head disapprovingly.

Before Kale could share his opinion on the situation, they heard Neelan's voice, and although in Ceruya, it was clear she was pleading with him. Suddenly, a scream rang out and both Kale and Lorin dashed through the door protectively.

"Neelan! Are you hurt?" Kale's question was answered without words.

Neelan cowered against the far wall, her father towering over her. Lelain stood to the side, obedient, fearful, and silent, as though she had become a completely different individual.

Zalura raised an open palm and Neelan's wide glassy eyes looked toward Kale as if to silently cry out for help. It was too late. Zalura's hand swung down, clapping loudly against the side of Neelan's face.

"No!" Both Kale and Lorin shouted.

Kale could no longer control himself. He quickly lunged forward to grip Neelan by the arm. He pulled her up toward him, ensuring his body stood between her and Zalura.

"We are leaving, now." Kale's voice was low and deep as he fought to maintain the temperature flowing to his palms. His icy blue eyes scorned Zalura, "Do not ever touch Neelan again." Kale pulled Neelan into his chest, gently stroking her soft hair while she uncontrollably sobbed.

"Filthy!" Zalura narrowed his hazel eyes, glaring toward Kale. "You are all filthy! She is no daughter of mine! Be gone from my sight!"

Kale glanced over his shoulder as they made their way to the entrance, "The only thing filthy within this home—is your heart." He slammed the door behind him.

Once outside, they were again confronted by the warm sunlight drifting toward the rooftops on the far wall of the city.

"Well, that went well," Illadar muttered bitterly.

"What now? Neelan," Kale gently gripped her shoulders, "I know you're upset right now, but you mentioned a plan. Is there still a way for us to see *him*?"

She sniffed, nodding silently.

"What are you talking about? This is the second time I have heard mention of a plan. I am no fool—you must tell me what is going on at once." Lorin demanded.

"Lorin," Neelan forced back her tears, "would you be willing to help us?" She swiped an arm across her face.

He grazed a finger over his golden brow in frustration. "Can you please just tell me what this is all about?"

"I need you to allow us entry into the Catalythe district. There is something we absolutely must do before leaving Tyrione. It is for the well-being of Ravondore." Neelan wishfully stared into his eyes.

"Neelan, please do not place me in such a situation. You know I am a guard of the kingdom. I was ordered to escort you directly to the gates upon leaving your family's home. You know very well what will happen if I disobey." He looked down, avoiding her eyes.

"Why must you always obediently listen to everything they tell you? Have you no will or desires of your own? Is this kingdom truly worth living bound by such tight restrictions?" Neelan's voice grew agitated.

"I am so sorry, I just cannot help you."

"Very well then." Neelan sighed. "I suppose it was reasons such as this why you and I could never be close friends. You would always do as they wanted, despite the best interest of others."

Lorin looked as though he had been the one slapped across the face.

"Now, it is my turn to be sorry," Neelan spoke softly as she suddenly gripped Lorin by the arm and pulled him into a secluded nook between two homes.

"What are you doing? Tell me this moment," Lorin commanded.

"I said I was sorry." Neelan repeated as she withdrew a small, golden, worm-like creature from within her cloak.

Lorin's eyes immediately widened. "Don't do this. You know I am bound by laws to do my job—I have no choice."

"That is where you are very wrong, Lorin. Everyone has a choice." She held the golden glowing worm on her palm.

"*Aluneya,*" Neelan whispered as the tiny creature began to twitch with life.

The worm leapt from her palm as it danced gracefully in the air, leaving a golden trail drifting in its path. Kale and his friends remained frozen in place as though caught in a trance-like state. Lorin seemed incapacitated as well while the worm progressed its way closer toward his face.

Neelan hissed another command and the worm slid between Lorin's lips. His silvery eyes twitched and his body quivered as though a chill had run down his spine.

Once the worm disappeared from sight, Kale, Thomas, and Illadar regained bodily function as their focus returned to normal. Lorin however, remained stationed in place as if he had become a doll-like statue. His eyes and mouth were all that seemed to have the ability to move and he frantically glanced from side to side.

"Neelan, why have you done this to me?"

"I have already told you, our mission is in the best interest of Ravondore. Any true follower of Enya should sense the truth in what I say. Farewell, Lorin." As Neelan turned to walk away, Kale couldn't help but feel selfishly good inside.

"Wait!" Lorin called out. "You cannot do this!"

"Someone is bound to hear that ruckus," Illadar warned.

"Indeed. Allow me to rectify the situation." Thomas turned toward Lorin's direction. "*Silant devorda.*" He grinned. "A gift from a mere *human.*" Thomas winked.

Lorin's mouth continued to move, yet no sound emerged from his lips.

"The spell's duration is random, although, I presume we have around an hour before he makes full use of his vocal abilities. It would be wise to make haste."

"Agreed. My enchantment will wear off as soon as the worm dies within his body," Neelan stated.

Illadar cringed. "Sounds pleasant." He wiped beads of sweat from his wide ebony forehead. "What is our course of action?"

"Follow me quickly, and try to refrain from appearing suspicious." Neelan briskly made way around to the temple, leaving the three men baffled. She had fully regained composure and was back to her usual bossy, determined, and nearly fearless self.

Kale smiled happily.

"Pardon my interruption—however isn't it a poor idea to enter the temple after what has just happened? I somehow do not believe your father is prepared to welcome us with open arms." Thomas cautioned.

"Shh." She held a finger to her peach lips. "We are not going in, we're going around. It is important for us to remain quiet. The other elves, much like myself, have heightened senses and are able to hear and smell from a distance. Now that they are aware of your human scent, we must make haste," Neelan whispered as she led them through the landscaped surroundings.

And she was the one who said not to look suspicious. Kale rolled his eyes as they weaved through the tall circular bushes.

Upon reaching the side wall of the temple, Neelan knelt down beside a mass of tangled, thorny vines and overgrown grass. She immediately glanced around with caution before tugging carefully on the vines.

"Allow me, dear." Thomas chuckled at her miserable attempt to remove the vines. "Please step aside."

"Thank you, Thomas." Kale crossed his arms. "Had we waited on *her*, we'd never get out of here."

"Ugh." Neelan scowled. "I didn't see *you* helping."

"*Kruedia esonek*." Thomas' eyes widened as a red glow illuminated from his palm. A sphere of flames shot forth into the tangled web. It incinerated everything in its path, leaving the remnants of plant life to singe and shrivel. A loud sizzle could be heard from the direction where the fireball collided and a thick puff of grey smoke rose to the sky.

"Nicely done," Kale praised Thomas, though slightly jealous. He could still clearly recall how easy it once was to conjure fire as a dragon.

"Lovely—now we are sending up smoke signals to alert the guards of our whereabouts." Neelan's sarcasm was thick.

"What is this?" Kale disregarded Neelan's concern, distracted by the burnt hole through a wooden door that had been previously concealed. As he peered down he could see that the hole was completely dark.

"This is a passage my mother told me about while we were alone in her home earlier." Neelan lowered her voice. "It should lead us directly to the Catalyst district, near Brig's home."

"Well then, why are we standin' around? Let's get movin'." Illadar gripped an old rusted handle and lifted the burnt door upward.

Inside they could see an uninviting rusted ladder that led down into the darkness. Without hesitation, Illadar began to climb down, carefully resting his weight upon the delicate steel. They watched from above as he descended until the short black curls upon his head could no longer be seen.

"Illadar? Hello?" Kale called down as his own voice echoed back at him.

They continued to wait impatiently as more time passed in silence.

"I'm going in after him," Kale stated.

He placed his feet upon the ladder which flaked and slightly crumbled beneath his shoes. With each cautious step on the unsteady ladder, he moved deeper into the unknown darkness. Finally, he sunk below all traces of light and could no longer see his own hands before his face.

"Watch the last step kid, it's about to snap."

Kale nearly lost his grip in surprise as he struggled to catch his balance with one arm. "Why in Pan's name did you do that, Illadar?! I nearly fell! And why didn't you answer me before?"

"I was investigatin'."

As Illadar spoke, Kale could hear him chuckling to himself.

"It's completely dark in here. What could you possibly be investigating?" Kale replied with agitation.

"Didn't anything I've taught you sink into that thick head of yours? You don't always need to see in order to know somethin' is there."

Kale knew that arguing with Illadar would only add to his irritation.

"Kale, are you all right?" Neelan anxiously called down.

"Yes, I'm here with Illadar. I'm pretty sure it's safe to come down."

Thomas shook his head, "How foolish of me, I should have conjured us light from the beginning. It would be wise to see what we are getting ourselves into."

"Don't even think about it, Thomas. We don't need to risk drawing further attention to our location. You should be grateful many families are preparing supper, so your previous mishap that sent smoke into the air hopefully will not cause alarm. Wait until we are down inside the tunnel before utilizing any more of your spells," Neelan scolded.

"Very well." Thomas chuckled at Neelan's feisty demeanor.

"You may go down next. Please make haste; if Lorin breaks from his enchantment and alerts the others we will have a very difficult time making contact with Brig, let alone getting out of here safely. We aren't even aware of what he looks like, so finding him may prove to be a time consuming challenge." Neelan gestured for Thomas to climb into the hole.

Thomas nodded, not wanting to waste further time arguing with the spunky and all too stubborn elf. The old sorcerer took cautious steps as he made way toward the bottom with ease.

"I'm coming down, now," Neelan softly called out as she gripped the rusted handle of the wooden door, pulling it shut as she dropped lower into the darkness. With the sun setting and a small hole being their only source of minimal light, she was quickly engulfed by sheets of black in all directions. As Neelan's foot came down upon one of the final ladder steps, the sound of clinging metal chimed. She yelped in fear.

Kale immediately knew a bar on the ladder had snapped. *You don't need to see in order to know something is there.* Illadar's words ran through Kale's mind. He allowed his sense of hearing and smell to dominate, and suddenly, through the will of his mind, it felt as though time slowed. Kale took a step forward, listening closely to the whooshing of Neelan's body as she fell. He inhaled, capturing her lavender scent as he reached out his palms.

"I've got you!" he exclaimed as her body collapsed into his arms. "Are you hurt?"

"No." She slid her feet to the floor. "Thank you, Kale—for saving me." She pressed her tender lips to his cheek, kissing so softly no sound could be heard. No one could see what had happened—a moment shared by only them.

"I—well—uhm..." Kale fumbled with his words. He was grateful for the surrounding darkness so the others could not see his fiery red cheeks.

"You all right, kid?"

"Y-yeah, let's get going."

Kale felt confused by Neelan's actions and unsure if this was simply a friendly gesture of thanks, or if what Lorin had told him was true. *Now is not the time to think of such things.* Kale told himself. Though Kale could not understand the reasoning, when he thought of her kiss, it caused his insides to flutter. He knew, however, the most important task at hand was to find Brig and not dwell upon such emotions.

"How do we get out of here?" Kale managed to focus on their mission.

"My mother told me that following the flow of water will lead us there," Neelan replied as though nothing happened between them.

They stood in silence, each listening closely to the faint trickle of water to their side.

"This way." Neelan pulled on the cloth of Kale's tunic.

Thomas lifted his palm, no longer heeding Neelan's warning. They were secure beneath the earth, and he mumbled softly. A small glowing orb immediately appeared to brighten their surroundings. "We don't need any further accidents occurring," He spoke with a smile as he glanced toward Neelan.

Kale blushed at the thought of his words, hoping the old sorcerer didn't know their secret.

The four could now see the long, arched tunnel made of slick algae-covered bricks. Centered between two thin ledges was flowing water that, despite the small glowing orb, appeared black as night.

They continued on for many minutes before seeing a faint light in the near distance. As they moved closer, it became apparent what they saw were flames within hanging lanterns. They came to a large gated drain which opened into what Kale assumed must be the Catalyst district. It was completely dark, aside from the dangling oil lanterns which hung before each building, there were no vibrant flowers or wide array of colors; everything appeared bland and neutral. The whole area seemed dreary.

"We've come to a dead end. How are we supposed to get out of here?" Kale gently tugged on two of the iron bars set firmly in place.

"Thomas, can you cast something to get us out of here?" Neelan narrowed her eyes. "Something that *won't* cry out to the kingdom that we are here."

"I apologize, but that will not be an option. Casting anything so close to the homes nearby will surely draw attention. Which reminds me..." He pinched down on the glowing orb. "Lights out."

Neelan bit her lower lip as she tried to come up with an alternate plan. Her mother had not warned her of this; most likely because she wasn't aware of what was down the old, closed off tunnel.

As time passed, they each grew more frustrated with the situation—losing hope of ever finding a way to get past the sturdy drainage gate. Kale pressed his forehead against one of the iron bars as he released a frustrated sigh. Then, it struck him—he could use his ability to melt through the iron and quietly break them free. There was no time for discussion; he needed to act with haste. He closed his eyes, focusing on the warmth which ran deep within him. Kale quickly began to feel the moisture from sweat building up within the cup of his hand. They were rapidly heating.

Suddenly, Kale felt something cold and firm press against the flesh of his face. He leapt back, throwing his hands up defensively in front of him.

"That's hot...yes, yes, hot indeed," An unfamiliar voice spoke.

The four companions looked between the bars to see a grey-skinned elf, old by the appearance of his leathery skin. The elf pulled his thin, bony fingers from the iron bars, sticking them between his dry cracking lips. Kale cringed; the elf's nails were long, yellowed, and incrusted with brown filth—yet he sucked on them without hesitation.

The old elven man glanced up; his white hazy eyes locked onto Kale, who returned the stare uncomfortably. His thin white hair was messy and stuck out in all directions which drew attention to his misshapen pointed ears, bent down at the middle. It reminded Kale of a wild dog he'd seen while hunting many years ago.

Neelan paused all movement as she stared toward the stranger. "You are a dark elf. Would you happen to be Brig?"

"I do not know who she is!" The old elf spoke, as if answering his thoughts aloud. "You!" He pointed toward Kale, disregarding everything Neelan just said. He pulled his face so close to the iron bars that Kale could feel his heavy breath. His crusted lips curled up, "I have been waiting for you—Firehart."

CHAPTER 21

MALAKHAR'S TRUTH

The dark elf withdrew a tarnished key from within his brown satchel and inserted it into the side of the drainage gate. They watched as it effortlessly swung open which caused Kale to grumble beneath his breath.

Both Illadar and Kale assisted Neelan and Thomas through before quickly following. The drainage drop-off was moist and cold, dampening the front side of their clothing as they slid up onto the quiet street. Though the area was gloomy and deathly empty of life, Kale found it quite comforting—it reminded him of the home where he still longed to return, dark and secluded.

"Hurry, hurry. Quick, quick." The dark elf urged them in the direction of a home with a brightly lit interior. Unlike the homes they had seen earlier in the day, this one was very plain with heaps of clutter scattered around the outer walls. It appeared many of the items had not been used for years; some had begun to rust or decay. Kale also took note of the small pile to the side consisting of flasks and jars.

"Are you taking us inside this building?" Kale inquired suspiciously. They were unsure if this was truly the elven man they sought.

"Yes, I am certain it is him! Be silent, would you?" the man spoke over his shoulder to a vacant area where no one stood. "Ahem," He looked toward Kale. "This is my home. Now let's get inside before seen by the others!"

The four glanced cautiously toward one another before entering through the dingy, mildew-tinged door. The room appeared relatively normal, despite the misleading exterior. It was surprisingly clean with a wooden table and plush bed covered in a well-tailored, green comforter. The walls were nearly hidden by shelves stocked full of thick books.

"All right, you've gotten us inside—now, tell us who you are and how you know who I am." Kale grew impatient with the dark elf's elusive behavior.

"Tell them? Yes, yes, I suppose they already know." He fumbled through a stack of parchment. "My name is Brig. Your name is Firehart."

Kale sighed, rubbing his forehead. "Yes, I believe we have already established who I am. I'm thankful you are the one we have been trying to find."

"Me too, me too—yes, yes." Brig was constantly moving about, always appearing to occupy his fingers with a task. "Oh, I do believe that is a fine idea." He once again spoke aloud as if someone were standing next to him, engaging in conversation. "Let us move below where it is safe from any possible interruptions." Brig glanced around the room as if expecting to hear someone listening in. "Right this way, if you would please." He led them over to a stone wall that held two flickering candles upon a small wooden shelf. Brig held his hand out, placing his bony fingers against the wood. "*Lavora miyeche.*" The stones suddenly began to shift, receding back and to the side, revealing a dark tunnel leading beneath the surface.

Kale began to feel confident that there was more to Brig than simply being an old kook.

"Move quickly, if you care to keep your limbs." Brig replied to his own warning with maniacal, high-pitched laughter.

Kale caught a glimpse of Illadar who was reaching back to ensure his claymore was snug in place and ready if needed. *Brig must make him nervous*, Kale thought as they walked down into a circular room.

With a wave of Brig's hand, the entire room illuminated with dozens of candles that flickered brightly. They could now see the many shelves filled with colorful flasks and vials. Beside a table were an exact amount of stools for each of them to sit.

"You knew we would come here—you were prepared for this," Thomas spoke as he glanced around the room.

"I have already told them!" Brig scratched his floppy, left ear. "Yes, I have already told you I knew." Suddenly, his face bore a very serious expression. "The red one came as I slept. The red one foretold me you would come Firehart—no, no, no," he shook his head, "Kale." His oval-shaped, hazy white eyes looked as though they were marbles in the candlelight.

"All right, I'll assume you also know why we have come to you, then?" As Kale spoke, something Brig mentioned tugged at his curiosity. "And who is this *red one* you speak of?"

Brig burst into another fit of laughter as he began randomly skipping around the room. He pinched at his cloak on each side, lifting it slightly up as though he were a young child wearing a gown. For an elderly dark elf, he moved swiftly. "I do, I do, I do." He sang in a high crackled voice.

"Enough with the games, old man," Kale hissed impatiently. "Answer my questions. It's very important we get the information we've come for." Kale fought to control his frustration. He exhaled, "Please."

"Oooo." Brig puckered his dry lips. He then burst into rhyme, "The red one is so fierce and grand, a mighty beast indeed. Coming as I sleep at night to reveal the dragon breed." His fingers walked up Kale's back as he spoke.

Kale jumped away in disgust when the long, chipped fingernails met his neck. He was baffled at how Brig could possibly know the truth about him. What bothered him even more was that the dark elf still had not answered a single one of his questions. Kale rubbed his forehead. "You're correct—I am a dragon. But this still does not tell me what we've come here for." He wasn't in the mood to conceal the truth when it was apparent Brig knew his situation.

Finally, Brig ceased his child-like behavior as he sat upon one of the wooden stools. "I will not discuss certain details of my dream with you." His voice was defensive and final. "However, I can discuss *you*, black dragon. You are fascinating." As Brig spoke, he shoved a yellowed fingernail into his ear which Kale could now see was filled with white hair. After a few twists of his wrist, the dark elf withdrew a firm chunk of ear wax and gently rolled it between his fingers. "There are two reasons why you have arrived here at my home tonight."

Kale was aware of one—to find a cure for Judith's curse; but the other struck no part of his memory. "I don't understand," Kale confessed.

"I think he is impatient too!" Brig spoke to the air.

Kale's patience began to wear thinner than before as he

angrily held a deep breath within his chest.

"What tempers dragons have." Brig laughed as he read Kale's expression. "We both are aware of the first reason you've come, so we will begin there."

"Yes, I was hoping you may be able to provide us with information on how to remove the curse from Princess Judith."

"All right, all right, I shall ask him, just be quiet!" Brig barked aloud to himself. "I know it may seem as though I am a very wise individual who holds all of the answers—but I'm afraid I do not."

"So, you can't help us then?" Kale looked distraught, his jaw tightened.

"Shut up!" Brig waved his hand toward Kale's face, "Not you, boy, not you." He cleared his throat. "Where was I? Oh, yes," His tongue ran across his chapped bottom lip, leaving a glossy film of saliva behind. "I believe I can be of assistance, however, I will in turn need your help as well. You must provide me with further information on this curse. Please share all you know as I am unaware of the details involving your friend's issue."

"Of course, I will give you more information; however, I am curious about something." Kale rubbed his chin, "Why are you helping us? What motive could you possibly have to assist complete strangers?"

Brig laughed. "You dragons are so sly! I will admit, I do have an ulterior motive." His wrinkled eyelids lowered. "As you may know, many of the dark elves are frowned upon within the kingdom. We live secluded within the slums of the city. The red one has assured me that if you rein victorious on your journey, a balance will be restored—it will allow our kind more opportunities for a real life within Ravondore."

"I see." Kale felt an overwhelming sense of relief. He had expected something far less practical from such a *unique* individual. "Well, if you know of the curse, then you must be aware it has been placed upon the Princess by a dark elf named Malakhar." As Kale spoke the name, Brig's foggy eyes grew wide.

"I was not aware of whom it was! That abomination still walks this earth?!" He leapt up from the stool, once again engaging in a bout of childish behavior as he slammed empty vials against the stone walls. As they collided, each glass piece shattered into thousands of tiny shards.

"What are you doin'? Stop before you hit one of us!" Illadar scolded.

"Enough already!" Kale held an arm up to shield his face as Brig smashed a vial next to where he sat.

Brig paused from his commotion. "Do you know who he is?"

"We know very little about him, which is why we've come so far to speak with you." Kale felt as though they were once again looping in circles. "I only know he is a dark elf, and I am to avoid his touch by all means. Please explain more about this individual. Time is short, and I must find how to remove the curse."

"Zipeee!" Brig momentarily ignored Kale as he flung another vial against the wall. "Stop acting foolish!" The dark elf scolded himself. "All right, Firehart, you're going to need to know about him so I suppose I shall share. Malakhar was born long ago on Necron." His voice sounded bitter as he spoke the name of the elven man in black. "Unlike the others of our kind, Malakhar came to this world frail, underweight, and colorless—some might even go as far to say deformed. Many wanted to feed him to the sea as a child, saying his appearance was that of a monstrosity. His parents, however, pleaded for him to remain and live amongst them. After a great debate, he was able to stay and as the years passed he grew in seclusion. His mother and father were rarely seen in town and kept their distance from the city. His only brother was ridiculed by the other young elves for defending him when cruel verbal accusations were made. They had been shamed by the others for their desire to keep the boy." Brig shook his head.

"In time, as with most children, young Malakhar began to disobey his parents and break the rules. His behavior toward his mother and father lacked remorse. It was as though he cared for no living creature and would often lash out in fits of rage within his home for no apparent reason. He would often sneak off, despite his parents' warnings, to explore the nearby towns and city. The others would laugh at his appearance and throw rocks at his body. Eventually, he could no longer handle their reaction and fled, not to be seen again by the townsfolk for quite some time. As Malakhar continued to grow, he became determined to rise above those who had wronged him and soon, his ability to memorize ancient writings surpassed that of even the dark elven council. Malakhar memorized nearly every powerful curse he could find and soon sought to master the dark art of Drell. He would often experiment with his malicious attempts at curses on the innocent small animals within the forest." Brig sighed.

"Sensing a malicious aura growing within Malakhar, the council forbade him to study the magic, threatening to exile him should he try." Brig fumbled with his thumbs as he spoke. "Quite honestly, I know this was because they were fearful—and had every reason to be!" He raised his pointer finger to the ceiling. "Malakhar had a strong lust for power and a record of disobedience. It was difficult to sympathize with such a cold hearted individual." Brigs eyes gazed off to the side and he began to speak as though he were the only person still within the room. "It was a chilling day upon that forsaken island when Malakhar's brother took notice of his absence. Malakhar had been told not to leave the boundaries of his home, yet was nowhere to be found. His father was alerted and immediately took action. Upon further investigation of small clues left behind, his father was able to track his location. Malakhar had managed to make it unnoticed into the Elder's Chamber—though, I cannot begin to imagine how he could have gotten inside. He was attempting to steal scrolls which held the most devastating spells of Drell. Malakhar was planning to kill us all. It broke his father's heart, but Malakhar had to be stopped. His father managed to slip away unnoticed and contacted the elders immediately." Brig paused a moment before continuing his story.

"The elder's dispatched guards who wore enchanted armor impenetrable by Malakhar's curses. They captured him before he could escape with the scrolls, locking him within a shielded cage for days without food or water for his crimes. Once he was weakened to the point where he no longer had the strength to lift himself, they placed his pallid, frail body within a small wooden vessel. On the base of this quaint boat was a hole just big enough to allow the water to constantly trickle in. He was then sent out to the mercy of the open sea—they intended for him to slowly wither and drown. Something, however, went wrong with their plan and he managed to make it completely across the sea, landing upon Ravondore—alive. This is when the human you call General Jedah found him. In return for rescuing Malakhar and aiding him in regaining health, a blood pact was placed into effect. Malakhar had no choice at the time and was bound to serve Jedah loyally until their agreement is fulfilled."

"What's a blood pact?" Illadar questioned as he hung on

every word Brig spoke.

Neelan answered before Brig could speak, "It is a sacred oath that all elves must obey. Should an elf choose to enter such a contract—they are bound to follow through or shall perish to dust. The high elves believe this binding agreement is held in place by their Goddess Enya; the dark elves believe it is the wrath of their God, Botanar."

"She is correct," Brig continued as he resumed picking at his hairy ear. "You are here because you need to remove a curse Malakhar has placed—a very powerful one from what I've learned." He inhaled, closing his eyelids.

Kale could hear him muttering softly to himself in the foreign words of Draxion, the language of dark elves. It sounded as though he was talking himself into making an important decision—yet again paying no mind that he was not alone within the room.

Brig sighed as he eventually sat upright. "To break the curse and return the Princess to her former self, you must..." he grabbed Kale's tunic and pulled him directly in front of his creased face, "...kill him."

CHAPTER 22

A WARNING ARRIVES

Kale tugged at his hair in frustration. "So, now we must find Malakhar *and* kill him?"

"Correct," Brig replied firmly.

"You're telling me we have to place all hope in fate's hand? I'm sure he has already begun his return to Jedah, to report our whereabouts."

"I do not feel you need to worry about this. As I have said before, Malakhar seeks power. Though he obeys Jedah's word for sake of his pact, I strongly believe Malakhar has his own agenda." Brig interlocked his bony fingers.

"Interesting." Thomas rested his bearded chin upon his knuckles. "I do wonder how everything will fall into place."

"We need to coordinate a plan of action as quickly as possible." Illadar curled his ebony lips into his mouth, growing silent as he pondered the new circumstances.

The silence was disrupted by glass shattering as Brig hurled another vial against the wall.

"Why in Pan's name do you keep doing that?!" Kale fought with his temper as he attempted to control an outburst due to the dark elf's crude behavior.

"Listen here!" Brig shouted before tucking his chin against his chest while whispering to himself. "Shh!" He shivered. "Please, listen to me." His voice was now calmed. "I need to speak with you, Firehart—it is of the utmost importance. I have made a promise to the red one. May we speak alone?" He motioned toward a small brown door between two of the long tables Kale had not noticed before.

"These are my friends." Kale glanced toward the three. "They are the closest individuals I have to a family, so anything you can say to me can be said before them."

"Very well. You have been assigned another quest. This task is one that must be completed by you; there can be no other."

Kale laughed in anger. "You have some nerve to stand before me and tell me what I must do with my own life. I have been *assigned* to nothing–I choose my own path. I'm already in a situation where I cannot even fathom how we will succeed."

"Let me speak, dragon child!" Brig's face shook as he spoke. "In a time when the darkness of despair lies upon us and it feels as though so much has been lost, you must open the window of your heart and allow in the light." His mood had completely changed. "Some things are worth fighting for—and I assure you this is one of those things."

"All right, I'm listening." Kale crossed his arms. "What exactly is it that this *red one* wants me to do?"

"There are more." Brig smiled.

The room grew silent and Kale caught himself awkwardly glancing around. "More of...?"

"More of you." Brig shook his head. "No, no, no, I mean more of your kind—dragons! You are not the last."

"What!?" Kale straightened his posture, sitting immediately upright. "How could you possibly know this? Where are they? Tell me now!"

"Kale mind yourself!" Thomas interrupted as he placed a firm grip onto Kale's shoulder. "Listen to what he has to say. Our time is running short, we must soon leave or risk Brig's safety here in Tyrione. We do not know if the guards already seek us."

Kale breathed as he gritted his teeth. "I understand. I'm sorry, Brig, please continue."

"Yes, yes, as I was saying, you are not the last dragon. Well—you weren't, before becoming a human, that is."

"I *am* still a dragon!" Kale snarled as Thomas cast him an admonishing glance.

"Control yourself, boy. I am doing you a favor by telling you this information." Brig pointed a dirty nail in Kale's direction. "Many years ago, three dragon eggs were to be transported to Eldawin by a human. Along his journey, a dragon who dwelled within the desert, the Emerald Prince, caught scent of his own kind and fought to retrieve them. He only meant to protect the eggs, unsure as to why a human had them to begin with. His attempt was futile as the eggs sunk beneath the Earth's surface, never to be seen again–until now. The red one is certain they have fallen into an underground cavern, safe and unharmed. Only you Firehart—born a dragon—can save them from extinction. You can reshape this world."

"Kale," Thomas gleamed with excitement for his friend, "do you remember the vision I shared with you? It's astonishing how suddenly we seem linked together now as this all unravels before us."

Kale wrinkled his forehead in thought, when suddenly it dawned on him. "General Jedah! The package he was assigned to deliver for his quest to become a knight. I'll bet that with your memories as our guide, we could find the vicinity where they sank." He glanced upward. "It all makes sense now; the reason the dragon attacked—he was protecting the unborn hatchlings of our own kind." Kale tightened his knuckles. "Jedah must be stopped or the Emerald Prince will have died in vain," Suddenly, Kale paused. "Wait a moment, how can we be sure that this isn't a trap? This *red one* you speak of could be working with Jedah in order to lead us to death."

"I can personally assure you the red one is not in league with General Jedah. The red one means well and even appears to have true concern for your well-being. However, the choice to proceed will be yours. I am but the messenger." Brig flicked another ball of earwax to the glass-covered floor.

Kale didn't need to analyze the situation any longer. Despite the uncertainties and possible dangers which lay ahead, there was absolutely no way he would be able to decline; especially if there were eggs remaining. He was willing to try, given the one chance that there was still hope for his kind.

"We should leave now. I'm sure the guards have been alerted of our absence." Neelan adjusted her bow.

"Indeed. It is time. If there are no enchantments which will prevent it, I can transport us out of the kingdom once we find seclusion outside."

"We should be all right. The enchantments bound to our city are to keep others out, not in."

Illadar, Thomas, and Neelan made their way cautiously up the tunnel, keeping a keen eye on the windows in case a guard patrolled nearby.

"Come here, boy." Brig spoke in a low tone. "Should you find Malakhar, please lay him to rest quickly. It is time his pain and reign of bitter hatred toward the world finally ends." Tears formed to pool in the corner of Brig's eyes.

"Are you all ri—" As Kale spoke, Brig held out a palm to stop him from speaking.

"Though, ashamed to have been related by blood to someone with such a cold, hollow heart—he is still my brother. We were born on the same day; twins, though not alike in appearance, nor personality. Some say twins share an eternal bond between one another. We never did. Neither of us cared to be near the other, and I made certain to keep my distance."

Kale stopped—shocked beyond words. He placed his hand upon the old elf's arm as he nodded his head.

Brig forced a smile; he understood the message Kale sent with his gesture. Kale would do his best to ensure Malakhar would receive a swift death.

~~~~~~~~~~~~~~~

Once they were certain no guards were in the immediate vicinity, the four quickly gave thanks to Brig. Even Neelan was grateful, though she remained distant. Within moments they walked around the side of Brig's home, squeezing between the wall of a neighboring house.

"Move quickly, we mustn't be spotted while limited to such a narrow space," Thomas whispered to the others.

They emerged onto another small street which bordered the back entrances of many homes.

"This should be secluded enough. Now, get us out of here, Thomas." Kale was anxious to return to the forest with the news they had acquired from Brig. His heart also leapt at the thought of seeking hope for dragon-kind.

"Come, gather and hold onto my arms tightly, as before." Thomas closed his eyes, prepared to begin chanting the magical language.

"Halt!" A voice rang out, softly echoing down the enclosed stone street.

Thomas' eyes shot open and the other three turned defensively.

"Lorin!" Neelan called out.

To their side stood the golden-haired guard. His silver eyes appeared weary and for the first time since Kale met him, his flawless face was blemished with dim purple rings beneath his bottom lids.

"Don't do this Lorin; I had to do what I did. You have got to trust me." Neelan continued to plead her case, but Lorin abruptly silenced her, placing a finger gently upon her lips.

"I am not here to turn you in."

Neelan tilted her head in confusion as she stepped back from the touch of his finger which had remained upon her mouth.

"I was spotted earlier by a patrolling guard. They know you placed an enchantment upon me and fled. I have stalled them until now; they are scattered across the city in search of you and your companions. I was sent here by the elders to personally scout Brig's home. They do not suspect I would seek to help you after what you had done to me." He glanced down as though hurt by her actions.

"Bu—"

"Please, let me finish Neelan, time is short."

She quietly nodded.

"I agreed so I could ensure your safe escape. I don't believe they are aware that your friend is a sorcerer." He gestured toward Thomas. "Although it pains me, I want you to promise you will not return here again. The elders informed the guards that should you enter these walls, your friends will be sentenced to death and you are to be imprisoned within the pit for the remainder of your life."

"They will not catch me." Neelan attempted to stubbornly argue, though her heart raced at the thought of being trapped in complete darkness for hundreds of years.

"Promise me!" Lorin's voice was demanding, inflicted with sorrow.

"I—I promise. I won't ever return to the kingdom again." Although Neelan despised her father and the memories Tyrione held, the finalization was frightening. This was goodbye forever.

"If you are here to ensure a safe exit, why in Pan's name did you stop us?" Kale was tired, hungry, and irritable.

"I needed to warn Neelan. You, however, can return if you'd like. It would be quite nice to see your head perched upon a stake at our gates to ward off more filth from coming our way," Lorin snickered.

"You'll die for that!" Kale leapt toward Lorin, wrapping his fingers around the elf's neck as he squeezed firmly.

"Enough!" Neelan shoved Kale off of Lorin, glaring at both men. "Now is *not* the time. Both of you need to stop behaving as though you were children."

Lorin looked to the street. "I apologize, Neelan." Without warning, he pulled her into a tight embrace. He leaned down to her long ear, "I also came to say farewell. Please be safe," he whispered, releasing his grip. "I'll ensure the council does not know you were here—Brig will not endure punishment for assisting your cause. Though, I cannot understand why you would seek a dark elf, I am sure it is important. Please leave now, with no worry of what shall happen here." He bowed before turning to leave down the dark street.

Neelan gave a final glance toward him before returning to her friends. "Let's go." Her words were monotone and short.

They each gripped tightly onto Thomas' arm as he once again resumed a clear state of mind. "*Kalora Xenari.*" He called out, then they disappeared from sight.

With a *zap*, they were flung through a void before being tossed onto the leaf coated ground of the Forest of Forgotten Whispers.

Kale, Illadar, and Neelan groaned in discomfort as they slowly staggered to their feet.

"At least you didn't vomit this time." Kale half-jokingly teased Illadar as he gripped his own stomach to ease the nauseating sensation.

"Make haste across the river, we do not need a third encounter with Rees'Lok," Thomas urged.

With everything that had happened, Kale nearly forgot about the snaggle-toothed orc.

The four hurried across the running water and made way through the protected area of the forest where the dryads dwelled. Though Kale displayed a casual exterior, his insides were fluttering at the thought of seeing Judith again.

"You came back!" A shaky voice called out.

Kale squinted through the darkness in the direction of the sound. A round figure moved closer until he could see the hundreds of creases on the old woman's flesh. The tip of her long crooked nose led to a bumpy bridge between two, close-set, black, beady eyes. Her thin, near balding, grey hair revealed many fat moles scattered across her scalp. This was quite the opposite of what Kale expected upon his arrival. He fought the urge to shudder and step away from the old woman he knew was truly Judith—the stunning Princess of Mirion.

"Y-yes, I told you we would return." He finally choked the words out, forcing a smile.

Judith wrapped her stumpy, sagging arms around Kale's torso. "I am so glad you have come back safely."

"Thank you." Kale awkwardly replied.

"I hate to come between such a warm reunion," Neelan crossed her arms, "but we should go inside now. We aren't staying long." She narrowed her eyes as she glanced toward Judith. "One night, at most."

Normally, Kale might have stubbornly argued, but his desire to put a stop to Jedah and find the truth behind the dragon eggs drove his will to keep moving forward. On top of all else, he was starving and exhausted—the thought of going inside to rest was incredibly appealing.

"I knew thou would return to us." Elanya stood within the entrance of the massive tree. Her cascading white hair and pale flesh stood out dramatically against the darkness which wrapped around the tree in all directions.

They entered the familiar circular common room when Judith began to moan as her elderly body collapsed upon the floor. She curled into a fetal position, whimpering softly as her limbs began to stretch in length. The deep wrinkles on her skin flattened as the flesh tightened over her muscles. Her sun-kissed, sandy blonde hair sprouted from her scalp, replacing the grey frizz.

"Do not look at me!" Judith cried out as the transformation completed its process. The frumpy clothing draped from her thin frame.

"Thou should leave thee to change attire." Elanya motioned

them to another, smaller room. "Thou saw a glimpse at ye pain Judith endures each day from ye curse. Let us speak now while thee recovers." She maternally glanced toward Judith.

"We're just going to leave her in this state?" Kale questioned in concern.

Elanya nodded, "'Tis something she hath gone through for years. Judith desires to be alone during this time; now come."

They obeyed and wearily entered the cozy, candlelit room. Within moments, three beautiful, brunette, dryad women carried in silver trays piled with fresh fruit. Kale's animalistic instincts took control of his motor functions, causing his arm to shoot out and grip a handful of berries. He immediately shoved them into his mouth, chewing loudly. The realization of just how hungry he truly was sunk in as the sweet juices ran down his throat.

"Thank you." He unclearly mumbled, taking careful note of Thomas' disapproving glare.

"I must speak to thee, now, before Judith hath finished resting."

Kale nodded, though disappointed he couldn't further indulge in the delicious food without interruption.

"Did thou find information?" Elanya softly spoke, leaning toward Kale.

"Mmm-hmm." Kale replied, swallowing the remaining portion within his mouth. He continued on to explain everything they learned during their time with Brig. Kale even shared the news of dragon eggs still existing within the world. In his heart, he knew the dryads were on their side and could be trusted.

"'Tis great news for both thou and Judith." She smiled. "To know there is hope brings joy to thine heart. Thou must make leave tomorrow. Eat and rest now; thou must decide which path to embark upon. To free Judith—or seek ye dragon eggs. Ye choice may bring great rewards—or despair. For every action, there shalt be a consequence." Elanya stood, silently returning to the room in which they earlier left Judith.

"Do ya' have a plan?" Illadar asked as he lifted a wooden mug to his lips.

"Not really," Kale admitted. "I honestly don't know what to do. Choosing to seek Malakhar first might result in someone else discovering the truth about the dragon eggs. If anyone managed to retrieve them before us, it could end all hope for my kind. I know Brig said only I could save them. But, if it's only a matter of them resting beneath the earth's surface, then I don't see why another person couldn't stumble upon them. On the other hand— if I don't hunt Malakhar now, we may not have another opportunity before he returns to Mirion. Once he reunites with the mass of Jedah's army, there will be no hope of saving Judith at this time." Kale sighed as he shoved more berries into his mouth.

"We will figure it all out, don't worry." Neelan sat by his side, smiling soothingly.

No sooner had Neelan begun to comfort Kale when Judith entered the room. She immediately made a straight path toward Kale, seating herself on his other side.

"I apologize that you had to see me like that. I was so engrossed with your return, I nearly forgot the effects which would occur upon me stepping within the tree."

"Maybe next time you should pay better attention to your surroundings." Neelan leaned forward, glaring past Kale at the Princess.

There was tension in the air and a heavy silence engulfed the room.

"This yellow fruit is fantastic. Sweet, yet soft and juicy." Thomas nibbled on a flat square slice in hopes of softening the mood.

"How long will you be staying this time?" Judith's lips curved into an alluring smile that caused Kale to uncontrollably stare.

"Answer her." Neelan nudged the back of Kale's head, intentionally breaking his focus.

His eyes fluttered. "Um, not too long. We will be gone by tomorrow."

"So soon? If I may be so bold, will you please tell me why? You have only just returned." Judith placed her hand gently upon his.

Kale uncomfortably dodged Neelan's jealous stares. "We have another mission I cannot discuss openly. I do hope you understand." He was still too unsure of the outcome to get Judith's hopes up.

"I see. Well, I do hope you will come back soon." Her hand caressed his.

"I will return. That I can promise you," Kale reassured the Princess.

"All right, Kale," Neelan tugged his arm, "I think it is time for you to get some rest now. We have a lot to do tomorrow."

After a brief debate, Kale finally gave in as he piled a few more helpings of fruit into his mouth before standing to leave. He entered the familiar sleeping quarters then slid his shoes off and climbed inside one of the hanging, woven hammocks near the wall. His head ached as fatigue and thoughts from their extended day fought within his mind. He pondered his newly acquired knowledge of potential hope for dragon-kind, making him feel closer than ever to returning to his true form as a mighty black beast. The image of three baby dragons filled his mind, causing a smile to form across his face. The overwhelming joy of retrieving the eggs and finding a way to hatch them swarmed within his mind as he drifted into a dreamless slumber.

~~~~~~~~~~~~~~~

"Thou must wake!"

A sharp whisper rang in Kale's ear which startled him awake. "Wh-what's happening?" He asked, running a hand through his sloppy black hair as he wrinkled his forehead in confusion.

"Shh! Silence boy. Thou mustn't wake Judith. I shalt explain the situation to her come morning." Elanya towered over him as he slowly swayed within his hammock. "Word hath come that there shalt be an attack upon Braxle before dawn's first light. Thou must go to protect ye town." She urged Kale to his feet. "Give me thy sword." Elanya held out her hand impatiently.

Kale scurried through the darkness, still disoriented by the abrupt awakening. He quietly approached the far wall where his weapon was leaning; secured within the steel sheath.

"H-here." Kale mumbled while squinting his eyes in an attempt to regain focus of his surroundings.

Elanya quickly took the sword from his grip as she led him into the circular common room. She wasted no time with her actions as she lifted the unsheathed sword horizontally atop her palms.

"*Shek ton morey istu kokanae rebooshtan.*" As Elanya spoke, the sword began to reflect a blinding golden light which surrounded the blade.

"Take thy weapon." Elanya handed it back to Kale as the golden light faded. "This shalt aid thou in battle. When thy powers grow strong and thy blade burns with warmth, thine spell shalt help protect it from breaking. However, thou must remember–thine spell cannot withstand intense heat. Should thou infuse thy weapon with full power, it shalt still shatter. Be wary, dragon child." She gave Kale a gentle shove. "Many shalt die if you do not make haste. Go now, and take heed for Malakhar will be present with ye arriving army; however, ye one called General Jedah shalt not. Malakhar comes for ye one who hath betrayed Jedah—and he cometh for thee, Kale Firehart."

CHAPTER 23

THEY COME FOR BLOOD

Kale emerged into the crisp night's air as he secured his sword and approached the others who were already dressed, armed, and prepared for battle. A red-headed dryad woman followed, carrying a bundle of sharpened arrows.

"For thee, madam." The dryad handed them to Neelan, as she humbly bowed.

"Many thanks." Neelan placed them into her quiver which was now stocked full.

"May thee be safe upon ye journey, and may thee return balance to ye world." The dryad woman smiled as she turned to leave into the forest.

Kale nodded. He knew it was on this night, he would need to rise and prove himself a warrior. There was no further time to prepare; he had to fight in order to protect the lives of innocent victims. He needed no second opinion on his decision; he would give it his all or die trying. The people of Braxle were the first to take him in and give him a renewed look at life. Kale would not allow Malakhar and the royal army of Mirion to slaughter them just to get at he, and Illadar. This time Kale was prepared to stand and fight. Never again would he remain in seclusion while those he cared for died.

"Thomas, do you have the strength to teleport and still stand to fight?"

"Yes, Kale, I believe so. Though transporting so many at once is draining, I should still have the reserves to conjure attacks upon the intruders. I do feel quite rested, despite the minimal amount of sleep. Besides, if need be I have this." He placed a hand over the polished steel scabbard of his dagger as he winked at Illadar.

They made their way cautiously outside the protected grounds. Each glanced around in hopes that they would not face another encounter by Rees'Lok and the red beasts.

"I think the ugly green mongrel is sleepin'... Let's get movin'. I refuse to let innocent citizens die at the cost of my own actions." Illadar wiped tiny beads of sweat from his upper lip as he spoke.

"I agree." Kale took in a deep breath of cool air. "We need to leave now; it is the only way I foresee making it to Braxle with enough time to move the townsfolk to safety." He glanced toward Neelan. "You don't need to come with us, you know. This is not your battle. Go live a real life away from all this chaos."

"Away from the chaos means away from you, as well, and that is not something I am willing to accept. I'm standing by your side, no matter what should happen." She gripped onto Thomas' arm. "I am ready to go."

Thomas chuckled before he rolled his neck, closing his eyes to prepare for the teleportation spell. In an instant—they were gone.

~~~~~~~~~~~~~~~

Kale gripped his forehead, "Ugh, at least it is easier to handle each time we travel this way." He staggered upon wobbly legs, fighting the feeling that at any moment his knees would give out. As he glanced toward the pointed wood wall, it seemed miniscule in comparison to Tyrione's massive stone barrier. "We have got to move with haste. Without knowing the location of the oncoming army, we haven't a clue of when they'll arrive."

"Indeed, Kale, every passing minute is extremely valuable. We must warn the others." Thomas breathed heavily, but began to walk toward the town entrance.

Illadar was on his heels and Neelan remained close to Kale at all times. The gentle night breeze sifted through her hair as she moved forth with determination.

At that moment, despite the fear which gnawed at Kale's gut, he realized for the first time how ravishing Neelan truly was.

"Neelan," Kale spoke softly as they briskly made way through the town, "please be cautious tonight. You are my friend and I don't want anything to happen to you. I don't want to lose you."

"You worry too much, I shall be fine. My bow has never let me down." She flashed a confident smile.

"Where are you takin' us, kid? Do we even have a plan?" Illadar kept his eyes peeled in all directions in case any sudden, abnormal movements should take place within the shadows.

"I do not think any of us were prepared for this to happen. I'm going to take us to Lord Zalimond's home. I've figured that if anyone knows the fastest way to alert the townsfolk of evacuation, it'll be him."

"This is going to be an interestin' night. Let's hope it all works out in the end." Sweat began to form on Illadar's dark, muscular arms. He was definitely feeling the tension of their situation.

Kale tried to focus on getting them to their destination as quickly as possible. He thought back to the tour of Braxle Theresa had given him, remembering each turn to take. A surge of disappointment weighed upon him in the back of his mind. He secretly wished General Jedah would have had the nerve to rear his ugly, bald head within Braxle. Kale thought of how sweet slicing his neck in two would be. However, he knew, realistically, there would be no chance only the four of them would rise victorious over the full force of Jedah's massive army.

Although freeing Judith of her curse would result in the general's execution, Kale would not be satisfied. Kale longed to avenge the innocent and dragon-kind. He desired to stare deep into the general's eyes as he forced the nefarious monstrosity into an eternal slumber. Kale laughed aloud at his own thoughts as he unknowingly bared his teeth in an animalistic snarl.

"Is this the place?" Neelan questioned Kale.

Kale had been so deeply wrapped in his own thoughts he failed to realize they were standing directly in front of the Lord's home.

"Yes, this is it." Kale glanced toward the house. "All lights appear to be off. He is about to receive one devil of an awakening."

"What had you expected? Most normal individuals are resting well by this time." Thomas rested a hand on Kale's shoulder. "Shall we proceed now?"

Kale nodded. His throat felt dry and his stomach twisted in knots as he approached Lord Zalimond's door. *There is no turning back now.* Kale's knuckles firmly rapped against the wood, creating a repetitive rhythm until they saw the flickering light of an oil lamp through an oversized window.

"Who is it? Are you aware of the time?!" A disoriented sounding male voice called out after several moments of silence. "This better be of the utmost importance."

The door creaked open to reveal a stout, middle-aged man with a plump, round face and thick black mustache. It was obvious they disturbed the Lord's sleep as his receding black hair stood out in all directions and his attire consisted of a long blue nightshirt.

Lord Zalimond held the lamp out toward Kale's face. "Who are you?" Thick-ridged wrinkles formed upon his forehead.

"My name is Kale, and we have come with urgent news. There is an army of men in route to Braxle who are prepared to attack. They are ruthless and will surely claim the lives of any commoners they cross."

The Lord's small beady eyes narrowed as he silently stared toward Kale — attempting to read his expression. Suddenly, he burst into a fit of laughter. "You expect me to believe this?" The skin between his eyes wrinkled, "Be gone! Braxle is a peaceful town; we have neither guards nor trained soldiers, why would anyone possibly dispatch an army to attack? It makes little sense. We have nothing of value anyone could possibly desire so badly."

Lord Zalimond had a natural way of coming off as irritating. This made Kale grateful that throughout his time within Braxle, he went unnoticed by the self-absorbed Lord. It was a rare sight for Zalimond to be seen roaming the streets.

"Lord, I assure you what this kid says is true." Illadar stepped forward to Kale's side.

"Galin! You've returned already?" He paused. "How can you

be so sure of what this young man says? And why did you abandon your job at the blacksmith forge?" His beady eyes now glanced across the four as if to ensure there were no others present whom he would recognize. "Are these your friends?"

Neelan tugged upon the hood of her cloak to ensure it safely concealed her pointed ears.

"Yes, they're all with me and we haven't much time to spare," Illadar quickly replied.

"Ah, I do believe I have seen the old fellow in town before." Lord Zalimond glanced toward Thomas.

Thomas grunted, trying not to take much offense to the Lord's ill-mannered words.

"We don't have the time for a reunion," Kale interrupted their conversation. "They could attack at any moment and we must evacuate the citizens."

"From which direction will this attack strike?" Lord Zalimond seemed to believe his warning by this point as his tone grew serious.

"Unfortunately, we don't have any information on their location." Kale knew that time was far too short to engage in an explanation about Malakhar, or even Elanya who informed them of the attack.

"Evacuating the people of this town is an unwise decision which I will not endorse. You could very well be leading the citizens directly toward the army—straight to their deaths."

They knew he made a solid point and did not further argue. Kale also knew that by the time they evacuated such a large group to safety, Malakhar and the army would have most likely burnt Braxle down to ash. Kale tugged at his black hair and groaned in frustration. He knew they could not prevent casualties, unless the people were each removed from their homes.

"Is there anywhere we could hide them?" Illadar suggested. "If we can't get 'em out of here, then we should try to find a means to hide them safely within the town."

"Not possible. There is nowhere large enough to accommodate such a number of individuals." Zalimond shook his head.

Kale could feel his temper rising when it dawned on him–the secret location Theresa spoke of, beneath the Lord's grand home. "There *is* somewhere!" Kale exclaimed with enthusiasm.

"Pardon?" Zalimond raised a black bushy brow.

"I am aware of the room you have beneath your home, hidden away from the townsfolk and unknown by most. From what I have heard, it should be adequate for the accommodations we need. The people could hide there until this is all over."

"N-no." The Lord stammered. "You have heard wrong. There is no such place."

"Don't lie to us, you greedy cur! What riches do you possibly think will remain if the town is demolished?" Kale's arm shot out as he gripped the Lord's night gown, pulling him so close he could feel Zalimond's breath against his face. "Listen," Kale growled, "there are many innocent people sleeping within their beds as we speak—women, children, and infants. Now, we will try this one last time and, so help me, you'd better tell the truth or I'll rip you apart." His upper lip curled , baring his teeth in anger. The scent of burning cloth filled Kale's nostrils. He quickly released his grip before any harmful damage had been done.

Lord Zalimond's face paled and tiny beads of sweat formed above his lip. "All right, yes, I have a treasury. It was built to secure my wealth, and could probably fit each citizen inside. B-but, how did you do that...?" He glanced toward the browned area of cloth on his night gown where Kale had touched.

"This is no time for such questions!" Illadar came to Kale's aid.

Lord Zalimond's eyes glanced to the ground in defeat. "Right... I shall dress and inform my wife of the situation, and then we will begin our alert."

"We must go now; do not worry about your appearance and your wife will be fine for the moment." Thomas gestured toward the petite, middle-aged woman who now stood behind Zalimond. "What part of *the enemy may arrive at any moment* do you not comprehend? We need you to join our party for the time being so the citizens are confident we speak the truth." Thomas' temper had been pressed and now he too was quite agitated by the Lord's careless behavior.

"All right," Zalimond replied as he turned to face his wife. He gave her a firm nod as if to tell her everything would be fine before stepping into his home. The Lord retrieved a hand bell located near his front door. "Let us go, then."

The Lord's method of alarming the citizens seemed inadequate, but there was no further time to come up with alternate ideas. They made their way briskly down the streets of town as Zalimond frantically clanged the inner ball of the bell. It seemed as though the realization of the situation had finally sunk into his thick skull.

Kale and the others began to run from door to door, banging their fists upon the wood to wake each family.

"You must leave for the Lord's home immediately; there is an attack in route now! Please wait outside his door. More information will be forthcoming shortly!" Thomas repeatedly called these words, reinforcing it to the more stubborn or confused individuals.

Mothers and fathers rushed to grab their children, while

others rummaged through their belongings to retrieve valuables or family heirlooms before leaving. The town was now in a state of panic.

"We will take care of things from here on." Kale told Lord Zalimond. "You should return to your home and ensure everyone gets safely inside." As the Lord turned to leave, Kale firmly gripped his arm, "And do not even think of attempting anything foolish." His voice was low and threatening.

"I am the Lord of this town; I will make certain they are safe within the underground chamber." He yanked his arm free and left for his home.

They continued down each street, double checking many of the homes to ensure each was empty. Kale even scouted the tavern to ensure no townsfolk were still indulging in a late night drink. As he confidently made his way back toward his comrades, he heard a man's voice calling to him. Kale spun around to see a group of nine men standing in a close gathered group.

"I told you it was him!" One of the men exclaimed. "You're the young man from the tavern that night, when the odd fellow in black came in."

The foggy memory of Kale's night out with Theresa raced through his mind as he began to vaguely recall a few of the men's faces. "Yes, it is me. I do appreciate the aid you provided that night, but I assure you it is in your best interest to follow the others to Lord Zalimond's home. You'll find sanctuary there from the oncoming attackers," Kale urged the men to make haste.

"Not happenin'." The heavy set man who had assisted him and Illadar that night crossed his arms. "We've all decided we aren't gonna' run and hide. We will stand and fight—Braxle is our home and no one is gonna' to take it from us."

"You have no idea what you're up against! Do not be fools—

the army that will soon arrive consists of well-trained warriors who will show no mercy under command."

"Let them come. Braxle will soon enough be their grave." Another man spoke up and the others supported his words with cheer. His massive arms bulged from a sleeveless tunic as he pounded a fist into his palm.

"Besides," the first man dove back into the conversation, "Lord Zalimond is already in the process of sealing them into some secret room of which he spoke. There is no turning back now." He ran a hand over his tightly, pulled-back, brown hair. "We might not be well-trained warriors—but we are strong and able. By the looks of your numbers, you could use additional support."

The last thing Kale needed was to look after a band of commoners who had no prior sword fighting experience. It was a death sentence for them. Despite his disagreement with the circumstances, Kale knew they were right to assume there would be no turning back at this point. He would need to make the best of the situation and begin preparations with the unknown time remaining before the attack. In the back of Kale's mind, he couldn't comprehend why Jedah did not choose to come for the battle. It was he, after all, who had sworn to slaughter the final dragon. The thought made Kale uneasy.

"Fine," he finally graced the men with a response, "if you are willing to risk your life for this town, then follow me." He quickly led the group toward the blacksmithing forge which he had grown to know very well. They rummaged through the entire workshop, taking anything they could find that was ready for battle.

Kale watched in dismay as only a couple of the men handled their weaponry appropriately. The others clumsily swung their steel around as though it were a toy. Kale's mood was lifted when he took notice of the neatly organized piles of armor. It was obvious that a new blacksmith had taken over the shop.

"Men, come here and find something that fits properly. This should assist greatly while in combat." Kale commanded. He was proud of himself for his ability to lead the group.

"Smart move, kid." Illadar's voice caused Kale to start in surprise. "I tried to find you in hopes we could scrounge some armor, but I see you're already one step ahead." He grinned.

"I needed to ensure these men are well-equipped before the army of knights arrives."

Illadar leaned back to peer around a large pillar in order to investigate the new additions to their group.

"'Ey look, boys, Galin is back too!" A blonde-haired man spoke as the others cheered. "Ya' were the best blacksmith we've ever had, I tell ya'! Barniber took the place over, but it's jus' not the same. He fled like a coward ta' the Lord's house already."

"Thanks, but this isn't the time for praise. We've gotta' keep movin'," Illadar replied.

Kale could tell Illadar forced his face to remain expressionless in order to hide the prideful smile which struggled to reveal itself. Kale had grown accustomed to Illadar's defensive tough exterior, but knew that beneath was truly a soft and warm individual.

"Kale, this should fit." Illadar tossed him a chest plate.

"Thank you—we've got to get going now."

Clad with the basic essentials, they gathered at the center of the town square, quickly met by Thomas and Neelan.

"The town has been completely cleared." Thomas lowered his grey brows. "You've brought others?"

"Yes, they are townsfolk who have chosen to stand and fight

alongside us," Kale replied.

"Well, we need to form a strategy as quickly as possible. With more in our party the options have broadened." Neelan's voice was calm and serious.

After remaining in heavy silence as they each weighed their choices, Thomas finally spoke. "I believe it would be in our best interest to keep watch, in order to see from which direction the oncoming attack will come. It will allow us a great advantage with defensive tactics when confronting them as they approach. We should separate and take post on each side of the town."

"That would be a good idea, only..." Kale paused, giving momentary thought to his words, "how will we communicate with one another? It's not as though we can speak to each other from such a distance. Do you expect us to run halfway across the town to send word the army has been spotted? By then they may already have arrived."

"A wise perception, young one." Thomas grinned. "Though, I do have an idea." He looked toward the group of men who had joined them. "We have more than enough within our party to spread out in pairs." Thomas then reached into his pouch, retrieving four strips of silky pearlescent cloth."

"We don't have time for games, Thomas. Please tell us what you're up to before we are ambushed." Kale rubbed the bridge of his nose.

"Myself, and you three," Thomas pointed toward Kale, Neelan, and Illadar, "along with four of the men shall make way to the homes that border alongside the picket wall. We will need to position ourselves atop the thatched rooftops in order to have a clear view of our surroundings."

"Can't we just stand on the surrounding perimeter? It would make things much more simplistic than attempting to climb atop a structure." Neelan placed her hands upon her hips.

"No, dear, that would be far too dangerous. We need the protection of the walls to provide an additional defensive advantage." Thomas fumbled with the four strips of cloth. "Now, as I was saying, once atop of the roof we will utilize these pieces of fabric. They will be used as signals." He raised his eyebrows, reading the expression upon the others faces. "I do apologize, but it is the best I could do under these circumstances. I assure you, however, they will suffice." Thomas then bunched the material into his fist as he closed his eyes. With a wave of his free hand, he softly spoke, "*Grevorta Kadexia.*" An immediate pale glow emitted from between the crevices in his fingers. "Keep these concealed as to not alert the enemy of our presence. Should you see any movement coming toward the town, take the glowing ribbon and hold it to the inner direction of the city. Through the darkness, we should each see the signal with ease. Using this method we can quickly determine where the attack will first hit. Though, they may enter through the town entrance, regardless, we must be prepared for anything. We do not know what type of weaponry they bring." He handed a strip of glowing cloth to Kale, Neelan, and Illadar, who eagerly inspected the item before shoving it out of sight.

"How are we gonna' get atop the houses?" Illadar was still unsure of the plan.

"All homes have a ladder in back for when the roof needs repair." One of the townsmen chimed in.

"What will happen once one side has revealed the signal?" Kale added to the questions.

"Meet in the town square immediately so we can gather forces. We are useless in pairs once they infiltrate the town," Illadar commanded.

Everyone nodded in agreement, preparing for their course of action. The remaining men were to station themselves within the square and await further instruction while keeping watch for movement within the town.

"All right, let's get moving. We've already expended too much time here." Kale motioned for his partner to join him as they began making way toward the eastern wall. The feeling of dread began to swarm around him as he and the townsman approached their destination.

With all the hustle, they had not prepared any strategy for once the army arrived. It seemed as though in the end, it would be every man for himself. The one thing Kale was certain of, above all else, was he desired to seek and destroy Malakhar.

Once they situated themselves atop the roof, Kale carefully adjusted his feet to avoid falling through the woven thatch. He glanced at the vast surroundings. As the cool breeze grazed his cheeks, he recalled the night he spotted Neelan perched atop the wall, watching over him. Kale smiled, taking in the moment, and realizing just how much she truly did care for him.

"How do you think this will end? My wife is hiding with the others at Lord Zalimond's home. I'd easily lay my life on the line before allowing any harm to befall her. She means everything to me." The slender man who had accompanied him finally spoke. He ran a hand over his short, slightly graying, brown hair. "I just can't believe this is happening to us. I'm not sure what we've done to deserve such an attack, it all seems so surreal." His eyes filled with worry as he spoke.

Kale dodged the man's stare, feeling torn and guilty inside. His heart ached at the realization of how much pain and worry he had placed upon the people of Braxle. He cleared his throat. "They should be safe within the hidden room. But, we will need to fight—that much is certain. Without defense, the army will burn this town to the ground." He glanced toward his palms at the thought of burning. Kale truly hoped the night would prove he had truly learned to master his powers. "You will be in charge of keeping an eye out for other signals. I shall watch for outside movement. Please alert me immediately should you see anything—as will I." Kale handed the man his glowing strip of fabric, taking caution not to reveal it from concealment at any time. "Please hide this, unless I give word to shine it for the others to see."

"Understood, Sir," the man replied.

Kale had never been called Sir before, let alone treated with such formal respect. It made him feel important.

The man sighed, "I don't really know who you are, but I give my thanks for your return. The fact that you've come back here to fight for our town and its people is noble." He forced a smile. "If it matters any, my name is Forwin."

Kale couldn't find the courage within himself to confess that the army's main motive was to seek him and Illadar. He wished they had known of Malakhar's plan sooner, or knew more details of their location to ambush the foray of men before they even reached the perimeter of the town. "My name is Kale." For the first time he looked into Forwin's eyes. "When the time comes to engage in battle, use your senses and watch every movement of your opponent. Do not make any rash or foolish moves. You will be no help in protecting your wife if dead."

They continued to wait beneath the starlit sky; each man keeping a keen eye on their surroundings. With every passing moment their anxiety increased, weighing on them heavily as they sat with uncertainty.

Suddenly, the faint flicker of a flame could be seen in the far distance which caused Kale to focus his eyes to further investigate. His heart began to pound against his chest and his breathing intensified. He was certain at this point that what he saw was the army; their torches became clear against the sheet of darkness—they wanted their presence to be known.

"It's them; they are coming from this direction. Quickly, reveal the signal!" Kale commanded.

Within seconds, Kale felt a hand tightly clench his wrist. "I think we are in grave trouble." Forwin's voice was hoarse as he spoke.

"What are you—" Kale's mouth hung open in shock. He was struck speechless.

From each direction, they could see the illuminate glow of the cloth shining back toward them. The army was coming from all sides. A feeling of despair swept over Kale as he fought to remain strong; he did not want to reveal any sign of weakness to Forwin.

The knights moved quickly toward them as they marched to a steady beat–closing in on them like hungry wolves. Kale and his comrades were the prey, trapped within one large cage. It was too late to run, too late to plan their next move. The time had come to fight or die.

CHAPTER 24

THE DARK ELF'S RETURN

"Quickly, make way to the town square!" Kale called out to Forwin.

Upon a final glance, Kale confirmed there were at least a dozen men heading in his direction. He swallowed hard, hoping his friends would return with better results.

Once they made their way down the side of the home and back to the square, the others awaited their arrival.

"This is unbelievable—what are we to do?" Neelan appeared distraught as she tightly gripped her bow. "There will be no way for us to split up and confront each group outside of town. If my calculations were correct, there are eighteen men approaching from my side. The group consists of mostly archers from what viewed through the darkness."

"Mine had over a dozen as well, though, I'm unsure of the weaponry they carry." Illadar added. "They are headin' directly toward the town entrance."

Kale grunted. His hopes had been trampled by the realization they were well outnumbered. He had expected a small army; he didn't fathom such a considerable contingent of forces.

"I believe I have an idea." Thomas chimed in on the conversation. "Neelan and I will return to our assigned post as quickly as possible. The rooftops are close enough to allow a clear view over the picket tips of the wall. With ranged attacks we should have the ability to eliminate some of the incoming targets. Any reduction will be beneficial once they are close enough to infiltrate through the entrance. I do not believe they are aware we know of their arrival, so I'm anticipating this will catch them with the element of surprise. We shall return here once they have moved in close enough to become a threat to our own well-being." He turned toward Neelan, "Fight cautiously—not recklessly. Go quickly, young one."

She nodded, dashing off toward the west wall. As Kale watched his two friends leave, he sighed, regrettably wishing he had told them to return safely. He knew Thomas would fend well for himself, but he feared for Neelan. Kale knew she had never used her bow for more than hunting animals. The thought of losing her began to pierce at his heart.

"All right men, hold a firm grip upon your weapons and prepare to engage in combat. We don't know their course of action, so the front entrance may be breached at any moment. Though the square allows us more room to fight, along with a broadened perspective of all sides of town, it would be in our favor to move forward and encounter them toward the entrance. The bordering structures will work as a barrier so we can close the area around us. They will be forced to confront us head on and in a more condensed formation. This will save us from havin' to take on all of 'em at once. It's too late for us to strategize any form of a surprise attack—especially with the lack of previous skill in battle, it would surely increase the odds of casualties."

Illadar paced before the group. Having already fought alongside Mirion's royal army, he was the only one fit to lead. Each man nodded in agreement, prepared to advance forward upon command. Illadar kept his claymore strapped securely to his back and instead withdrew the spiked flail which dangled to his calf.

"Let's move!" Illadar ordered as he took the first steps toward the town entrance.

~~~~~~~~~~~~~~~~~

Neelan nimbly stood atop the spiked wall as she watched the knights creep closer in the darkness. Because of her exceptional vision, she was able to clearly target each of the men. Neelan bit her lower lip in disappointment as she took notice to the chainmail that covered their bodies. She knew it would prove to be a great challenge for her. She carefully inspected their neck, hands, and a limited section of their faces, making a mental note that these were the only areas where armor was not present. Neelan forced the thought into her mind that these men were just like animals and she was the huntress. *I never miss a target.* She continued to prep her morale with positive reinforcement. Neelan flipped her cloak over her shoulders as she slid an arrow out of the quiver, resting it precisely atop her fingers as she began applying tension to the string.

She knew that upon first strike, the group of knights would become frantic and quicken their pace to attack.

"Here we go..." She whispered as her fingertips released the string. The arrow shot forth through the darkness toward her first target and Neelan watched as it pierced into his cheek. The knight stumbled back as he staggered in a swaying motion before collapsing to the ground. Before the other men had time to react, she launched another arrow which zipped recklessly past the helmet of another knight.

Concentrate! Neelan tried to focus under the intense pressure, steadying her hand which fought to tremble. Another arrow released, this time landing its mark and striking a knight through his eye socket. *Bull's-eye.* She swallowed hard at the realization that she had now killed two humans.

Within seconds, Neelan watched as many of the knights swung objects from around their backs. She quickly realized they were holding crossbows and readying for an attack.

"I am not going down so easily." She stared forward with resolve as she fired another shot that landed an instant killing blow.

"Fire!" a man's voice called out.

Before Neelan could react, a bolt flew past her cheek nearly grazing her flesh. Her heart raced and her breathing quickened. She began to fire a series of arrows, sending more of the men to their grave, while giving others mere flesh wounds. She managed to utilize her exceptional senses to dodge oncoming attacks which were much slower than her own.

As the men retaliated with another wave of bolts, Neelan lost her footing while trying to dodge the attacks. The split second in time it took for Neelan to regain balance caused her to lose concentration just long enough to miscalculate her movements. She returned focus toward the attack in time to watch as a bolt pierced through the tender meat between her rib bones. The impact caused her body to fall back as she tumbled onto and down the thatched roof, landing forcefully upon the ground. Pain seared through her torso as the blood began to saturate through her grey bodice. Neelan gritted her teeth as she mustered the strength to snap the bolt's end off, leaving the tip embedded in her tissue. She knew removing it entirely at this point in the battle would cause her to lose too much blood. Not wanting to cause her friends more worry in the already tense situation, Neelan pulled her beige cloak around her shoulders, which allowed the fabric to drape over the wound.

She inhaled, forcing her mind to change focus from the incredible pain as she ran back to her friends. They needed to be warned of the remaining archers who could easily launch a rain of arrows upon them at any moment.

"Neelan!" Kale's face lit up as she approached. "I am really glad you are safe. What is the status?"

"I believe nine of the eighteen have been killed, four wounded. Each man wore chain mail, so, as we've expected, they are well equipped with armor." She had a difficult time speaking while enduring the pain.

"Are you all right?" Kale questioned her odd behavior.

"Yes, I am fine." Her eyes shifted in another direction. "I'm just winded from my run back here."

They both turned as the sound of rapid footsteps could be heard. Thomas approached, wiping dripping sweat from his face with the sleeve of his tunic. "I come with a positive report." He heavily gasped for air before continuing on to explain how he managed to completely eliminate all approaching archers from his direction using a spell numerous times which caused the ground to explode from beneath their feet. "There was however, one issue which arose. While I was able to rid the burden of approaching archers, there was one individual who remained unharmed." He shot a glance toward Kale. "Malakhar was within the group of men. He deflected each blast with ease, remaining uninjured throughout my entire efforts. He still approaches. We must ready ourselves. I believe it would also be wise for me to return toward the western wall to finish off the men Neelan was against. It would be unfortunate if we were caught beneath a sea of bolts." He glanced down, quickly tucking his hands beneath the long sleeves of his tunic. The poison from exerting his magical abilities had begun to take effect, though not nearly enough to put him at his capacity. Thomas knew he must be able to continue casting to help ensure the safety of his friends.

"All right, Thomas, but do not over exert your magical abilities." Kale cautioned him in concern. "I do have one question before you go. Do you think Malakhar has learned the dark elven magic, Drell? Brig said he was only skilled with releasing powerful curses upon individuals, yet he deflected your magic so effortlessly. It seems suspicious."

"Very perceptive of you, Kale. We must take great caution while facing such a foe. It's been quite some time since you've encountered him, just as you have grown in power, he may have also—be careful, dear friend. I do not feel this attack is a random act of cruelty. My intuition tells me it was carefully planned."

"I will utilize my training to its fullest tonight." Kale gripped his sword with a grin. "You be safe too—old man."

As Kale watched Thomas disappear into the darkness, the sound of pounding footsteps could be heard trampling over the clay entry street. Kale cursed himself for not thinking of a solid plan to delay or prevent entry into the town. He knew, however, there would have been no possibility for Neelan and Thomas alone to ward off every enemy. No one else within their party had skill with ranged weaponry aside from minor hunting tactics with sharpened sticks. Although Kale knew there had been no time for preparations, the thought of ambushing the oncoming knights seemed more appealing than ever; yet he knew at this point it was far too late.

"Ready yourselves men, and reposition to face the oncomin' attack." Illadar tightened his hold upon the flail. He was prepared to fight with every ounce of his strength. This battle was for the wife and child he had so tragically lost—it was for those who had suffered by the hands of Jedah's men—and to protect the innocent hiding beneath the small town.

"I am ready, let them come—for they shall die tonight." Kale's eyes burned with hatred at the thought of Malakhar looming nearby. He gritted his teeth, forming a tightened grin as he envisioned his sword slicing through the dark elf's body. He had let Malakhar slip through his fingers once—but never again would he allow the past to repeat itself. He wanted justice, and longed for revenge.

As the sound of footsteps drew closer, it felt as though a heavy blanket draped over them, causing the air to feel hot and difficult to breathe. Neelan was the first who caught a glimpse of the reflective metals as the warriors approached in a well-formed protective stance. Their shields created a nearly impenetrable barrier that closed in on where they stood. Within seconds, they were met by a wall of steel.

"I knew Malakhar's plan would prove successful. Your weak heart shall be the death of you—foolish Illadar." A familiar voice spoke. The barrier of shields parted just enough to allow sight of a man who bore a wide, rotten-toothed smile.

"Saldin!" The veins on Illadar's neck throbbed as he stared resentfully toward the general's lieutenant.

"It's quite amusing you know—I can still remember the squeals from your wife as she was acquainted with the general's blade. Now the time has come for you to meet the same fate as I pierce my steel through your pathetic heart." Saldin laughed hysterically.

"You're mine!" Illadar's muscles flexed as he yelled out in fury. He raised his flail, taking off in a charge toward Saldin while disobeying his own words of caution.

Before making it to the wall of shields which protected the lieutenant, a white blast shot from behind the knights. Illadar stopped in his tracks as he watched many of the enemy men fly in all directions upon the spell's impact. Some landed upon the ground with minor scrapes, while others lay lifeless, their limbs scattered about.

"Thomas! I thought—" Kale's voice was cut off by the loud sound of a horn Saldin now held to his lips.

"Guard up!" Saldin shouted as each knight swiftly ducked beneath their shields.

Within seconds the sky lit up and Kale immediately recognized the flickering vibrancy of flame. Many bolts began to descend upon their heads.

Thomas instantly teleported to Kale's side, dampened with heavy sweat. "Gather around me!" He shouted. "*Alaria!*" Thomas called out as he extended his palm toward the sky.

They watched in relief as a swarm of fire coated bolts ricocheted off an invisible barrier that protected them from harm.

"I thought you planned to rid us of the surrounding threat, Thomas!" Kale's eyes were wide as he glanced at the damage. Some of the arrows struck the surrounding homes and flames quickly fed upon the thatched roofs.

"The archers are taking caution to stay out of my sight. I was only able to strike down one group before they grew wise to my presence," Thomas spoke quickly. "I must go now and salvage what I can of the town before it is too late." Without another word, he briskly left in the opposite direction of the scattered knights.

"Get them!" Saldin called out as he staggered to his feet. His greasy hair hung sloppily over his leathery skin as he directed his glare toward Illadar.

A horde of men flocked toward Kale and his comrades with a blood thirsty craze filling their eyes. The battle erupted as weapons crossed, and soon Kale and his party began to drift apart as each fought for their lives. Kale struggled to stay close to Neelan as she dodged and parried attacks in attempts to distance herself far enough to fire another shot from her bow. As Kale warded off an incoming attack from one of the knights, he kept a close eye out for Malakhar. He knew the vile dark elf had to be nearby. Kale's blade slid against his opponent's until they both pushed back to increase the amount of space between them.

"You don't have to do this," Kale tried to reason with the knight. "The people within this town are kind and good-hearted; they don't deserve what you bring upon them."

"Silence!" The knight replied as he thrust his blade forward. "Those who are not allied with General Jedah are our rivals. All who oppose shall meet the fate of our steel!"

The knight's loyalty to such a malicious man infuriated Kale to a point of pure rage. He could feel his palms beginning to grow warmer with each passing second. *Yes, keep going.* Kale continued to focus his ability as they reengaged in combat. He smiled as the searing heat began to course through his blade, creating a faint red glow.

The illuminated weapon drew the attention of another knight who came to aid his comrade. It was now a battle of two against one.

Kale was thankful to see the second knight who joined in was the person previously attacking Neelan. Joy swept through him as he saw from his peripheral vision that she was now standing away from the chaos within the temporary sanctuary of a darkened alley. He could see she was preparing to reengage her bow for an attack. His wandering mind got the best of him, allowing one of the knights to dodge Kale's oncoming attack, riposting toward Kale's chest. Although Kale managed to side step the thrust, the attack had been swift enough to slice against his bicep. Blood instantly trickled down his arm—fueling his adrenaline. He couldn't afford another reckless move. Elanya had enchanted Kale's weapon for the very purpose of being able to withstand his power. The time had come to utilize her gift for the good of Ravondore.

"Now, you die!" Kale's body was infused with fury as his sword swung toward the knights' with amazing speed. He applied full force with both hands as the blade sliced through the chainmail ringlets of the first man, melting his flesh. The powerful attack continued on to his comrade who stood by his side—sending him to a similar fate. Kale stood above the two knights who had been sliced into halves. "I tried to reason with you—scum."

Kale immediately moved to another target charging toward the rear of Illadar, who was still engaged in combat with Saldin. Despite Kale's attempt to ease the burden upon Illadar, many knights continued to focus upon him.

Eventually, Illadar backed into a wall, surrounded by warriors who had the sole desire of striking the killing blow.

"For you, my love." Illadar spoke as he violently swung the flail.

The flail collided into the gut of a nearby knight; the force immediately caused the man to fold over, dropping his sword. Blood spouted from the knight's mouth as his body collapsed to the ground.

Illadar focused on the next enemy, who swiftly met a similar fate. The flail had impacted against the knight's leg, shattering the bone and causing severe open wounds which oozed crimson. Illadar ducked and side stepped out of the oncoming attacks, fueled by his desire for revenge.

There were now only two men left between Illadar and the cowardly Saldin, standing safely back as he watched with amusement while his pawns fought faithfully. As one of the knights thrust his sword forward, Illadar met the attack midway as the weighted ball of his flail swung many times around the warrior's blade. Illadar tugged the sword effortlessly out of the knight's hand. He gripped the hilt, pulling it free from entanglement. Illadar then used the knight's very weapon to riposte and plunge the tip of the blade through the man's throat.

The knight shivered in shock as he reached for his oozing neck before buckling to his knees. Illadar was fueled by the thought of ridding the world of foul beings like Saldin and his loyal men. He swung his massive arms as though a mindless berserker, hell-bent on destroying the wicked. The flail collided with the side of the remaining knight's face, smashing into his skull until his features were unrecognizable. The spikes sunk so deeply, the weapon was nearly irretrievable.

Saldin flashed a yellowed grin as he raised his sword. He gazed forward through greasy brown hair as he charged Illadar.

"You will die now, traitor!" Saldin yelled while swinging his weapon toward Illadar's head.

Illadar spun away just in time, but felt the force of air swoosh by his cheek. As he regained his footing, Illadar reached behind his back to withdraw the mighty claymore which easily outreached the long sword.

"I'm not goin' down that easy." Illadar mocked Saldin as their swords clashed.

Their battle intensified as each man fought to land a killing blow. While Illadar excelled in strength, Saldin maintained an exceptional speed and parried each strike. Both men were exceptionally skilled and well trained in combat techniques.

Within the alley, Neelan struggled with the pain from her wound and amount of blood loss. Despite her agony, she continued to fire off a series of arrows toward the knights. The surrounding darkness provided her with ample camouflage so the men could not easily spot where she stood. As she reached to withdraw another arrow, a strong force pushed her violently forward. She fell to her hands and knees, watching as her arrow spiraled away. Neelan released a shrill cry as a spurt of blood gushed from her wound.

Both Kale and one of the townsmen from Braxle heard the sound and immediately fought to make way toward her.

A knight, who had caught onto Neelan's stealthy tactic, towered over her with a crazed look of perversion in his eyes. "Too bad such a pretty little thing will die tonight. We could've had some fun." He let out a sinister laugh. "Then again, when this is all over, maybe we still can. I prefer a woman who remains still while I have my way with her." More laughter burst from his wide lips as he raised his sword.

Kale and the townsman dashed toward Neelan as the knight swung downward. The townsman arrived first as he lunged forward, deflecting the blow mere inches away from Neelan's head.

"Fight me, you cowardly cur! How dare you lay harm to an

injured opponent—a woman, nonetheless!" The townsman yelled angrily as he flourished his weapon toward the knight.

"It's your death wish." The knight grinned as their swords chimed against one another.

Kale hurried to Neelan's aid as he gently lifted her to her feet. "Are you all right?" He kept a firm grip around her waist until certain she could stand upright.

"I am fine." Neelan grunted. "Thank you."

"Get yourself to safety; I'm not allowing you to fight any more," Kale demanded.

"Do not command me. I am fighting until this battle is over," Neelan stubbornly replied.

Before Kale could scold her, a cold steel blade swung toward his face, grazing his cheek with the tip. He stepped back, protectively pushing Neelan to the side. Kale glanced up to see the same knight who had engaged with the townsman only moments ago. From the corner of Kale's eye, he saw the valiant man who had tried to save Neelan lying lifeless and limp upon the ground.

Kale groaned angrily as he stepped forward while torquing his sword back. The edge of Kale's blade ripped through the knight's neck before there was any time to prepare for the blow.

The heated weapon sliced into the warrior's muscle and bone with ease, giving him a swift death. The sickening scent of burnt flesh filled the air as the knight's head rolled to the ground.

"So, you do still retain the power of flame. How very interesting. And here I was thinking my familiar, Sarus, was fooling me," a raspy voice sounded to the side.

Kale's eyes instantly turned toward the noise. There, stood a figure in black whose long, pale fingers stroked the black feathers of a crow perched upon his shoulder.

"Malakhar!" Kale called out as he tightened the grip on his weapon. "That bird..." Kale recognized the crow which he recalled sighting on many previous occasions.

"How thoughtful, you know my name—I am touched." Hoarse laughter escaped from the dark hole within the draping hood. "And it would appear you've also been acquainted with Sarus as well." Malakhar continued to stroke the bird. "Did you truly believe I would allow you and Illadar to leave this pathetic town without being watched? I am no fool, you ignorant dragon. I could have killed Illadar that night, but I needed you alive. There were far too many disgusting humans around for me to complete my mission alone, and having no weapon on hand, I was not about to attack the entire, worthless town. I allowed you to leave while Sarus kept a careful watch upon you both. This provided me the time to increase my magical abilities—which I lacked upon our previous encounter."

"Allowed us? There is no way you could have slain Illadar that night; he would have easily had your head—or whatever it is hiding within your cloak. For such strong words, you sure fled like a coward." Though Kale wanted to strike Malakhar where he stood, he needed to find the answers he desired. "Why hasn't your *master*, General Jedah, come?" Kale snickered, purposely attempting to agitate the dark elf.

"He is not my master, you filthy dragon!" Malakhar's voice rose as he spoke. "I am in debt by oath to that human. Once I deliver you to him, I shall be free of these chains he holds upon me. When that moment arrives, he shall be sorry for attempting to use me as a pawn for so many years. Once I am able to retrieve the scrolls of Drell, he will become my servant—along with the rest of the world who will bow before my power." More laughter followed.

"So Jedah is unaware you have found me?" Kale pried the subject to confirm his suspicions, all the while keeping distance from Malakhar's reach.

"I do not answer to you!" Malakhar waved his hand and the crow took flight above the rooftops. "You are already aware of my past, thanks to my pathetic twin brother, so I suppose there is no longer the need to hide myself." He curled his long, deathly pale fingers around the edge of his hood, allowing it to fall back upon his shoulders.

Kale cringed as Malakhar revealed his hideous, misshapen face.

Malakhar's nose was excessively lumpy and coated in a scab-like crust. His long ears did not slant upward as Neelan's did, but instead seemed to droop down toward his neck like heavy flaps of flesh. The dark elf's face bore many deep purple veins which seemed to press against his near transparent skin. His eyes were the most taunting feature—soulless, and black as the night. It wasn't only his iris that was black, but the entire eye itself. The shade contrasted dramatically against his flesh. His appearance could be summed into one word—*evil*.

"I must admit, I was expecting a rather different response to my...monstrous features. Then again, you are not truly human." Malakhar's colorless lips curled up into a smile which revealed jagged teeth that looked as though they had been smacked with a stone. Each tooth appeared crooked or chipped—all equally yellowed. "You are not human, nor dragon. You don't fit in with either side—maybe, you and I are more alike than you realize, Firehart."

"The *only* thing you and I share in common is that we both desire to change this world. Yet, your intentions benefit only yourself. It's inhuman." Kale focused as his sword began to softly glow. "You sicken me!" He could no longer contain his anger. He lunged forward, aiming for the cold-hearted, dark elf.

Malakhar opened his palm as a thin sword formed within his grasp. The blade matched his cold eyes—black. It was the most unique steel Kale had ever seen.

Malakhar's speed was astounding and he deflected Kale's oncoming attacks with ease. "Did you assume I would simply stand and allow you to strike me down? Tsk, tsk, how foolish, you silly dragon. As you have become stronger since we last met, so have I." He leapt back to dodge another of Kale's thrusts. Malakhar then extended his arm outward as shards of ice shot from his palm toward Kale.

Kale dove to the ground, rolling out of the attack before scurrying back upon his feet. "So you *have* obtained the ability to conjure magic. Just as I thought."

Their swords crossed once again as Kale continued to focus on intensifying the heat which ran through his steel blade. This was a battle he knew he must win, for his friends—and for Ravondore.

"If you're so powerful, why did you come here with the aid of Saldin?" Kale snickered, panting heavily while deflecting Malakhar's attacks. "What a coward you are."

Malakhar laughed. "Saldin; that filthy fool has come on his own terms. He desires to slay the weak-hearted Illadar and obtain Jedah's praise. He longs for prestige from the other knights in order to remain the general's favorite little pet. It was his decision to exclude Jedah from knowing of this plan. He desires to prove himself with this victory." Malakhar's footwork was flawless as he gracefully weaved to each side of Kale's strikes. "I have come with the sole desire of defeating you so my oath will finally come to an end. Jedah desires you alive so he may claim the killing strike—I merely desire the satisfaction of weakening you for the trip. My magical abilities have grown enough to keep you alive for the journey back to Mirion—with or without your limbs." Malakhar snickered.

"The only one who falls tonight shall be you." Kale pushed his weight in Malakhar's direction, forcing the black blade inches away from the dark elf's face.

Malakhar's black eyes narrowed as his scabby nose flared. He yelled out in a foreign tongue and an invisible force struck Kale, sending him flying many feet away.

Kale's back landed hard against the ground as his hands lost grip on the hilt of his weapon. He watched in disbelief as his sword spun away from him.

"No!" Kale cried out as he reached hopelessly for the weapon.

Malakhar slowly advanced toward Kale, who was now staggering to stand with his back against a wall.

"What a pity this fight should end so soon. I expected more from you, Firehart," Malakhar sneered.

Kale was prepared to attack using nothing but his own scorching hands, though he knew getting past Malakhar's blade would be an obstacle.

The most sinister look Kale had ever seen crossed Malakhar's face as the dark elf took a swift step forward, extending an open palm.

"Do not let him touch you!" Neelan shouted frantically as she used the last of her strength to dive into Malakhar. She threw her weight on top of the dark elf as they both tumbled to the ground.

As the hood of her cloak fell back upon her shoulders, Malakhar cringed.

"A high elf—disgusting. What a foolish girl to throw your

own life in danger for an unworthy man...if you can even call him that. What a pity; I'll have to deal with you now as well." Malakhar gripped her neck, mere seconds before Kale managed to retrieve his sword. The dark elf squeezed tightly as Neelan cried out in anguish.

"Get your hands off of her!" Kale charged at Malakhar who was still hunching over Neelan like a hungry tiger.

To Kale's surprise, as he swung his sword forward, it sliced into Malakhar's back, singing the fabric of his cloak while piercing through his flesh. Blood immediately began to leak from the gash as Malakhar screamed in pain. Kale took advantage of the dark elf's brief moment of disorientation as he slammed his foot forcefully into Malakhar's rib cage. Malakhar instantly hit the ground, growling in anger as he reached behind to feel the damage which had been done.

Kale quickly knelt by Neelan's side. "Neelan—Neelan, please answer me!"

Neelan softly groaned—her long lashes fluttered as her eyes struggled to keep focus. "Kale, I cannot move my arms or legs. He has cast a curse upon me."

Kale stood as his wide eyes finally took note of the wound between her ribs. Half of Neelan's torso was now soaked with her own blood.

She was so badly hurt, and yet she risked the last of her strength to save me...

An entirely unfamiliar emotion flowed through Kale's body as he found a renewed rush of adrenaline. Seeing Neelan in this state made him certain he never wanted to leave her side—never wanted to lose her. He knew now, Lorin's words had been true. She loved him—and he loved her too.

"Please hold on, Neelan, for me. We will get out of this together."

Kale looked toward Malakhar, who had begun to pull himself up. Kale had no hesitation as he leapt forward into the air, bringing his sword above his head while lunging down toward the dark elf.

Malakhar's arm shot up with amazing speed, despite his injury. His black sword yet again deflected Kale's blow.

"How sentimental; a dragon and an elf in love—it's almost...humorous. You sicken me, Firehart. To have such power as a dragon, such strength, and yet here you stand before me as a pathetic human. What a waste."

"This fate was not my choice." Kale angrily pushed his blade closer toward Malakhar's chest.

"Ah, now you see a glimpse into my own life. I certainly did not choose this grotesque body. As I've said before—we are not so different." Malakhar's black eyes pierced Kale's.

Kale shot a brief glance toward Neelan who helplessly lay upon the ground. "You get through each day fueled by revulsion for the world. There is nothing you desire to save. I am fighting to protect everything I have grown to love. Do not compare us again, you depraved abomination." His voice was low and deep. "This ends now."

He focused more energy than ever before into his weapon as it rapidly changed from red to yellow. Kale stepped back, allowing room to swing as he lunged the blade toward Malakhar's torso.

Malakhar side stepped to avoid the blow as he raised his blade to collide with Kale's. Both men continued to swing violently at one another, equally determined to rise victorious.

Suddenly, as both swords crossed, Kale's blade snapped. He stepped back in shock as the remaining half folded over in a melted clump. He had disregarded Elanya's warning to take caution while utilizing his powers. Her enchantment was not able to sustain such a high degree of heat.

"No..." Kale whispered to himself as Malakhar's blade thrust forward—plunging into the right side of his chest. Kale grunted as he felt the blade tear through his flesh and muscle. "My time to die shall come," Kale wrapped his hands around Malakhar's blade, enduring further pain as the razor-edge dug into his palm and fingers, "but today is not that day."

Holding the blade, Kale pulled Malakhar toward him. The tip of the blade dug deeper into Kale's body, causing him to feel painfully nauseous. He wanted to close the space between them so he could take hold of Malakhar's cloak and ignite the dark elf into a standing torch. *I still cannot reach him.* Kale gritted his teeth. *At this rate I will kill myself, or be cursed.* Before Malakhar could react, Kale lifted his leg, slamming his foot forward with all the strength he could muster. As the sole of his boot collided with Malakhar's gut, Kale released his grip upon the blade which sent Malakhar flying backwards.

The inhuman strength of Kale's kick had been so severe Malakhar immediately spat blood as he pathetically attempted to lift himself upon all fours.

"K-Kale, please come to me quickly!" Neelan's voice was hoarse as she called out from the same area in which Malakhar left her immobile.

Kale rushed to her side, gently brushing the hair from her eyes. "What is it? I must finish this battle before he recovers, I must get you help."

"Pull me up; we are going to use my bow. Should you attempt to use close combat he will only place a curse upon you as well. Quickly now before he is able to stand, this may be our final chance at victory..." Neelan struggled to speak.

"I've told you, Neelan, you are not fighting anymore. I will do this alone."

"Shut up, Kale! I have a single arrow left and I am not about to trust you to make the shot. Quite honestly, you are a horrible archer."

Kale knew arguing would only cause her to unnecessarily exert herself. They also greatly lacked time as he could see that Malakhar had conjured a minor healing spell upon himself.

The dark elf staggered to his feet, still holding his blood-drenched sword within his grasp.

"All right." Kale carefully placed an arm under her body as he lifted her into a seated position.

"Take my bow, and then lift my arms into place. I still have movement in my torso and will take aim, you finish the shot. We get one chance Kale—just one."

Kale lifted her arms upon his own as he gripped the sturdy wood frame of the bow. As Neelan maneuvered the bow toward Malakhar, Kale pressed his cheek to hers as they both concentrated upon the arrow.

One shot. Kale repeated in his mind.

Malakhar regained his strength and walked swiftly toward them with his sword held out to the side. His blackened eyes were wide with rage.

"The games are over, Firehart. General Jedah will have to suffice without the killing blow, for it is I who now starves for the honor." He cackled maniacally.

Kale felt Neelan's warmth against his face and could feel her breath, panting in sync with his. He closed his eyes, allowing his hands to infuse with power which he carefully directed solely onto the arrow itself.

"Now!" she commanded.

Kale's eyes shot open as the arrow launched from the bow. Upon leaving Kale's fingertips, the arrow ignited into flames. The swift escape of the projectile saved Neelan's hands from any burns. They watched as the arrow flew toward Malakhar with blinding speed, piercing precisely through the center of his pallid skull, incinerating the flesh. The dark elf flew backward, slamming forcefully into the stone wall behind. A loud crack could be heard as his skull impacted. Within seconds Malakhar's limp body fell to the ground succumbing to the flames which fed off his garments.

"It is over." Neelan smiled sweetly at Kale as she caressed his cheek with her fingertips. The curse had been completely lifted upon Malakhar's last breath and she could once again move her limbs.

"Thank you for risking your own life to save me. I—I never want to lose you. I could not have done this without—"

Kale watched in horror as her eyes rolled back into her skull. "Neelan?!" He began to gently shake her limp body. Kale's eyes glanced down toward her wound which still secreted blood. "Not now, not after all we've accomplished. We did it, Neelan, we won. Please, wake up!" Kale pressed his forehead to hers as he gently stroked her silky hair. "Don't you dare leave me..." He whispered as a tear rolled down his cheek, falling upon her eyelash. Kale's heart raced. He couldn't understand why he had never noticed it before–Kale was undeniably and deeply in love.

Straining with all his might to hold Neelan within his arms, he fought to stand. He nestled her body against his chest, cradling her as he walked out of the secluded area. He needed to find Thomas quickly so the sorcerer could aid Neelan before it was too late. With each step Kale took, more blood seeped from his open wound as it trickled down his torso and leg.

"It's going to be all right," he whispered to Neelan. "We are going to be together forever, you'll see." For the first time in Kale's life, he knew what it meant to love and to truly ache in pain at the thought of losing someone.

As Kale emerged into the main section of the town square, he gazed upon the many deceased, blood-drenched bodies of knights and townsmen. He took another step forward and felt his legs begin to tingle. His vision grew more blurred with each patter of his footsteps, until he could no longer stand. Kale collapsed to his knees, using the final amount of strength within his body to ensure he would hit the ground first. He tucked Neelan against him, protecting her from harm as he allowed himself to fall backwards. Kale pulled her body tightly into his arms as they both lay amidst the many corpses.

"I am so sorry..." He softly kissed her forehead as everything went black.

CHAPTER 25

TO FREEDOM

"His eyelids are moving! Kale is waking."

Kale could hear a woman speaking over him as he wrinkled his forehead, allowing the sunlight to flood his eyes. "Wh-where am I?" His pupils dilated to view a familiar cleavage-stuffed bodice leaning over his torso. "Theresa?" He glanced around at the recognizable walls of the inn.

"Everyone, he is all right!" As Theresa spoke, cheers erupted from all around. "We're all glad that you're alive. And, yes," She flipped her dark ponytail over a shoulder, "I forgive you for your crude behavior in the tavern." She playfully smiled. "I'm just grateful you returned to protect us."

"I am glad you're all safe." Kale struggled to sit upright in the narrow bed, but a spike of pain struck his chest, causing him to groan loudly. A flood of memories rushed through his mind. "Neelan!" Kale ignored the pain as he climbed to his feet in a panic. "Is she all right?!"

Two arms slid around his waist from behind. "You're awake!" Neelan's voice chimed.

Kale immediately spun around, disregarding the spiking pain that throbbed from below his pectoral as he stared down into the violet eyes of Neelan. "I thought I'd lost you." Kale softly spoke. A wave of emotion coursed through him at the sight of the woman he so longed to be with for eternity.

Without hesitation or regard to the others who stood around him, Kale gently tilted Neelan's chin upward as he leaned in and pressed his lips to hers. He had never felt so happy in all of his years alive; despite the awkward grunts which could be heard from Theresa.

Neelan closed her eyes as she rose up upon the ball of her feet, giving completely in to the kiss.

"All right, all right, give it a rest you two." Theresa placed her hands upon her wide hips.

Kale glanced around at the many familiar faces which surrounded them. Thomas and Illadar gave him a friendly wave while chuckling to themselves. Soon, the crowd enfolded Kale and the room suddenly felt incredibly small. Many praises and words of gratitude filled the open air.

"Excuse me." A woman spoke.

Kale felt a gentle tug on the back of a new black tunic he wore.

"May I please have a word?" She questioned.

Kale turned to see a middle-aged woman in a long rose-colored dress standing before him. Her eyes were red and swollen which revealed a heavy sorrow. Kale nodded, allowing her to take him by the hand as they weaved through the crowd of individuals who continued to converse amongst themselves about the previous night events. As Kale passed, many of the townsfolk gave him a firm pat upon his back; most unaware of the injury that surged with pain. Kale was surprised to see no blood saturated his new tunic. The wound felt much better than before he collapsed, which made him wonder what had occurred since the battle.

As they left the inn, the woman led Kale toward the town square where he saw six, long, rectangular boxes, all aligned in a perfect row. The woman stopped walking and turned to face Kale. Tears began to stream down her cheeks as she took Kale's hand into hers, squeezing tightly.

"My husband, Forwin, will be laid to rest within the earth's soil tonight." Her voice shook as she spoke.

Kale's heart sank as he realized the boxes were actually coffins which held the bodies of the townsmen who had fallen in the battle. Forwin died trying to protect the woman who stood before Kale–and to protect the town which was his home.

"It's my fault." Kale could not contain the truth that tore at his emotions. "The army came here because of me. Had I not come to live within Braxle, none of this would have happened. I tried to save everyone–I truly did." He lifted the woman's hand near his face. "I cannot change the past, but please accept my sincerest apologies. I never meant for any of this to happen."

At that moment, Kale wanted, more than ever, to turn back time to when he was a dragon. Having his current knowledge, he gladly would have accepted Thomas' plea for them to both escape to another continent. He would easily sacrifice the ability to remain on Ravondore in order to avoid all the terrible events which had happened because of his existence.

"I believe you misunderstood my intentions, young man." The woman rubbed her index finger across her lower eyelid. "I wanted to thank you, for coming back to ensure our safety.

Without your return, we all would surely be dead. The rumors of General Jedah's army are not for the faint of heart. They show no mercy. You could have run and left our fate to their steel blades, but instead you placed your own life in danger for us. You are a noble and courageous man, Kale. I am certain that Forwin died proud to have fought by your side." She glanced to the ground. "While I now ache in the pain of my sorrows, I know he would never regret his choice to join you–therefore, nor do I."

Kale swallowed hard, touched by the woman's kind words. "He was a brave man. I am the one who is honored to have known such a loyal and determined human–person. Even if our time together was short, I shall never forget him." Kale struggled to look into her eyes, still filled with guilt. The anguish she felt, regardless of her attempts to remain strong, struck Kale's heart with each glance of her tear-filled eyes.

"She's right you know." One of the surviving men sauntered toward them. He stared glumly down at the coffins. "Though, it's painful to see our friends have moved on from this life, most of us support you and have nothing but respect for your decision to return. We don't know, nor do we care to, the reason such an army seeks to kill you, but we feel you are truly a good person."

"Indeed, you will always be welcome to return to Braxle, once your conflict with the general of Mirion has been resolved," Lord Zalimond spoke as he approached Kale. "You shall have a home here, should you desire to return." His lips curved upward into a smile from behind his bushy mustache.

"Thank you. The words you have shared with me today will remain in my heart. I am forever in debt to your people for what I have caused. Again, I am so very sorry." Kale humbly bowed.

"It is time to go now." Thomas approached Kale, placing a hand upon his shoulder. "We must return to the forest."

Kale glanced over to see Illadar and Neelan standing by Thomas' side.

"Arthur, one of the men who fought valiantly alongside of us, has provided three horses from his stable as a token of gratitude." Thomas gestured toward the man standing off to the far side of the square. "I am far too fatigued to return us with magic. Even with the potion provided to me at the inn, I still have not fully recovered." He rubbed the top of his right hand as he spoke.

"I would like to thank Arthur for his kindness, however, I would also like to say goodbye to Mortimer as well. I noticed he has once again provided clean clothing and my body has been bathed. Have you seen him?" Kale glanced around curiously.

"Morty is currently assisting the apothecary to aid the wounds of two men who were injured in battle. Although, I am certain he would enjoy seeing you awake and well, we must leave him to tend to such an important task." Thomas nudged Kale's back to urge him in the direction of Arthur. "Now, let us be on our way so the townsfolk can resume a normal life once again.

Kale approached Arthur and thanked him for the horses and his support in battle. As Kale watched Neelan pat the mane of the black horse, his mind began to dwell upon the previous nights events. "I just don't understand." Kale exhaled, rubbing his forehead which throbbed terribly. "Where did the bodies of the knights go?" He gritted his teeth, "And where is *his* body?"

"We moved 'em this mornin' to the outside of town–Malakhar's as well. I'm guessin' they intend to burn the lot of 'em tonight." Illadar read the expression upon Kale's face. "Yes, kid, Malakhar is as dead as they come. You don't have to worry about him anymore. I've gotta' say though–you did one impressive job on him with that power of yours. Most of his head was charred beyond recognition." He grinned, softly chuckling.

"What about Saldin? You killed him, right?" Kale questioned.

Illadar flashed a disheartened glance. "I'm afraid not, kid."

"What?! Why not? What happened?" Kale spoke quickly; shocked by the news.

"Calm yourself, Kale. We have all been through a lot." Thomas took a hold of the conversation. "We tried to stop him, however once he noticed his comrades were dwindling in number, he fled."

"The cowardly cur ran away," Illadar jumped in. "The remainin' knights followed in retreat."

Kale gripped his hair, yelling out in frustration.

"It will be all right." Neelan placed a hand upon Kale's back. "We have made great progress, and Malakhar is gone. I am sure Saldin will run back to Jedah. We'll end up taking them both down at once. We must now return to the Forest of Forgotten Whispers. I am sure that Elanya," she sighed, rolling her eyes, "and Judith, will be anxiously awaiting our arrival." A playful smile crossed her face as she attempted to lighten the mood. "Now let's get going already! All this time, I thought I'd fallen for a dragon–little did I know he was truly a slow turtle in disguise!" She laughed at her own childish joke as she leapt atop a stack of hay. Neelan then slid her foot through a stirrup before slinging her leg over the brown saddle.

"How are you able to move with such agility? I saw the blood coming from your side last night." It was the first time Kale took notice of the new clothing she wore.

"You can thank Thomas." She winked toward the old sorcerer. "Although he had exerted himself in battle, he never left our side. He used the last of his stamina to heal the worst of my wound and safely remove the embedded bolt tip. He healed your injuries too."

Thomas' face was overwhelmed with a cherry tint. "You should know I would never step aside while friends suffer. Besides," he glanced toward Kale, "who would I have to amuse me with their human inadequacies?" He laughed, holding a hand up before Kale could speak. "Joking of course–well, somewhat anyway." He smiled. "Which brings me to a more serious subject; you mustn't over exert yourself. Your outer layers will still need time to heal. Mortimer has provided us with bandages and ointment to ease the pain."

Kale smiled at the thought of how unconditionally caring Mortimer was. He was disappointed he would not be able to give thanks in person, but knew they must make haste toward the forest before twilight arrived.

Entering the forest at dusk would increase their chance of an attack by the red beasts and Rees'Lok. The group knew they would be at a severe disadvantage while recovering from their injuries. An encounter with the orc would surely bring death upon them.

Kale clumsily mounted the horse, seating himself in front of Neelan as he took the reins within his grasp. He continued to mimic every movement Illadar and Thomas made, kicking his heels into the horse's side. The horse huffed and shuffled his feet as though he could sense Kale was not truly human.

"It's all right, boy." Neelan ran her fingers along the horse's side as she soothed the creature.

"Farewell, once again, Braxle." Thomas glanced over his shoulder. "May we return in the future under more joyous circumstances."

They trotted through the exit as many of the townsfolk gathered to wave goodbye. Kale caught sight of Theresa blowing him a kiss which caused him to look away bashfully.

Neelan growled as she kicked into the horse, causing the steed to trot faster. "We're off! Hold on tightly," She called out as she wrapped her arms firmly around Kale's body, pressing close to his warmth.

~~~~~~~~~~~~~~~~~

The four were relieved to see the enchanted stream which bordered the Forest of Forgotten Whispers. After a very weary-eyed horseback ride, they were ready to visit Judith, and then lay within the hanging hammocks for a needed rest. Now that they were familiar with their surroundings, the journey proved to be less time consuming. As they crossed the forest's magical barrier, they were surprised to hear the sound of birds chirping within the gloomy trees.

"Things seem different this time. I hope the noise doesn't attract the red beasts or Rees'lok to our location." Kale spoke, rubbing his eyes as his horse slowly trotted behind Illadar's.

"Yes...this is very odd indeed." Thomas inspected their surroundings.

Darkness swarmed the forest, and after maintaining a steady pace they could see the massive tree trunk come into view. They were equally grateful at how swiftly they made it to the center of the Forest of Forgotten Whispers. On their previous journey to the tree, it had taken nearly an entire day of searching.

Golden specks drifted around, guiding their way with a lit path. As they approached the mass of vines, the plants squirmed and twisted, allowing them passage. They quickly dismounted and Kale gave a gentle pat on the horse's crest.

The animal returned the affection by nudging his nose against

Kale's arm.

"It appears as though he has grown quite fond of you, Kale," Thomas laughed.

"Kale!" Judith hurried toward them. Her golden hair appeared silk-like under the glow of the trees mysterious floating specs. "Look at me! Just look!" The expression upon her face revealed pure bliss. "I can walk the soil of the earth as myself once again! How can I ever thank you? Elanya confessed everything once she was certain the curse had been lifted." Judith held her arms out as she spun her body gracefully on one foot. "It feels so good to be outside once again. Not upon a tree limb, but truly outside in the world–it is amazing!" Judith fell into Kale's arms, staring up toward him. "Please, come back with me tomorrow. My father will insist on meeting you." Their blue eyes met as she flashed a beautiful smile. A hopeful expression remained upon her face as she continued to gaze at Kale.

Kale could feel Neelan's scornful eyes burning into the back of his skull with a jealous rage.

"We had no intentions of you returning alone, so of course we will come." Kale lifted Judith to her feet and took a step closer toward Neelan.

"Shall we head inside?" Thomas could sense the usual tension rising when Neelan and Judith were near Kale.

"That is a fine idea," Kale quickly replied as he led the way.

They were instantly greeted by an enthusiastic group of dryad women who were each dressed in a flowing, white silk dress that trailed to the floor. Fruit had been set out on banquet sized silver platters and colorful floral garland draped the room. Elanya soon entered the room in a pale blue gown which hung loosely off her shoulders. It shimmered in the candlelight with each stride she took. She was thrilled by their return and announced the night would be spent celebrating before sleep. They all began to enjoy the festive atmosphere, feasting and laughing together.

Eventually, as the candles dimmed, the celebration came to an end and one by one the dryad women left for their own trees. Judith also fell victim to the temptation of sleep after she once again thanked the four for their courageous victory.

"Dost thou have a plan for tomorrow? It shalt be a grand day of importance and thou must make haste to thy kingdom of Mirion." Elanya tucked her long white hair behind a pointed ear.

The mood within the room shifted as the conversation grew serious.

"A plan?" Kale's response came across as ignorant and a look of disappointment was immediately revealed upon Elanya's face.

"Thou cannot approach ye kingdom of Mirion as thou art now. All four of thee shalt be captured and killed by Jedah or his men whom devote loyalty to he."

"She's right." Illadar added. "We were all seen by Saldin, whom I'm sure will return before us and alert the general of what has happened; in his own words of course. Saldin will never admit defeat." Illadar crossed his dark muscular arms as he leaned back. "The guards will be placed on watch for us to arrive. A clever plan is necessary to obtain entry into the kingdom."

After a heavy bout of silence where each pondered their options, Elanya stood.

"Thy mind works mysteriously—one might say, quite ironically." Elanya spoke softly, chuckling to herself. It was the first time they heard Elanya laugh which made the four slightly uneasy as to the reasoning behind it.

Elanya left the room without a word, returning shortly after with a brown leather satchel. "In ye days to come, when thee reaches ye kingdom of Mirion, drink this." She handed the sack to Thomas. "Thou shalt find enough for each to retrieve a sip. I must warn thee–ye effects shalt only remain for two hours."

"What exactly is it?" Kale grew concerned at the thought of ingesting an unknown substance.

"A concoction which shalt transform thy body."

No way–not again. Kale shook his head at the thought of having to go through another bodily alteration, unless it was to return him to his dragon form.

"Pardon my curiosity, however, I do believe I speak for all of us when I ask what exactly it is we will become?" Thomas wrinkled his forehead in concern.

"Of course thou may." Elanya smiled. "Thine drink was giveth to women I have known in ye past. Thee used ye mixture to enter areas unnoticed–as mice."

"We are going to become mice?" Neelan dove into the conversation, now appearing alert to what was happening around her. "Great." She crossed her arms unhappily.

"Thou must remember, the effects last but a mere two hours. Then thee will return to normal."

"Have *you* ever used the potion?" Kale was skeptical of the entire situation. He did not desire to spend the remainder of his life as a small vermin.

"Boy, thou mustn't forget that thine body is but a shell. I am a dryad." Elanya responded.

"I suppose that means no?" Kale wanted answers and grew frustrated by her odd manner of speaking.

"Correct." She nodded. "Thou must rest now. Judith shalt be anxious to depart shortly after waking." Elanya glanced down at Kale. "Judith hath become like a daughter to me. I shalt dearly miss her. Please ensure she returns to her father safely. Thee must take heed while travelling to ye kingdom. Ye one called Jedah is foul, yet intelligent; thou will send his warriors to ensure Judith hath not left thine forest. Take caution and do not travel along ye main roads."

Kale opened his mouth to speak.

"We shalt be fine, Kale Firehart." Elanya spoke as though she had once again read Kale's thoughts. "Ye knights are unaware Judith hath been rescued by our kind. Should ye warriors attempt to enter thine home, they shalt perish."

A worried expression was painted upon Elanya's face as she gazed out toward the open entrance.

"I must also warn thee–since thou hath been away, the forest hath behaved abnormally. I believe ye issue revolves around Rees'lok. Neither he, nor his red beasts hast been seen hunting. Something is happening within thine forest, yet I hast not yet drawn a conclusion. Be wary upon your departure."

After Elanya left they briefly engaged in a tactical conversation as they decided it would be most wise to ride upon horseback to one of the smaller farms outside of the kingdom. A small farm would have less likelihood of drawing suspicion. They also assumed that any farmers on the surrounding areas of the kingdom would be ignorant to the alert placed in effect for Kale and his companions. It was agreed upon they would pay the owner of the farm a satisfying sum of coins to keep their horses within their stable while they executed their mission into the kingdom as mice.

It took a great deal of coaxing to convince Kale it was their safest option to put an end to Jedah. He finally gave into the plan –though obviously apprehensive about the transformation.

Once they felt confident with their strategy, they each made way to the room full of hanging hammocks. All four easily drifted into a deep slumber. They soon would begin their journey to reshape the depravity of Ravondore.

CHAPTER 26

INTO THE KINGDOM

Over the following days they cautiously travelled toward Mirion, stopping only to allow the horses to drink and to rest at night. It was an enduring journey, but they were each determined to end Jedah's reign of corruption and tyranny. The group eventually came upon a quaint farmhouse on the surrounding grounds outside the kingdom. They could see many delicious looking crops growing that made their stomachs rumble. As they drew closer, the sounds of pigs grunting and cows lowing could be heard.

Thomas was the first to dismount; moving swiftly despite his age. He draped the horse's reins over the stake of a fence which surrounded the field of vegetation. He made way toward the small, wooden farmhouse.

"I shall remain behind. Anyone within this region would surely recognize me." Judith pointed to a thick cluster of shrubs. "I will remain there until you've returned." She pulled a hood over her head.

Kale nodded, hastily walking to catch up to the old sorcerer.

Thomas' wrinkled fingers rapped gently upon the door and they could hear immediate movement. As the door cracked open, they could see the sliver of a middle-aged man's face. He appeared intimidated and confused by the four strangers who stood at his doorstep. Thomas politely informed the farmer they meant no harm and explained they were in need of care for their horses. At first the man questioned their motives in concern, stating there was a perfectly fine stable within the kingdom.

Thomas responded to the farmer's suspicions by creating a fictitious story. He explained that during a previous visit to Mirion, his horse grew ill after staying within the kingdom stables. Therefore, he did not trust to leave them there again. He told the farmer they were travelers who were interested in browsing the marketplace for rare goods.

The farmer wrinkled his face as he continued to inspect the four.

"I am not so sure about this." The farmer rubbed his stubbly chin. "My apologies, but I cannot help you."

As the farmer attempted to close his door, Thomas held a firm hand forward.

"Perhaps this will persuade you." Thomas reached into his pouch tied to his waist and withdrew a handful of coins.

The farmer's mouth dropped open as he swung the door wide open. "I shall show you to the stable." He swiped the mound of coins from Thomas' palm.

After securing the horses, they bid the farmer farewell as they hastily met with Judith, concealed behind the shrubbery.

"I was beginning to wonder if you would ever return." Judith flashed Kale a playful smile which caused Neelan to grunt. "Is everyone ready?" The Princess withdrew a satchel from inside of her cloak.

"I don't think I will ever be ready for this. Let's just get it over with. I can only hope that no one stomps on us along our journey. Mice..." Kale sighed. "From a dragon to a puny mouse." He looked toward the kingdom of Mirion, easily identified behind a field of scattered trees.

"I sure hope Elanya is certain of these effects." Judith puckered her lips as she took a large gulp of the liquid concoction.

No sooner had Judith swallowed, her body began to tremble as she buckled to the floor in a seizure-like state. As Kale and Illadar reached out to grab her, thousands of tiny coarse grey hairs began to sprout from her skin. Her limbs began to shrink and mutate; taking the form of a mouse, until she was no bigger than the size of Kale's hand. Judith squirmed free from her clothing, which had fallen to a crumpled pile upon the ground. Her little pink nose twitched as she let out a squeak.

"It worked!" Judith's voice was shrill and unrecognizable.

"What in Pan's name are we supposed to do about clothing? In two hours we will be standing before the King unclothed." Kale rubbed his forehead as he heavily exhaled. Though they had discussed their options before, the realization of the situation caught him off guard.

"As I have mentioned before, I am hopeful Judith will assist us. I recall the castle having an abundance of wardrobes." Thomas replied.

"Yes, do not worry." Judith twitched her long whiskers as she spoke. "When the time comes, I will take care of everything. But for now, please drink quickly! I have already consumed the potion and time is passing."

Neelan was the next to drink and quickly met the same fate as Judith.

"I cannot believe I'm doing this." Neelan's chirpy voice was even more high-pitched than Judith's.

Kale couldn't help but laugh at her abnormally fluffy brown fur.

"I do believe it is our turn now." Thomas allowed a stream of liquid to glide down his throat. He immediately passed the satchel over to Illadar before the transformation could take effect.

They all stared, waiting impatiently. Nothing happened.

"What's goin' on here? Let me give this stuff a try." Illadar swallowed a large gulp before passing it on.

Kale wasted no time drinking the remainder of the potion. "Oddly refreshing." He said as he licked his lips.

They stood in silence as the seconds passed.

"Great, it didn't even wo—" Kale gripped his stomach in pain, glancing over to see that Illadar and Thomas were in the same predicament. His chest quickly began to burn in the most nauseating way.

"What's happenin'?" Illadar groaned.

They hit the grassy ground and all three rolled around in discomfort. Their bodies began to tingle as they twisted and squirmed in distress. Finally, the pain ceased. Kale was the first to stand, rubbing his eyes which were oddly out of focus and blurred.

"Nothing, I kn—" Kale stopped speaking as he clapped his hands over his lips which now felt tender and plump.

As his eyes came to focus, he could not have been more astonished by what he saw. There, before him stood two other women who remained frozen in place with their jaws hung.

*It can't be...*Kale shook his head as his mind raced.

All three men had completely transformed into females.

"This is the most hilarious sight I have ever seen!" The tiny brown mouse which was Neelan squeaked in amusement. She could not take her small beady eyes off the former men who now stood in oversized clothing which draped from their feminine frames.

Kale heavily sighed. He knew that there was nothing he could do at this point about the situation. "Well, I suppose it could be worse–I could look like Thomas." He chuckled, staring upon the old sorcerer's physique.

Thomas had short brown spiraling curls that frizzed horribly at the ends. His lips were incredibly thin and his nose was beakish and crooked with two plump moles near the tip. A generous protrusion of nasal hair made it appear as though he was hiding some form of an animal within his nostrils.

"This is in no way amusing!" Thomas shouted in a high feminine voice which stunned even himself.

"I'm gonna' have some words to share with Elanya when this is over," Illadar finally spoke as he examined his new body. He was now a heavy-set woman with smooth ebony skin and curves in all the right places. His shoulder-length hair was straight and black, curling inward just below his jaw line.

"You know, Kale, I am actually quite jealous of you! You make a beautiful woman." Neelan half-jokingly squeaked while staring at his head full of perfect silky black hair that cascaded down his back in wavy locks.

"Enough everyone!" Judith took command as she ignored the choked laughter of both Illadar and Kale as they continued to stare toward Thomas. "We haven't much time left and I refuse to accept we have come this far only to be caught and imprisoned– or worse." Judith stood upon her two hind legs. "You three," she motioned a paw toward the former men, "go behind the bushes and put on whatever will fit from my and Neelan's clothing. It may not be a perfect fit, but it shall have to do. We must convince the guards you are truly women and not draw suspicion."

Kale quickly swiped Judith's white blouse and pants, moving behind the foliage to change. As he did, he could hear the loud hissing from the brown fluffy mouse. Neelan was obviously jealous he hadn't chosen her attire instead.

Thomas traded in his garments for Neelan's clothing, leaving Illadar to use his own tunic as a dress while wrapping Judith's cloak around for concealment.

As the three emerged from the bushes, the two mice scurried up Kale's clothing to his shoulder. Both Neelan and Judith tucked themselves behind his neck to hide within his long thick hair.

"Kale, you must wear Neelan's cloak to conceal your shoulders. The blouse you wear was tailored specifically for me and the guards will certainly take notice. No common peasant would wear such an elaborate style," Judith warned.

Their brief walk past many small peasant homes was spent listening to Thomas stubbornly complain about his predicament, which Kale found to be rather amusing.

They soon approached a massive curtain wall which towered above their heads. Atop the bordering wall stood several armor clad guards who immediately stood at attention upon spotting Kale and his comrades. Upon reaching the gate house, the five friends could see movement from within the arrow slits which increased the tension amongst them.

"State your business!" One of the guards called from the lowest opening within the watch tower.

Within seconds an older man wearing a steel helm peered out a small window hole. He silently inspected each of the women from head to toe, awaiting a response.

"Tell them you have come to purchase crop seed." Judith whispered into Kale's ear which caused him to twitch as her whiskers brushed against his ear lobe.

Kale did as instructed, still taken aback by the sound of his own feminine voice. He knew it was vital for them to convince the guards they were farm peasants who bore no threat.

"Our families sent us here to purchase seed from the market to grow crops to harvest before winter." Kale batted his lashes at the guard while flashing a flirtatious smile. *I cannot believe I'm doing this.* His insides fueled with anger which he forced into submission.

"All right, but the market will close at dusk. You'll need to leave the kingdom before then or you'll be sitting in a cell for the night." The guard's cheeks flushed as he playfully winked toward Kale. "A pretty little lady like yourself shouldn't be out once nightfall is upon us anyway. Give me a moment and I'll let you in."

"Thank you." Kale replied melodically as he wiggled his fingers to gesture goodbye. *How degrading,* he thought with a sigh as the guard disappeared.

Having no weaponry and with time running out, Kale knew he had to lay the act on heavily in order to get them inside and finish things once and for all with Jedah.

"This is quite humiliating," Thomas quietly mumbled to himself.

"Just go along with it, old man, we're runnin' out of time," Illadar snapped back while taking caution to speak softly so no guards would hear.

"That's easy for you to say–look at you!" Thomas whispered in annoyance. "My nose hair is so long it looks as though I have a mustache. And let us not even get into these things." He glanced toward his rather flattened cleavage. "They resemble the pancakes Morty would make us."

Luckily for Illadar and Kale, who fought to suppress their laughter, the massive steel portcullis began to lift. They watched as the massive spikes rose above their heads. Four guards immediately appeared to greet them, each heavily clad in steel.

"Welcome, please make haste to the market. All peasants must leave prior to dusk." The guard narrowed his eyes as they were yet again inspected from head to toe.

"We won't be long." Illadar attempted Kale's approach as he flashed his pouty lips while pulling the cloak tightly against his skin to accentuate his voluptuous curves.

It was obviously working to their advantage as the guards persona softened and they soon began to develop a sense of flirtatious comfort.

"If you ladies should need an escort tonight, we will be here."

"Yeah, you could show us where you sleep at night." Another guard added while leering at them. "I'd like to see what's under that cloak." He winked toward Illadar who in turn took an immediate step back for fear of releasing his anger and punching the guard square in his face.

"You can have the ugly one." A third guard gestured toward Thomas as he slapped his acquaintance on the back.

His laughter was infectious and soon all four roared with laughter.

"Well, we must be going now, before it grows late. Farewell, gentlemen." Kale forced a smile as he gripped Thomas, who looked as though he was prepared to unleash a deadly attack.

They walked briskly through the city until the laughter was drowned out by the bustling commotion of the marketplace.

Mirion exceeded any image Kale had ever imagined. The market was filled with many stone shops with sizeable windows in the front so people could view goods while passing by. Even the ground they walked upon was made of beautiful smooth salmon and white stones. In all four corners of the market were flowing waterfalls splashing into an elaborately detailed fountain.

"Now is not the time to view the sights of our kingdom, Kale. Think of what will happen if we should all transform here, with all of these people around," Judith scolded.

"It's so magnificent, though!" Neelan squeaked as she peeked her furry head through Kale's dark hair. It was her first time viewing a human kingdom and she was mesmerized by the sights.

"We can sightsee another time, but you must remain hidden now!" Judith snapped.

"You really are no fun." Neelan complained as she tucked back against Kale's neck.

Kale knew Judith was right as he quickened his pace, making way across the large open market. Luckily for the three transformed men, there were so many individuals around they easily maneuvered through the crowd without drawing notice. They took great caution to behave as casually as possible in order to avoid drawing unnecessary attention. Though the three men had become women, Thomas' rather hilarious appearance was anything but the norm.

The massive grey stone castle sat upon a large motte. Its squared peaks loomed above all else within the kingdom. A large flag, which bore the crest of Mirion, fluttered upon each of the four guard towers.

"We are here! Hurry, Kale; enter the keep." Judith was so excited she did not realize her tiny claws were digging into the skin on Kale's neck.

"Stop doing that!" Kale quietly snapped as he tilted his head back.

They approached the narrow castle entrance from a bridge that led across the motte. Many guards were positioned within the courtyard, keeping careful watch of their surroundings. A magnificent floral garden centered the courtyard which gave it a bright, cheerful feel. Within the garden was an impressive brick well that appeared to be the source of the castle's water.

To the side, through a series of freestanding columns, Kale could see the training quarters where pages endured accelerated training to become a knight. As they walked, Kale continued to watch the men actively practicing to improve their combat skills against stationary pells. Kale and his friends wandered forward, uncertain which direction to go. Judith and Neelan huddled within the camouflage of hair to remain unnoticed by the guards. Suddenly, through the sound of beating weapons, Kale heard a familiar voice–one he would never forget.

"Hurry up, you worthless peasant boy. If you continue to linger behind your comrades, I may have to schedule another visit to see your eldest sister." A sinister laugh escaped the tall, bald man's lips. "I'd bet she has yet to recover from the last time, so I advise you to strike the target on your next attempt, before you waste more of my time." His hand lashed forward, striking the child across the face.

Kale's plump lips curled as he snarled, locking eyes upon the one he hated above all others–General Jedah.

"I am going to kill him—I *need* to kill him. I shall do it now, with my bare hands." Though he spoke as a female, Kale's voice was hoarse and filled with rage.

"Not if I get to him first, kid. I'll crush his ugly bald skull in." Illadar's eyes were so filled with hatred, they had become red and glassy.

"Enough, you two!" Thomas quietly insisted. "You will ruin everything we have worked so hard for and surely be killed if you allow your emotions to take hold. I have endured being on the run, fighting in a deadly battle, and looking like *this* for our cause. I am not going to tell you both again to calm yourselves and keep moving." His very thick and masculine eyebrows narrowed.

Kale breathed heavily as the two mice squeaked pleas for him to continue walking. He softly growled as he ground his teeth. Fury continued to consume him and he could feel his temperature quickly rising. Kale began to shift his eyes around, taking a mental count of the surrounding guards.

"I can't take it anymore!" Illadar spoke angrily under his breath as his desire to seek revenge upon Jedah intensified beyond anything he'd ever felt. Memories of his wife raced through his mind and consumed rational thought.

Illadar suddenly dashed forward in a crazed rage.

Thomas held up his palm without hesitation as if he had been anticipating the scenario. He quietly spoke so no others would hear, "*Adorin Vexinar*".

Illadar immediately fell forward onto the stone floor as many of the guards flocked toward them. Without hesitation and before another incident could occur, Thomas placed the same spell upon Kale who immediately lost control of his own motor functions. The two men were now mute puppets in Thomas' hands.

"Pardon us," Thomas explained as he quickly attempted to recover the situation, "my dear friend here was overly excited to view the pages in training. You see, we come from poverty-stricken families and to be within the kingdom walls is such a privilege. We tend to get carried away with our emotions on the few trips each year we are able to visit here."

Thomas knew that with his hideous appearance there would be no point in attempting any flirtatious tactics. He easily coaxed Illadar to his feet, gently tugging him in Kale's direction.

"What in Hades is all this commotion?" General Jedah called out.

Thomas gulped as the worst scenario, next to being caught, was upon them. The old sorcerer wistfully hoped his spell or the transformation potion would not wear off while in the presence of Jedah.

The general carelessly shoved the guards aside as he closed in on the three women until standing mere feet away. His battle-worn face, with its long scar, was even uglier than Kale recalled.

Kale's insides felt tormented as he stood so close to the man he desired to decapitate, and yet, he could not move his own body to do so.

"Who are you three?" Jedah squinted his right eye as he stared toward them.

Thomas forced himself to bow before the general. "Good day, General. We have come to speak with the King's steward." He paused to glance upon Jedah's expression. "Although I must say, we are thrilled to have the privilege to lay eyes upon you today. What an unexpected treat." He wondered if he was laying the flattery on too thick.

Jedah's eyebrows pressed toward the center of his face as his forehead wrinkled. "Whatever you wish to say to the King, or his steward, can be told to myself. I'm certain King Valamar would prefer it that way. I cannot fathom anyone within the castle walls having the desire to lay eyes upon such a grotesque woman." He eyed Thomas in disgust.

Flattery was obviously not an option with the general. They watched in torment as Jedah cackled at his own cruelty.

Thomas struggled for the right words to say as a tingling sensation began to manifest within his legs–they were running out of time.

"We have been sent here on behalf of our families to speak about a disease spreading amongst the crops. Many of the farmers feel as though it may hinder vegetable production for the market." Thomas struggled to keep focus as the tingling sensation spread to his arms.

Jedah stared silently for a moment as he analyzed the facial expressions on Thomas and his companions.

"General, pardon my interruption, but your assistance is required at the archery range."

Thomas immediately recognized the voice–Saldin. The greasy-haired lieutenant stood near the training area, awaiting the general's response.

"The men await your arrival. We must prepare in case *they* attempt to return and disrupt our plans." Saldin added.

The five knew Saldin referred to them.

General Jedah raised his hand, gesturing for Saldin to wait as he returned his focus toward Thomas. "I suppose I'll allow you to speak with the King's steward. I do not have time to deal with such a petty situation, nor do I honestly care if half of the useless peasants wither from starvation." He pointed toward the castle doors and motioned for them to leave. "Be quick, and then get out of my keep. I do not wish to view your ugly face again. Should I see either of your friends causing further ruckus–I shall do with them as I please within my chamber." His lips curled as he smiled tauntingly at Kale.

"Thank you, General Jedah, we shall be quick." Thomas bowed, forcing back his own desire to unleash the full fury of his magical abilities upon the general.

Thomas took the hands of Kale and Illadar as he led them toward the large doors. Cautious, but walking quickly and without arousing further suspicions, Thomas felt many wrinkles return to his skin. The man standing guard at the door immediately granted them access after having seen them with the General. They hastily entered the large royal hall, sighing in relief as the door closed behind them.

"I am far too old for this." Thomas spoke and could now see the effects of the potion on Kale and Illadar were wearing off as their facial features began to distort.

"Move quickly and silently to the room at your right before the patrol guards find us!" Judith's vermin body had tripled in size and hung noticeably out of Kale's quickly receding hair.

Thomas pulled Kale and Illadar in the appropriate direction, when he felt a firm tug.

"Get your hands offa' me." Illadar pouted angrily. "What was that all about?! I coulda' had him!"

"You can thank me later for saving your life–and ours. Now, move quickly," Thomas instructed.

Though still enraged, Illadar followed them into a stuffy square room, filled with many pieces of wooden furniture.

Kale soon regained the ability to move and was equally bitter about the situation. Never had he imagined he'd be so close to Jedah for a second time and not have the ability to strip the general's life away.

Judith and Neelan leapt from Kale's back, both nearing the size of a large cat with scattered patches of fur. Judith immediately scurried off into an almond colored closet and Neelan followed without invitation.

"There is another wardrobe across the room with men's clothing." Judith called out with a voice that sounded much like her own. "Move quickly, we have no time to spare. Jedah will surely grow suspicious if we are inside for long."

Rustling and movement could be heard as the two women searched within the closet for gowns to wear. Their limbs had returned, though still covered in random bits of overly long hair.

"Here Neelan, you may have this one." Judith handed her a blue dress. "I wore this in my late childhood to a royal ball. It's quite lovely and should fit you."

Neelan mumbled under her breath as she snatched the gown from Judith's grip. They quickly changed and emerged from the large closet, prepared to find the King.

Kale and Illadar took one glance toward the two women before bursting into a fit of laughter. Judith and Neelan hadn't fully transformed to their original bodies and had enlarged bucked teeth, along with rat-like facial features. The men however, were no better off as they now appeared to be very masculine women. All five enjoyed a moment of laughter over how utterly ridiculous they each looked.

As they engaged in their brief moment of comic relief, the door creaked inward. A short, round woman wearing a plain beige dress and white bonnet pushed the wooden door with her backside as she carried an armful of clothing into the room. Upon turning herself around to face the room, her eyes grew wide with fear.

"Hel—" The woman's attempt to cry out for aid was stifled by Thomas' palm.

"We mean you no harm." Thomas' green eyes met hers as he spoke. "Please forgive my actions, however, I have no choice but to temporarily restrain you."

The servant's eyes grew even wider, her breathing turned to rapid pants.

"Now, now, please do not be frightened," Thomas continued. "We come with no foul intentions, but we must speak with King Valamar personally. We cannot risk any obstacles to interfere with this mission, for the fate of your entire kingdom depends upon it. What I am about to do shall not harm you and will not last for long." He waved his free hand before the servant's face. "*Silant devorda.*" Thomas slowly removed his hand. "Please step inside of the wardrobe."

The servant opened her mouth to yell, soon realizing she had lost all ability to speak. She gripped her throat in alarm as she frantically glanced around at the group who had still not fully transformed.

"As I have said before, dear, no harm will come to you. Once the spell has lost its effects, you will have the ability to call for assistance." Thomas then tied the servant's hands behind her back with a ribbon from one of the gowns hung inside the closet. "Please do not linger–step inside the wardrobe."

The fearful servant gave a quick glance in Judith's direction before obeying the request and slowly stepped inside.

Once the servant entered the small space, they used a wooden chair to secure the two doors. Thomas gave a firm tug upon the doors before feeling confident they would not budge.

"We'd best go now, before she stirs. Follow me." Judith cleared her throat as she shook the feeling of guilt. She cautiously led the way through the hall and past two thrones to a golden door. Red velvet banners draped down on each side, each bearing the Mirion crest.

A single guard stood to the side, holding a polearm vertically parallel to his body.

"Name and purpose?" His words were short and firm. He continued to stare at each of the five comrades as the side of his lip raised in disgust. "*What* are you?" He held the polearm out toward Judith's throat. "Speak quickly, beast."

Judith took her forearm and firmly shoved the weapon to the side. She quickly moved past him, pushing open the golden door and entering the royal chambers.

"Let's go!" She called out as she took off in a sprint, ignoring the screaming guard who followed close behind, down the candlelit corridor. "Father!" Judith cried out as she entered a large bedroom through a wooden door.

A tall older man, wearing a white tunic and red velvet surcoat spun upon his heels. His baggy eyes widened, "Guards!" He called out as Judith flung her arms around him.

Three guards, including the man who had been chasing them, piled into the room. They closed in on the group, forming a triangular barrier, their weapons drawn.

"Release the King or die!" One of the guards demanded.

"Father, stop this at once, please—it is I, Judith, your daughter!" She pleaded.

"How dare you try to deceive me! My daughter is de—" The King's jaw dropped as the last remnants of the potion's effects faded and there before him stood the restored body of the golden-haired Princess. "This is impossible!" The King shouted.

One of the guards took advantage of the distracting moment to seize Judith and restrain her on the floor. He aimed his sword toward her chest. "Shall I kill her, Your Highness?"

King Valamar's green eyes pierced Judith's.

"Father, please—don't do this! Remember when you would hold me as a child and tell me to think with my mind, but to look with my heart? Now is the time to look with yours." Judith's eyes began to tear.

"Withdraw your weapon at once!" The King extended his

arm to help Judith to her feet. He appeared dumbfounded as he continued to inspect her from head to toe.

"This is just not possible. Am I dreaming?" The King reached out to touch her face.

Judith broke down into tears as she explained everything in detail.

"My precious daughter," his hands rest gently upon her cheeks, "I should have seen within your eyes all along that it was truly you. How I have missed you." He wiped a tear from beneath his eye. "All this time, I was such a fool. I thought I had lost you, my darling."

They embraced in a loving hug, both equally grateful for their reunion. Once their joyful emotions settled, the King's face filled with rage.

"Jedah." He clenched his fists which shook with anger, "The man who I entrusted with my very life has dared to betray me. He shall pay dearly for these actions." He glanced toward the three guards. "Gather the knights who have served directly below my authority. At this time, I cannot place trust in those who have been led by *him*." His lips snarled as he emphasized the end. "I want both Jedah and Saldin arrested and placed into separate cells at once." The King paused a moment to approach Kale and his friends. "I thank you all dearly for protecting my beloved daughter. I wish to see each of you tonight at the banquet hall, there is much to discuss. Please feel free to help yourself to any of the castle amenities." He then directed his attention toward Thomas who had managed to find a grey robe in the wardrobe. "I would recognize you anywhere, old friend. It is wonderful to see you again, Thomas. And who is this here?" The King looked toward Neelan. "An elf within Mirion?"

Neelan glanced down in embarrassment. She completely

forgot about concealing her ears with all that had happened.

"Do not shun, my dear. You are welcome here within the kingdom. Please make yourself at home. I am honored to see you have journeyed so far in the efforts to save my daughter."

"Thank you, Your Highness." Neelan hesitantly bowed, still bashful of her appearance, yet filled with joy by his words.

"Please forgive my departure. However, there is much I must tend to under these new circumstances. Thomas, I do hope you will join me once I've finished. There is something I would like to speak to you about." King Valamar rushed off, commanding Judith to stay behind in case the situation should result in bloodshed. He assured her he still had an overpowering amount of loyalty within the walls of their kingdom.

"Wait!" Kale called out as the King turned to exit the room. "Just what exactly do you plan to do? Jedah must be brought to justice at once—and I desire nothing more than to be the one to end his miserable life. I have come too far now to simply stand back while you and your men, who were foolishly betrayed, take action." Kale's heart raced as he spoke.

"Learn your place, boy!" King Valamar bellowed.

"Kale, do not speak to the King in such a manner. Have you forgotten the meaning of respect?" Thomas scolded while placing a palm onto Kale's shoulder.

"Thomas, you of all people should not expect me to stand here while the man who slaughtered all dragon-kind is finally able to meet justice."

"This is not a matter for you to deal with. I appreciate all you have done for my daughter; however, you are in Mirion now and shall obey my authority." Without another word, the King turned and briskly left the room.

"I am under no one's rule." Kale clenched his teeth as he

pulled free from Thomas' grasp and stepped forward toward the door.

"That is as far as you shall go, commoner." One of the knights placed his blade before Kale's throat.

"Kale, please stop this!" Judith called out as both she and Neelan rushed to Kale's side. "There comes a time when you must swallow your own pride and place trust into the hands of another."

Judith knew her father was quite capable of handling the task on his own. The truth of Jedah's cruelty was revealed and she knew they had succeeded in stopping him before he obtained enough power and manipulation to steal the citizens' loyalty. The kingdom was still under Valamar's rule and Judith was confident Jedah would soon be apprehended.

"Fine. I will remain here for now..." Kale's voice was still filled with anger. "But should word not arrive soon that he has been captured–I will find and kill him myself."

"I give you my thanks, Kale." Judith smiled sweetly. "Let's move to more suitable accommodations while we wait." She motioned the knights to stand at ease and led them to a separate, yet equally large room.

"Do not even think about running, Kale." Neelan warned while tightening a firm grip upon Kales wrist.

Kale sighed, shaking his head as he continued to follow Judith to the next room.

A grand four-post bed, draped with sheer white fabric, seemed well-suited for a woman of royalty. Fine hand-crafted furniture filled the room and shone as though freshly polished. Although her father thought her to be dead, he never had the heart to remove her belongings and ensured the room had been properly kept.

The five companions sat upon the plush lavender colored bed as they anxiously discussed the situation. Both Kale and Illadar fought the strong urge to dash out of the castle and confront Jedah. At that moment, they equally desired to bash his head into the stone floor.

Their conversation continued and soon Kale found himself so engrossed in discussing their thoughts on how the King would handle the situation, he lost track of time. After an hour had passed, one of the royal guards rapped upon the door.

"You may enter." Judith spoke with renewed authority.

"Your Highness, please accept my sincerest apologies for my previous actions." The guard bowed.

"It was understandable. You were only attempting to protect my father, and for that I give you my thanks." She smiled sweetly which caused the young guard to glance down in an attempt to conceal his reddened cheeks.

He cleared his throat before standing upright. "Milady, the King has sent me to request the presence of Thomas within the library."

"Jorin," As Judith spoke, the guard bore an expression of surprise as if he had not expected her to remember him by name. "Please report the current status of General Jedah."

"Yes, Milady; Jedah has been apprehended by ambush and is currently being held within a cell, surrounded by the King's trusted guards."

"What about Saldin?" Kale could no longer bite his tongue. "Did you get that coward as well?"

"I regret to say, he managed to escape. We have scouted the entire city with no positive report. However, the King has dispatched more men to scout the surrounding farmland as well."

"How can we be sure the remaining warriors give loyalty to

us and are not aiding Saldin?" Judith pressed the concern.

"That, my Princess, is the other issue. The knights in support of the general must have fled with Saldin. Our numbers have decreased and we are unable to locate any of them. It's as though they had anticipated being discovered and planned a secret escape route. I cannot promise everyone who remains pledges loyalty to your father; however I do feel most, if not all of our enemies have fled. Your father has every able guard and knight on alert and we shall remain on high security for the night. If they attempt anything foolish, it will be the last move they make." Jorin focused his attention toward Thomas. "My apologies, however I mustn't stay any longer for the King is waiting. Please, follow me." He bowed before escorting Thomas away.

"Do you think he is trustworthy?" Illadar questioned once Jorin was gone.

"Yes, I am certain of it. He was recruited and trained by one of my father's dear friends specifically to become a personal guard to the King. He has had little, if any, interaction with Jedah or his men."

The next hour was spent in awkward silence as they each pondered their own thoughts of what the King and Thomas could possibly be discussing in private. They knew it had to be something of dire importance for the King to place it in priority over further reuniting with his daughter.

Eventually, Thomas returned with a look of glee upon his face. "It is time to join the King for dinner." The lines on his cheeks thickened as he smiled with a certain twinkle in his eyes.

Kale was so hungry he didn't bother to inquire about Thomas' dramatic change in mood, or the fact the old sorcerer once again wore a silly pointed hat that matched his grey robe.

~~~~~~~~~~~~~~~

Once properly seated around a polished banquet table, Kale's curiosity finally got the best of him.

"Can anyone please explain what exactly is going on? We have gone through torment and back to make it where we are now. I think it is fair to say we deserve more information," Kale shoved a roll into his mouth as he spoke.

"Kale," Judith narrowed her eyes as she scolded him, "though he is my father, do not forget that you are in the presence of a King–mind your manners!"

Kale looked down chagrined at his rude behavior. He could hear Neelan laughing under her breath from the seat to his side.

"It is quite all right, Judith. After all this young man has gone through, I think it is quite fine for him to enjoy himself tonight." King Valamar winked at Kale. "I also believe he deserves to be provided with further information." The King adjusted himself in his heavily cushioned chair.

"First, I would like to personally welcome you to our kingdom. I am honored to have each of you here tonight. You have returned the most precious person in this world to me. Judith's mother died while in labor, so she truly is all I have." He cleared his throat. "I am also pleased to see that despite your differences," the King glanced toward Neelan, who sunk down into her seat, "you have all come together as one unified group. Please, dear, do not feel as though you must hide yourself within the walls of our kingdom."

"Thank you for your kindness toward me..." Neelan softly spoke, then slowly adjusted herself upright in the chair.

"Now, let us move onto the more serious matters at hand. I request the presence of each of you immediately following dinner. I want no time wasted in sentencing my former general. The longer he remains within this kingdom, the more risk of his escape. I want this matter handled now, so tomorrow we may execute his punishment. We have yet to find Saldin or the group who disappeared with him, though, I am very confident they are no longer within our walls."

"What is going to happen to Jedah?" Kale quickly caught his overly forward behavior as he cleared his dry throat. "Your Highness," He added.

"I am sorry to inform you I cannot discuss the subject at this moment as Thomas and I are still establishing the full details. However, I can assure you he will not harm another soul after tomorrow."

Why him? Kale wondered as he stared blankly toward Thomas.

Within minutes, a grand feast was placed upon the table and they each enjoyed a wide variety of satisfying dishes.

Once finished, the King dabbed his chin with a cloth napkin before standing from his seat. "I must excuse myself now, and tend to further preparations. Please continue to enjoy your feast. Once you have finished, Judith will escort you to your sleeping quarters where you will find appropriate clothing for tonight's event. I would like you to meet me within the grand hall. Sentencing will begin shortly after."

The King cast a glance of warning toward Kale and Illadar. "Though, I am grateful for the return of my daughter, we cannot risk anything going wrong tonight. I will inform you now that Jedah will be present and I expect you both to suppress whatever aggressive actions you may desire to execute. Should you attempt to disrupt my ruling in any way, you shall find yourself sleeping within a prison cell tonight. I will warn you–they are not accommodating. This is my kingdom and the issue will be dealt with diplomatically–despite my urge to slit his throat for placing my own daughter and the people of Ravondore through such strife and agony." The King flipped his red velvet robe over a shoulder and left them to finish their meal as he exited the room.

Kale could barely ingest another spoonful of potatoes as his stomach turned in knots at the thought of being in the same room as Jedah. The night would soon bring a cascading series of changes none of them could have imagined.

CHAPTER 27

THE KING'S PLAN

The group was escorted into two separate bedrooms joined by an unhinged doorframe. One room was assigned to Neelan, and the other for the men. Within each area they found a rolling wardrobe filled with both men and women's formal attire. After sorting through, they each found something of interest that fit well enough to wear.

Neelan tapped upon the frame of the open doorway. "Are you decent?" She called in.

"Yes, my dear, they are both dressed. You may come in." Thomas replied.

As she entered, Kale couldn't help but uncontrollably stare.

Neelan's hair was pinned elegantly back with a sparkling clasp, crafted in the shape of a rose. Her pastel yellow gown hung in a slightly crumpled heap at the floor, but fit perfectly in all other areas. The form-fitting upper half led into a very full skirt which had draped fabric and a small bow in the back. Neelan looked as though she belonged with royalty.

"Do I look silly?" Neelan placed her hands upon her flushed cheeks.

"N-no—sorry." Kale quickly dodged her eyes and glanced away bashfully. "You look really beautiful."

"You think so?" Neelan gripped the gown, lifting it from the floor as she spun around. She then approached Kale, whispering softly into his ear, "You're not so bad yourself." She winked at him, smiling seductively as she ran her fingers along his neck.

Kale's heart pounded as his breathing tightened within his chest. Neelan's soft caresses sent chills down his spine.

"I do not mean to interrupt such a...moment, however we really must be leaving now." Judith cleared her throat from the doorframe.

~~~~~~~~~~~~~~~~~~~

As they entered the royal hall, Judith, who had escorted them, immediately moved toward her throne. Kale and the others followed Thomas to join a group of lesser royalty, consisting of nobles and lords. Judith lowered herself upon the golden throne and many shouts of awe erupted within the large hall. She humbly smiled toward the crowd as she adjusted her elaborate teal gown.

"She has truly returned!"

"The Princess lives!"

Voices could be heard in all directions as the anxious citizens stared toward Judith.

"Silence, please." King Valamar stood and raised his hands above his head which bore a magnificent golden crown. Even from a distance, the variety of jewels which were socketed into the gold itself could be seen. Then, before the audience, he briefly informed them on the situation leading up to Judith's return.

Kale glanced around as the whispers of many enraged individuals filled the room.

"Bring in the culprit!" The King bellowed.

A dozen warriors who were heavily armored surrounded Jedah. The former general was shackled at his wrists and ankles. He wore filthy tights and an oversized tunic hung on his body like a large sack. The room grew silent as they all watched Jedah shuffle his way along a long beige carpet to the thrones. The guards forcefully pulled on Jedah's arms, restraining him in place as they neared the King.

"You go no farther, betrayer." One of the guards warned.

Kale's heart once again burned with pure fury at the sight of Jedah who wore an expression that bore no guilt for his actions.

"Do as you will–*your highness*." Jedah sneered as though this was nothing but a game.

King Valamar's face shook in anger and Kale could see he was struggling to maintain composure.

"Ah...Princess." Jedah released a sinister laugh. "So good to see you again. Did the dragon decide to release you?" More laughter followed. "Those filthy beasts; it is a shame one of the disgusting creatures still roams this world." His eyes shot directly toward Kale with a burning, untamed fury.

Kale's pale blue eyes narrowed. *He must know...* Kale returned the bitter glare, baring his teeth as he fought to remain still out of respect for the King.

"Do not speak!" The King's voice was loud and demanding as he pointed a finger toward Jedah.

"What shall you do? You are a foolish King who allowed yo—" Jedah groaned in pain as one of the guards slammed the pommel of his sword into Jedah's back.

"The King said to silence yourself." The guard ordered.

"I've given this situation deep thought and have come to the conclusion that death is simply too good for you." As King Valamar spoke, Kale and Illadar appeared as though they had just been struck in the face.

The surrounding audience appeared just as dumbstruck by the King's words.

He does not deserve to live. Kale thought with a grimacing look. *I hope the King has a plan and is not truly as foolish as I have come to believe.* He silently awaited an explanation.

"You have betrayed our kingdom—betrayed me. You've kidnapped and endangered my daughter. In addition, you have tormented, slain, and destroyed the lives of many across Ravondore. Without remorse, you have taken the lives of women and children. You've committed all of these heinous acts without my acknowledgment and have blemished the good name of Mirion. I cannot imagine how many wish for the fall of our kingdom after what has been done. Our kingdom stands for peace and justice. We only seek aggressive tactics when absolutely necessary and I was a fool to have trusted your word. For this treachery, you shall be sentenced to a life in torment until your body perishes–think of this as a prolonged execution. By tomorrow's light, you will be sent to a cavern hidden away within the snow-covered continent of Sundra. The frost elves–mighty and powerful, will ensure you remain locked away, enduring countless days of agony until your time on this world has ended. When they arrive here tomorrow, no soul in Ravondore shall ever lay eyes upon the likes of you again." The King's eyes pierced Jedah's with a malevolent stare that only a father who had thought he lost his only child could feel.

Neelan knew the frost elves were cold and emotionless beings within her race. They were not vicious or aggressive, unless provoked, and usually maintained a thriving desire for balance within the world. However, unlike the high elves, they had no remorse. The frost elves could torture and take life without a second thought.

Kale struggled to accept the situation as he shifted anxiously from one foot to the other. His heart raced with doubt and an uneasy feeling of uncertainty swarmed within his mind. Having no prior knowledge of the frost elves, he assumed the worst. With the many devoted followers Jedah had accumulated, the thought of the former general finding a way to escape seemed to be a sure reality.

Neelan took notice to Kale's anxious movements and rose up onto her toes to whisper words of ease into his ear. She briefly explained the great power frost elves possessed. The gesture slightly eased Kale's nerves, though he still could not understand why King Valamar did not simplify the situation by sentencing Jedah to an immediate execution.

"My decision is final." The King spoke with assured confidence, despite the uncertain whispers amongst the crowd.

"It'll be all right..." Neelan softly spoke to Kale and Illadar.

King Valamar clapped his hands twice. "Take him away. I cannot bear to see his face any longer." He then faced the audience. "You are all dismissed. We will meet again at dawn's first light."

~~~~~~~~~~~~

"What is he thinking?!" Kale tugged at his hair in frustration once they left the hall.

"Calm yourself, Kale. The King has the best intentions of Ravondore in mind," Thomas replied.

"By allowing Jedah to live?" Kale slammed his fist angrily into his palm.

"Death is swift, where Jedah is heading will be far worse. The frost elves will show him no mercy. He will live each day in agony. Though far in distance, the frost elves have been at peace with Mirion until word of Jedah's vile actions reached them. Now that they are aware of King Valamar's ignorance in the matter, the treaty of peace has yet again resumed. They believe in maintaining balance within the world, much like the high elves. However, unlike Neelan's kind, the frost elves will come when summoned to punish the wicked. They will not, however, engage in war as it is against their beliefs. The frost elves will come only once the enemy has been captured and judgment passed. Think of them as the hand of punishment. They are far more powerful than Jedah could dream and I do not foresee how he could possibly escape without first meeting a terrible death." Thomas placed a hand upon Kale's shoulder. "You should not worry yourself over the situation. We have succeeded and Jedah will be gone tomorrow."

"How does the King even know they will arrive to aid with Jedah's purgatory? And how could they possibly make it here by tomorrow mornin' if they're comin'' from another continent?" Illadar joined in.

"Between only us," Thomas lowered his voice, "decades ago when the treaty was first agreed upon, a previous King of Mirion was entrusted with a scepter only to be used in a time of need to restore balance. The enchanted item allows the true King to contact the Frost Emperor. Unlike my own limited abilities, the frost elves are able to teleport themselves to any location without ever having to set foot or view the area beforehand."

Thomas' words managed to reassure both Kale and Illadar enough to refrain from pressing the subject any longer.

The group was so fatigued from their arduous journey they each hurried to their freshly prepared beds. Neelan kissed Kale softly on the cheek before her own departure, assuring him a second time everything would be all right.

Kale lay back on the plush maroon comforter as he stared up toward the sheer fabric draped from each of the four wooden bedposts. As he continued to dwell upon the King's final judgment, his eyes struggled to remain open until he could no longer fight against them. His body went limp as he drifted into slumber.

Kale tossed and turned on the large feather mattress as a series of dreams involving Jedah's escape tormented his sleep. In one of his more vivid dreams, Jedah managed to smuggle a cell key and silently slip out beneath the guards' noses as they mingled amongst themselves. Jedah cleverly made his way inside the royal chambers and crept to Kale's bedside. Kale could clearly hear the words Jedah spoke, *"All dragons shall die by my hand. You cannot escape me."* Then–the steel blade thrust down toward Kale's chest.

The dream became so intense, Kale woke abruptly, covered in beads of cold sweat.

"Kale?" A soft voice called through the darkness.

"Yes, Neelan, I apologize for disturbing you, I was having a horrible nightmare. Everything is fine, you can go back to sleep now."

Neelan sat down upon the edge of Kale's bed, placing an arm gently around his bare torso. "You're worrying about this too much, Kale. You shall see, he will be gone tomorrow morning and we can all move forward with our lives. Don't lose sight of your next quest. You can save dragon kind from extinction–you and only you."

Kale's chest burned; he had nearly lost focus on the eggs.

"What would you do without me?" Neelan flashed a gentle smile which could be seen through the darkness. "You are a mess." She quietly laughed as she placed her hands upon Kale's cheeks. She lightly brushed her nose against his, pressing her body firmly into his torso which felt firm and warm. "Don't forget I am here for you." She spoke so closely that he felt her hot breath against his lips. "Please get some rest; I'll be just in the other room if you need me."

"Thank you." He stroked a hand through her hair. "I'm glad you're with me."

"Goodnight." She smiled once again before returning to her own bed.

Kale stared toward the ceiling as he listened to the repetitive rumble of Illadar's snoring in the bed parallel to his. Eventually, his eyes began to roll and despite his desire to remain awake and avoid further torment within his dreams, he dozed off.

~~~~~~~~~~~~~~~

Kale's eyes fluttered open as he stared forward into a blinding bright light. As the light dimmed, Kale could see he was surrounded by nothingness—only white in every direction, there were no walls.

"Hello?" He called out. "Can anyone hear me? Neelan?"

"I am here with you, my young Firehart." A soothing female voice sounded in all directions, yet no one could be seen.

"Where are you? Who are you? And where am I?" Kale held

his hands out in front of his face as he searched to see if anything –or anyone was there.

"Please do not be afraid, little one."

Kale spun around to see a woman staring back at him with nurturing golden eyes. She had red spiraling curls and a gentle smile which creased at the corners, revealing her matured age. It took Kale a moment to realize he had seen the woman before.

"Zasha, it's you again!"

"You are quite right, Firehart." She chuckled as she placed a hand upon his cheek. "You have come such a long way since your journey began. I am so proud of all you've accomplished– you truly are a noble one. You have grown more than I could ever have imagined."

"Why have you been helping me–or whatever it is you *are* doing?"

"Because, my dear Firehart, it is you who can change the world. You have the ability within your heart of gold to right what has been wronged. On such a vast earth, there will always be good and evil. When the wicked such as Jedah arise, so will a valiant hero. In this case, that hero–is you." Zasha took Kale's hand into hers. "I know you will save the dragon race Jedah fought to destroy. I will aid you when able, but you must find the true strength within yourself to succeed." She released his hand, gripping her black scarf which had been wrapped many times around her neck. "I have something to share with you." Zasha exhaled as she slowly removed the fabric from her body to reveal a steel collar.

Kale's forehead wrinkled. "I don't understand. What is it?"

Zasha turned without words and began to walk away.

"Wait!" Kale reached toward her.

"There is a secret I have been keeping from you. Please know it was for your own benefit, and the overall good of Ravondore. The timeline of events needed to happen as they did, and I knew once you were aware of the truth, you would come to find me." Zasha turned to face him from a distance as she gripped firmly upon the collar.

She closed her eyes and Kale watched in astonishment as the steel ring began to glow, splitting into two halves. As the pieces hit the white ground, her body rapidly transfigured into the last thing Kale could have ever imagined–*a dragon.*

Zasha's massive form towered above him. She was mighty and red with large spikes along her spine. Her eyes were a vibrant yellow which was surrounded by toughened scales. Her bat-like wings flapped once before tucking snugly against her torso. She was nearly twice the size Kale had been before his human transformation.

"This can't be real..." Kale's mouth felt dry as he swallowed hard. He reached out to touch the snout of what had been a woman only moments ago. "Why are you hiding as a human? And why have you not come to see me in person?" Kale began to grow angry as his mind raced. "If we are the last of our kind, shouldn't we search for the eggs together?" He withdrew his hand. "Just what sort of games are you playing?!" Kale yelled furiously as the realization struck him. He felt betrayed to know that all along, there had been another living dragon within the world, yet he was led to believe he was the only one. Throughout his journey he had bore the weight of thinking he was the very last of his species, when all along it had been untrue–*she* knew from the very beginning.

"Please understand; this was never intended to cause you pain. It had to be done and I assure you all will be answered once you are here. Just know that, at this time, I am unable to physically be with you. I have missed you so very much, my dear, sweet, Firehart. Once you find the remaining dragon eggs, soon after, you shall find me too. Then we can be together again." Her voice was now raspy, yet soothing.

"Again? I have never met you outside of these visions within my dreams." Kale tightened his fists in frustration.

The large red dragon softly huffed as she lowered her head near Kale. "We met long before you can recall young one–you are my son, dear Firehart."

Zasha began to vanish right before Kale's eyes.

"No! Please wait! You can't tell me something of such importance and then leave me again! Come back!" Kale swung his arms around frantically where she had stood in an attempt to grip onto her.

"It is time for you to wake now. Please be strong, my little one."

Just as mysteriously as she had arrived, Zasha was now gone.

CHAPTER 28

KALE'S ULTIMATE DECISION

"Mother!" Kale cried out as his eyes shot open in a panic.

He stared at his friends surrounding him with concerned expressions upon their faces. Kale could see that the night sky was slowly becoming overwhelmed with pink hues; the sun peeked above the horizon. The morning rays of dawn shined in upon the large room through a square framed window.

"Thomas," Kale heavily panted, still shaken from his restless sleep. "I had another dream of Zasha." Kale looked down gripping his sheets tightly. *Could it all have been a dream? No, that can't be—I don't know how, but I am certain it was real.* "I have something to tell you." Kale paused a moment in thought before glancing up at Thomas. "She is my mother–and a dragon, currently in human form, like myself. I believe it has something to do with a collar she wears beneath her scarf. I must find her."

"How can this be?" Thomas' eyes widened. "Are you certain you are not confusing your dreams with reality? I cannot understand why something of such importance would not be revealed to us much earlier."

Kale explained all details of the dream, including Zasha's foretelling of the opportunity they would soon have to find her. He also informed them of her promise to reveal all answers they desired to know about her secrecy.

"I honestly do not know how I'm supposed to handle this. Do you really think she could be my mother? I've always assumed my parents must have fallen in the great dragon war. To think she might actually be alive...feels so surreal." Kale planted his face within the palms of his hands. Though his heart told him that Zasha was truly his mother, his mind still had doubts. "There is so much happening right now. How am I to remain sane when everything is so confusing?"

"I cannot answer if she is your mother, or if what you saw was merely a dream. However, I promise you we will find the answers together." Thomas smiled, and Kale could see Neelan and Illadar nodding their heads in agreement.

"Kale, we are all here for you and will do all we can to unravel this mystery. I have told you before–I'm not going to leave your side." Neelan ran her fingertips down his back and for the first time since he woke, Kale saw that she and Illadar were clad in the clothing they had worn prior to drinking the potion. Neelan giggled at his expression. "Yes, our clothing was returned before dawn's light. Our horses are also waiting within the kingdom's stable. But for now, we must quickly leave for the keep. Judith left earlier and will be waiting for us in the main hall."

~~~~~~~~~~~~~~

Judith greeted them with a warm smile; she appeared stunning as always. Her arm length white satin gloves complimented the pale peach gown she wore, accessorized by an elaborate gold necklace.

"It is time my friends; the moment we have all longed for. Father is already in the keep and the frost elves should arrive at any moment. We must hurry." Judith motioned them to follow her.

The door opened to reveal a horde of citizens gathered behind many guards who ensured they each kept behind the large rectangular shaped area. They instantly spotted King Valamar upon a wide raised platform with four guards to each side.

Two guards approached Judith's side as she continued to lead the way toward her father. As they walked past the citizens, many bowed while others tossed freshly picked flowers in her path. It was obvious those loyal to the King truly cherished her as their Princess and were thrilled by her return.

"Hello, father." Judith curtseyed, taking position by the King's side. "I shall see you all soon." She softly spoke while smiling at Kale before directing her attention toward the crowd. She raised her gloved hand to greet them and cheers immediately rang out within the keep.

One of the guards led Kale and his comrades to the side of the raised platform. They were positioned toward the front of the huddled citizens who eagerly awaited what was to come.

King Valamar held his arm out and the crowd immediately grew silent. "Bring in the culprit!" He bellowed, pushing his red velvet cape over a shoulder.

Four guards, in full suits of armor, approached. They pushed a wheeled wooden stand with two crossed stakes that held Jedah securely in place with thick black chains. The former General's cold, heartless eyes gazed around at the angry crowd who immediately erupted with chaos. The bordering guards struggled with their shields to push the citizens back as they shouted and threw rotted produce at Jedah. Despite the crowds' response, Jedah still bore no expression of remorse for his actions.

King Valamar glared upon him with disgust. "Jedah Bladewell, you are hereby exiled from the kingdom of Mirion, and I am sure I speak for the other ruled territories when I say you shall never set foot upon the continent of Ravondore again." As the audience cheered, the King once again raised his hand in authority. "It now begins."

The crowd grew deathly silent as a layer of ice mysteriously began to form in front of the wheeled stand where Jedah stood. The small, frosty circle rapidly began to creep outward, expanding across the stone floor. Many citizens staggered backwards in fear as the ice moved closer toward the perimeter where they stood.

A nearly simultaneous exhale could be heard as the frozen layer stopped inches short of the guards and citizens. The inexplicable frost then began to creep upward along the wooden posts, and soon each breath Jedah released came out like a thick fog from his mouth.

"You cannot stop me." Jedah sneered. "I will rise again–and you all shall die." His dark eyes scowled toward the King.

The chains binding his wrists and ankles soon became coated with a layer of ice–then the unknown presence was finally revealed.

Two tall, slender male elves appeared, one to each side of Jedah. As their claw-like nails touched the chains, they snapped effortlessly in two. Though Jedah was free from restraints, he did not move, remaining immobile as if paralyzed in place.

Kale watched in silence as their pale blue robes fluttered gently, though no breeze was present. The high collar of their attire slightly concealed their pale faces, yet did not obstruct their long pale-blonde hair from flowing past their shoulders. Wrapped around their heads was a pointed crown which matched the color of their robes. The look within their nearly translucent eyes appeared detached from all emotion, and their hollow cheeks gave a menacing appearance. They spoke no words as their hands waved toward Jedah's motionless body. The crowd continued to watch in silence as frosted rope emerged from the ground, slithering around Jedah's appendages and binding his limbs tightly together.

Jedah appeared to regain movement in his body and yelled out in agony. It was the first sign of weakness Kale had ever seen from the vile man. Jedah's muscles flexed as he struggled to break free, still grunting in pain. He looked toward the sky, releasing a loud scream which caused spit to fly from his mouth.

The frost elves placed a hand on each side of him and then, just as mysteriously as they had arrived, the frost elves and Jedah began to fade into a glacial mist. The final sounds of Jedah's piercing screams could be heard echoing off the stone walls before they disappeared from sight.

"It has been done." The King spoke while holding both hands above his head. "My people, we are free from his cruelty. I make this promise to you today; I will strive to right the wrongdoings Jedah has brought upon Ravondore. Though, I cannot undo the horrible losses which have occurred, I will not stop until Mirion, and our brethren across this vast continent, rejoice in a new world where balance will be restored." As the King spoke, Kale saw Illadar look away from the others to hide the pain he felt at the thought of his deceased wife.

The crowd erupted with vigorous cheers and Kale relaxed as relief swept over him. He still had an uneasy feeling in the pit of his gut, but he tried to remain optimistic about the situation. Before Kale and his friends could slip away in the midst of the rejoicing citizens, King Valamar caught sight of them.

"My dear friends, please, join me." The King motioned the four toward him, which left them with no choice but to respectfully obey.

As the crowd settled, the King was handed a long sword by one of his personal guards. He continued on to explain to the citizens of Mirion that it was Kale and his friends who rescued the Princess and fought bravely against Jedah's men.

"Kale, Illadar, and Neelan, it is my honor to offer you three a place here within the castle as knights to the royal family. Thomas and I have already discussed this matter and he is prepared to support your final decision." The King looked toward Neelan. "To have humans and a high elf living together harmoniously would be a stupendous milestone for our world."

Neelan quickly glanced away to hide her reddened cheeks. Though, she longed to live among humans in peace, Neelan still hadn't come to terms with accepting what she truly was. In her heart, she still felt as though the crowd might be looking upon her with distaste. However, if there was one thing both she and Kale had learned throughout their journey, it was to not hastily judge others. Thus, she shook her thoughts and turned to face the muted citizens who awaited their reply for a place within the kingdom.

Kale was the first to take a step forward. "Your Highness, the honor presented means more to me than you know and I truly thank you from the bottom of my heart. However, I apologize, but I must decline." Kale could hear gasps from surprised individuals within the audience.

"You see," He continued, "it is not that I do not enjoy my time here in your magnificent kingdom, but I have something of dire importance I must do." He smiled. "I suppose it is safe to say I'm a free spirit. I would like to remain unbound, where I can aid all in need of my help across Ravondore. Throughout my journey, I've opened up my heart more than I could have ever imagined. I never wish to stand back while others suffer." Kale's blue eyes met with the King's. "Should you ever need me, though, I will always be of service. You are truly a noble King." Kale bowed.

Neelan moved toward Kale's side, "King Valamar, I thank you dearly for your kindness. You are a truly wonderful and accepting King who has made me feel welcome within your kingdom, and among human kind–something I never thought possible. However, I too must decline your gracious offer. My heart follows Kale to the end, and I will not leave his side."

Illadar's decision was not as easy. Mirion had always been his home. This was the kingdom where he had built so many wonderful memories. He glanced upon Kale, Neelan, and Thomas as his dark lips slanted upward into a smile. Illadar suddenly became certain of his future. Without his wife, Mirion held nothing more than visions from his past; it was time to move forward with his life.

"I will be stayin' with them as well, Your Highness."

Kale looked to his side, surprised, yet thrilled, with Illadar's decision.

King Valamar and Judith smiled as they nodded toward the group in approval. Though the three would not become knights of Mirion, one by one the King had them kneel before him as he dubbed each a hero, eternally welcome within the walls of the kingdom.

The King moved closer to Kale so that only the two could

hear his words. "I have something to give you before your departure. Please wait for me within the great hall. Your friends may join you as well."

Kale nodded as he and his friends were escorted back to the large castle door. The keep roared with cheers and cries of gratitude as they made their exit.

~~~~~~~~~~~~~~~

Shortly after they entered the hall, Kale began to anxiously pace in a large circle. *What could King Valamar possibly have to give only to me?*

Neelan urged Kale to settle down and relax as she tugged gently on his arm.

"Do you know what is happening Thomas?" Kale pressed the old sorcerer for answers.

"I mustn't say a word. The King will reveal what is happening very shortly." He winked. "I can assure you, however, it will be well worth your wait."

Kale tilted his head back in frustration as he rolled his eyes. "You know I hate when you do this."

"You are far too impatient, young one." Thomas laughed to himself.

Luckily for Kale, he didn't have to endure the pressing curiosity for long. Judith and King Valamar soon entered the room. Illadar immediately dropped to a knee as they approached.

"We will have none of that today. For now, we speak as friends. Please stand." The King smiled warmly. "I am grateful we finally have the opportunity to speak without interruption, Kale. I will not waste your time with meaningless chatter as I am aware of the quest you desire to embark upon. Regrettably, I know all too well of the dragon eggs you seek."

It all began to make sense to Kale—this was the conversation he and Thomas had in private; the old sorcerer had told him everything. Despite the King's knowledge of Kale and his journey, he was still unsure as to the full extent of what was happening.

"Do you remember the vision I shared with you of Jedah embarking upon his final mission to become a knight?" Thomas questioned.

Kale nodded as he suddenly recalled it was Thomas who aided the King with the enchanted item on Jedah's quest. Thomas was the one who could piece together the puzzle on events that had happened since.

"Yes, Kale, Thomas helped me fill many gaps which I have been uncertain about since that very day Jedah left on the delivery mission." King Valamar spoke as though he could read Kale's expression. "The package was to be delivered to Eldawin as a peace offering. It was in hopes of having them unite with our kingdom. At that time I was unaware they were the eggs of a dragon; they had been mislabeled as gryphons by my father's advisor many decades ago. My intention was to give the Lord of Eldawin this gift so they would have the ability to travel between our cities with ease. Quite honestly, if I had known these were dragon eggs, I would have kept and attempted to hatch them myself. To have dragons protecting our kingdom would have been a vital advantage to ward off any opposing threats who may seek to attack."

"We are not petty animals that you can train. A dragon is not a creature which one can own." Kale snapped as he interrupted the King.

The thought of King Valamar's words sickened him and for a

moment, made him remember why he loathed humans so.

"Yes, I do know this now—and I am deeply sorry. I'm certain you will be able to find the eggs. You are both brave and determined." His expression was comforting and his voice revealed sincerity in the words he spoke. He truly was apologetic for his actions in the past. "I would like to present you with something very rare and extremely valuable in hopes of making amends for my horribly poor decisions in the past." The King's hand disappeared inside of his cape. Within seconds he withdrew a short, thin vial illuminated with a vibrant blue substance. "Thomas cares deeply for you and has informed me of your situation. He has told me what you truly are and how you long to return to your true form."

Thomas placed a hand upon Kale's shoulder as he smiled toward him.

"This potion is the last of its kind in existence. It has been kept within a chamber, along with many other powerful concoctions and enchantments for centuries. The room itself is guarded by powerful magic—only to be accessed by a true King of Mirion." The King's cheeks were spotted with pink and Kale could tell he felt a sense of pride in his statement.

"Pardon my interruption, but I still don't understand what all of this is about. What exactly am I supposed to do?" Kale began to grow uneasy with the situation as he nervously shifted in place.

"Do not be wary." The King's eyes filled with excitement. "The potion, Kale Firehart, will permanently return you as you once were–a dragon. It has the ability to reverse all magic placed upon an individual. You will no longer have to live a life as a human and can resume your true form."

Kale's eyes grew wide as he watched the King carefully pull open the cork. "Drink this and you will have the wish you have so longed for. The effects will not occur for at least an hour which will give you an ample amount of time to safely exit the kingdom. Please accept this as my humble apology for all I have caused you to endure." King Valamar extended his arm as he carefully held the vial toward Kale.

"See now, you stubborn dragon, I told you I would help find a way to change you back." Thomas spoke happily, his green eyes twinkling with glee.

Kale's heart raced. The offer caught him completely off guard and he was left with no time to gather his thoughts or prepare his mind for such a life altering decision. He began to glance nervously around in a panic, his insides churned nauseously.

"Do what your heart tells you. I am staying by your side regardless of what you choose." Neelan caressed his cheek, wrapping her other arm around his as their fingers interlocked together.

Kale had endured major transformations, not only in appearance, but within himself. Kale was and always would be a dragon. It was how he had been born into the world and no amount of magic could change that. His outside appearance as a human mattered little to him now. Throughout his journey, he came to realize that how one looks does not reveal who a person is.

Because of this new found insight, he was confidently able to make his decision.

"I choose—" Kale paused. Though he made up his mind, the reality was still frightening. "I choose—Neelan." He glanced toward Neelan whose face lit up with surprise. "I want to be with you until the day I leave this world. The thought of never being able to caress your body or to kiss your lips is unacceptable. I love you, Neelan, and I always will."

Her violet eyes sparkled like he had never seen before and a blissful smile appeared upon her face. She leapt into his arms, pressing her chest to his as their two hearts—though different beings—beat as one.

"Are you certain of this decision?" The King questioned as he withdrew the vial.

Kale's eyes glazed over with guilt. "I sincerely apologize, Your Highness; I did not intend to insult you in any way. I truly do appreciate your generosity with such a rare and generous gift. But, I am more certain about this decision than I have ever been before."

The King smiled, chuckling softly. "There is no need for apologies. This vile has been collecting dust for centuries and I could not have chosen a better person to have used it. You have traveled far and learned more than most do in a lifetime. This is a joyous time."

Thomas took the vial from the King's hands. "I truly am proud of you, Kale." He momentarily left to secure the vile within a temporary magical barrier until the King could later return it to the chamber.

Judith approached Kale, flashing her perfect smile toward him. "I am so happy for you. I shall always be here, should you need anything." She softly laughed as she looked at Neelan's jealous expression. "As a friend, of course," She added. "You are all welcome to rest here tonight, if you desire, before taking leave for your next journey. We will be celebrating Jedah's exile with a grand feast and celebration."

"Your offer is kind, and we are grateful, however, I do not think my patience will allow me to postpone leaving any longer. Though I have chosen to remain in this form, I am still a dragon

at heart, and I must do all I can to restore my kind to this world."
Kale glanced off to the side, "I also need to find out if she–Zasha
–is truly my mother." Though he had his doubts, his heart told
him Zasha spoke the truth. The thought alone filled him with an
anxious joy.

"I understand. Though I wish you were able to remain here
with us awhile longer." As Judith spoke, Neelan wrapped her
arms around Kale's arm protectively.

"You are all welcome to gather any provisions or weaponry
you desire from the marketplace at no charge. I would also like to
send you with a gift." The King withdrew a black velvet pouch
which jingled with the sound of many coins. Filled to the point
where the pouch bulged, gold coins peeked from the top. "Please,
take it; I will not accept no as an answer." King Valamar
chuckled as he saw Kale's mouth open to argue. "I have more
than enough here so you do not have to worry. You have all
worked hard to bring back someone who is priceless to me, so
again, I give you my deepest gratitude."

They each thanked the King for his generosity and kindness
as they engaged in a bittersweet farewell. Judith's eyes began to
swell with tears and Kale tried his best to assure her they would
all meet again, though, taking caution to watch his words around
Neelan.

After they each exchanged a few final words, the four
comrades left for the marketplace.

As they walked through the bustling center of the city, many
of the citizens bowed before them while giving words of praise
for their deeds. They wasted no time in filling their sacks with
food for their journey then making a stop at the kingdom
blacksmiths where Kale sorted through their impeccable variety
of weaponry. After great thought, he found the perfect sword

replacement. Though he knew it would most likely not have the durability to withstand the heat from his powers, he would manage until he could find a proper solution.

Soon after, Neelan insisted they browse through the many shops and stalls. Kale, though impatient to depart on their quest, agreed. He was unable to resist the excitement and joy in Neelan as she happily skipped through the market. For the first time in her life, she felt confident to walk among humans without concealing her elven characteristics.

Once Neelan had her fill of exploring, the four retrieved their horses from the stable. Each horse had a high-quality, new, leather saddle stuffed with soft wool. They thanked the groom and stable hand for the care provided and mounted to leave the kingdom.

Many of the citizens gathered to bid the four farewell. As they reached the gate at the curtain-wall a sad realization hit them. Judith would not be travelling alongside them. After their journey from the forest to Mirion, the four grew accustomed to her companionship. They knew, however, she was returned to where she rightfully belonged.

~~~~~~~~~~~~~~~~~

As the group trotted past the open farmland, Thomas steered his horse toward Kale's.

"Kale, I can sense something is bothering you. Tell me, what is on your mind?" The old sorcerer glanced upon Kale with genuine concern.

"I can't lose the feeling something is not right." Kale paused a moment. "I know Saldin and his men have escaped, but the whole situation feels wrong. Though the frost elves may be powerful, there is something within me, screaming inside–telling me Jedah should have been slain at his sentencing. I can almost feel his anger taunting me. I do not think this is the last we will see of him."

"Kale, I have said it before–the frost elves possess incredible power no normal human can contest. Everything will be fine." As the final words left Neelan's lips, they heard it–the sound of something hitting the ground.

"Thomas!" Illadar called out as he leapt from his horse.

"What happened?!" Kale yelled in a panic.

They rolled Thomas' limp body over just in time to see the needle-like dart that protruded from his neck.

"I hear something approaching quickly." Neelan spoke softly. "I think it's–"

Those were the final words Kale heard before *they* arrived.

The Chronicles of Kale: A Dragon's Awakening

Aya Knight was born in South Florida, where she spent the majority of her childhood. At a young age she developed a strong passion for fantasy and a love of writing. Through movies, books and video/computer games she would escape into an alternate reality filled with adventure, magic and epic quests.

As Aya entered adulthood, she expressed her enjoyment of writing through becoming a freelance journalist. She wrote about a broad variety of topics that gave her a brighter insight of the world. Eventually a story began to develop within her mind involving characters to which she immediately grew attached. Aya knew that she needed to compile her thoughts onto paper. She grew so intrigued with the evolving storyline that she placed all hopes within the hands of her imagination, leaving journalism behind.

Aya now lives in Central Florida with her husband and two sons where she continues her passion of writing.

9144607R0

Made in the USA
Charleston, SC
14 August 2011